MW00398012

Premiere

A COLLECTION OF ROMANTIC TALES FROM
ROMANCE WRITERS
OF AMERICA®

Romance Writers of America®
14615 Benfer Road
Houston, Texas 77069

PREMIERE: A ROMANCE WRITERS OF AMERICA COLLECTION

TABLE OF CONTENTS

WHAT IS A ROMANCE NOVEL?

DEPENDING ON WHOM YOU ask, you'll receive answers that range from the outdated and inaccurate term "bodice-ripper" to something like improbably handsome and wealthy boy seduces improbably beautiful and virtuous girl and they live happily ever after.

Romance Writers of America® defines romance fiction as smart, fresh, and diverse, with a central love story and an emotionally satisfying and optimistic ending. Some say romance novels are pure fantasy because of that happy ending, but the truth is that romantic love is everyday magic and happy endings happen every minute. Falling in love is one of the core elements of the human condition; it touches us all.

Romance novelists know this, and their stories and characters are as distinct and varied as every individual on earth. It isn't as simple as boy wins girl. Writers of romance are masters of character development, because that is the driving force of a love story: the myriad changes and sacrifices flawed protagonists must make, the evolution of their self-awareness and goals due to their love, and their view of the world as colored by their circumstances, backstory, and social mores. Love raises the stakes in a way nothing else can. It inspires us to a level of heroism that is rarely achieved by any other motivation.

It is the richly detailed characterization that makes the romance genre so hugely successful and widely read. Romantic love isn't fantastical. It's real and unbiased, and so is the genre. There is a romance for every reader, an imperfect hero or heroine we can see ourselves in.

Within the pages of this collection, you'll find some of the diversity in romance. Like a sampler box of decadent chocolates, this anthology is a taste of the variety of characters and settings to be found in the genre. All the stories are tied together with the theme of a wrong number, but the authors take wonderfully different routes in their exploration of that premise.

I hope you enjoy all the stories as much as I do.

Settle in and fall in love.
Sylvia Day

RAVISHED BY THE GEEK

VICKI LEWIS THOMPSON

New York Times Bestseller, RITA® Finalist,
RWA Nora Roberts Lifetime Achievement Award Recipient

To: Jamie_Smith2@DevcoIndustries.com
Subject: Project Update
Hey, Jamie! Just finished writing the hottest scene EVER.
Tell me what you think, girlfriend! Too bad this is fiction.
Wouldn't mind experiencing it for real, you know?
XX00
Viv

JAMIE AUTOMATICALLY HIT FORWARD and typed Jamie_Smith without the 2 after it. When he'd hired on as the new IT guy, personnel had mentioned there was a woman named Jamie Smith in accounting. Because he was the second Jamie at the company, he'd ended up with a 2 on the end of his email addy. He'd met the other Jamie, a twenty-something bubbly sort whose hair changed color so often he had trouble recognizing her in the hallway. She and Viv, who worked in the legal department, were best buds who'd known each other since high school.

He had no trouble recognizing Viv in the hallway. He'd spotted her his second day. On his third day, he'd been lucky enough to stand behind her in the cafeteria line, and they'd talked about movies. Turned out they both liked action-adventure with some comedy mixed in.

If he'd had the looks and confidence of Drew Hanover, Devco's top salesman who'd quarterbacked his college football team to a Rose Bowl victory, Jamie would have asked Viv for a date. She didn't appear to be seeing anyone. But he was a glasses-wearing computer geek and knew his limits. Vivian Crowley—blond, green-eyed, and built like a Victoria's Secret model—was out of his league.

But that didn't stop him from admiring her from afar or discussing movies with her whenever they happened to see each other in the cafeteria. Viv shouldn't be sending personal emails through the company system, but plenty of others did it, so he couldn't blame her too much. He'd just delete this one and forget about it.

Or maybe he'd read it first. Viv hadn't mentioned that she liked to write, but sometimes people were shy about their creative side. She hadn't intended for him to see this, but there it was on his screen by no fault of his own, and he was curious about what she considered *the hottest scene EVER*.

Thirty minutes later, he had to agree with her assessment. She'd written the hottest scene EVER, and he was using all his mental tricks to shrink his bad boy. If someone came into his cubicle, he was so not leaving his chair.

He wouldn't be forgetting that scene anytime soon. The hero had agreed to satisfy his lover's fantasy by meeting her in a darkened hotel room as if they were strangers. They weren't supposed to speak or use names, although moaning and crying out had been allowed and encouraged. In the dark, where she couldn't see his face or anticipate his moves, he'd driven her wild with inventive sex play.

Jamie had kept his cool during the furry-gloves section. He'd been only semi-aroused during the feather-boa part. The whipped cream had ramped up the action quite a bit, and by the time the guy brought out the flavored body paint, Jamie had desperately needed a cold shower. When the episode was over, the man had silently dressed and exited the room, leaving the woman wrung out with pleasure.

Of course, Jamie imagined that Viv was the woman, but now that he'd read her scene, he couldn't let on. If he saw her in the cafeteria at lunchtime today, he'd have to act natural, as if he hadn't recently imagined her writhing naked on a hotel bed while someone licked flavored body paint from all her private places.

Okay, he could do this. On his high school debate team, he'd been known as the Ice Man because, when necessary, he had the mental discipline to hide his emotional reactions. If he talked to her, he'd erase this scene from his mind, and she wouldn't notice anything different about him.

But that was two hours from now. In the meantime, he was free to think about this subject as often as he liked. The more he considered it, the more fascinated he became. Judging from her comment in the email, she'd never actually done those things with a guy, but she'd like to. And at this moment in time, he was the unlikely dude with the inside info ...

Viv sat at an elevated table in one of San Francisco's trendiest bars with her best friend, Jamie. "You didn't email me back about my scene. Did you read it?"

"Almost didn't get to it. A damned payroll glitch sucked up most of my day, but I managed to skim it before I shut down my computer." Jamie grinned. "It's smokin'.."

"Oh, good." Viv's shoulders relaxed. Jamie was her beta reader. Without her, Viv wouldn't know whether what she'd created was worth submitting.

"In fact, it's the best sex scene you've ever written. I have to believe you'll sell this book. You get better and better with each manuscript." Jamie signaled for the waitress.

Viv sighed. "From your lips to God's ears. I've never worked so hard at something in my entire life. I feel as if I have two jobs, but only one of them is paying me anything."

"Yet. Have faith." The waitress came over and Jamie ordered them each an appletini before turning back to Viv. "By the way, you accidentally sent that email to Jamie Two."

Her face grew hot. "Damn!"

"Ah, don't worry. He probably just forwarded it and dumped

his copy without looking at it. That's what I do when I get his. Who has time to snoop into someone else's mail?"

"But what if he didn't dump it? What if he read it? I'd be so embarrassed."

"Listen, Viv, you're hoping to get published, right?"

"That's my goal."

"Then what happens when everyone can read your stuff, including Jamie Two?"

"I'll use a pen name." She hadn't thought of one yet, but she'd worry about that when she signed a contract.

"So nobody will know it's you?"

"You will, obviously, but you won't tell if I ask you not to."

"Of course I won't. I'll even pinkie swear if it'll make you feel better."

Viv smiled. "Not necessary. I trust you."

"But won't you want to tell your folks?"

"Well, yeah, and my sister. But my *grandparents*? No way, not with all the sex I have in there. Nobody at Devco has to know, either. I just hope to hell Jamie Two didn't read that email."

"I'll bet he didn't. He forwarded it to me first thing this morning, and I don't think he acted any different at the cafeteria today. I mean, he has a crush going on, but that's always been true."

"I know." Viv thought about the times she'd caught him gazing at her with poorly disguised longing in his soft brown eyes. "It's sweet."

"It's *very* sweet. I think he's sort of handsome. I mean, in a geeky kind of way. I'm thinking Clark Kent."

"Yeah, I know what you mean. I do like his hair, and once he took off his glasses to clean them, and it totally changed his look. Plus he's super smart."

Jamie studied her. "He likes you a lot. Ever think of dating him?"

"Nah. He's nice, and I'm flattered that he's crushing on me, but he's not … dashing. I want somebody with adventure in his soul. Someone who would ravish me."

"Like the hero in this current book."

"Exactly! Find me that guy, and I'll be in seventh heaven."

Two weeks later, Viv came into work, headed straight for the ac-counting department, and made her way over to her friend's desk. "I have to talk to you. Come with me to the ladies' room. Now."

Jamie's eyes widened and she pushed back her chair. "Okay."

Once they were safely in the restroom, Viv looked around to make sure they were alone.

"You're making me nervous," Jamie said. "What's with all the secrecy?"

"Look at this." Viv pulled a cream-colored envelope from her messenger bag, took out the folded sheet of elegant stationary, and handed it to Jamie. "I don't know what to do."

Jamie scanned the handwritten letter. Then her gaze lifted. "Jamie Two?"

"Isn't it obvious? He *did* read my scene, and now he's inviting me to meet him in a swanky hotel room tonight!"

"He didn't sign it."

"Of course not! The whole point of the fantasy is to meet as strangers. All I have is a room number." Viv reached in the pocket of her linen jacket. "And a key."

"Are you going?"

"No! I mean, probably not, but ... what do you think?" Viv's chest tightened with anxiety, but underneath her nervousness lurked a spark of excitement.

Jamie folded the letter and tapped it against her palm. "He'd be the safest stranger you'd ever rendezvous with. Nobody gets hired at Devco without a thorough background check."

"I'm not worried about that. He's a sweetheart."

"Then what's the problem? He's giving you a chance to live out your fantasy. In my opinion, that's heroic."

"It would be, if he can pull it off, but this is Jamie we're talking about. He's a geek. What if it's a disaster? That would be horrible for both of us. We'd have to keep working in the same building, eating in the same cafeteria, meeting by accident in the hallway. It would be hell."

Her friend handed the letter back and turned to the mirror to fluff her hair, which was strawberry blond this week. "I guess you shouldn't risk it, then." She leaned closer to the mirror and pursed her lips.

"Would you? Knowing the potential consequences?"

Jamie met her gaze in the mirror. "You said you wanted dashing, and this is dashing. You said you wanted to be ravished, and he sounds as if that's what he has in mind. Think of what he's risking by sending you this letter. If you *don't* go tonight, how do you think he'll feel?"

Viv had considered that. Picturing him waiting in vain made her very sad. But the thought of actually going to the hotel ... she honestly didn't know if she could do it. After all her talk about wanting a dashing hero to ravish her, she might turn out to be a chicken.

Jamie faced her again and took her gently by the shoulders. "We have to get back to work, toots. You don't have to make up your mind right this minute. See how you feel as the day goes on."

Viv nodded, but she didn't think a few more hours would make any difference. She'd continue to debate whether to play it safe or take a leap of faith. Meanwhile, she had to live with the fact that Jamie Two was going through a different kind of agony.

He'd thrown down the gauntlet, and he wouldn't know until eight tonight whether she'd decided to pick it up. She'd eat at her desk this lunch hour to save both of them awkwardness in the cafeteria. No matter what she decided, though, she gave him props for courage. As for her bravery or lack of it, the jury was still out.

CHAPTER TWO

SEVEN FIFTY-SIX, AND JAMIE was sweating bullets. What had he been thinking, booking this room and mailing that invitation? Obviously Viv had known that he'd sent it, because her friend would have mentioned the email mistake, and conclusions would have been drawn from that. It couldn't be anyone *but* him.

So here he was, about to face total humiliation because she wouldn't come. But once he'd put the invitation in the mail, he'd set the stage for the slight possibility she *would* come. The laws of probability were against it, but based on that one-in-a-million chance, he had to complete his preparations. Every detail had to be exactly as she'd written the scene he'd now memorized.

He'd dressed as she'd described the guy—bare feet, black sweats, and a black, tight-fitting T-shirt. The T-shirt looked decent on him because, contrary to the stereotype of pigeon-chested computer nerds, he had pecs. Not huge ones because he only worked out three times a week. He found the process boring, but it did mean he could go to the beach and not have bullies kick sand in his face. Because he felt less vulnerable wearing his glasses, he'd leave them on until she came through the door. If she ever did.

If and when she arrived, he'd remove his glasses right before he switched off the bedside lamp. After that, the room would be too dark to see anything even if he had on glasses. He'd memorized the layout, and with a little caution and luck, his perfect recall ability would keep him from slamming into furniture or doing a face-plant on the thick carpet.

She had a dress code, too—knit sheath that could be pulled over her head, flat shoes, trench coat. No underwear. That last detail threatened to give him a woody whenever he thought about it. So mostly he didn't think about it.

Her dress code wouldn't matter if she ignored his letter. He'd gambled on the possibility that she wouldn't be able to resist her own fantasy, even if a geek offered to provide it. But now that he'd come to the moment of truth, he realized how flawed his thinking had been. She'd want her fantasy, but only if it came wrapped in the right package.

Seven fifty-eight. Everything he'd need was stacked on the bedside table—furry gloves, feather boa, whipped cream, flavored body paint, and condoms. He'd tucked one condom in the pocket of his sweats for insurance purposes, in case things got a little crazy and he couldn't easily locate the box in the middle of all the other paraphernalia.

It all could be for nothing, and he braced himself for the disappointment when she didn't show up. He wouldn't leave right at eight, though. He'd give her ten or fifteen minutes' leeway in case she was caught in traffic.

Crossing to the window, he parted the heavy blackout curtains and gazed down twenty stories to the street below. The night was cool, and fog had crept in from the bay to blur the diamond and ruby necklace of cars headed in and out of the city. She could be down there, climbing out of a cab and walking toward the hotel entrance, her heart pounding and her palms sweaty, just like his. She could be down there, but he had a tough time believing that she was.

Seven fifty-nine. If she'd been in a generous mood, she would have arrived early. But as the digital clock on the bedside table clicked over to eight, then eight-oh-one, any hope he'd tried to keep alive withered. Eight-oh-two. Okay, that was it. She'd decided not to—

A key card slid into the lock. He held his breath. Really? His elaborate scheme might actually work? His pulse shot into overdrive. *She was here.* Now it was all up to him.

Whipping off his glasses, he laid them on the bedside table and hit the light switch, plunging the room into darkness. His glasses rattled a little on the nightstand because his hands were shaking. Please, God, let him be able to do what she wanted without fumbling. Hell, it was *really* dark in here.

The door opened, and a slice of light from the hallway revealed Viv's silhouette. She wore her trench coat with the collar turned up, which made her look like a spy in a Grade B movie. Her breathing was audible even from fifteen feet away.

He didn't move, as if she were a wild animal he'd startle. But his heart throbbed painfully and he was getting dizzy. *Okay, Smith. Do* not *pass out.*

She closed the door and clicked the safety latch. The sound was really loud in the dark silence. According to what she'd written, she would take off the trench coat, the dress, and the shoes. Then she'd stand very still while he approached. They weren't supposed to say anything.

He reached for his glasses again. Although the room was blacker than a dead monitor, maybe with his glasses on, he'd catch a glimpse of her. No dice. He could hear the slide of fabric and the sound of her quick breaths, but saw nothing. He clenched his jaw in frustration and returned the glasses to the nightstand.

The rustling stopped. He was in a locked hotel room with the woman of his dreams, and she was *naked*. His body tightened everywhere, but especially south of the Mason-Dixon Line. The noise from his pounding heart and rushing blood blocked all other sounds. He had to regain control of himself or he'd never be the suave lover she wanted.

Slowly he sucked in air and let it out. And again. There. Now he could hear *her* breathing, and it was quite agitated. He didn't know if she was scared, nervous, or aroused. In the dark, a person breathing hard could be any of those things.

He'd never realized that before. The analytical side of his brain kicked in, and he recognized the lifeline it had tossed him. If he could reimagine this dramatic episode as a scientific experiment, he might not make a total ass of himself.

Show time. He focused on locating exactly where she was in this very dark room. He was deprived of sight, so he listened. As he walked soundlessly in the direction of her breathing, he figured out something else. In the dark, his poor eyesight didn't matter. He wasn't a nearsighted geek anymore. He was her fantasy man.

Her familiar aroma became another tantalizing beacon in the dark. He'd always thought she smelled great, but he'd never identified that scent precisely. He'd been too caught up in her dazzling blondness.

When she was cloaked in darkness instead, identifying her

scent was easy. Her skin smelled like ripe apples ... and something more. It was subtle. Unmistakable. He breathed it in and felt the rush of an emotion he'd never experienced with a woman—power. He'd aroused her.

Okay, maybe he couldn't take total credit. She'd written the scene, and he was merely acting it out for her. But he must be doing a good job so far, or she'd be laughing at him instead of trembling in anticipation. He envisioned pheromones swirling everywhere.

He could also swear that her body heat acted like a magnetic field pulling him toward her. Her minty breath told him which way she was facing. Obviously he'd never stood right in front of her when they were barefoot. His eyes had begun to adjust, and he could almost see her face, but he'd become fond of using his other senses. Arms at his sides as in the scene she'd written, he closed his eyes and followed the scent of mint as he lowered his head.

Her breath was warm against his mouth. His jackhammering pulse made him quiver, and he did his best to remain still. He was about to kiss Vivian Crowley for the first time, and he didn't want to do it while he was shaking.

Her breath hitched.

Instantly he ascribed all kinds of motives to that little gasp. They all boiled down to one overriding fear—she'd changed her mind, but she thought it was too late. Of course it wasn't too late. They hadn't signed a contract or even made a promise. He could break the code of silence and ask if she wanted to forget the whole thing.

He could do that, but he wasn't going to. Instead, he would close the gap between them and touch his lips to hers. He would take his time. He would learn her mouth and discover how she liked to be kissed. He would kiss her that way until she was hot for him, until she peeled off his shirt and sweats just as she'd written.

Then he would lead her to the bed. He'd guide her down to the thousand-thread-count sheets and make love to her in all the ways she'd imagined. He would pleasure her as she writhed beneath him and begged for more. She would teach him how to touch her, where to touch her, until he gave her orgasm after orgasm. He would be her fantasy man.

CHAPTER THREE

AT THE LAST SECOND, Viv chickened out. To her surprise, she was no longer worried that the experience wouldn't live up to her expectations. The exact opposite, in fact.

Because she couldn't see Jamie, he'd lost every trace of geekiness. He was making all the right moves. He even smelled terrific. She'd never noticed that before. In the silent fantasy world she'd helped him construct, her favorite geek had become sexy as hell.

As a result, she was incredibly turned on. Embarrassingly so. She'd imagined him having to work for this. She couldn't possibly be craving him so much that she was shaking. She couldn't possibly want to strip him down and have her way with him. She couldn't attack Jamie. It wasn't part of the script, and she'd feel like an out-of-control fool.

Therefore, she'd just step away, put her clothes on, and walk out of here before he found out her situation. Once she'd made it home and had given herself time to process, she'd apologize to him. Then she'd ask him out. Obviously she was far more attracted to him than she'd realized, and they *should* explore the possibilities. Just not right this minute, when her libido was raging.

She'd opened her mouth to tell him thanks but no thanks, at least not now, but then he kissed her. Oh. *Oh.* Suddenly she was fully involved in the hottest, most delicious, most seductive kiss of her life. Where had he learned *this*?

Never mind. She didn't care. She just wanted it to go on forever. She clutched his shoulders and pulled him closer. Why wasn't he holding her? Oh, yeah. According to the scene, he wasn't supposed to touch her yet, just kiss her. To hell with that.

Gripping his biceps—nice muscles!—she guided his arms forward. Apparently that was all the direction he needed, because after that, she didn't have to worry about whether he'd touch her or not. Turned out he was especially gifted in this area, too.

He stroked and massaged, cupped and fondled until she pulled away, gasping. She was going to have an orgasm any second, and he was still dressed. Time to fix that. Before she came, she wanted to take the same liberties with his body that he'd taken with hers.

Grasping the hem of his T-shirt, she pulled upward, and he obligingly leaned over and held out his arms. She yanked it quickly over his head and tossed it on the floor before flattening her palms against his chest, his very manly chest.

Mmm. She never would have dreamed this kind of terrain had been there all along, hidden behind a white dress shirt and a pocket protector. She tunneled her fingers through a thatch of springy chest hair and discovered more than enough muscle to satisfy her. She'd never been into body builders, anyway.

That lovely chest of his was heaving, and his heart thumped heavily against her palms, but that was only fair. He'd played havoc with her breathing a moment ago, and she intended to do the same with his. If he could rub his thumbs across her nipples, she could rub her thumbs across his.

He groaned and cupped her backside, bringing her in tight against the soft jersey of his sweats. What lay beneath that jersey wasn't soft at all. Or the least bit small, either. Yum.

She wanted what was under those sweats, and she wanted it now. This wasn't at all how the scene had been written, but she was past caring about the stupid scene. She slid both hands under the waistband of his sweats and took charge. Oh, *yeah*. She'd never guessed he was walking around with this kind of treasure under his boxers.

His next groan sounded tortured, and she suspected, given how hot and rigid he was, that she'd pushed him as close to the edge as he'd pushed her. He verified that when he backed away, his breathing rougher than an oxygen-deprived mountain climber.

He fumbled in his pocket, and the crinkle of foil sent joy surging through her, especially to the juicy parts. Once he was suited up, she grabbed both his hands and tugged him down to the carpet. They didn't need no stinkin' bed.

He kicked away his sweats, and then he was there, settling between her thighs. He sucked in a breath and then he drove deep. Glorious! Two quick strokes and she came, arching upward with a triumphant cry.

But he was far from finished. As he kept thrusting, she wrapped her legs around him and held on tight. He was good at this, too. So good. She wasn't at all surprised that tension coiled within her a second time. He had an amazing package and knew exactly how to use it.

So she might have a little rug burn from sliding on the carpet. So what? She was heading for another breathtaking orgasm, compliments of a guy she'd completely underestimated. She could deal with a little rug burn in exchange for being loved by Jamie.

Then he slipped his big hands under her bottom and lifted her gently up off the carpet, all the while continuing that relentless rhythm that turned her inside out. In the midst of the most intense lovemaking she'd ever experienced, she was being cared for! How great was that?

Dazzled, she gazed up at him, but he was only a shadowy form in the darkness. She couldn't see his face, couldn't see those gorgeous, nearsighted brown eyes, couldn't see his cute little smile. And now she wanted to. She wanted to watch his expression as he buried himself in her over and over. She wanted to look into his eyes and share the glory of his climax.

But they were in the dark. That's how she'd decreed it should be. And they hadn't spoken a word to each other because she'd emphasized how mysterious silence could be. Yes, maybe so, but she loved his voice. She'd never realized that, either, until now.

He was close to coming. She could tell from the sudden change in his breathing and the rapid movement of his hips. Gripping her bottom, he shifted his angle a little, and ... oh, wow ... He'd found a spot he'd missed before, and she was ... *coming*. With a wail, she surrendered to the force of an orgasm that whirled her in a cyclone of pleasure.

With a deep bellow of satisfaction, he drew back and thrust deep once more. Then he shuddered and gulped for air as his spasms blended with hers. Slowly he lowered her hips to the carpet and followed her down. They lay in a tangled heap, slick with sweat and breathing fast.

He rested his head on her shoulder, and she combed her fingers through his hair. He really did have great hair. There were plenty of great things about Jamie. She'd only begun to find out what they were.

In one particular way, she knew him very well. Exhibit A was the current position they found themselves in. She'd never had first-time sex that was this wonderful, and the reason was obvious. She'd liked him all along, but she hadn't allowed herself to think of him romantically. The geek stereotype had tripped her up. No more.

She had so many questions now. She'd never asked about his family and whether he had any siblings. She wondered what he'd been like as a little kid. A little whiz kid, probably, and she wanted to hear about that.

The more she thought about the gaps in her knowledge, the more impatient she was to fill them. What did he like to do for fun besides go to movies? Well, and have amazing sex. *That* had been big fun. But what were his favorite foods, his ideal day? Did he love dogs or cats?

They had hours of catching up to do. And all the while they were playing the getting-to-know-you game, they could take breaks for more of what they'd recently enjoyed here on the carpet.

It was a lovely picture she'd painted for the two of them, but she couldn't figure out a decent segue. How were they supposed to get from having crazy-good sex in the dark with no dialogue to a meaningful conversation in which they shared significant facts about themselves?

Finally she took the plunge. "Jamie, we have to talk."

He sighed mightily. "I know."

She felt that sigh all through her body. It wasn't a happy sigh. "I didn't mean it like that." She kept finger-combing his thick hair. "I just—"

"I screwed up your fantasy. I didn't do any of the things you wanted. No furry gloves, no feather boa, no whipped cream, no flavored body paint. They're all here, over on the nightstand. But I rushed to the main event, and now it seems sort of anticlimactic to get into the other stuff, plus we're talking, which we're not sup-posed to do, so I suppose the whole strangers-in-the-dark thing is ruined, too. I'm sorry, Viv."

She was flabbergasted. "You have *got* to be kidding."

"About what? I didn't deliver what I promised in my letter."

"Jamie, look at me."

"I can try." He lifted his head. "You're pretty shadowy, though."

"Good point. We need some light on the situation. Since you're the one who scoped out the room first, maybe you'd better be the one to turn on a lamp."

He didn't move. "Hold on a sec. Don't be hasty. Maybe we can still salvage the fantasy. If we leave the lights off and stop talking, we can pretend we didn't have this conversation and just go on from here."

Now it was her turn to sigh. "I don't care about the fantasy anymore."

"Right." He sounded discouraged. "Because I ruined it."

"No, if anyone ruined it, I did! You were following directions and kissing me with your arms at your sides, remember? Who changed that dynamic? Not you!"

"I could have resisted. Wait, no, I couldn't. Once you pulled my arms toward you, I was done for. Okay, so you're the one who messed up the order of things, but we can get it back."

"I don't want it back. What actually happened was way better than the scene in my book."

"It was?"

"Yes! Jamie, the sex we just had was fabulous! I loved every sweaty minute of it."

"You did?" He lifted his head and peered down at her. "Damn, I wish I could see you."

She smiled. "So turn on a light, genius."

"Okay." He eased away from her and stood up. "I will in a minute."

She thought it was cute that he didn't mention the little condom chore he had to perform first. His voice came from the even deeper shadows of the bathroom. "And FYI, technically I'm not a genius. I'm a couple of points shy."

She sat up and ran her fingers through her hair. "See, those are the kinds of things I want to know. What's your favorite food?"

"Mac and cheese. I get it all the time at the cafeteria."

"I know you do, but if you had a choice of anything in the world, what—"

"Still mac and cheese." He crossed the room, his footsteps a soft whisper on the thick carpet. "Ready for the light?"

"Yes." She shaded her eyes as the bedside lamp flicked on, and by the time she took her hand away, he was there, kneeling beside her, his brown hair tousled and that precious little grin on his face. How had she missed the fact that he was so good-looking?

He gazed at her as if transfixed. "Damn but you're gorgeous."

"Thank you, but what I really want to talk about is—"

"Where we go from here, right?"

"Yes. I—"

"Everything's cool, Viv. This didn't turn out quite the way you might have expected, and so I didn't get to leave gracefully, but I can still grab my stuff and go. As for work, I can act as if nothing ever happened between us."

She stared at him. "Why would you want to do that?"

"So I won't make you uncomfortable."

"I don't think you understand."

"Sure I do. You wanted to experience this fantasy with someone, and although it went in a different direction, we sort of did it. Mission accomplished, more or less. We move on."

"Do *you* want to move on?" She had trouble believing it considering the way he'd always looked at her before and the way he was looking at her now. He had it bad.

He glanced away. "That's not the issue."

"I'm afraid it is, because if I could have what I want, I'd like to be with you. But if you don't want to be with me, then—"

"What?" His shock was almost comical.

"I want to be with you, Jamie. I want to spend time getting to know you. I'd love it if we could have more of that amazing sex. I think we could have something special between us. But that's just me. You have to weigh in on the matter."

He continued to look as if someone had smacked him upside the head.

"Did you hear me?"

"Yeah, but it's not computing."

She captured his face in both hands. "Then try this on for size." And she kissed him with all the energy she could summon. She used her tongue quite liberally, too. When she finally drew back, the glazed look in his eyes had been replaced by a sexy gleam. She took a deep breath. "Get it now?"

"It's starting to penetrate." A slow grin joined the sexy gleam. "So you liked what we did?"

"I didn't just like it. I *loved* it."

"So you might want to try it again sometime?"

"I would. Say in about five minutes."

His eyebrows lifted. "With furry gloves?"

"Furry gloves, feather boas, whipped cream, flavored body paint. Whatever you've got."

Standing, he held out his hand. "Good, because I'd hate for that stuff to go to waste."

"So would I." She placed her hand in his. "You went to a lot of trouble. The least I can do is let you ravish me."

He laughed and drew her over to the bed. "Didn't I already do that? It sort of felt that way."

"Okay, you already did, but feel free to do it again. And again. And again." She tumbled onto the mattress, gazed up at her adorable geek, and prepared to be ravished for the rest of the night.

After that, who knew? He might want to continue doing it for weeks, months, even years. He just might be the guy who was destined to be her ravishingly perfect happily ever after.

New York Times bestselling author **Vicki Lewis Thompson** divides her writing time between nerd heroes and cowboy heroes and is threatening to dream up a book about a nerdy cowboy. The recipient of Romance Writers of America's Nora Roberts Lifetime Achievement Award, she has more than a hundred published books and has at least a hundred more story ideas swirling in her head.

Connect with her at VickiLewisThompson.com, facebook. com/vickilewisthompson, and twitter.com/vickilthompson.

UNDER A WICKED MOON

LILA BELL

RITA® Finalist

THIS WAS SO WRONG. Stacia Byrne should be using the blender to mix margaritas, not a potion to keep a supernatural assassin from killing her! Growing up in group homes and foster care, she'd never imagined her life would get even more messed up once she was an adult. But in the five years since she'd turned eighteen—

Frantic knocking reverberated through the cubbyhole of an apartment. *Kyann.* It seemed a safe bet that the person on the other side of the door was the psychic, half-blood succubus who'd sworn to help her. Stacia doubted assassins bothered to knock, particularly the one coming for her.

Liam MacTíre's face loomed in her mind. The last time she'd seen him had been almost eight years ago. At seventeen, his ink-black hair and ice-blue eyes, not to mention his towering size, had lent him an air of danger; yet she never would have believed he could hurt her. Well, not physically. Emotionally, he'd crushed her by leaving in the dead of night without even a good-bye. Had he known what he was back then, or had he been as shocked as she was when she learned of her own heritage?

"Open the damn door!" Kyann sounded uncharacteristically frazzled. Normally the redhead oozed cocky self-assurance and sex appeal. Stacia had been complaining for weeks that it didn't help their attempts to lie low when her friend kept introducing herself to men as "Kyann, like the pepper," in her sultriest voice.

Fingers shaking, it took Stacia a full minute to unfasten the deadbolt, knob lock and security bar. Removing the intricate barrier spell, however, came as easily as breathing. For a woman who'd spent most of her life with no freaking idea she was a sorceress, she was coming into her powers nicely. Which was why the Tribunal wanted her dead.

Despite her attempt to lead an uncomplicated life as a Dallas bartender, Stacia was subject to ancient laws that predated the Texas Legislature by centuries. Though most people were blessedly unaware of the Tribunal's existence, it was the sacred group of immortal elders, practically deities, who ruled supernatural beings. Some of Stacia's ancestors had thought themselves powerful enough to overthrow the Tribunal. The rebellion had been brutally quashed, but just last month, one of her relatives had violated the terms of the treaty. Everyone in their bloodline was marked for death. The Tribunal maintained order by never hesitating to make an example.

Kyann scrambled inside, clutching a small bag. "You owe me *huge*, blondie."

"You got them?" Stacia would have experienced a rush of relief if it weren't already late afternoon. According to Kyann's vision, Liam would be here before sunset.

The psychic had once explained that she often had simultaneous visions. *It's like alternate endings on a DVD, but there are hundreds of them, and they all play at once.* She hadn't foreseen any course of action that led to Stacia escaping or hiding for long. Liam would track her like a bloodhound. Or, more accurately, a wolf.

Stacia needed to face him—armed with a potion and a desperate plan. The idea that she could kill Liam was laughable. Even if she magically tapped into the necessary strength, she doubted she could bring herself to do it. At one time, he'd been the most important person in her life. Now, he was one of the Tribunal's twelve Enforcers. To kill him was to declare open war. Being half human had helped her hide this long, but if she provoked the Tribunal further, the remaining eleven Enforcers would devote their considerable life-spans to hunting her down and gutting her mercilessly. Each assassin possessed a unique mystical weapon; she'd heard they favored blades.

No pissing off the scary, stabby people. Instead, she'd drawn inspiration from a childhood fairy tale and the memory of asking her foster-mother why the huntsman who was supposed to kill Snow White had saved her. Stacia had been surprised he would risk the wicked queen's wrath to help. Stacia had seen far too many who refused to so much as inconvenience themselves on another's behalf. But if the Champion spell worked …

Kyann thrust the bag into Stacia's hands, glancing furtively over her shoulder as if the dragon-shifter she'd seduced might appear in a burst of flame. "My vision about you being the only one who can save my life in the future better be true, because you are a lot of trouble. Here. Four dragon scales, as requested."

"Four?" Ah, gods, no. "You mean five! *Tell me you meant to say five.*"

"Y-you said you needed four. Didn't you?" Kyann looked pale and apologetic. She was often so preoccupied by incoming visions and trying to keep possible realities straight that she grew confused. "They're, um, big scales, relatively speaking. Maybe four biggish ones work just as well as five smaller?"

They weren't discussing how many cloves of garlic to put in a pasta sauce—this was life and death!

But since four was all she had, Stacia had no choice but to try. She peered into the bag at the iridescent scales. Her plan was to inject Liam with a potion that would turn him into a gallant protector, full of chivalrous compassion. Wolf-shifters were naturally loyal. If she could just redirect his loyalty to her …

Would four scales have any effect? If the resulting potion wasn't enough to compel him to actively defend her, perhaps it would still generate enough compassion for him to let her go. A clean break might be better anyway. She'd learned a lot about wolf-shifters, including that the myth of being forced to turn every full moon was complete bunk and that they mated for life. If she bewitched Liam to stay as her protector but separated him from a mate in the process, the she-wolf would come after Stacia with more fury than the Enforcers.

Kyann shuddered, her face going blank and her eyes shining an otherworldly silver. Judging by her furrowed forehead and clenched fists, she was having a particularly intense vision.

"You okay?" Stacia asked when her friend's gaze returned to normal.

The corner of the psychic's mouth lifted. "That's what I love about you. A big, bad werewolf assassin is about to come huffing and puffing at your door, but you still find time to worry about someone else." Kyann squeezed her hand. "I'll be okay. How can I not be when I know that on the darkest day of my life, you'll be there to rescue me? But, right now, I'm needed somewhere else. Urgently."

"Go. If this potion works, your presence here is unnecessary, and if it doesn't … well, you should be as far away as possible." She swallowed. "At least *some* of the paths you've seen end with Liam sparing me, right?"

"Some." Kyann grabbed the doorknob, adding over her shoulder, "This isn't good-bye, blondie. I'm eighty-six percent positive."

Trying not to think about the other fourteen percent, Stacia rushed to add the scales to her assembled ingredients. She was glad she had time to fill the syringe she'd procured last week. This would be far more difficult if—

Heavy footsteps crashed in the outer hallway. She gulped. He wasn't even trying to be subtle.

Every impulse in her body told her to run for the window and take her chances with the fire escape. But she couldn't risk falling three stories while grappling with a trained killer. Still, if she just stood here waiting, his suspicions might be roused. She was scrambling for the bedroom and possible hiding places when the door splintered into fragments.

A hysterical giggle bubbled in her throat as she thought of how meticulous she always was with the locks. How had she believed that a sliding security bar would even break his stride? She'd placed a barrier spell around the apartment, too, but it was likely the Tribunal elders provided their Enforcers talismans strong enough to break through. It was next to impossible for a twenty-three-year-old bartender to compete with beings who'd practiced magic for thousands of years.

Also impossible? Believing that the muscular giant in front of her had ever been a seventeen-year-old boy.

Thick black hair framed a haunting face—his features would have been beautiful if they weren't so full of menace. At fifteen, she'd watched him play a shirtless game of basketball, and it had taken a week for her heart rate to go back to normal. She hadn't known then that they shared the bond of each being half human, half *other*. She'd only known she felt a deeper connection with Liam than any of the countless people she'd met while being jostled through the system. There had been one or two occasions when she'd believed— hoped?—he felt it, too.

But there was no sign of any connection visible in his ice-blue eyes.

"Witch," he growled. "You know why I'm here." He held out his hand, and a silver dagger appeared in it.

If he throws that, I'm screwed. She needed to be close enough to inject him. Knowing she couldn't outrun him, she flattened herself behind the battered leather couch.

There was a startled pause, then a harsh, staccato laugh. "If you were shooting for an illusion or vanishing spell, it failed." The floor beneath her shook as he advanced. "Why forestall the inevitable, witch?"

"Quit calling me that. I'm a sorceress." Not that she'd ever asked to be. No one had given her a choice in her family's blood feud with the Tribunal. "I'm Stacia. Y-you remember me, right?"

He lifted the couch straight into the air, and he sneered down at her with something shockingly close to hatred. "How could I forget?"

CHAPTER TWO

LIAM HAD BEEN SELECTED for hunting down Stacia because, like her, he was half human. Mystical beings were attuned to other mystical beings, but when the "blood was diluted," as one elder put it, more pedigreed Enforcers had a difficult time finding their quarry. In cases like this, the Tribunal sent Liam or the half-human, half-incubus Nik Becker. Nik, however, had recently found his fated "soul-half" and opted for early retirement.

When Liam had learned the target was the little witch who'd betrayed his secret, he would have volunteered even if he hadn't been asked. Red haze clouded his vision, the memory of being strapped to a table, the doctor's taunting voice. *Who do you think told* us *about you?* With a growl, he flung the leather sofa away.

A sharp pain seared his calf. In the split second he'd been preoccupied with the past, she'd rolled toward him and … stabbed him? She was chanting frantically as Liam brought his blade down—but it fell uselessly from his suddenly numb fingers. A burning path shot from his leg to his head, and his limbs were heavy. She'd poisoned him! The room spun with nauseating speed, and just when he thought that he, an immortal wolf-shifter assassin, might disgrace himself by puking in front of his target, everything went black.

Liam woke with the scent of her pounding in his body like a heartbeat. Even after seven years, he knew it intimately. When they'd been in the foster home together, he'd tutored her in math, and sometimes the sweet, heady smell of her—like vanilla but more unique—had made it impossible to think. His eyes flew open, and he turned his head, ignoring the painful dizziness in his need to find her. *Stacia.*

But she was gone. Her absence was a pain far worse than the throbbing in his head or residual sting in his leg. *No!* He shot to his feet. He couldn't be without her again. Closing his eyes, he inhaled deeply. He would track her. If not in this form, then in his wolf shape. Night had fallen, and he knew how to blend with the shadows, away from human eyes. Tomorrow night was the full moon, and he was brimming with power—and a purpose even more compelling than his sworn duty to the Tribunal.

At seventeen, for both their sakes, he'd battled the voice inside that whispered Stacia belonged with him, to him. But something had reignited that fever-bright certainty. A single thought consumed him. *Stacia Byrne is mine.*

Dragon scales—every bit as potent as rumored. Even three hours after witnessing her potion in action, Stacia was startled by its effects. She hadn't expected it to work so rapidly. If, in fact, it had worked.

She'd paused only long enough to check for Liam's pulse, then she'd bolted with a prepacked duffel of clothes, charms, and emergency cash. Had he awakened since she left, or was he still out cold? The Champion spell had both a potion component and an incantation. Since her potion hadn't followed precise directions, she had no idea how Liam would react toward her when he regained consciousness. It had seemed wiser not to stick around and find out.

Kyann's voice echoed in her head, repeating her silver-eyed warning from last week. "There is *no* possible outcome where you outrun the wolf."

Unable to help herself, Stacia glanced through the centimeter of grimy motel window that wasn't covered by the thick curtain, noting the brightness of the almost-full moon. Wolf-shifters were at their strongest this time of the month, would be damn near unstoppable tomorrow and the night after that.

Stepping away from the window, she huddled deeper into her jacket. Although the autumn days weren't too cold, the crisp night air held a bite that was inescapable in the drafty motel room. She eyed the bed dubiously. She wasn't sure she was willing to recline on a mattress that could be rented as cheaply as what she'd paid for this ugly room. And while resting to restore her energy might be the prudent thing to do, there was no way in hell she'd be able to sleep.

Feeling ragged and alone, she momentarily regretted tossing her cell phone in a trash can after sending Kyann a quick *Still alive* text. Stacia wasn't sure the Tribunal, who hated to bother with mundane, mortal details, used phones to track people, but why risk it?

A muffled shout came from the unit above her, making her jump. Cocking her head, she listened closely, her face heating when she decided the noise had been a sound of pleasure, not struggle. Kyann had joked about the irony of their being roommates—the sexually voracious part succubus and the virgin, a "new-age odd couple."

So what now, O great sorceress? She hadn't realized how accustomed she'd become to asking for Kyann's advice, finding out at least *some* of the possible outcomes of her actions. Now she was flying blind. Her mind and pulse both raced.

Meditation. Get centered. She reached into her bag and pulled out a candle, a bag of crushed lavender flowers, and a piece of jade. Meditating worked better when she was outdoors or when the ceiling above her wasn't vibrating with the sound of strangers having sex, but at least—

BOOM.

Light-headed with adrenaline and fear, she whirled to see the door crumple inward. Her gut clenched when Liam exploded into the room. Earlier, he'd looked like what he was reputed to be—a cold-blooded killer. *You know why I'm here, witch.* He'd sounded resolved but not emotionally engaged. Now? He looked *pissed.*

He had a serious case of the crazy-eyes, and she should be running like hell, but where could she go? The motel room was tiny, and if she backed into the bathroom, she was sealing herself into a dead end. But as he hurtled toward her, irrational survival instinct propelled her into the bathroom anyway. She was in the process of trying to shut the door when he wrenched it off its hinges.

The man was murder on doors.

"Never again." With the snarl in his tone and the predatory gleam in his gaze, it was easy to imagine him in wolf form. "You do not escape me again, Stacia."

So much for her last shred of hope that four dragon scales were an adequate substitute for five.

He pounced, and she squeezed her eyes shut, not wanting to see the blade that ended her life. At least she could manage that small measure of escape. But there was no cold steel, only the curve of his fingers grasping her shoulders. And then the unfathomable shock of his mouth, hot against hers.

CHAPTER THREE

"WHAT IN HELL IS goin' on here?" a twangy voice demanded.

That's what I'd like to know. Stacia was so dazed by the turn of events that she felt like she was having an out-of-body experience. She saw the motel manager standing next to the ruined door with a shotgun. On some level, she registered that Liam had shoved her behind him … protectively?

Liam snarled. From her position, she couldn't see his expression, but all of the blood drained from the manager's face.

"Wh-what's wrong with your eyes?" he demanded.

Charging forward in a blur, Liam bent the muzzle of the rifle before the man had the chance to squeeze the trigger. "Leave, mortal."

The manager didn't have to be told twice. Dropping his hold on the now-defective gun, he hauled ass.

Stacia swallowed, trying to radiate confidence. "He'll be back once he's called the cops." Or the Marines.

"Then we will not be here." Liam tugged her back into the main room.

"We?" So the plan was no longer to kill her and be done with it?

"We will not be separated, Stacia. Not ever again."

Considering that he was half shifter and she was half sorceress, their life-spans might go well into the hundreds of years. *Never* was a serious proposition.

"I d-don't understand. Aren't you going to … ?" She couldn't speak the words. So she made the universally recognized *Psycho* stabbing motion.

His eyes flashed crimson. "Kill my mate?" He sounded outraged. His fingers clenched around hers, and she wondered if he knew he was hurting her. "*Never.*"

His mate?

Poor, deluded wolf-boy. She'd really screwed up that spell. She'd been shooting for compassion, not passion. *Five scales equals "chivalrously protective," but four is "crazily possessive."* Good to know.

On the plus side, he no longer wanted to dagger her to death.

"Liam? Ow. My hand."

He immediately relaxed his hold but didn't let go, keeping his wild-eyed gaze on her as if afraid she'd vanish.

"I'm *not* your mate." There was a time when it would have been her fondest wish. "What you're feeling ... I cast a spell."

"No kidding." He scowled. "Stabbed me in the godsdamned calf."

"Right!" At his dark glare, she tried to sound more contrite. "I mean, yes. Desperate circumstances and all. It confused you. When you get far enough away from me, you'll probably start to feel more yourself."

"No. And it's not up for discussion." He reached into the pocket of his leather jacket and withdrew a crystal. "*Dormite.*"

Her last conscious thought was a wry comment on turnabout and unfair play.

Liam's most expedient course of action was to steal a car. The pock-faced man with stained teeth he took it from reeked of meth. Guy shouldn't be driving anyway.

Liam buckled Stacia into the passenger seat, breathing in her scent, noting the soft warmth of her skin. Her lashes were dark crescents across her cheeks as she slept, and he missed the green flame of her eyes almost as much as he craved her taste. Kissing her earlier, which he'd dreamt of for nearly a decade, had merely whetted his appetite.

It was a sign of the sorceress's burgeoning power that she only slept for thirty or forty minutes. The Tribunal charm he'd used should have had her slumbering for hours.

She stirred in the passenger seat, her voice groggy. "Where we goin'?"

"I don't know," Liam admitted. When was the last time he'd been without a plan? Even as a teenage captive, he'd strategized. *Tear out the throats of my kidnappers, find others like me.* It was good to have goals.

His last foster home had been the one he'd shared with Stacia. During a full moon, he'd snuck out, compelled to run, to shed the four walls that suffocated him. But someone had grabbed him in the woods. He'd been chloroformed by his foster-mom's brother, a doctor with crazy ideas about Liam's "superhuman" blood helping those who were sick.

"Someone will find me, and you'll be locked away," Liam had railed as his blood was drained, weakening his body and his hope. The doctor had scoffed that no one cared enough to come looking for a belligerent seventeen-year-old runaway. Liam had seized on the name that came instantly to mind. "Stacia cares."

"The shy blonde?" The doctor had chortled with dark amusement. "Who do you think told us about you? She's terrified of you, sees you for the freak you are. But don't worry, I'll give you purpose."

Liam had spent months in the doctor's secret lab before breaking the man's nose and a few ribs during a full moon. After that, the doctor had sold him to even less scrupulous scientists from another country—possibly another dimension—but Liam had been rescued a week later by other shifters. They'd taken him to the elders, and he'd dedicated his life to justice in the Tribunal's name.

Stacia called him confused, but she was wrong. He remembered everything clearly. He knew it had been his job to kill her— just as surely as he knew she was his mate and that he couldn't wait another night to be inside her.

"You are mine," he said aloud. The words calmed him, soothed the restless violence below the surface.

"N-no. Liam, I'm not." Regret laced her tone. "I never would have cast that spell, but I was fighting for my life."

He nodded approvingly. "Fierce little witch." His priority was keeping her safe. He didn't begrudge any trickery that helped protect her, only her past betrayal.

She sighed. "You're still calling me 'witch.' This isn't progress."

"I could call you my Stacia." He was too attuned to her, his senses too heightened, to miss her small shiver of pleasure.

"This is a lot for me to take in. When I woke up this morning,

I half expected to be dead by now. You kissed me!" Her tone was dumbfounded.

Had it really been that big of a surprise? From the way she'd ogled him when they were younger, he would have guessed she'd imagined it as often as he had.

His fingers tightened on the steering wheel. "You didn't like my kiss?"

She turned to look out the window even though there was little to see in the darkened landscape. "I didn't say that."

Pride swelled within him. And desire. He wanted to kiss her again, claim her.

"Liam."

Hearing her say his name was a pleasurable jolt of electricity along his nerve endings. "Yes?"

"I need you to concentrate. Are you *sure* you don't have another mate out there? The spell may have clouded—"

"Enough about the spell! My kind mates for life. Not even your powers, little witch, are sufficient to blot out the memory of something so vital. The mate bond is irrevocable." Eternal.

She gulped. "Irrevocable?"

He gave her a grim smile. "Bet you're wishing now you'd been nicer."

"What? *You're* the one who tried to kill *me!*"

He stiffened at the reminder. "I've already given my word that won't happen again. All I want to do is …" *Bury myself inside you.* "Protect you," he finished. His lust for her burned like a flame, and it would only grow worse. Tomorrow was the full moon. Wolf-shifters might not involuntarily transform into literal beasts, but they were hard-pressed to deny their most primitive instincts beneath the silvery rays of the Sanguine Moon. "In order to build a future, I can forgive you the past."

She reached out and socked him in the shoulder.

"What in the seven hells?" he asked mildly. Well, he considered it mild. From the way she recoiled, Stacia might disagree.

"You left me," she sputtered. "Abandoned me without a good-bye. I knew our foster-mother would never let us date in the traditional sense. But you were almost eighteen. You were going to be free soon, and I foolishly believed—"

"Kidnapping is not the same as abandonment."

Energy crackled around her, hinting at how powerful she would become. "Kidnapping?" Her voice was low and dangerous, and he'd never found her sexier.

"The doctor. Our foster-uncle," he sneered. "He said *you* were the one who told him about me. My strength and speed and increased energy around the full moon."

She clapped a hand to her mouth. "Gods, Liam. I— Stop the car, please."

He obligingly steered them onto the shoulder, wary. If this was a ploy for her to try to escape again, she was in for a rude awakening.

CHAPTER FOUR

KIDNAPPED? FOR A MOMENT, Stacia feared she might be sick.

That night came rushing back to her, the clammy anxiety she'd felt when she'd realized Liam had snuck out. At first, her worry had been selfish. He'd been on thin ice with their foster-mother, and Stacia was terrified that if he got sent away, she'd never see him again. But as midnight came and went, she'd begun to worry instead for his safety. Hating herself, she'd tattled to their foster-mother, deciding that even his exile from the foster home was better than his dying of exposure in some ditch.

A noise echoed in the car, and Stacia belatedly identified it as her own hysterical laughter.

"Something is ... funny?" Liam asked dubiously.

"Why is it always a ditch? None of the people I know who've shuffled off their mortal coil actually died in ditches, but that's always the figurative go-to. I was scared *you* were dead in a ditch."

"You worried. About me." He said the words reverently, like a prayer.

"Of course I did! But, looking back now, remembering the doctor's questions ... I told them you hadn't been yourself. You'd been aggressive, fighting with some of the other boys, and the doctor asked me so many things. I babbled answers as fast as they came to me, hoping something I said would help them find you. Now I realize he'd asked leading questions before, too." Infatuated as she was, it hadn't taken much encouragement to get her to discuss Liam. "I swear I didn't purposely hint at what you were! I didn't even *know*."

"I only found out once the shifters saved me, but when I learned about your sorcery, I thought clairvoyance might be one of your talents." He caught her chin between his thumb and forefinger. "You didn't betray me?"

"I would never—"

UNDER A WICKED MOON   33

His lips crushed hers in a searing, open-mouthed kiss. She grabbed his shirtfront in her fists and held on for dear life. She'd never been kissed with this kind of intensity. Even as she responded physically—her skin flushed with arousal, her breasts tightened in anticipation—she couldn't help feeling trepidation. She was completely inexperienced with men, and this one seemed ready to devour her.

A wicked thrill zinged through her at the thought.

"W-wait." She pulled away, trying to catch her breath. An outrageous possibility occurred to her. "Liam, are you a virgin?"

"Hell, no."

"Oh. I thought … this mating-for-life thing?"

"Once we mature into our shifter abilities, we don't make love during a full moon. Not unless we know we've found The One. Sex during a full-moon phase seals the bond. And right now, it's all I can think about." His eyes glittered with sensual promise.

She swallowed hard. The first fantasies she'd ever had were about this man. And, dear Lord, his kisses … But what if he were simply reacting to her botched spell? He'd been back in her life less than a day, and his emotions might not even be his own. Coming together in a lifelong bond seemed—

Actually, coming together sounds pretty damn good.

Giving herself a mental shake, Stacia cursed her libido and Kyann's bad influence.

"Can we find a place to stop for the night?" she asked. "To tell you the truth, it's been weeks since I got a decent night's sleep, and this is a lot to process."

"That I can do, and it'll be a damn sight nicer than the dump I found you in," he promised. "But only one room. You sleep in my arms, my bed."

The thought of those strong arms wrapped around her? Heaven. "Deal. As long as we're *only* talking about sleeping."

"Deal," he parroted. "For now."

When morning sunlight warmed her face, Stacia stretched without opening her eyes. The second she realized she was alone, she sat bolt upright. Where was Liam? Had it been a dream?

Nope. All real.

Shirtless and barefoot in a pair of jeans, he was pacing at the food of the bed, his demeanor agitated. His color was ashen, and the fluid grace he normally moved with had developed a few twitches overnight. Was this a symptom of her spell wearing off? Was he wrestling with his assigned task of eliminating her?

"Liam?"

He swiveled to face her, his eyes blazing blue. "Stacia. I didn't mean to wake you. But I couldn't stay so close to your body. I ..." His gaze swept over her in a bold, nearly tangible caress.

That was why he looked so strung out, because of how badly he wanted her? Beneath her concern, a secret, sinful part of her gloried in the effect she had on him. A few men had made half-hearted attempts to get past second base, but no one had ever wanted her like this.

After Liam's disappearance from her life, it had taken a long time before she'd noticed another guy. Even then, she'd tried to behave perfectly, giving no one an excuse to brand her a troublemaker. As she'd approached her eighteenth birthday, before she'd known about her heritage, she'd felt something was *off* about her. Being uncomfortable in her own skin made it difficult to get naked with anyone. Since then, she'd been occupied with learning to manage her magic and, most recently, running for her life.

Now Liam was on the run with her, a fugitive from his dangerous employers and on edge. Her impulse was to soothe him. Without thinking, she bounded from the bed to hug him and surreptitiously check his temperature. He looked feverish. The moment her arms brushed the bare skin of his shoulders, he hauled her against him for another kiss. Heat spiraled through her. As his tongue slid possessively against hers, she melted into the embrace. When he nipped at her bottom lip, she instinctively rubbed against him, loving the feel of his hard, male contours against her softness. Liam was well over six feet tall—every part of him was massive. Still, the sizable erection pressing against her made her breath catch.

She broke off the kiss, staring downward. Desire and panic warred within her. When he caught her gaze, his lips quirked in a half smile. He took her hand and gently pressed it against him. Even that slight touch drew a moan from him. Unable to stop herself, she cupped him more firmly through the denim. His hips rocked.

"Stacia." He murmured something in a language she didn't know. "What you do to me."

The problem was what she *wanted* to do to him. "Liam, I spent my teens crazy about you. I consider it an act of the greatest fortune that you came back into my life." Granted, it would have been nice if he'd shown up at her door with roses instead of kicking it down, but … "I can't make love to you, though. Not without reversing the spell first. Even if it means you'll go back to—"

"I would never hurt you."

Gods, she wanted to believe him. "Less than twenty-four hours ago, you felt differently."

"I'd never found anything as strong as my loyalty to the Tribunal. They've been, for all intents and purposes, my pack. But what I feel for you, what I've *always* felt for you trumps that. Less than twenty-four hours ago, I believed you'd betrayed me." A hint of vulnerability flashed in his eyes. "The doctor said you were scared of me, wanted me gone."

"You were the best part of my life," she whispered. "What I looked forward to when I woke up each morning and thought about as I drifted to sleep each night."

He buried his face in her hair but mercifully refrained from kissing her. She wasn't sure she had the strength to stop him twice. "Do you have what you need to do the reversal?"

"Not with me." The ingredients could be volatile and didn't travel well. "But I know of a cabin that's a safe house for sorceresses." She didn't add that it had been established because of the Tribunal and assassins like him. "It's kept well stocked, but it's a few hours away." At his crestfallen look, she sighed, wishing there weren't so many miles to cover. "Hey, Texas is a big state."

"Texas isn't all that's big."

A shiver of anticipation danced across her skin. If they didn't get out of this room soon, it was a toss-up which one of them would drag the other back into that king-sized bed.

CHAPTER FIVE

THE DRIVE TOOK FOREVER. An hour in, Stacia noticed Liam's hands trembling. Sweat beaded above his upper lip. She pulled over and made him switch places so she could drive.

"Too damn difficult," he muttered. "Being trapped in here with you. The full moon is getting closer and I *need* ..."

Wondering if fresh air and a break from their proximity would help, she stopped again. But he didn't want to get out and stretch his legs. Instead, he tugged her as close to him as the car interior would allow, dotting kisses down the slope of her throat and palming one breast through her T-shirt.

Her breathing grew ragged. Paradoxically, he looked more in control of himself.

"Better now," he told her. "It's like withdrawal. If I go too long without touching you, tasting you—it gets bad. Worse as night approaches."

So they made frequent stops. It might have qualified as the best road trip of her life except that as the day lengthened and the sun dipped below the horizon, Liam became too antsy to calm. By the time they rolled into the gravel driveway beneath the light of the moon, his clenched fingers were ripping into the passenger seat. Tension like she'd never seen was etched into his features.

She spoke the words for the entry incantation, and Liam checked the premises for her safety. Relief swamped her when she confirmed all the necessary ingredients were on hand. She knew the reversal spell well—it was one of the first a sorceress learned, in case anything ever went wrong. The potion wasn't inherently complicated, but it would need to simmer for at least an hour. Casting a sidelong glance to where Liam paced in front of the fireplace, she wondered if he'd make it another sixty minutes without shattering under the strain.

They both stared at the small iron pot, willing it to boil in spite of popular advice to the contrary. When she noticed he was digging his fingers into his thighs in an effort not to grab for her, she ached for him.

"Would it be better if you touched me?" she asked. "Like when we stopped—"

The rest of her question was lost in his kiss. Maybe it was a mistake, offering permission to do the one thing he'd been trying so valiantly *not* to do, but she hated watching him suffer. And it was hard to regret their kiss. He toppled them back against the deep rug, her sprawled across his body. As the fire crackled in the background, a different kind of flame licked through her.

Liam rolled them over, pinning her with his weight yet miraculously not crushing her. "Need to see you," he rasped. That was all the warning she got before he swooped the T-shirt up and over her head.

She had the distant and absurd thought that she wished she'd packed nicer bras for fleeing home, but he didn't seem disappointed with the pale pink cotton. He eyed her hungrily, and her nipples hardened beneath his avid gaze.

He peeled down one cup, baring her breast and swirling his tongue around the stiffened peak. Tunneling her fingers through his hair, she held him close as she arched up to meet him. His mouth was more magical than any spell in existence. His tongue and lips and, dear gods, his teeth—her body was buckling under a pressure so wickedly sweet that it wrung incoherent cries from her. When he stopped, she thought she might actually sob.

But then she was distracted by his dragging her jeans away.

Yes. Wait. "Liam, we can't make love."

He nodded acknowledgement, his thick hair tickling the sensitive skin of her abdomen. "Just need to taste you. So wet," he murmured approvingly. Then his mouth was moving against her, and it was somehow even better than when he'd been at her breasts. It only took a few minutes to send her soaring, and he growled in satisfaction when orgasm overtook her and she throbbed beneath his tongue.

He slid a finger inside her, then another, pumping them in rhythm to the fading aftershocks that redoubled and began to build again. "Need to be here, need to feel you pulsing around me."

The word *irrevocable* danced at the edge of her sanity. She wanted Liam inside her with a passion that bordered on madness. But not enough to shackle him to her if it was a mistake.

Feeling guilty and selfish, she batted his hands away. "We can't do that. But maybe I could touch you?" she volunteered, hoping to give him the same kind of release he'd brought her.

"No! I'm at the edge of control already. I might forget myself." His expression was so darkly intense that she scrambled into her clothes, afraid to tempt fate.

At the end of the hour, she had to dissuade him from drinking the hot liquid straight from the iron pot.

He captured her gaze over the top of the mug. "After I take this, and my feelings for you haven't changed in the slightest? You. Are. Mine." He drained the liquid in a single swallow, and she fought the urge to sidle away, trying to show trust.

He went to his knees, his head thrown back and his eyes squeezed shut. He was pale but eerily silent.

"Are you all right? Liam, talk to me."

"I *was* under the influence of your spell." He opened his eyes slowly, his words slurred.

"Oh." Then she should be thanking the gods she'd stopped him earlier. Instead, disappointment roiled through her.

"I feel the difference now." Blinking, looking more himself, he gave her a heart-melting smile. "You *are* my mate, Stacia Byrne. I think I knew that at seventeen but repressed it because I was so angry. It's like the injection you gave me somehow knocked that knowledge loose—violently. It clawed at me from the inside. But now, it's … perfect." He grabbed her hand and placed it over his heart. "You're right where you're supposed to be."

Joy bloomed inside her. She was really his?

And he is mine.

She launched herself into his arms, and he swept her up, carrying her to the nearby couch. Soon, she was naked, pressed between buttery-soft leather and Liam's sculpted muscles. Seeing him nude for the first time heightened her desire and her twinges of apprehension. But by the time he pressed into her, she was so slick with need there wasn't actual pain, only a moment of discomfort.

With his mouth on hers and his clever fingers at her breasts, the sensation quickly evaporated into pleasure. Soon, she was soaring again—and this time he went with her, gasping, "My Stacia," in a low rasp that made her toes curl.

For a shining moment, the world was perfect. They lay entwined and grinning like idiots. Then reality struck.

She cleared her throat. "Not to ruin the afterglow, but now what? As far as I know, the Tribunal still wants me dead."

He smoothed an errant lock of hair away from her face. "I won't let anyone hurt you. I'd die first—and I'm not easy to kill. But our safest bet is going off-plane. The Tribunal is the law in this dimension, but there are other realms, some quite beautiful. The elders don't want people to know how chaotic things are right now, but they're dealing with a vampire uprising and a missing princess. On top of that, they've lost two Enforcers this year. Three, counting me. I think they're distracted enough that we can get away, as long as we do it quickly."

"I have to come back, though. Eventually." After she'd had time to develop her powers and a plan. "I owe a friend a favor." According to Kyann's visions, in five years, Stacia would save her life.

But for now, Stacia would go. It wasn't a perfect solution, fleeing in exile, but she would be with the only man she'd ever loved, secure in the knowledge that his feelings for her were genuine and soul-deep. For now, that was all the happy ending she needed.

Lila Bell is the author of hot paranormal romances *A Wicked Hunger*, *Wicked Vengeance*, and *Wicked Persuasion*.

Lila is also a pen name for award-winning, five-time RITA® finalist Tanya Michaels, who writes sexy contemporary romance for Harlequin Blaze (*Good With His Hands*, 04/15) but leaves shape-shifters, incubi, and mystical assassins to her alter ego. You can follow Lila on Twitter @WriterLilaBell.

A RIGHT HONORABLE GENTLEMAN

COURTNEY MILAN

New York Times Bestseller, RITA® Finalist

London, 1863

IT WAS LONG PAST midnight, and the windows of all the other houses on Grosvenor Square were dark. But Miss Catherine Hooks had no time for weariness. No matter how long her day had been, her most taxing chore lay ahead of her still.

In this house, the oil lamps lining the hall still burned merrily. Below, the last sounds of the day made their way up the stairwell: the brush of broom against floor, the sharp bark of the housekeeper giving orders, the clink of silver as the butler counted it back into the case.

But there was no slinking back to join her fellow servants. Cat fingered the paper in her hands and continued down the hall.

A door opened ahead. Cat's breath caught—but it was Mrs. Walters, the cook, who stumbled out. Not *him*. Mrs. Walters's face was fixed in a grim smile, a determined grit of teeth that she held long enough to pull the door shut behind her. As soon as she did, all hint of pleasantry slipped away. Her fingers touched her temples; her eyes, somewhat shielded by the graying curls that peeked out from under her white cap, shivered shut.

Cat came up to her. "He's bad tonight, then?"

Mrs. Walters's lips thinned in misery. "I tried so hard—did *everything* right. I was sure he could have only praise about the dinner ..."

"You know how he is," Cat whispered soothingly. "He's responsible for all of England. Sometimes he … forgets that the country's not always at stake. He'll be better tomorrow." He usually was.

A tremor ran through Mrs. Walters. "Oh, Miss Hooks." She put her head in her hands. "He sacked me."

Cat blinked. "*What?* No. You know he doesn't mean it."

The other woman shook her head. "This time? I'm not certain. Don't go in there now, dearie—he's in that dark a mood."

Cat should have been afraid. She knew her employer's moods as well as any of the eight servants who kept Mr. Glennon's London home in order. But the thought of Mr. Glennon in one of his black, bitter moods sent a little thrill down her—one that had very little to do with fear.

"Come," Mrs. Walters was saying. "He won't have heard you. Creep back the way you came, and he'll be none the wiser."

Cat held up the paper in her hand. "I can't. I've been—"

The door opened abruptly behind them.

"She's been summoned," a deep, pitiless voice said. "If you're going to gossip about me, have the goodness to do it belowstairs, where I can't overhear every word."

Mrs. Walters winced. Cat turned to face her employer. The Right Honorable Mr. Edward Glennon stood in the doorway, towering above her. She saw his eyes first, black and piercing, his gaze as sharp and unforgiving as a blade of ice. His hair was salt-and-pepper, his mouth set in a frown. He saw Cat staring at him, and folded his arms over his chest.

"Well, Hooks?" he demanded. "Are you going to stand there like a dumbstruck puppy, or will you come in?"

A dumbstruck *puppy?* Cat narrowed her eyes at her employer.

Mrs. Walters gave Cat's arm a final, comforting squeeze. Cat brought her chin up and swept into the room.

In the years that she'd worked for him, his office had never changed. The same heavy leather-upholstered chair sat behind a desk of oak; the same dark carpet graced the floor. The paintings never moved by so much as an inch. Mr. Glennon's desk was always clean—an alarming feat, considering the quantity of paper that crossed it. A wicker basket held his voluminous outgoing correspondence, organized neatly by destination. At this time of night, it was full once again, even though the post had gone out at seven in the evening.

Mr. Glennon seated himself in his leather chair but, to Cat's annoyance, left her standing like a supplicant.

She shifted her shoulders and faced him like a soldier. "You asked to see me, sir."

"I've heard a disturbing report." Those dark eyes focused on her.

Cat suspected that the other members of the Privy Council spared not a thought to the details of their households. Mr. Glennon, however, was both a widower and the Chancellor of the Exchequer. Details were his duty. He didn't know how to lay that duty down—not even past midnight, not even when it was a question as mundane as the proper polish to be used on silver. Certainly not when it came to Miss Catherine Hooks, who was charged with the care of his only son.

She folded her hands. "I assume," she said, "that you are referring to the chickens. An unfortunate incident, sir, caused by high spirits. I've dealt with it."

Her employer snorted. "Dealt with it, have you? High spirits are well and good, but Peter is a Glennon, Miss Hooks. He has a capacity for mischief that cannot be controlled by the namby-pamby means employed by foolish, soft-hearted governesses."

Namby-pamby. Foolish. Two more insults.

Cat kept her expression severe. "On the contrary, sir. You, of all people, should know my heart is anything but soft."

A glint of appreciation flickered across his features, but it was swiftly quashed. "How many times must I tell you? When you find yourself over your head—when you realize that your disciplinary methods are as inadequate as your mind is weak—you must come to me."

Cat held his gaze. She waited, counting out her own heart-beats as she did.

He didn't blink. He ought to scare her. With his considerable attention focused on her—attention that was powerful enough to shift the future of the entire country—her pulse raced. But it wasn't fear she felt … just her own peculiar foolishness.

"You may stop pretending to that ridiculous temper," she finally told him. "I handled it with my usual aplomb. The only reason you're yelling at me is because you want to know what I did."

A smile touched his lips. A notch in her favor; she'd broken him first. "Well," he said a little too gruffly. "Perhaps." His eyes hadn't left hers. "Perhaps," he repeated.

In that word, twice spoken, in that long look he gave her, lay all the things they dared not say to one another.

Cat looked away first. "If you must know how I punished him, I had him write a letter to his grandmother."

After four years of working together, he'd learned to suspect her of deviousness. He tilted his head. "Explain."

"In this letter," Cat said, "I had him explain to her how much he missed being called Petey-kins."

He shut his eyes and smiled ruefully. "Ouch."

"And how he had been thinking, there were likely to be so many Peters at Eton, that it would be best if she addressed all correspondence to him at that institution by that beloved pet name."

The smile on his face flickered, threatening to disappear. "Oh," he said more slowly. "That's almost too cruel."

She shrugged. "I haven't sent the letter. It's hidden in a safe spot. But he knows that the next time he doubles the work the servants do, it goes out with the post."

Slowly, Mr. Glennon leaned back into his chair. "Hooks, remind me never to anger you."

Only it wasn't those simple words she heard. There was a caress in them, one she couldn't have identified in tone or look. Still, she heard the compliment of his regard slide around her. That kind of thought might make another woman foolish, but Catherine was never foolish.

"If you don't wish to anger me," she said calmly, "stop calling me foolish, weak-minded, and … oh, what was the other one? Ah, yes. A *dumbstruck puppy.* It's beneath me, sir."

He looked up, his eyebrows rising. She doubted that any of the other servants ever took him to task.

But nobody had ever thought Cat was important. She'd been orphaned young, passed from family to family until her failure on the marriage mart pushed her into service. She'd learned long ago that if she didn't insist on fair treatment, she'd never get it.

Mr. Glennon could change the fate of the country with a frown. He stared at her now; she met his gaze without flinching. Flinch? She could scarcely breathe with his eyes on her, those piercing, brilliant eyes that could turn the stiffest spine into jelly. The only thing that kept her upright was the knowledge that she was a governess, and a good one.

"You're right," he said. "That was badly done of me. My apologies."

And fair. Even to Cat, a mere governess. Even when nobody else was present to mark his fairness. A stupid reason to fall in love with a man, but there it was. Nobody had ever thought Cat was important, but sometimes, Mr. Glennon made her think she could be.

She cleared her throat. "It's just as well you asked to see me. There is something else we must talk about."

He sighed. "Walters. I know. I lost my temper." He looked upward. "Inexcusable on my part, really. It was an important dinner; half the Privy Council was here. I'm the Chancellor of the Exchequer; you'd think my household could distinguish between a trifle and a tart, particularly when I sent a note expressly specifying the former. But—"

"But your handwriting is execrable," Cat finished, "and your son released a flock of chickens in the scullery. You should thank her for having a meal at all."

Another sigh. He scrubbed at his forehead. "Damn it. Apologize to Walters for me, will you?"

Cat tapped her fingers together. "I will do nothing of the sort. You were in the wrong. *You* owe the apology."

"Damn." His gaze lingered on hers, almost inviting. But what he said was, "Get out, then. I suppose I'd better get down there."

"Sir, there's another matter." Her hands prickled. Her heart thumped heavily in her chest.

His brow furrowed momentarily before clearing. "Ah. You need advice. What is the matter?"

"I don't need advice." She took a deep breath. "I need a reference."

He blinked. He set his hands on the surface of his desk, spread them flat, and then blinked again. "A reference?" he repeated slowly. "Whatever do you need a reference for?"

"The usual reason. I'll want another position when I leave."

"Leave?" He shook his head. For the first time that evening, he took his eyes off her, his nostrils widening in annoyance. "Why the devil would you leave? Is someone making your life difficult? I shall take care of it. Is it the pay? I'll—"

"Peter is eleven," Cat said. "Almost twelve. He'll be going to Eton in three months, and when he does, there will be nothing for me to do."

He ran his hands through his hair, shook his head. "No. You can't leave."

"I can. I will."

He glared at her.

"I must," she whispered. "I …" No, she couldn't say that. "I hate boredom." It was all she dared say. Anything more would overturn the pact of silence between them.

He pushed to his feet and paced to the window. The back of the house faced the mews; she couldn't imagine that he saw anything of interest at this time of night. Still, he stared for a moment before turning back to her.

"Be my housekeeper."

"I should like to see that," Cat replied evenly. "As if I would take Mrs. Evans's place."

He made a motion with his hand. "Surely we need someone in the scullery."

"I am one of the best governesses in the country. I am thirty-nine years old, far too ancient to be laboring over soapy dishes in hopes of promotion upstairs, simply because the man I'm working for can't … can't …"

She cut herself off, letting that sentence trail uselessly in the air. That wasn't the way things worked between them. They argued. They sparred. They certainly didn't speak about their feelings.

But perhaps he didn't agree. His face grew grim. He walked

toward her until he stood within arm's length. "Can't what?" he murmured. "Come now, Hooks. After four years of locking horns with me, surely you don't fear speaking now."

It wasn't words she feared. It was the truth that lay between them, those seconds of silence when they didn't speak.

Oh, he tried not to show his feelings. He never smiled at her overmuch, never leered at her with lecherous intent. He called her into his office and brought her to task as often as any other servant in his household. He was a gentleman, and consequently, he'd only given her those unintended smiles, that extra smidgeon of his attention.

But now, his dark eyes were fixed on her, waiting an answer that was beyond all propriety.

"You don't need me to stay," Cat heard herself say. "You need to visit a brothel."

He didn't laugh. He didn't flinch. And most telling of all—he didn't deny it. His jaw grew rigid, and his nostrils flared, but he didn't take a single step toward her. Nonetheless, the air around them heated—as if acknowledging the attraction that arced between them had given her desire substance.

"Did I ask to bed you?" he finally said. "Have I ever implied as much? I abhor masters who importune their subordinates. It's a misuse of power."

But as he spoke, his gaze fell to her lips. A shot of heat went through her, and for one instant, she imagined what would happen if he were less exacting in his moral standards—if she were less strict in her conduct. She imagined the touch of his lips, the warmth of his arm around her, drawing her close. She imagined a home that she never had to leave ...

His eyes traveled up to meet hers, and his gaze hardened.

"Just as well," she said. "I am not the sort to bed my master. No matter what my personal feelings on the matter might be."

"Of course."

"This is what honorable people in our position do," she said. "I find another position. You provide a reference. I leave."

"That's our only choice?"

Cat had never been stupid. He was her employer. He called

her names, for God's sake. No matter what his private feelings, in some way, she would always remain his servant. *She* had to remember that she was important, because nobody else would.

She refused to acknowledge the stinging of her eyes. "I leave," she told him, "and we remember each other with fondness."

"With *fondness?*" He let out a harsh breath. "That's what this is?"

Before she could lose her nerve, she took a step toward him. He didn't move to take her in his arms. He didn't reach out to touch her at all. He simply stood in place, watching her.

She let her fingers brush his cheek. "With great fondness," she whispered.

His hand came up and caught hold of hers. His eyes glittered. For a moment, his touch was warm on her fingers, his head bowed close to hers.

For just one moment, the words he did not say hung between them. They lingered like a seduction, crackling against Catherine's skin. His arms didn't come around her. His lips didn't touch hers. Only his fingers played over hers, his breath whispering against her cheek.

"No," she said aloud, denying herself as much as him. "I'm just your governess. That is all I will ever be, so I must insist on being the best governess I can be."

He let out a breath. "Catherine." His fingers slid down her wrist. "You'll never be just anything to me."

She couldn't speak, couldn't move. He was the one who straightened, the one who turned away, his movements deliberate and angry. His jaw clenched; he glanced at her unhappily.

But they'd said all they could say. Everything else between them … well, that wouldn't happen.

He tilted his head. "Get out," he said. "I have work to do."

CHAPTER TWO

THERE WAS ONLY ONE thing Mr. Edward Glennon could do about Miss Catherine Hooks's resignation: refuse to see her again.

The alternative would have been damning. She'd wound herself so tightly into his life that he couldn't imagine a world without her. And now that they had openly acknowledged the truth—that he wanted her and she wanted him—he was very much afraid of what might transpire. A gentleman didn't take liberties with his servants, no matter what the circumstances.

And yet every time he saw her, he could think of nothing else. *Seduce her,* his less honorable impulses demanded. *Seduce her into staying.*

Gentlemanly conduct prevailed—but only because he refused to see her.

He waved her away when she told him she'd answered a few advertisements. He left the room when she told him that there might be some inquiries.

When a solicitor inquired about her character, he forced himself to answer with the truth. *Miss Catherine Hooks is the finest governess I have ever had the pleasure of encountering,* he wrote. *I cannot imagine a world without her.*

He sent the message, and then, in a fit of pique, promptly burned all the correspondence—his drafts, the letter from the solicitor, everything.

When she knocked on his office door a few weeks later, he tried to shut it in her face. She insinuated her foot in the way.

"Under my contract," she gritted out, "I must deliver notice—"

"What?" he'd demanded. "What are you saying, Miss Hooks? You're talking so quietly I can hardly make out what you're saying."

"I *said,*" she shouted, "I am *leaving!*"

At least when he was baiting her, there was no possibility of taking her in his arms and trying to change her mind. He gave her his most supercilious look. "What's that? You're breathing? Why are you shouting at me about such trivialities?"

"God, you are impossible!" She turned and left in a huff.

Two hours later, she returned with a letter. He ripped it up in front of her face.

"I can still leave," she told him as the pieces fluttered to the floor, "even if you refuse to acknowledge that I've given notice."

It wasn't her notice he refused to acknowledge. It was her—the woman who had wound her way into his life.

"I'm busy, Hooks," he said with a growl. "Get out."

He worked through the party the other servants had in her honor, even though he could hear her voice drifting up the stairs. He sat at his desk with his door open, scribbling grim responses to correspondence, listening to the sound of her laughter filling his home.

It was the height of foolishness to wait in the front parlor the next morning. The new family—he'd refused to ask about them—had sent a carriage for her early. He watched from the window as the footmen loaded her trunks into the boot, as the servants clustered around her, dealing out embraces and good wishes. They backed away; she stood before the carriage, all alone on the gray cobblestones of the drive.

She couldn't leave. She *couldn't.*

And then, as if she were thinking the same thing, she turned and looked at the window where he stood. He wasn't sure how long they stood there—she frozen, looking at him, he with his fingertips pressed to the cold glass, wishing that she would come back to him. But she didn't. And when she turned away—when she opened the door of the carriage—that was when his heart realized that she was actually going to go.

He tore out of the house, down the front steps. He was scarcely in time to catch her hand as she was ascending into the carriage.

"Catherine." He struggled to draw breath. "Catherine, don't go."

He could feel her pulse pounding in her wrist, could mark her breaths by each puff of white in the cold morning air. She looked at him, her eyes sparkling.

"I've accepted an offer of employment," she told him. "They are expecting me this morning."

She didn't pull away from him, and he couldn't make himself let go.

"I am a governess." Her voice shook. "That is what I do. Please don't make me regret this any more than I must."

A gentleman didn't importune his servants, and until she left his grounds, Miss Hooks was still his servant. Edward hated having principles. He absolutely hated them. Slowly, he released her wrist.

"Where will you be staying, then?" he asked.

The family that employed her lived in London—he knew that much. She'd be close. They might …

She looked away. "You were right to stay away. I can't bear to say good-bye to you once. I don't wish to say it a second time."

"Where will you be staying, you stubborn minx?" he demanded.

She pulled her hand away. "I am not your servant any longer," she told him, "and I'll thank you not to address me in that fashion." Her eyes were glittering, and he wanted to kiss her more than ever.

"Don't be ridiculous." He gritted his teeth. "The details don't matter. Where are you staying?"

She shook her head, but she slumped, giving in to him at last. "Rotherhithe Street," she whispered. "Number 77 Rotherhithe Street."

Edward meant to pursue her immediately, but almost as soon as she left, the budgetary negotiations that had been proceeding apace broke down into the worst sort of parliamentary acrimony. He counted off each passing week with a growing sense of frustration. He knew where she was. He would see her eventually. As soon as this was all ended …

The instant a free hour appeared, he ordered his carriage. At first, he felt only anticipation. But as the streets passed, excitement gave way to concern. Rubbish piles on street corners, dingy stone, shutters that hung precariously from abused, rusted hinges … This wasn't the sort of neighborhood where he'd expected to find her.

He arrived on a stinking street and couldn't quite believe it when his driver came to a halt in front of a nondescript building. A once-proud brass placard on the door of number 77 Rotherhithe

Street declared that Joseph Harris, draper, would be pleased to sell bolts of his finest linen to the public on Tuesdays through Thursdays. A hand-scrawled note tacked beneath the tarnished brass sign contradicted this flatly: "Liquidation to be held this Wednesday at noon."

Edward stared at that card and then looked up the filthy brick of the building. It didn't look like the sort of place where one of the finest governesses in England would have taken a position. She must have been bamboozled. She was probably wondering what to do. He found that he quite liked the idea of saving Miss Hooks from her difficulties.

He knocked smartly on the door. The door made a dull, wooden thud—one that he doubted could be heard. Nobody came. He waited—one, two, three seconds—and then knocked again. He let a full half minute elapse before fetching his walking stick and pounding on the door with greater force.

"Hurry up, hurry up!" he muttered.

His arm ached with the effort of beating on the door by the time it creaked open. A man peered out at him. He was unshaven, and his nose looked to be in desperate need of a handkerchief.

"Cease that infernal noise!" the man said, glowering at Edward. "Can't you read? You'll get your money after Wednesday, but there's not a penny to be had before, no matter how hard you pound."

Edward brought himself up to his full height. "I am not here on an errand of business, but on one of mercy. Tell Miss Hooks that I have come to rescue her."

"Eh?"

"Miss Hooks," Edward said impatiently. "The governess. I have come for her."

The man's scowl deepened. "There's no governess here. Just me and Mrs. Harris. We've got no little ones. No call for a governess." The man spat on the threshold, inches from Edward's boots. "No money to pay one, neither."

"There must be some mistake," Edward said, inching away from that unsanitary globule. "I have it on the best of authority ..."

He looked at the weedy man in front of him—the dirty, stringy

A RIGHT HONORABLE GENTLEMAN

hair; the grimy shirtsleeves—and realized that there were two possibilities.

Either Miss Hooks had been bamboozled by this slovenly idiot in front of him or she had lied about her address.

I don't think it would be a good idea to see one another, she'd said, and like a fool, he'd demanded her direction.

Number 77 Rotherhithe Street, she'd said. He'd heard her clearly; she was too precise to have been mistaken herself. There was only one other possibility: She'd lied to him. Deliberately.

For a moment—just a moment—he couldn't believe it was possible. He was the Chancellor of the Exchequer, damn it, and she should have been … she should have been …

I'll thank you not to address me in that fashion, she'd said, and he'd called her ridiculous.

More exchanges flooded back in his mind. The way he'd talked to her. And—most recently—the assumption that if he just growled at her loudly enough, she'd give in to him.

She'd made herself the best part of his day, and he'd repaid her with insults. If he hadn't been paying her salary, she wouldn't have tolerated his company at all.

He swallowed. The truth came to him on a tide of shame. The way he'd treated her? He would have lied to himself, too.

CHAPTER THREE

BY THE TIME SEVERAL more weeks had passed, Edward had reconciled himself to her absence. He woke without having to remind himself that she was no longer present. He passed hours without thinking of her—easy enough when his days were so full. He had almost convinced himself he was on his way to forgetting her.

In his spare moments, though, he slipped up. One afternoon, when he was walking through Hyde Park at a brisk pace, he thought he saw her.

It had been days since he'd seen a woman and thought her Catherine, days since his heart raced in furious anticipation. And yet here he was again—catching sight of a female and imagining it was she. She was coming down the path toward him, too far away for him to make out her features. The woman's dark blue walking gown looked like one Catherine owned—the one with the little crinkly bits of fabric decorating the cuff.

It wasn't her, he told himself. The women he saw were never her. It didn't matter that she had Catherine's blond hair, that she wore her hair in a simple chignon, the way Catherine always wore hers.

Catherine had never had a bonnet like that—a wide thing of straw and silk flowers that shielded her face. As soon as he was near enough to see her face, he'd know that it wasn't her.

He marched briskly on, refusing to acknowledge the race of his heart. And then the woman in front of him stopped and looked at him. Her parasol slipped from her grasp. Her mouth rounded in surprise.

Ten steps closer, and he could see the nose he knew so well, the golden-brown of her widening eyes.

"Sir!" said the woman who should not have been Catherine and yet indisputably was.

"Miss Hooks." The words slipped out of his mouth. He took a step toward her.

She looked utterly befuddled—and completely dazzled. Her smile poked out involuntarily.

It hadn't changed, that electricity arcing between them. He found himself pacing toward her, step by step, reaching for her hand.

She let him bow over it, didn't protest when he found he couldn't relinquish it.

"Miss Hooks," he repeated. "How do you do?"

"Very well, thank you." She managed a flummoxed curtsy. "How do you do?"

"Well."

For a moment, they stared at each other in awkward silence. Every second stumbled past like a wasted opportunity. At any moment, she'd make her excuses and disappear once more. And in that instant—holding her hand, wanting to hold more of her, remembering everything he had said to drive her away, Edward realized that he was in a hell of a predicament: She didn't want to see him, and he couldn't let her go.

He cleared his throat. "How do you like your new position?"

She smiled. "I like it very much!" she told him sunnily. "I am working with the two best young ladies in all of England. They are such dears; you would not believe how lovely they are. It is the best position I have ever—" She stopped at this and coughed.

"I'm glad to hear it," he told her gravely. "Rumor has it that your last employer was something of a rag-mannered bear."

A single eyebrow rose. "Mr. Glennon," she said in mock reproach, "I would never speak ill of a former employer."

"Why not? You did it often enough when you worked for me."

That smile flitted across her face again. "Yes," she said quietly. "I did."

He had an appointment with a crowd of bankers in ten minutes—the sort of appointment that could not be put off. He abhorred decisions made in the heat of the moment.

He consulted his pocket watch and offered her his arm. She looked at it—very, very slowly—and then, with a shake of her head, as if she was admonishing herself, she reached out and took it. It felt right to have her beside him, right to fold his gloved hands over her fingers.

"I have missed you," he said quietly, as they walked along the bank of the Serpentine. "I've missed you every day since you left."

She let out a breath. Her fingers tightened on his arm. She didn't say anything, though—not until they left the main path and wandered into a wood.

"I see," she finally said, "that you haven't taken my advice and visited a brothel."

"Damn all brothels," he said, turning to face her. "Brothels are impractical. For one, I'm the Chancellor of the Exchequer, and I cannot be seen visiting one. For another, brothels don't have you, and so they will be, by definition, inadequate to my needs."

She turned to him, her eyes wide. "Mr. Glennon. Please don't do this."

He could feel that clock ticking in his head, his next appointment bearing down on him.

"Miss Hooks—Catherine." He swallowed. "I have had a great many hours to think about you. About the many things I did wrong. I have come to a conclusion."

She shook her head. "We mustn't. I gave you the wrong house number for a reason, because—"

"You did it," he said, "because the Chancellor of the Exchequer is an ass."

She let out a breath and looked away. "You have to be. There's too much at stake for you to suffer fools gladly. I understand." Her voice was low. "I have always understood. It's your work."

"It's my work," he agreed. "But someday, the government will change, and I'll look up and find myself without a pile of work, and set in my ways as an unbearable ass. I told you a thousand times while you were with me that you were naïve, foolish ..." He trailed off before he reminded her. "I never told you—not once— how extraordinary you were. How much I admired the way you could solve problems without once resorting to insult or physical threat. Miss Hooks, I am ashamed."

She was looking at him with rounded eyes.

"Wednesday is your half day, is it?"

She let out a slow breath. "I don't know what to think."

"I don't know what you should think, either," he responded. "But seeing as how I am going to ask you to marry me, I thought I would give myself a sporting chance at getting a yes."

She colored and stopped walking. Her mouth closed, and she looked up at him.

"If you tell me no," he continued, "I'll leave and throw myself into my work. Really, for the sake of England, you should reject me now. But if you tell me yes …"

He took a step closer to her. She tilted her head back, almost swaying toward him. He set the back of his hand against her cheek, brushed her face tenderly. "If you tell me yes," he whispered, "I'll do my best to leave the ill-tempered rants to my associates."

She let out a shaky breath. "You can't marry me."

"Let me worry about what I can do. Concern yourself with what you want."

She pushed away from him. "But I have to—I cannot—" Her hands wrung together. He waited, the minutes to his meeting diminishing, second by precious second.

"I've never had a beau before," she said slowly. "I have no idea what to expect."

"Never had a beau?" He frowned at her. "How is that possible? You're rather nice-looking."

"Nice-looking, am I?" But a little smile came over her face. She looked directly at him, her chin lifting in a challenge. "*Perhaps* it was because I had a reputation as bossy. No man wants a bossy wife."

"Wrong, Miss Hooks. At least one man does." He reached out and took her hand. "Unfortunately, there are twenty-three bankers waiting for me, and if I wish to avoid another money panic …"

"Yes. Go."

He raised her hand to his lips. "Until next Wednesday, Catherine."

It was only her gloves he touched. Still, when he relinquished his hold on her, her cheeks flushed a most satisfying pink.

She watched him, her eyes bright, and for the first time in weeks, he felt hope—luminous, lovely hope.

"Next Wednesday," she agreed.

"You brought your secretary?" Cat asked dubiously.

It was a cool autumn day, and the Right Honorable Mr. Glennon wore a bright blue scarf against the chill. He also had a pair of thick gloves, which he was not wearing at all. He bore them in one hand, beating them against the palm of the other as he spoke.

"One moment, Miss Hooks," he said, and turned back to his younger companion. "Address the last message to Mr. Newdegate."

The young man beside him shifted and scribbled in a book with a pencil.

Mr. Glennon dictated precisely, punctuating each sentence with a smack of his gloves. "Over the last years, our exports to France have increased threefold. The ad valorem duty that France applies to English silk goods is thirty percent. Do the math for him—he hasn't the head for it himself—and then suggest that he remove his thumb from his ..." A pause, and both men glanced at Cat.

Mr. Glennon's secretary coughed politely. "From his nose, sir?"

"His arse," the Chancellor of the Exchequer replied. "She's heard the word."

Catherine found herself smiling in direct contradiction to the resigned shake of her head.

"Right, then," Mr. Glennon said. "I'll be back in twenty minutes."

The younger man bowed and left at a brisk pace. Mr. Glennon turned back to her. *Mr. Glennon.* She had to think of him that way. She wasn't even sure why she'd agreed, why she was entertaining these thoughts. And if she let herself call him Edward, even in her own mind, she doubted she could resist further intimacy.

Instead, she arched an eyebrow at him. "You're busy."

He sighed. "It's this damned French treaty. Parliament avoided the issue in '52 because exports were low. Now, though, with America blockaded, the world has changed. So must our trade treaties." There were dark hollows beneath his eyes; he rubbed his forehead and drew in a breath. "It won't always be this bad."

She put one hand on her hip. "You've scarcely slept."

"It'll be over in a few weeks, and I'll sleep through service next Sunday."

Four years and some months she'd spent working for him. He never did get around to catching up on his sleep.

"Next time, send your excuses. I'll understand."

He cast her another unreadable look. "Catherine, I think you do *not* understand."

Her name on his lips—*that* she understood all too well. A thrill went through her. But she was not going to give in simply because he addressed her in an intimate fashion.

He took a step toward her. "In the last five years, I have not wanted for people to tell me 'Yes, sir.' In all that time, there has been only one soul who I could count on to tell me 'No.' 'No, sir, you're being unreasonable.' 'No, sir, you had no right to shout at Mrs. Walters.' 'No, sir, there's no excuse for you to talk to me in that way.' If I have retained any hint of humanity, it's because of you."

Cat swallowed.

"I don't need your understanding. I need you to look at me and tell me in no uncertain terms when I've become unbearable."

"In that case," Cat said, "next time, remember that Mr. Newdegate is a member of Parliament and an important man in his own right. You'll do better at convincing him if you don't put his back up."

He grimaced but didn't gainsay her.

"There. I've said my piece. Now go work out your treaty with France."

His jaw set mulishly. "Did you not hear what I just said?"

She made a shooing motion. "Go on, then. I'm an adult. Your country needs you."

He didn't scamper off as she'd expected. Instead, he offered her his arm and walked her not in the direction of the government buildings but away—across the bridge over the Serpentine, into one of the forest glades that dotted Hyde Park. The branches were bare by now, and the sun beat through them.

"It's my job to think of priorities," he told her. "To decide whether to listen to the weavers or the miners, the bankers or the workers. Every little aspect of the economy must be put in its proper place and attended to when necessary." There was a fierce quality to his voice. Trees surrounded them, and they were suddenly, temporarily, alone.

"You don't need to justify your work. I understand."

"You don't," he said with a jerk of his head. "Obviously you don't. I tell you this in my professional capacity. For the next twenty minutes, you are more necessary than all of England."

Her mouth dried. Her throat closed. She'd never had anyone tell her she was important, let alone necessary.

"I'm ... I'm ..." Her voice sounded odd. "I'm just a governess."

But it was this she'd feared most in his office all those months ago—not that he would seduce her with a kiss or a caress. This was what all those silences had meant. All those times she'd told herself that her work made her important, he'd been arguing right back at her.

"You are not *just* anything," he said in low tones. "No, Catherine. You're the only woman in all of England who will tell me when I've gone too far. I need you as I've never needed anyone. I don't know when I fell in love with you, but I'm never going to stop. I'm never going to want to."

She hadn't known how much she needed those words until he gave them to her. Her breath hitched, and she looked over at him.

"So stay," he said quietly. "I know how much I must do to prove I'm worthy of you—but please, walk with me a while."

All her life, she'd had to remember her own importance—to insist on it with everyone she dealt with. What would it be like to have one of the most powerful men in the country believe in it, too?

She glanced over at the Right Honorable Mr. Edward Glennon—at his dark eyes, intent on her face, at the determined set of his mouth. At the way his gaze caressed her.

Heaven, she thought. It would be *heaven.*

"You're not my employer any longer." Surprisingly, her voice didn't shake.

"Yes." He watched her warily.

She took a step toward him. "So you cannot order me what to do."

"I didn't mean to order."

"I won't stay with you a while," she heard herself say.

He inhaled.

"I'll stay with you forever."

His eyes flashed. He reached out; his hands took hold of her wrists. But she was the one who moved forward, the one who looked up at him, the one who closed the gap between their lips. The heat of his mouth met hers.

"God, Catherine," he murmured, his breath whispering against her lips. "I don't deserve you. But I love you—so much."

And then his mouth took hers full force, his arms wrapping around her with a ferocity that took her by surprise. He kissed her hard at first, and then slower still, seducing her with the promise of years to come. It took all her will to pull away.

"Don't be ridiculous," Cat told him. "You'll deserve me. I love you too much to let you do anything else."

Before she started writing fiction, **Courtney Milan** got a graduate degree in theoretical physical chemistry from UC Berkeley, and a law degree from the University of Michigan. She's been a law professor and a scientist, but her favorite job is the one she has now: writing historical romances full time.

If you'd like to learn more about Courtney Milan, or to sign up for her newsletter to find out when her next book is released, please visit www.courtneymilan.com.

STATION 12

AMBER LIN

ISOBEL MONROE WAS DONE waiting. She wasn't sure why she'd ever started. A wink and a few heroic stories and suddenly she was Matt's convenience girlfriend. Mostly this involved waiting for him to show up or call, which he did with increasing irregularity. Well, she was done.

Though she couldn't entirely blame him. If she'd been his convenience girlfriend, he'd been her convenience boyfriend, too. No demands, no expectations. No drama, as long as she pretended she didn't know he slept with other women sometimes.

Done.

Her tires crunched over loose gravel in the parking lot. Opening her trunk, she peeked inside the cardboard box. A pair of running shoes, a toothbrush, a razor. Everything Matt had kept at her house, the sum total of a six-month relationship.

The box also contained the Fireman of the Month calendar, a gift that had seemed cute at the time. Now, it just annoyed her. Okay, so he was hot. She got that, but he hadn't been doing her any favors. She took care of herself in the limited time she had after work and made up the difference in the summers.

If there were such a thing as a Third Grade Teacher of the Month calendar, she liked to think she'd warrant one of the lesser months, like maybe October. Yeah, she was solid October material, and she didn't deserve to be jerked around.

Red letters spelled out *Fire Station 12* over the brick building. The bottom of a red metal garage door peeked from the ceiling, rolled up as men in loose pants and snug T-shirts worked on the shiny truck. Appreciation stalled her steps as she took in the sight of sweaty muscles and tanned skin. She wanted something deeper in a relationship. She *deserved* something more meaningful than a recurring booty call. But Matt's carved physique would be missed.

"Can I help you?"

The masculine voice caught her attention. One of the firemen hopped down from the truck with impressive agility for his size. Tall. Wide in all the right places. His T-shirt clung to his chest, and she found herself jealous of thin cotton fabric.

He approached her, wiping his hands on a rag. She didn't recognize him from the calendar, which had to be an oversight. Maybe some people would find his eyes too deep-set or his nose too broad, but conventional beauty didn't apply to him. He wasn't pretty; he was magnetic, and she felt his pull down to her bones.

Stop staring. Snapping her mouth shut, she tried to focus on the task at hand.

She cleared her throat. *Can I help you?* "Hi, I'm looking for Matt."

"For Matt." His voice was flat.

"Yes, please."

She tried to keep the frustration from her voice, but from the surprise in this man's vivid blue eyes, she'd failed. Her frustration wasn't for this guy, even if he wasn't exactly being forthcoming. It was for Matt not answering her calls.

She would have worried he'd been hurt on the job except he'd left a couple vague return messages—both while she was in class, when she couldn't have answered the phone. How else was she supposed to give him back his stuff? She felt bad for coming to his workplace. But after fifteen missed calls and the sinking realization she didn't even know his address, she'd had to do something.

She softened her voice, aiming for casual. "I need to drop something off for him. He left some stuff at my place." Let his coworkers think it was just a hookup—or he could explain it however he wanted. She didn't care. What she needed was closure.

No, what she really needed was to move on. Stop waiting. Start living again.

The firefighter rubbed his square jaw, a slightly sardonic tilt to his lips. "And you are?"

"A friend," she said shortly, inviting no further question.

Of course, he didn't look fazed in the slightest. "Whose name is … ?"

He waited. And damn, those eyes were blue. Her kids had a project where they made murals of different parts of the world. His eyes were the crystalline depths around the Fiji islands. His tanned skin was a sandy beach, but his lips … they had no likeness. They were a mystery, where X marks the spot, and instinctively her body tightened, already reaching for this newfound goal.

Which was exactly how she'd gotten herself into this mess.

"Izzy," she admitted with a sigh. "Isobel Monroe."

"Isobel," he repeated, as if trying it out. Tasting the name on his tongue. "He never mentioned you."

Oh, great, as if her ego hadn't already hit rock bottom. She gestured to the box she held. "Listen, I'll just leave this for him. He'll know what it's for."

The fireman looked dubious. His lips pursed in something like puzzlement, and she noticed he'd missed a spot while shaving that morning. Bristle shadowed the area where a left dimple would go, while his square jaw gleamed smooth. She wanted to touch the rough spot, to feel the abrasion on her lips. She liked the inconsistency of it, too. It made him human instead of a bronzed Adonis—the way, she could admit now, she'd always secretly viewed Matt.

Her mouth felt dry under the curious gaze of her nameless inquisitor. He seemed suddenly too immense, too *knowing*. Desperate for escape, her gaze lit on a row of tall cubbies in the corner. Yellow jackets muted with black residue hung in a row. Shiny black boots lined up neatly below them.

It was a public space. No doors like lockers would have. But names had been scribbled above each stall, making them personal. *There.*

She gestured. "I'm just going to leave this here for him. In his cubby over there. He can just get it whenever, no hurry."

The fireman still wanted to block her way, she could tell, so she sidestepped him. She moved as she talked, almost babbling now, bumping into a rolling cart in her haste.

Embarrassment had been simmering for days—for a lot longer than that, if she were honest. And it had boiled over with the man's guileless admission that Matt had never mentioned her. That she meant nothing to him. Really, the way he'd brushed her off had proven that. As had the way he'd treated her the entire six months.

Maybe it only seemed worse under the heat of that piercing gaze. Humiliation formed a tight knot in her stomach, but she forced herself to walk with her head held high, chin up. At Matt's cubby, she shoved the box into the bottom, behind the boots, even. Hiding her misery in plain sight.

At least she didn't see any pity in the blue eyes. Only curiosity—and confusion. *Who are you to Matt? Why are you leaving him?* The only questions he could ask her would make her shame deepen.

She managed to excuse herself with some semblance of politeness. Something like, "Thanks so much for your help," even though he hadn't wanted to help her. "It was great to see all … this. Lovely truck. Really, it's very …"

And that was how her sentence ended. *Lovely truck. Really, it's very …*

Ugh, how articulate. The school board would be so impressed with their Teacher of the Year. Well, at least it was over. She crossed the loose gravel quickly and reached her car. Key in the lock. *Almost there.*

"Wait. Hold up!"

Damn. Too slow. He'd finally recovered from his shock, and he would ask those questions now. He'd ask how she'd managed to get a box of Matt's stuff but couldn't even get him on the phone to arrange a pickup time. And she'd be forced to make excuses—or worse, she'd be forced to tell the truth. She opened her mouth, ready for that magic explanation where she didn't look pathetic or angry or hurt, but nothing came out.

"Will you go out with me Friday night?" the fireman asked.

She blinked. "Excuse me?"

"Friday night. I usually work weekends, but I can exchange shifts with someone, no problem." He was holding the cardboard box under his arm. "I get that this is probably bad timing. Unless I'm reading this wrong, there was maybe a breakup, and you and I just met. But the thing is, if I let you drive off, I'm probably never going to see you again."

"And that's ... bad," she said slowly, trying to catch up.

"Very bad." His expression was solemn, and the heat in his eyes gave proof to his words. It *had* been curiosity in his eyes before, but not only interest in his coworker's affairs. That curiosity had been for her, and the realization sent a flash of heat through her body. Oh, yes, she still had it. Miss October, indeed.

And this guy was no slouch. Broad shoulders and a lean waist. The loose-fitting pants added to the appeal, making him look solid and unmovable. Dependable, when she should know not to depend on guys anymore. She really should have learned her lesson by now, but the sexy, forthright man in front of her made her want to run through the book one more time, just to be sure.

Matthew Gaines supposed the regret in her eyes should be some consolation. Still, he braced himself for the rejection.

"I'm sorry," she said. "You're right, this is a breakup. I don't think it's a good idea to start something new."

He understood that. He just didn't like it. And he'd never been one to take the easy way. "At least give me your number. I'll wait some appropriate amount of time and then call you. How long were you with this guy? I'll wait one day per month you were with him."

She looked amused. "And what if I've been with him five years? Are you really going to remember me after two months?"

"Yes," he said honestly.

He'd seen his share of long legs walk through the open garage door of Station 12, and hers were especially lovely. Then she'd intrigued him, asking for him by name when he knew for damn sure he'd never seen her before. He would have remembered. He'd let her leave that box in his compartment simply because he was curious. And maybe because he wanted to check her out when she bent over.

He liked that. He also liked the way her smoky eyes had darkened when she'd checked him out first. Most of all, he liked the way she held her head up high, even though he sensed she was flustered. She wasn't comfortable, but she wouldn't be cowed. A silk exterior and steel underneath. He'd learned to recognize strength in his years at Station 12. He respected strength, but that didn't stop him from wanting under her skirt.

Her shoulder lifted. "I've got to admit, I'm kind of a mess right now. It ... it wasn't a good breakup. I'm not sure when I'll be ready to date again."

Shit. He'd seen enough tragedy to know it could happen to anyone. He showed up to work every day with the full knowledge it could be his last. He knew how rare a chance could be, just a blink of an eye. And this one had already closed shut. He bit back his disappointment.

"I understand." He held up the box. "But you probably want to take this back."

Her face reflected confusion.

"That was my cubby you put this in," he explained. "I'm Matt Gaines. Station 12. Nice to meet you."

"How is that possible?"

"I'm guessing the Matt you're looking for works at one of the other stations in the city. They stop at twelve—this one. Maybe eleven? Ten? There's a few other Matts in the firefighters' football league." More than a few. Mix-ups were common, though they'd never been this alluring.

"Oh, God." Her expression was stricken. She groaned. "I just made a fool of myself in front of a stranger. For nothing."

"Don't feel bad, Izzy. We're not strangers anymore."

She sent him a dire look. "This isn't funny."

"I'm not laughing," he countered.

A grudging smile tilted her lips. "Okay. It's mildly amusing."

"You *did* just manage to reject two Matts in the span of five minutes. If anyone's a loser here, it's not you."

She didn't laugh, though. Her eyes filled with a soft, wispy sadness, the same way they'd been when she'd first walked up to the station. He wished he could be the one to wipe it away, but he couldn't. Either as Matt-the-firefighter or as a random guy she'd just met, he had nothing she wanted.

Except the cardboard box. It was light, he noticed distantly. *He didn't deserve you.* The thought came to him suddenly, fiercely. It would remain unvoiced, but he knew it was true. Because the box was light, because of the sadness in her eyes. Because of the rumors that circulated about Matt from Station 10.

It wouldn't matter for him. She would leave and find the right station. She would move on, but he would never get to know what might have been.

Isobel managed to leave the firefighter, but just barely. He stood in the parking lot with the sun beaming down on him while she drove away, glancing hungrily into her rearview for a final glimpse. And she managed to find the right fire station this time, Station 10, confirmed because his picture was right there in a news clipping pinned to the wall. And because the receptionist knew Matt.

"I'll make sure he gets this," the woman promised, her eyes laden with understanding and pity.

This wasn't the first time she'd been the recipient of such a box, Isobel guessed. The box of shame, because Matt hadn't told her where he lived. But he'd told her where he worked. That had been a point of pride for him, a bragging point. For that reason alone, she wanted nothing to do with firefighters at this point. Especially ones named Matt.

But she couldn't stop thinking about Station 12.

That was how she thought of him. Blue eyes. A wry smile. And a request to see her again so raw and so earnest that she ached with the memory. That was Station 12.

She really wasn't ready to date again, so soon. And she had a

strong feeling that dating Station 12 would be intense. Not the occasional meet-ups she'd done before but a serious courtship. The word
was almost foreign to her. *Courtship*. Like some throwback to chivalry
and ball gowns. It would be that way with him, without the pomp
and circumstance. In his actions, where it counted. Even when he'd
been demanding a date, he'd kept his physical distance from her.
She'd realized that later, thinking back. He'd never wanted her to feel
crowded or threatened—and she hadn't. She'd just felt wanted.

And he was a firefighter. He worked to protect people every
day. She wouldn't really vilify an entire profession based on one
failed relationship. He was a modern-day knight, the bulky gear
and helmet his armor. She admired and respected what he did. She
feared it, too, because if she did date Station 12, if they got close
and something were to happen to him—

No, there was no point thinking about it. It wasn't going to
happen. It would be months before she was ready to date again, and
even then, she wasn't sure Station 12 was the man to do it with.

Still, Friday night was particularly hard.

I could be on a date right now. Instead, she curled up on her
lumpy sofa watching late-night reruns. The TV flickered.

"We interrupt this broadcast ..."

Her hand was already on the remote, the up arrow to change
the channel beneath her forefinger. A hundred times, she'd probably
seen a serious newscaster ready to report some story—and changed
the channel because she found it so depressing. It affected her past
that moment, these random tragedies of strangers. They drenched her
ordinary day with melancholy. She'd become an elementary school
teacher so she could make a positive impact in her own small way, but
she wasn't sure she was up to the darker, scarier side of life. Of death.

She'd already mentally checked out, ready to turn the channel,
when the flare of orange flames caught her eye. A fire. Her hand froze
over the remote. Her whole body tensed, heart pounding in her ears.
As she watched, the camera turned away from the reporter to point
directly at the flames. The picture went out of focus for a second, just
a blur of yellows and reds, like looking into the sun. Then the lens
pulled back, and she could see the apartment building with flames

behind it. She could see the spray of water trying to douse the fire. The fire truck was barely visible in the corner of the screen.

The intersection flashed across the bottom of the screen. Near to Station 12.

It meant nothing. She didn't know the specifics of fire-station zoning. Maybe the call had somehow gone to a different station. Maybe Matt of Station 12 wasn't working tonight. But she knew he was. He'd said as much. And there was no way they'd call to a different station when that one was so close.

He was there. She squinted, but the people were only moving shadows over a dark lawn. She couldn't make out any of them. Couldn't tell if that shadow was him or that other one. Or what if he wasn't among them? What if he'd gotten injured and was even now at a hospital?

"Matt," she whispered.

No longer Station 12. He was Matt, and calling him anything else had been a desperate attempt to distance herself from the magnetic stranger. A failed attempt.

Numb fingers scrabbled for the volume button. The reporter was talking about safety regulations and old apartment buildings. Nothing about the people standing on the outskirts of the video, families clustered together. Nothing about the firefighters risking their lives to save them.

Risking their lives. What if he ... ?

No, she couldn't think it. He was fine. He had to be fine.

He wouldn't have been working tonight if you'd gone on a date with him. He would have exchanged shifts. They'd be having awkward first-date conversation over the appetizer course right now, and if anything happened to him, she'd never forgive herself.

"Heads up."

Matt glanced at his partner in time to catch the damp rag tossed his way. "Thanks. Why don't you go ahead? I'll handle the reports."

"Seriously?"

Matt wiped his eyes, but they still stung. They always did, and the only thing that fixed it was a hot shower and a long-ass sleep.

Still, he was reluctant to head home to his empty apartment. His partner, on the other hand, couldn't sit still.

Derek's eyes were bloodshot, his stance tense with the exhaustion they were both feeling, but the light in his eyes was all for the woman waiting at home.

"Get the hell out of here," he said.

Derek grinned. "Melli will be grateful. She'll make you those cupcakes you like so much."

"I'm counting on it."

With a salute, Derek jogged to catch a ride with one of the badges.

On the sliding scale of bad-to-worse, the apartment fire ranked bad. Not worse. Almost everyone was out by the time they arrived, sirens blaring. Dusk had fallen, blanketing the earth in a serene yellow glow. Still enough light to see by.

The only person left inside was an elderly woman, who fought Matt as he pulled her out. They did that sometimes. Derek was in charge of rounding up her "two, no, three of 'em" yapping dogs. The dogs had also fought for their right to stay inside the burning building. He'd seen those reactions many times, but he almost preferred them to the desolate acceptance on the faces of those outside.

This was the part of firefighting he disliked, the way his mind would pick apart reactions in the aftermath. A little boy standing on the curb with a limp, sodden teddy bear. A woman with serious asthma problems getting hooked up to life support in the ambulance due to smoke inhalation. He'd become a firefighter to help these people, but he needed distance to be able to return to the job day after day. He needed to unwind after a fire. Instead, his mind kept running in circles of anxiety.

By the time he cleared the scene, nightfall drew the world in flashing red and orange lights smattered across a black canvas. An official hand-off was made between the first responders and the investigators who'd deal with the follow-up.

He rode shotgun in the fire truck on the way back to the station. He closed his eyes and tried to think of something else. One image rose to the surface. Sad brown eyes. Silky honey-blond hair he'd love to run his fingers through. And coral-pink lips that pursed when she tried not to like him. She was something else, all right. Ethereal, like a painting come to life.

The truck jolted over the steep gravel driveway. Matt did a double take through the window, disbelieving. That beat-up Honda sat in the same parking spot it had last time. The slender silhouette of a woman perched on the trunk, as if his mind had conjured her.

Damn, he hoped this wasn't some oxygen-deprivation hallucination. But she seemed so real. She'd seemed real to him last time, too. He'd gone through life watching blurred colors and flashing lights, like riding a carousel and looking out. Only to one day look over and realize someone else was on the ride next to him, her edges defined, dark eyes full of melancholy and promise.

Matt approached slowly, casually, careful not to spook her. She'd run once. He didn't want her to leave again.

She stood up and wiped her palms on her jeans, as if she were nervous. "Hey."

"Hey back. What brings you by?"

"I changed my mind. About the date. That is, if you still …"

The abrupt end to her sentence made him smile, and somewhere deep inside him, tension eased. Yeah, this he could do. A date with a pretty girl, a nervous one. Even coated with sweat and soot, he could handle this.

"I'd love to take you out. Pick any place you want. I can be ready in four and a half minutes. You can time me."

"Actually, I kind of took care of that." She stepped back to reveal a box on her trunk. Unlike the brown cardboard box from her last visit, this one was white with a colorful label he recognized. "And I think you look great just the way you are."

Even in the dark, he saw the flush creep up her cheeks. A slow smile spread across his face. He was the guy who always had a comeback, but he couldn't have spoken just then.

She rushed to fill in the silence. "I got you a masala burger, because I like them. And a paneer wrap because I like them, too. But if you don't like Indian food, or spicy stuff, we could go—"

"I like Indian food," he cut in, because he could talk now.

Because she kept surprising him, and he didn't want her to stop. "I like spicy food. But most of all, I like that you came back."

Yeah, Isobel had come back. She'd run before. She could own that now. Run scared because this Matt had been bold and confident—just like the Matt who'd cheated on her. Grabbing life by the horns, flouting the rules. These were the hallmarks of men who pumped adrenaline every day. They *needed* that high. At least, that was how she'd explained away the old Matt's behavior.

Or then again, he might just be a jackass.

The truth was she didn't know this Matt from Station 12. He might hurt her, break her heart. She couldn't protect herself from that, but if he had enough courage to run into a burning building instead of away—well, then, she had enough courage to meet him with curry snacks after.

He opened the box on the hood of her car. "Fuck, that smells good. Pardon the language. I just realized I'm starving."

She grinned. "It does smell fucking good. I should get a medal for not digging into it by now. Though I did grab a few fries."

Grabbing the paper-wrapped burger, he turned to sit on the trunk. "Do you mind?"

"Not at all." She grabbed the wrap and hopped up beside him.

He ate ravenously, and she followed suit, spices bursting on her tongue. Warmth from his body seeped into her side. The smoky scent of him along with a chemical tang wrapped around her, forcing her to acknowledge his mortality. A protector, a knight. It still scared her, but instead of making her run, it made her want to pull him closer. To grant him the boon of herself in the age-old language of thanks. She scooted herself on the warm metal until her hip was touching his. She wanted to experience everything with him, to hold that moment in her hand and close her fingers around it.

She jumped as the heavy garage door groaned and began to roll shut. "Oh, do you need to go?"

"Nah, the guys will handle it. They know I'm out here with you, so they won't bother me. There's a rule at our station about that."

"For when women visit you?"

"For when people bring food."

She laughed and reached for the glass bottles she'd tucked inside the box and handed him one. The mango juice ran down her throat, thick and sweet. A few guys left the station and headed to a parking lot in the back. She waved along with Matt when they drove by.

Then it was only her and him, alone beneath the heavy sky. A few specks of starlight peeked through the city's atmosphere, but she wouldn't have traded the view for anything. She liked the busy streets with their energy and diversity. She liked brash, handsome firefighters named Matt who worked at Station 12.

He wiped his face with a napkin and grimaced as it came away black. "Shit. I should have taken you somewhere. Or at least showered. I swear I can be more civilized than this. Next time."

Next time. Her chest felt full with something she couldn't name.

"For now, though, tell me about yourself. What you do, what you like. And if you want to help a guy out, your favorite type of flowers."

Hah! What a charmer. She could see right through him. And she was still charmed.

"Well, I'm a third-grade teacher at Pilsner Elementary. I love the kids, hate the politics, but it comes with the job." He nodded, his eyes serious, and she figured he'd understand that. Public service wasn't so different. "We get to start *Charlotte's Web* next week."

He put a hand over his heart. "Ouch."

"What? It's a great book," she protested.

"The spider dies at the end. It's not super happy fun time."

"Death is part of life." She flushed, because who was she to tell a *firefighter* about death? But she was right about this. "Children have to deal with death as much as adults. Sometimes even more, because it affects them more."

The teasing glint faded from his eyes. "That sounds like the voice of experience."

"Maybe. Yes. My parents died when I was ten. They were coming back from a movie, and their car crashed." It didn't escape her that firefighters were often called to the site of crashes. She swallowed around the knot in her throat. "I don't remember much about them. I feel like I should remember more."

"I'm sorry."

"Well." She pushed the clouded thoughts away. "My mother was a teacher, too. And her mother before that. So I feel closer to them when I teach. It feels kind of like … like a legacy they left for me."

She waited for him to laugh at her. No, she knew he wouldn't. But he might not understand what it meant for her to have that, how it had shaped her life.

When he turned to her, his expression was serious. His eyes searched hers, though not for meaning; he knew what she meant. He looked for her consent, which she gave in the sudden stillness of her body and slight tilt of her head. Expectant awareness raced over her lips, a burst of light against a dark and lonely backdrop.

His lips met hers in a gentle brush, a touch like a question, one they asked of each other. *Who are you?* But not with words, and they answered the same way. *I know you.* His mouth moved over her bottom lip, testing, tasting, and she held steady for his advance. Let him take the lead, because he'd been to hell and back tonight. She let him set the pace, because he'd asked her to show him what she liked, and what she liked was this. Warm lips against hers. His breath against her skin. A hand sliding behind her neck, holding her open. Sweeter than any bouquet of flowers, his kiss teased and claimed, explored and conquered. She'd still take those flowers, though. She'd take everything he could give her.

"Calla lilies," she murmured, her lips brushing his as they formed words. "I'm a sucker for calla lilies. Any color. They get me every time. Slam dunk."

"Thank you," he groaned, his mouth claiming hers again.

He didn't go softly this time, didn't give her time to refuse. He nudged her mouth open until his tongue slipped inside, confident and hungry, exactly like the man. She tasted the spices from the food he'd eaten, bold like his actions. *More*, his lips demanded, and she obeyed with a moan.

She trembled everywhere—her lips, open and aching. Her hands where they clutched his shoulders. And inside her, too, at her core. She trembled with a need that had never been slaked. She'd never thought it could be, but the way he took her mouth proved it could. Without hesitation, he found every secret space inside her, lighting it up. He asked for more and then took it before she could answer him, *yes, please, take me.*

When his other hand slipped around her waist, she pressed herself against him with a sense of stark relief. It was harder to be apart from him than together. The air felt like sandpaper against her pebbled skin, the night sky blinding. In his arms, she found surcease, a shelter against the loneliness that had always been with her.

His every touch tested her, to find out what she liked. He asked with his words, with his hands. *If I touch your breast like this, would you like it? If I rub my thumb against your nipple, do you want more?* And she did, thrusting herself against his palm, begging now.

If he had the courage, then she would find it, too. It wasn't just about fires or food. If he could explore her body, then she could do the same to him. He lent her his strength, and she used it to seek the hem of his T-shirt, to lift it up and find bare skin, the ripple of his abs. He felt damp to the touch, lingering sweat and soot, but she didn't mind that at all, because of the way he had earned it, because it was *him.* She soaked the dampness up with her skin, as if her skin were a sponge, as if she could take a piece of him inside her.

Her hands drifted lower to the place where his pants were snug. She knew he liked it because he groaned into her mouth. His tongue sought hers and spoke the words he could not say. She obeyed those, too, because he was a man who reached for what he wanted, and she would follow his example.

She slipped her forefinger into the waist of his pants and ran it gently, side to side. Against her finger pad, the thick fabric was still warm with his body heat. And on her knuckle, she felt the ridges of his muscles, taut with excitement, with need. It was a tease, for him, for her; there was only so far she would go out in the open, even though no one was around this late.

She couldn't take what she wanted, couldn't give him what he needed, but her finger in his pants, tugging him closer, touching him barely—it was a promise. She would do more with him, and soon. She wanted everything.

He deepened the kiss, pressing her open and making her vulnerable. He bent her backwards until the warm metal cradled her back. His hand slid beneath her shirt, rough fingers sliding over her belly. She laughed breathlessly, tickled by the calluses there, excited by them. He bent his head and kissed the soft, pale flesh he'd exposed to night air. He opened his mouth and placed wet kisses in a line across her belly. She wanted him to move higher, to her breasts—or even better, lower. But they wouldn't do that here, in public. Later. *Next time.*

Headlights flashed as a new car pulled into the parking lot. Matt pulled back and straightened her shirt, shielding her from sight as the guy got out and headed toward the station. A teasing whistle pierced the air, and Matt flicked the finger at the guy with a small, embarrassed smile.

He helped her sit up, apologetic as he explained. "The next shift. There'll be more guys coming in now."

She straightened her clothes, a flush heating her cheeks. "Sorry. I should get going anyway. It's late."

"You'll let me see you again." He said it as a statement, not a question. But in his cerulean eyes, she saw the question mark, a hint of doubt that made her melt inside.

"I'm counting on it," she said softly.

Matt was strangely reluctant to let her go. He knew why—because she'd disappeared once already, like Cinderella into the night. He wanted to invite her into the station, or better yet, bring her home. But there'd be time for that later, because she'd left her phone number this time, the metaphorical glass slipper on the stairway.

Right now, her eyes were shadowed with exhaustion. And worry, too. She'd told him about seeing the news report. If he got serious with her—and he planned to—there would be more where that came from. It was an unavoidable part of the job. He'd do what he could to minimize that stress, and that started with sending her home to sleep.

He waited in the parking lot until her red taillights disappeared. Then, as soon as he'd checked in with the guys and headed home, he called her, because to hell with mandatory waiting periods. He wasn't going to wait to call her, to see her again, to make something happen between them, and he suspected she didn't want to wait any more, either.

"My dad was a firefighter, too," he said when she answered the phone.

"So you get the legacy thing."

He heard the pleasure in her voice, could see the slight smile in his mind. "I do, though in my case it was more of a mandate. My dad practically raised me in the station. It's still a second home."

"Oh, yeah? I'd love to see it. Well, more than I did the first time. Maybe you can show me around sometime."

"I'd love to. After I show you my regular home, though, even though it isn't much. I need some time with you without those bastards catcalling. That reminds me … did that box of yours happen to have a calendar?"

A pause. "Oh, God. You found that?"

"Behind my boots," he confirmed. "It must have fallen out. I figured either that or one of the guys was ribbing me."

"Throw it away. I don't want it anymore."

"Exactly what I was hoping to hear, sweetheart. If you need a firefighter to look at, you've got me."

"Twelve months of Station 12," she said in a teasing voice. He liked that voice. He wanted more of it. Twelve months sounded just fine to him for a start.

"I'm counting on it." His voice came out rough, which was just how he felt inside, sideways and spilled over. She'd managed to get under his skin in just a short amount of time. The simplest things, from her stubborn chin to her secretive smiles, tore down his walls. If he spent more time with her, how much deeper could she go? The thought should have terrified him, but he'd figured out long ago what made him tick. He liked the thrill, and she was the biggest risk he'd ever taken.

One thing was for sure, it would be a hell of a ride.

Amber Lin is the author of new adult, contemporary, and historical romance. *RT Book Reviews* called her debut novel, *Giving It Up*, "truly extraordinary." Amber believes everyone deserves a happy ending, even if it feels impossible. Especially then. All of her books contain redemption and steamy ever afters. Oh, and pie. Find out more about her books and sign up for her newsletter at authoramberlin.com

WRONG NUMBER, RIGHT GIRL

MONICA MURPHY

New York Times Bestseller

Ty

"I DARE YOU TO get that chick's number."

I watch the girl Jace is talking about. She's short and stacked, with long blond hair that falls in sexy, perfect waves to the middle of her back and plump lips slicked with bright pink lip gloss I can see from where I'm standing. And we're clear across the room from each other.

"She looks like my type," I drawl, bringing my beer bottle up to my lips and taking a swig. I'm already a little drunk, and we've only been here a little over an hour. But we've each had almost three beers, so we'll be shitfaced in no time. "I bet those glossy lips would look real good wrapped around my dick."

The moment the words leave me, I wince. I'm sick and tired of acting like this. But it's become my role among our friends, and it's easier to just go with it.

Four years in college acting like a complete asshole in regard to women is getting beyond old, though.

"I knew you'd think that." Jace laughs and nudges me in the side with his elbow. "That's why I thought she looked perfect for you."

The girl catches us looking, and I flash her my best, biggest smile. She rolls her eyes in response, making Jace laugh harder, the jackass.

"I think you're losing your edge," he says.

I ignore him, keeping my gaze locked on the girl. She's wearing a tight white T-shirt with a deep V-neck and a short denim skirt, exposing all kinds of tanned skin. Her shirt rides up when she lifts her arm and runs her fingers through her hair, offering me a glimpse of a belly ring flashing in her navel.

Fucking hot. Normally I'd already be over there, standing at her side, making all my usual moves, saying all the usual things. Lately, I haven't been motivated. I'm starting to feel guilty for all the things I've done and said in my not-so-distant past.

But Jace is drunk and full of expectations. This is what usually happens with us when we're out drinking together. I approach the prettiest girl first, and he goes after one of the friends. It's a win-win for us.

Tonight, I'm realizing I'm pretty much over it.

"Go talk to her." Jace shoves at my shoulder, nearly sending me toppling, but I right myself before I fall on my face.

Damn. I guess I'm drunker than I thought.

Offering Jace a murderous glance, I polish off the rest of my beer in one swallow. "I am," I mutter before I hand him my empty beer bottle and head toward my new supposed favorite blonde.

The bar is packed, but it's always packed on Thirsty Thursday. I shove through the crowd, shout a few heys to some guys I know. The music is loud. A girl I screwed around with last semester offers me a flirtatious hi, and I know if I can't score with the blonde, I have that one waiting in the wings.

Wait a minute. I don't necessarily want to score with the blonde. And I definitely don't want another girl waiting in the wings, either. What I should do is get the hell out of here.

But I don't.

Finally I reach my target, stopping in front of where she's standing with a small group of friends. Her back is to me, and I drink her in, my gaze settling on her very fine ass in that very short skirt. She doesn't turn until one of her friends spots me. A tall brunette with a skeptical expression on her pretty face and curly-ass hair leans over and whispers in Blondie's ear, her gaze never leaving mine.

I stare at her, thinking she's actually much prettier than the blonde. Not my usual type with her willowy body and dark hair, but she has a wholesome look to her. Hell, she's even wearing glasses.

If I even attempted to bring someone like her around to my friends, they'd laugh at me. I'd never hear the end of it.

Slowly the blonde turns, her smile too bright, a little false, and I blink, focusing on her rather than her friend. My confidence falters, and I realize quickly she's not interested.

Lately, hardly any of them are, and I wonder if they can tell I'm not interested, either. That's gotta be it.

"Hi," I say in greeting, feeling at a loss for words. And that never happens.

Her smile fades. "Hello," she says coolly.

"So. Don't think I've seen you around here before. What's your name?" Huh. Original. Wonder if it's all the beer I've consumed. Or all the girls I've consumed. Banged. Whatever. Maybe I'm finally running out of flirting material.

Maybe I need to stop looking for the next quick fix and focus on finding a nice girl for once. That would thrill the hell out of my mom.

"Kristi." Her smile is completely gone now. All I can see are those overly glossed lips of hers. They look sticky. No way do I want to kiss that.

Not that I really wanted to in the first place …

"Well, nice to meet you, Kristi. I'm Ty." I nod, shoving my hand into my pocket so I can pull out my cell phone. Since Jace dared me to get this chick's number, I'm doing it. Not that I'll call her. I'm not that interested. "I'd love to talk to you, but this place is too fucking loud."

It's my standard line, one I always use in a too-loud bar, which is every bar downtown, especially Thursday through Saturday. Though usually I have my arm around the girl by now, looking deep in her eyes, trying to get that brief connection I'm always striving for. They always seem to go for it when I ask if they want to take our conversation somewhere more private.

"Maybe we could get together some other time," I suggest.

Her brows rise. "That sounds fun," she says weakly, like she doesn't really mean it.

"Give me your number, and I'll text you this weekend." I might. Depends on if I'm bored or not.

Christ, you're an asshole.

"Awesome." She rattles off her number, and I enter it into my phone along with her name, offering her a quick smile when she finishes.

"My friend is waiting for me." I wave a hand in Jace's general direction. "I'll text you tomorrow."

"Promise?" She bats her overly-caked-with-mascara eyelashes at me.

"Yeah. Sure," I say. I can't stand when girls want me to promise them shit I can't deliver on. Every chick does it. Even Mom.

And I hate it.

Lauren

"You actually gave him your number?" I can't believe it. I heard him ask Kristi for it, but I didn't pay much attention to their conversation. First, I couldn't hear them very well; it's so noisy in here. And second, even I've heard of Ty Webster. He's a player. Loves nothing more than to hook up with a different girl every day of the week. He's a total pig.

And he would so not be interested in me. I'm not his type considering I'm not short, blond, nor do I have huge boobs. He's tall and made of solid muscle, smoking hot, and I'm just ... me. Tall, flat-chested, with boring, uncontrollable curly hair.

The complete opposite of Ty Webster's type.

That even I know his type shows just what a total dog he is.

"No." Kristi turns to look at me, a smirk on her too-glossy lips. "I gave him *your* number."

"Wait ... what?" I shriek, but no one can really hear me. The music is hella loud, and so is the crowd. I grab hold of Kristi's arm and tug her close, yelling in her ear, "Why did you do that?"

"Why not?" She shrugs, looking rather pleased with herself. "I didn't want him harassing me."

"So you'll let him harass me instead?" He'll be incredibly disappointed, too, if he ever texts my number and finds out it's me and not Kristi.

"You're a big girl. You can handle it."

I don't say anything in response, and she tugs her arm out of my grip, flashing me a smirk before she moves toward the bar. She's my cousin, and I swear half the time she invites me out with her friends just so she can have someone to pick on, dump on, whatever.

Every time I go out with her, something like this happens. She goes out of her way to humiliate me, give me a bunch of crap. I complained to my mom last week when I talked to her, and she told me I should give Kristi another chance. So I did.

And this is her last one. I'm done. Just because I don't know a lot of people doesn't mean I can't have any type of social life without Kristi.

Well, I hope not.

Taking a sip from my drink, I glance around and notice Ty Webster standing directly across the room, looking straight at me. I pause, my glass still held up to my lips, my eyes going wide. He's totally watching me. Why? I don't get it. And he's alone, too, leaning against the wall, one hand shoved deep in his jeans pocket, his tall, muscled frame deceptively casual. I say deceptive because he looks ready to spring into action at any given moment. All that contained energy just seems to vibrate beneath the surface, waiting to be unleashed.

I wonder what it would feel like. To have all the vibrant potency that makes up Ty Webster unleashed all over me.

Ugh. Why in the world are you thinking of him like that?

I've seen him at bars before, specifically the last time I came with Kristi and her equally bitchy friends. Usually he's checking out another girl, sizing her up before he approaches like he just did to Kristi. It's his typical mode of operation, one that everyone is aware of.

Doesn't he get sick of this? According to Kristi's friends, he's been at this for a few years, pretty much his entire college existence. Doesn't he want a regular girlfriend?

If I could roll my eyes at myself, I so would. Listen to me. The very last thing he probably wants is a regular girlfriend. Someone that'll tie him down and make demands on his time. My ex broke up with me exactly because of that. I wanted too much, he'd said. It wasn't that I was needy, but did we have to spend so much time together?

I'd been almost relieved when we broke up. If he hated being with me so much, then good riddance.

Chancing a glance in Ty's direction, I see he's still staring. Bet he won't come talk to me, though. Being seen with me might make him look like he's slumming.

God, I hate that I even thought that. Where the hell did my self-confidence go lately anyway?

I decide to unabashedly stare at him right back, letting my gaze roam over his features. He keeps his dark hair almost military short, and he has a classically handsome face. All sharp cheekbones and angled, hard jawline. The slightly crooked nose that looks like it's been broken a time or two plus those intense dark brown eyes, offset by a lush, beautiful mouth.

Put that all together with his massive, muscular frame and it's downright devastating. No wonder all those girls can't resist him. He's gorgeous and he knows it.

A slightly crooked smile curves his lips, and he tips his head toward me. I glance over my shoulder, thinking he's smiling at someone else. Maybe Kristi.

But no. There's no one standing behind me, no one looking his way. He's smiling at me.

I smile back, just a quick flash before I duck my head, my long, curly hair falling in front of my face. I wait a few seconds, tuck my hair behind my ear as I lift my head to actually find him approaching. Headed right for me.

Oh. My. God.

Locking my knees, I try to keep my legs from going wobbly and wait for him. My heart is racing, and my mouth has gone dry. I take a big drink from my glass, polishing off the last of the vodka cranberry I ordered earlier before I set it down on a table beside me. I can feel the remnants of vodka clinging to my lips, and I lick at them real quick, feeling like an idiot. Thankful he didn't see me.

I don't know how to talk to gorgeous, womanizing guys. The past men in my life are all average dudes. Not sexy football stars who strut around campus like they own the place.

Ty stops directly in front of me, his dark gaze roving over my face, and I feel my cheeks heat. "Hey."

His voice is deep and rumbly. I can literally feel it wash over me, making my skin tingle. "Hi," I say softly just as he leans in closer, maybe to hear me better, I don't know.

But I swear I hear him inhale, and I can't help but wonder if he's actually ... smelling me?

That's kind of hot.

"Want to get out of here?"

I gape at him. Didn't he just ask Kristi out? I mean, really? What a jerk. "Not with you," I retort.

He slaps a hand to his chest, his expression one of mock offense. "Ouch. I wasn't trying to get in your pants. I just thought we could go somewhere and, I don't know ... talk, maybe?"

"Talk? Really?" So what? Should I be insulted that he doesn't want to hook up with me? Talk about confused. I wonder if it's the liquor that's making my head spin.

Or maybe it's the guy.

"Yeah." His smile falters a little. "Really. What's your name?"

I don't know if I want to tell him. "Did someone put you up to this?"

Now his smile has completely slipped away. "What are you talking about? I noticed you when I talked to whats-her-name earlier. And I saw you watching me, so I thought I'd come talk to you."

"*You* were watching *me*." I jab him in the chest with my index finger and feel nothing but hot, solid flesh beneath the thin fabric of his T-shirt. Good lord, he's like a brick wall. A hard brick wall of muscle.

"Does it really matter?" He sounds incredulous.

And I'm being ridiculous. But this isn't feeling so right anymore. Not at all. I'm out of my element, and this guy will probably treat me like a joke. I don't need this.

So without another word, I turn around and flee, pushing through the crowd toward the bar entrance, not once looking back. I don't think I want to see his reaction.

I'd rather forget this night ever existed.

CHAPTER TWO

Lauren

YOU'RE GOING TO THINK I'm a total asshole, but I have a question for you.

I stare at the message that came from an unfamiliar phone number, my brain foggy as I wonder who it could be. So I decide to ask.

Who is this?

Flopping back down, I tug my comforter over my head and snuggle into my pillow, my cell still clutched in my hand. I dreamt of stupid Ty Webster last night. And in my dream, I agreed to leave the bar with Ty. He took me back to his place, where he proceeded to kiss the very sense out of me, right before he peeled off my clothes and screwed my brains out. His hands and mouth everywhere, whispering dirty words in my ear, touching me in all the right places that left me an aching, gasping mess.

That's how I woke up. An aching, gasping mess, feeling hollow since none of what happened actually, you know, happened. Talk about a letdown.

Now I'm getting random texts from numbers I don't know, disturbing my rare chance to sleep in. I don't have any classes on Friday, so I take advantage of it as much as I can.

My phone dings and I check my text.

I met you last night. Don't tell me I'm already that forgettable?

Oh. Crap. I think, no, I know who it must be. Ty. And he believes he's texting Kristi. This is totally awkward.

Right … the dark-haired guy who barely talked to me and asked for my number?

Ha. He's lucky I didn't tell him to screw off.

Yeah. Uh, this is going to come off as a total jerk move but …

I wait for his question, my heart tripping over itself in anticipation.

What's the name of the brunette who was with you last night?

My heart threatens to stop. So now he's asking Kristi what my name is. I can't believe this. This is a total jerk move.

I also kind of—okay, really—like it.

Which girl? I type.

The tall one with the pretty dark hair. Curly.

My skin warms. He called my hair pretty. I shouldn't let his words affect me. They're most likely meaningless. For whatever reason, he thinks he's interested in me. Probably just wants to get in my panties.

But I kinda like the thought of him getting in my panties, right? Ugh. I really am just like every other girl who's fallen for his pathetic lines.

I think you're talking about my cousin, I finally answer. The one who wears glasses?

Yeah. The pretty one who wears glasses. She's your cousin? Ah, shit, you must think I'm a total ass.

Maybe. I should. Kristi definitely would. But he's talking to me about me.

So I'm going with this.

Yeah. Kind of. But if you like her, I don't really have a problem with it.

Really? Okay. What's her name?

Should I tell him? I was reluctant to last night.

Tell me why I should I give it to you. From what I hear, you'll probably just try to get her naked and use her, then forget she ever existed.

Whoa. My thumb hesitates over the send button. Should I really be that harsh?

Why not? I firmly press the blue send button and wait for his answer.

Damn, girl. I like that you're so protective of your cousin.

I burst out laughing. If he knew how Kristi threw me under the bus by giving him my phone number instead of hers, he wouldn't say that.

I'm trying to change my ways. I think your cousin is just the girl to help me.

He's either really good with the lines or he's being sincere. I'd rather think the latter.

Of course, this is just wishful thinking on my part, but I may as well have fun with this while I can, right?

You really think she can help you?

I hope so. But I get it if you don't want to tell me her name.

She's a big girl. I guess I don't need to protect her. I hesitate a moment before I continue.

Her name is Lauren.

Ty

Lauren. I like it. Somehow, the name fits her.

And since our encounter last night, she's all I've been able to think about. And I never do this with any girl. I am the total cliché. Love 'em and leave 'em. Wham, bam, thank you, ma'am. Whatever old lines you've heard describing a player, they're also describing me. I'm a user and I can admit it.

Where I once was proud of this, now I'm not. I'm actually kind of horrified by my past behavior. I need to make amends.

I'd like to start first with this girl, who's so completely different from any other girl I've been interested in before. Lauren.

Can you give me her number? I text in reply.

You ask for mine last night and now you're asking for hers? What sort of douchebag are you?

Damn, this girl doesn't hold back. Though I'm pretty sure I deserve it.

Yeah, I guess you're right. Forget it.

No response, and I set my phone on the end table, then grab the remote and turn on the TV. Forget it. I'll watch something mindless and, if I'm lucky, take a nap. I slept for shit last night, my brain too occupied with visions of the girl with long, curly brown hair. Instead of scowling at me, she's smiling, her dark eyes sparkling.

Doubt that's ever going to happen, though.

My cell beeps, and I glance at it, surprised to see it's a reply

WRONG NUMBER, RIGHT GIRL   91

from Kristi. She must hate me but not enough to cut off all conversation with me. Yet.

I glance at my phone and read the message.

Are you really as bad as they say you are?

What exactly are you talking about? I'm evading. I'm also stalling. I should be honest, but it's so hard.

Your reputation with girls and that you've been with a bunch of them.

Shit. I decide to go ahead and bare all.

What you've heard? I pause for a heavy moment before I continue typing. Multiply it by ten.

I hold my breath, waiting for her response.

Um. Wow. O.O

Unbelievable but I'm laughing. Wow and the little face is right. I hate it. My reputation has turned into an absolute embarrassment.

I get it if you don't want to give me your cousin's number, I type. I'm probably not worthy of her.

It's true. I'm probably not.

She's really smart and studies all the time. School's important to her, Kristi types. And she just broke up with her jerk ex-boyfriend before she moved here. She doesn't have time for guys like you.

Ah, so she's a hard worker, she's been burned, and she's probably fragile. I am the last sort of guy she would be interested in.

Yeah. I get it.

My heart sinks. I can tell this is going to be the gentle letdown. I've never had that happen to me before. To my friends, yep, I've seen it time and again. I've done it to girls plenty of times, too.

This shit … it hurts. Why did I never realize it?

Hey.

Hope lights up within me despite myself.

Yeah?

She's here with me. And she says she wants to meet up with you.

I squash down all that hope. This could be a trick. Kristi acted like she hated me last night. Why would she help me connect with her cousin Lauren? It makes no sense.

The last twenty-four hours don't make any sense. I don't know what's wrong with me. Have I lost my damn mind? Do I really want to pursue this girl I don't even know, who I spoke to for maybe five minutes tops?

Her face flashes in my mind. The sound of her voice. The way she looked at me …

Yeah. I do.

Are you jerking my chain? I finally ask.

Dead silence is my response. Not a good sign. With a resolute sigh, I carefully set my phone back on the end table and resume channel-surfing, my brain too preoccupied with thoughts of Lauren, the pretty girl in the glasses, to find something good to watch.

Twenty torturous minutes later, my phone beeps. I eagerly grab it, my heart racing, my palms fucking sweating. I think my body might've been taken over by aliens, but I really don't care.

Meet Lauren downtown at Pete's Coffee Shop tonight. 7 p.m.

I stare at the words, my vision going hazy. She wants to meet with me. At a freaking coffee shop, but I'll take what I can get. Like a jackass, I wait a solid fifteen minutes before I respond to the text. I don't want to seem too eager.

I'll be there.

CHAPTER THREE

Ty

I'M SITTING AT A table just outside the coffee shop, tapping my foot nervously, getting a weird satisfaction every time my knee connects with the cold, metal edge of the table and makes a loud clanging noise. No one is outside with me anyway, so it's not like I'm disturbing anyone. It's too damn cold, the early fall air nipping at my skin as a soft breeze washes over me.

It's fifteen minutes past seven and still no Lauren. I fucked it up somehow. Kristi probably lied. She didn't talk to her cousin. Lauren has no idea I'm interested in her. She probably still hates me after our stupid argument at the bar last night.

Hell, I can't do anything right.

Growling under my breath, I grab my to-go cup and take a deep swig of my mocha with the extra two shots. It's fucking delicious, strong as hell, and I savor the taste, the warmth it gives me. I'll give this girl ten more minutes, and then I'm out of here. I refuse to let her stand me up. I refuse to look like the loser in this situation.

Too late.

Those two words irritate the ever-loving crap out of me.

I think of Lauren that night in the bar. Last night. Was it really only last night? Did I really only say a few words to her? I remember the look on her face. Her pretty pink lips, all that gorgeous, curly hair my fingers literally itched to touch, her scent. Fuck, her smell. I'd literally inhaled her like some sort of creepy stalker, she smelled so damn good. Thank God she hadn't noticed. I can't even peg what her scent was. All I know is that I want to smell her again. Bury my face in her hair, her neck …

"Hi."

Her soft voice breaks through my cloudy thoughts, and I glance up, my knee going still as I drink Lauren in. "Hey. You made it."

She grips the back of the chair she's standing in front of, a funny little smile curving her lips. She looks uncomfortable, and I worry that I'm the one making her feel that way. "Sorry I'm late."

"No problem," I say easily, forgetting all about my irritation and anxiety of twenty seconds ago. "You want something to drink?"

"Yeah. I'd love something." A visible shiver moves through her as she glances around, the dark night closing in around us, making me feel as if we're the only two people in this world. Forget the noisy coffeehouse, the bright lights shining from the windows. The loud but muffled voices coming through the walls and everyone milling around inside. It's just us, me and Lauren. "But I really don't want to sit outside. It's kind of cold."

I could keep you warm, are the words that want to automatically pop out of my mouth, but that sounds like the Ty of old, so I keep my lips shut.

This is new Ty. And he's not about to try and get with this girl too soon, only to discard her once he's through.

I frown. Did I really just refer to myself in the third person in my brain? Clearly I'm losing it.

"Let's go inside, then. I bet it's warmer in there." I stand, my knees bumping the edge of the metal table and making it jolt and clang so loudly I swear I almost knock it over. Smooth. Since when did I turn into such a klutz?

Lauren slaps her hand over her mouth to stifle a laugh, and embarrassment swamps me. "Are you okay? Did you hurt yourself?" she asks when she finally lets her hand drop away.

The embarrassment flees, replaced with tentative warmth. Is she really concerned? Or just asking because she's polite? "I'm fine. Thanks." I head to the door, opening it for her. "Ready?"

She walks toward the door, stopping right before me so she can stare deep into my eyes. Hers are as brown as mine, maybe even darker, and they flash at me from behind her glasses. Her hair is pulled back into a low ponytail, but a few curls escaped, framing her flushed cheeks. "If this is how you usually act around girls, I must say your moves aren't working real well. At least, not with me."

I barely restrain the urge to roll my eyes. Her bluntness both irritates and fascinates me. "Trust me. This sort of behavior is completely unusual for me."

"Just like you going out with a girl like me is unusual?"

Frowning, I study her. "I never go out with girls."

"Especially girls like me," she asserts. Again.

I'm not quite sure what she's going for here, but I'm almost afraid to ask.

Before I get the not-so-wonderful chance to answer her, someone clears his throat, drawing our attention. A man is standing in front of us, clutching a to-go cup in each hand.

"If you two would bring your conversation either inside or outside so you're not blocking the door, I'd appreciate it," the man says irritably.

"Sorry, dude," I say as I move out of the way. Lauren does the same, mumbling an apology as the man scurries out, his head bent against the wind. We step more fully into the coffee shop, letting the door fall closed behind us.

"Ah, it's so warm in here. Much better." She smiles at me and I'm dumbstruck.

Has any girl smiled like that at me before? So genuine, so real? The kind of smiles I earn are flirtatious, sexy, or fake. I'd grown used to them. I thought that's how all girls were.

Not this one.

Lauren

I don't know what to think. I still can't believe I'm here, at a coffee shop with Ty freaking Webster on a Friday night, surrounded by college hipsters pretending it's cool to hang out drinking coffee on a Friday when what's really cool is drinking yourself into oblivion at one of the many bars just down the street.

He's listening to everything I have to say like he's interested. His gaze rarely leaves mine as he asks me endless questions. I answer them all, returning with questions of my own, and though he struggles with some of them, he answers me.

And oh, my God, I like him. He's pretty driven. And smart. He's going to work for his family's commercial landscaping business when he graduates and will eventually run it when his father retires. He knows he's lucky that he has a ready-made career and doesn't have to struggle, and I envy him that.

But then he admits if he had his way, he'd be a high school football coach. A P.E. teacher, even. He doesn't want to disappoint his father, though, so he gave up that dream after his first year in college.

That confession made me a little sad. That Ty had to give up his secret dream, a rather admirable one, also makes me like him more.

Scary.

I like how attentive he is, mixed with all that barely restrained intensity. A few times, he reaches across the table and touches me. A casual brush of his fingers on my hair, a deliberate stroke across my knuckles, causing shivers to steal through me every single time.

I want more.

But I also feel a twinge of guilt. I'm lying to him. He thinks he texted with Kristi, but that entire conversation from earlier was with me. I want to come clean, but I'm afraid he'll be mad. He's been nothing but honest, revealing all his faults. All his regrets. For whatever reason, he wants to open up to me, and I like it.

"We should go," he finally says after we've been sitting at the tiny table for hours, our coffees long finished, the coffee shop nearly empty.

Glancing around, I see we're two of the last customers inside. The employees are cleaning up, preparing to close. "I guess we should."

He leads me out of the shop and into the cold October night, resting his hand low on my back as he guides me down the sidewalk. "Where's your car?" he asks.

I nod toward the small parking lot across the street. "Over there."

"I'll walk you over. Make sure you get there safe." He never removes his hand from my back, his hot fingers seeming to brand my skin even through my thick sweater. I steal a glance at him, admiring his strong profile, the thoughtful but determined expression on his face.

If I don't watch it, I could find myself falling for this guy, which is the craziest thing ever.

"This is my car," I say, coming to an abrupt halt. I was so enraptured with staring at Ty I almost walked past my own vehicle.

"Ah, okay." He offers a little smile and removes his hand from my back as I move away from him, digging through my purse for my keys. I find them quickly and turn to face him, the smile falling away from my face when I see his solemn expression. "I had a good time tonight, Lauren."

The sound of his velvety deep voice saying my name is something I like far too much. "I did, too."

He grabs my hand. "I really don't know how to do this, but I want to see you again."

I try to hide my smile, but it breaks across my face anyway. "It's pretty simple, Ty."

"It is?" He squeezes my hand and then pulls me closer. "What do I do?"

"You ask me out again."

"Well, I want to ask you out for tomorrow, but I'm afraid I'll look too eager?"

There goes that blunt honesty again. I really like it. "I'll say yes."

"You will?" A hopeful gleam fills his gaze, and he pulls me even closer, until I'm colliding against his chest, and he swoops his arm around my waist. "Then go out with me tomorrow, Lauren."

I nod slowly, my breath hitching in my throat as he lowers his head to mine. "Okay," I whisper just before he kisses me.

And oh, God, can he kiss. His lips are firm yet soft and so, so persuasive. The kiss is gentle, almost chaste, and I part my lips for him, offering him a blatant invitation.

He doesn't take it, much to my surprise. Merely pulls away from me slowly, his gaze smoldering as he stares at me, his lips damp. My stomach flutters, my lips tingle, and I want more.

I can tell this is it, though. He's leaving me wanting more. I think I'm leaving him wanting more, too.

"I'm taking this slow," he whispers as he reaches out to brush his fingers against my cheek. "I rush it and I'm afraid I'll fall back into my old habits. I don't want to do that to you, Lauren."

My heart feels like it's going to seize in my chest at his words. "Okay," I whisper back.

"I can come pick you up tomorrow," he says as he tucks a

wayward curl behind my ear, his finger brushing against my skin. "Give me your phone number, and I'll text you."

Everything within me stills. I don't want to tell him the truth *now*. It'll ruin the moment. He might hate me.

"I'm, um, busy tomorrow. All day. Can't I just meet you somewhere?" My mind races, trying to come up with excuses, but the moment the words leave me, I know they sound lame.

He frowns, his hand dropping away from my face. "I'd rather pick you up."

"It's just. Um. I don't want …" How do I get out of this without looking like a total bitch? What do I say?

"No, I get it." He steps away from me, his expression going completely void. Oh, God, did I make him mad? "You don't want me to know where you live or whatever. You don't even want me to have your freaking phone number."

"That's not it." I shake my head, worry crawling up my throat, stalling my words. "I-I … You have my phone number."

"No, I don't." He shakes his head. "Kristi never gave it to me."

"That's because she gave you mine."

CHAPTER FOUR

Ty

"WAIT A MINUTE." SHOCK courses through me as I stare at Lauren, still trying to absorb her words. "What are you saying?"

"When Kristi gave you her phone number last night, it wasn't hers." She pauses, remorse written all over her face. "It was mine."

"So when I was texting Kristi …"

"You were really texting me," she finishes softly.

Ah, shit. "You must think I'm an idiot."

"You must think I'm a liar," she murmurs.

I don't. Not at all. "You called me a douchebag."

She shrugs. "You never denied that you were one."

A chuckle escapes me despite the serious conversation we're having. "So you're the tough one watching out for your cousin."

"Watching out for me," she admits with a little shrug. "Your reputation is well known around campus, around town. I had no idea why you would be interested in me."

"Because you're the complete opposite of any girl I'd ever been with before." Unable to resist, I reach for her and pull her back into my arms. "That's a good thing, Lauren. Trust me."

"I want to trust you." She rests her hands on my chest, her fingers curling into my sweatshirt. "You've been nothing but honest with me from the get-go. So I'm the liar in this particular situation."

"I forgive you." Dipping my head, I brush my mouth against hers, capturing the little sigh that escapes her. I'm the one who should be asking for forgiveness. About my past, the things I've done and said. That this girl wants to spend time with me despite it all is blowing my mind.

And filling my heart with hope for my future.

Giving in, I deepen the kiss, sliding my tongue inside her mouth and tangling it with hers. She tastes sweet. Like mint and a lingering hint of coffee. Her hands slide up my chest to curl around my neck, and I step closer, pressing her against the side of her car. She gasps against my mouth, a little laugh escaping her. "Cold," she murmurs, and I tighten my arms around her, holding her as close as I can.

"I'll warm you up," I whisper as I move to kiss her fragrant neck. "That's a promise."

One I'd like to keep for a long time.

Lauren

Open your door.

I glance at my cell phone, a smile tickling the corners of my lips when I see who the message is from.

Why? Is there a creeper waiting on my doorstep?

A creeper who's ready to take you out to dinner is his reply.

A burst of laughter escapes me, and I go to the front door, throwing it open to find Ty standing there, his phone clutched in his hand, dark head bent as he's typing away.

My phone dings and I look at it.

You look beautiful.

"You haven't even really looked at me yet," I chastise, my entire body feeling light and airy at his words.

He glances up, those deep brown eyes meeting mine. "I don't need to look at you to know you're beautiful."

Aw. Who knew Ty Webster was such a romantic? "You are too sweet," I say as I grab his hand and pull him inside my tiny apartment, slamming the door behind him.

"You ready to go?" he asks as I push him onto the couch, then settle in beside him.

"Maybe we should order in." I press into his side, tilt my face up to accept his gentle kiss.

"Really?" He drops another tender kiss onto my lips. "Lauren, are you sure we're not moving too fast?"

That he has to ask is adorable. "What do you think?"

"I think this could be the beginning of a beautiful friendship," he answers, kissing me again.

I pull away from him with a frown. "Friendship?"

"It's a line from a movie. *Casablanca.* My mom's always been into classic movies." His cheeks actually turn ruddy, and it's the cutest thing I've ever seen. "I sound pathetic right now, don't I?"

"No." My skin warms, and I curl all around him. "I think it's the cutest thing ever. And you're right."

"I am?" His deep voice is full of surprise.

I slowly nod, aligning our lips until they're almost touching. "This definitely has the potential to be a beautiful friendship," I whisper just before I kiss him.

And hopefully much, much more.

New York Times, USA Today and international bestselling author **Monica Murphy** is a native Californian who lives in the foothills below Yosemite with her husband and three children. She's also a workaholic who loves her job. When she's not busy writing, she loves to read and travel with her family. She writes new adult and contemporary romance and is published with Bantam and Avon. She also writes romance as *USA Today* bestselling author Karen Erickson, and is published with Samhain Publishing and Entangled Brazen and Bliss.

A LIGHT IN THE DARKNESS

REGINA SCOTT

Night's Court, England, Christmas Eve, 1814

MAJOR SIR PERCIVAL NIGHTINCOURT heard his name being called. The word rose to a wail and was accompanied by the pounding of running feet.

"Percy!" His younger sister, Amelia, hung in the doorway of his study a moment before throwing herself across the Oriental carpet and into his arms. "Oh, Percy, I'm ruined!"

Percy patted her back, resolved to the wilt of his cravat under her tears. "As you are married to a fine Christian gentleman of considerable fortune, I shall assume this has nothing to do with your virtue or finances."

She pulled back to blink her wide blue eyes. "Oh, Percy, of course not." Her pretty face pinched. "But it is absolutely terrible, after all my planning. We are at wrong numbers." She peered up at him as if expecting a scold.

"A terrible sin, to be sure," he obliged. "And at Christmas."

"Precisely!" She pressed her fingers into the fabric of his bronze-colored quilted banyan. "You will help me, won't you? I simply cannot settle the matter without you."

Lord Wellington would have been delighted to see Percy hadn't lost the diplomacy that had made him the general's trusted right hand through the last few years of battles on the peninsula. He did not run his fingers back through his already disheveled brown hair that his sister had brought him yet another problem to be solved, the twentieth in the last fortnight since she and her husband had joined him at their family home in Devonshire. He did not so much as glance at the desk beside him, where a profusion of notes, maps, and correspondence gave evidence that he was hard at work writing a book. He did not remind her that he had already refused to join the small house party she'd planned for Christmas because he was determined to finish a draft by New Year's.

"I'd be delighted to help, Amelia," he said, "only I'm certain I should not usurp your husband's place. Surely James ..."

She shook her head so hard her dainty blond curls bounced about her face. "No, no, James cannot help me. He'll be partnering Mrs. Grasland, of course, just as I will be partnering Mr. Grasland." She frowned. "Percy, are you attending?"

Most assuredly. He knew her guests were to be a friend she'd met on her debut and the woman's family. As he'd been battling across Spain when his sister had joined Society, he had not met the friend. But he would never forget the name of Grasland.

"Forgive me, Amelia," he said. "My mind wandered for a moment."

Immediately she was all solicitude, touching his hand, lips trembling. "Oh, my poor dear. Is it bad?"

The last thing he needed was her pity for the melancholy that had assailed him since his return. Percy pulled back his hand. "Do not trouble yourself. You were telling me about your guests, the Graslands. Is Mr. Grasland related to Colonel Grasland of the 88th Rifles, by any chance?"

She waved a graceful hand. "I have no idea. All I know is that Harriet decided to bring her new companion, a poor relation named Eleanor who had nowhere else to go, and we will be odd numbers at table if you don't come down. I know you're working on your book, but surely you can put it aside for Christmas. It isn't as if the outcome of the war will change."

No, Percy reflected as she scampered toward the door, obviously content that she had convinced him. Wellington had defeated

Napoleon and sent him off to Elba; that would not change. But so much about the war had changed Percy that he could not seem to let it go. He'd thought the peace of their family home on a stretch of cliff overlooking the channel would calm his restless spirit, yet his nights were punctuated by dreams of canon fire and bayonet flash and his days with a dark urgency. He felt as if he might implode if he couldn't do something. Putting his thoughts down on paper had seemed the wisest course.

Yet if Eleanor Grasland truly was waiting downstairs, shouldn't he offer to sit with her? After all, he'd once offered her his heart.

Eleanor Grasland felt as if her past was closing in around her as she followed her cousin and his wife down the wood-paneled stairs for the dining room at Night's Court. She'd hoped to stay upstairs with the children and the nurse, but Harriet had assured her that Percy would not be partaking of any of the festivities. Yet still she felt his presence.

Though their hosts had had the house decorated with evergreen boughs and red velvet ribbon, brighter were the regimental banners hung in the stairwell, proclaiming the units in which his grandfather and father had served. Crossed sabers protected the entry hall. On tables along the silk-lined wall to the dining room, gold plate inscribed by the monarch described heroism on behalf of the nation. Surrounded by such trappings, it was small wonder Percy had insisted on purchasing a commission six years ago at her father's urging. Seeing these reminders of war now only emphasized to Ellie why she had refused his suit.

"Sit next to me at the table," Harriet directed her as they approached the dining room door. Their hostess had assured them they needn't stand on ceremony and could enter as they liked. That hadn't stopped Harriet from dressing for the occasion in a gown of white silk embroidered with gold that made Ellie's pale gray lustring look all the more understated. "That way," her cousin's wife continued as she paused in the doorway, "you can be spared the trouble of conversation and be near should I have need of you."

Ellie nodded. It was all the response Harriet seemed to expect

even though her expectations in every other area verged on demanding. The eldest by a number of years in a large family, she had all but
raised her siblings and was now mother to three. From the moment
Ellie had appealed to her cousin, Edmund, for help, Harriet had
appropriated Ellie as her own lackey, to order from pillar to post as
she pleased. It was a dark, narrow existence, but at least Ellie had the
food, clothing, and home her tiny inheritance had denied her. She
was grateful the Lord had provided for her, for all she sometimes
regretted the avenue through which that help had come.

Now she followed Harriet and Edmund into the dining room, a
cozy space where candlelight glowed on walls the color of creamy jade
and holly clustered around the silver epergne in the center of the long
damask-draped table. Ellie found herself seated midway down, with
Harriet on her right and Edmund across from her. Her cousin was a
quiet man, small, lean; the way his eyes darted about reminded her of
a mouse caught in a trap. There was no doubt the cat so pleased with
her prey was his heavyset wife who even now sleeked back her frizzed
ginger hair with one plump hand. Ellie wasn't sure how Harriet had
managed to become friends with Percy's sister and her husband. Blond
and bright, they both beamed at their guests now, their well-tailored
clothes and dainty manners exquisite. At least the pairing would make
for an interesting evening. Perhaps Harriet would even forget about her
for a time and give her a little peace. She lowered her gaze to her lap in
preparation for hearing the blessing. Instead, another word split the air.

"Percy!" Amelia proclaimed.

Ellie's head jerked up. There he stood in the doorway, looking
much as the memories she still hugged to herself. His dark hair fell
carelessly across his brow, his lips curved just the slightest as if he
were sharing some secret. The scarlet coat and white breeches of
his uniform were even more recognizable. Those gold epaulets at
his broad shoulders and braid at the cuffs proclaimed him a major,
the silver frogging down the black front, a member of the general's staff. He inclined his head to the room in general, then came
around to sit next to her as Amelia introduced the other guests.

"And Miss Eleanor Grasland," his sister concluded with a
smile to Ellie. Ten years her brother's junior, Amelia had been only

fourteen and here in Devonshire when Percy had courted Ellie. She had no way of knowing she'd introduced more than a stranger. Yet Ellie knew. She couldn't seem to find her voice as Percy gazed at her.

She was thankful their host, Mr. Endicot, said the blessing then, and the footmen began serving. Their hostess had selected a fine roast and all the trimmings for Christmas Eve. Yet Ellie couldn't force a bite past her lips. Beside her, Percy also chose little of the many delicacies to add to his gilt-edged plate. Up close, she could see that his face, once so boyish in its charm, had grown harder, the youth tempered into a man much as her father's weapons master might temper a sword.

As if he caught her staring, his lips curved upward again. "Am I so different, Ellie?"

She dropped her gaze to her cooling dinner. "No more so than anyone who has ventured onto the battlefield, I imagine."

His hand pressed against the tablecloth as if to anchor himself. "Too true, I fear. Yet I admit to surprise to find you here. I'd have thought you married long since."

"Life can prove surprising even for those of us not privileged to serve, Major," she murmured.

"Sir Percival," he said. "I recently resigned my commission."

He no longer followed the drum? Ellie raised a brow. "Now, that is surprising."

"Salts!" Harriet barked.

Ellie knew how to react to the command. She pulled the reticule from the lap of her gown and drew out the little porcelain box with its brass grill. Harriet, she was convinced, had never fainted in her entire life, but something about reducing Ellie to this role pleased her to no end. She held the open box under Harriet's long nose, waited for her to sniff and roll back her eyes as if seeking heaven's aid as she usually did.

Instead, her cousin's wife glared at her over the box. "Listen to nothing he says," she hissed. "You know you do not wish to end like your mother."

Ellie's hand started shaking, but she managed to pull back the box and slip it into her reticule as Harriet turned to the others with a smile to assure them it was only the excitement of their excellent company that had made her feel faint. Of course Ellie didn't wish to end like her mother, scouring the papers for word that her husband had survived this skirmish, that battle, shriveling away like a plant for lack of water. She'd promised herself she would never marry a soldier. Her convictions had made it easy to refuse Percy's suit but altogether too weak to stop her from regretting it later.

But Percy was no longer a soldier. Was it possible they might find a way back to each other now?

Percy had chapters to compose, correspondence to review to dovetail experiences. Surely he had discharged his sacred duty by keeping his sister from being odd numbers at table and could now escape upstairs.

Yet he found himself escorting Ellie to the withdrawing room after dinner, past windows that showed the velvety night pressing in around the court. How could he have stayed away from her? Ellie had always been lovely, from her hair the color of the wheat waving along the cliff to her eyes like the sea at dawn. From the first, her whimsical smile, her soft voice, and the elegant sweep of her fingers had combined to draw him to her like a candle in the window on Christmas Eve. He was no more immune to her now.

But he did not much like her benefactors.

He could feel Mrs. Grasland's gaze on him as he led Ellie to a brace of satin-striped chairs near the velvet-draped window, but he heard Amelia strike up a conversation, and the two women were soon giggling like girls over shared memories.

He had shared so much more with Ellie. She'd been the daughter of the famous hero Colonel Horatio Grasland, who had been in England then for a recruiting drive. Grasland was a member of all the best clubs, knew just how to turn a tale to entice his young audience. Percy hadn't been the only one eager for excitement, adventure. But what had kept him coming back to the Grasland town house after his first dinner with the colonel was Ellie.

"He's a magician, you know," she'd warned him when he'd told her his intent to purchase a commission in her father's regiment. "He conjures amazing feats, but if you look closely, you'll find it nothing but stray bits of wire and wax."

He'd discovered his fair share of conjurers over the years, from Spanish noblemen willing to sell their country to France to French soldiers more interested in plunder than patriotism. Along the way, war had lost its glitter. Yet the desire he'd felt then, to make a difference in the world, had never left him.

Neither, it seemed, had his desire for Ellie.

With Harriet safely caught up in conversation, Ellie could focus on Percy. How easily time slipped backward. From the day they'd met, there was nothing they could not share, except the love for war. They both preferred their books to be rousing romantic adventures, their politics verging toward Whig, and their faith in the Lord to lead them. Now they shared as easily, their lives since they had parted, the activities of old friends, the loss of loved ones, his mother and her father.

Conversing with Percy was unlike talking with anyone else. He gave her his full attention, leaning toward her, smile playing about his lips, gaze intent on hers. He was quick to laugh at her jests, could be counted on to nod approval to her heartfelt choices. He was always ready to ride to the rescue should she need him but equally willing to let her solve the matter to her own satisfaction. Just sitting beside him made breath and thought come easier.

Yet when he shared his stories about life with Wellington, she heard something behind the words, saw it in the shadow that crossed his face. There was tension in him, like a spring never released. She could only wonder at its source.

Somewhere in the world beyond the glow of Percy's smile came the tolling of church bells. Percy rose and drew back the drapes as his sister and the others gathered around. Through the wreath that hung against the glass, starlight brightened the countryside. In the distance, squares of colored light showed where the village church was preparing to celebrate services.

"It's midnight," Amelia said with the delicious shiver of a child anticipating sweets. She stood on tiptoe and pecked her husband on the cheek. "Happy Christmas, my love."

He wrapped an arm about her waist. "Happy Christmas, dear."

Even Harriet and Edmund reached for each other's hand and stood a moment gazing out at the night, where a single star shown brighter than any other.

Warmer was the way Percy gazed at Ellie.

How could he have been so blind? He'd thought his career could sustain him, yet he'd always felt something missing. He'd prayed for guidance many times in the field, but it seemed his answer had been waiting for him in England all along.

Still, he couldn't assume she still felt for him. He was no longer the man Ellie had admired. For all he longed to take her in his arms, the restlessness inside him murmured caution. How could he ask Ellie to join him on his journey when he wasn't sure where the Lord was leading this time?

Amelia turned from the view to offer them all a smile. "Our mother loved Christmas and insisted on keeping the old traditions. She did not count the time a success unless she was surrounded by family and friends."

James patted her hand. "She would be proud of you, Amelia."

Her smile trembled. "I hope so. I want this, our first Christmas without her, to be perfect."

So that was why she'd been working so hard. "And how could anything my clever sister planned be less than perfect?" Percy teased her.

She blushed, then turned toward the door and clapped her hands. The footmen marched in bearing a bronze basin and various accoutrements.

Ellie clapped her hands as well. "Oh, Snapdragon!" she cried as one of the footmen set the basin on a table in the middle of the room and the other went to the fire for a brand. "Father loved this game."

"So did we," Amelia assured her as they all surrounded the vessel. Percy could see the dark dots of the raisins floating in the amber sea of the brandy. "Remember, Percy?"

He smiled as the footman approached with the burning brand. "Of course. You were only six when Mother let you put in your hand. You snatched half a dozen before the rest of us managed one."

Amelia giggled. "But you always won." She glanced around at her guests. "No one could beat Percy for diving through the fire."

The footman evidently took this as his cue, for he touched the brand to the alcohol. Blue flames leaped up, dancing against the metal, and Amelia's guests gave an appreciative gasp.

Percy couldn't gasp. He couldn't breathe. All he could see were the flames. He'd been with Wellington at Burgos Castle, the only time the general had been forced to retreat short of achieving his goal. Muskets flashed long into the night, like blue flames dancing to some macabre tune. So many wounded, more killed, his own attempts at negotiation useless.

"Excuse me," he managed and strode out into the corridor.

But even there, the air felt hot, suffocating. He leaned one hand against the silk of the wall and tugged at his stock with the other. Why couldn't he leave be? What more did God expect of him?

"Here." Ellie was beside him, thrusting a little box at his face. The fumes burned his nostrils, made him recoil, and brought reality sweeping back at him. He straightened to stare at her.

"Did you just administer smelling salts?"

Ellie felt her cheeks warm at the incredulous look on his handsome face. Indeed, with Percy towering over her, dressed in his regimental finery, medals decorating his broad chest, her actions seemed ridiculous.

"Habit," she admitted, tucking the box away. "Forgive me. You did seem in distress."

He shook his head. "A momentary lapse, I assure you."

She could well believe that. He seemed to be gathering his

dignity around him like a cloak. From inside the room, she heard Mrs. Endicot start the song that accompanied the game. Harriet's voice joined in, surprisingly sweet.

Ellie reached for Percy's hand. "Let it go. Come back with me and play Snapdragon."

His smile was more grimace. "I'm not much in the mood for celebrating."

She could almost feel the darkness gathering around him. She gave his hand a squeeze in encouragement. "It is Christmas, the night our Savior was born. What better reason to celebrate?"

He stared at their joined fingers, and she was suddenly aware of his body next to hers, the quiet of the corridor, the beating of her heart. As if he felt the same, his gaze rose to hers, his brown eyes deep. Slowly, he brought her fingers to his lips. The pressure of his kiss stopped her breath.

"Dear Ellie," he murmured. "Always the optimist. You deserve a happy Christmas. Go, enjoy the game. I am fit company for no one tonight." Before she could question him, he released her and strode away.

"Salts!" The cry pierced the air, and Ellie started. But for once, she didn't run to do as she was bid. *Forgive me, Lord, for ignoring my duty, but Percy needs me more.* She set her reticule on a table by the door so the footmen could find it if the salts were truly needed and hastened after Percy.

The way led up the stairs to the highest part of the old manor. Tucked under the thatched roof lay a long study. In the light from the fire and the single candle on the desk, she could make out books nestled on shelves under the dormer windows. At one end of the room stood a massive stone fireplace, the warmth spreading along the Oriental carpet that ran in a narrow strip of color down the center of the room. At the opposite end, she sighted an open doorway and the footboard of a great box bed inside. She certainly wasn't going to follow Percy in there!

"Percy?" she called, but he did not answer.

She wandered to the desk that sprawled across the back of the room and gazed down at Percy's work. It seemed he was writing a book. The pages lay scattered across the desk, along with maps, diagrams, and sketches. More maps were tacked inside the dormers, pins denoting important spots in France, Spain. She picked up a piece of the parchment.

"I still remember the night we heard the French were advancing," he'd written. "I'd gone with the other officers to the Duchess of Richmond's ball. Surrounded by good Society, it was easy to forget for a time that danger was marching closer, that likely tomorrow we would be bowing before our Maker rather than a pretty dance partner. I saw the courier arrive, felt the word run through those assembled like wildfire. It was time; it was war. And we were all that stood between Brussels and Bonaparte."

Her hand was shaking; she could not continue.

"Eleanor."

She looked up at Percy in the doorway of his bedchamber. Gone was his military finery, to be replaced by a quilted banyan of a smoky bronze that made him a shadowy figure as he advanced.

She held out the sheet to him. "It seems you still love war, Percy, more than you ever loved me."

He had to make her understand. The book, his life, meant nothing if that was what she thought of him. He moved to her side, took the page from her hand.

"No one sane loves war, Ellie," he said, laying the paper down with the others.

"Yet you cling to it." She waved a hand at the maps along the wall. "You surround yourself with it."

The sigh escaped him despite his best efforts. "The things I've seen stay with me, Ellie. I cannot seem to escape them. I need some way to make them right, yet the war is over, and nothing can be done. You were wise to counsel me against going. Back then, all I saw was the glory."

He felt the shudder run through her. "Father was the same way. He couldn't stay in England when Mother was ill, couldn't remain after she died. There was always one more battle to be won for England, one more tyrant to put down. And then he was killed, and I had no one."

Not even him. "I know that's what you feared, why you refused me. But you deserve better than to be the bearer of smelling salts."

She spread her hands. "I had other offers. I could not think it fair to marry a man simply to improve my circumstances."

"Then you never fell in love." He wasn't sure why that disappointed and encouraged him at the same time.

She glanced up at him. "Only once. With you."

The softness in her gaze pulled him closer. He could not stop himself from taking her in his arms, bending his head to hers. The caress of her lips wiped away the darkness, filled him with hope, with light.

Anything that is lovely, excellent, or worthy of praise, think upon such things.

That is what he'd forgotten, that light dwelt in darkness. This closeness with Ellie was what he had missed, why he'd fought, why he'd come back. He couldn't seem to let her go.

But he knew he had no right to hold her like this. He drew back, feathered his fingers across the satin of her upturned face.

"Oh, Percy," she said, opening her eyes and drawing him into the depths. "I fear I'm the one who was naïve. Reading what you wrote, I begin to understand why my father and you had to leave, had to stay away. And I realize why I couldn't go with you. I lack that kind of courage."

"Courage enough," he insisted, unwilling to hear anything bad said of her. "You stayed behind, waited with no way to influence the action except your prayers. But I assure you, they are a more potent weapon than Wellington's best canon."

"They must be," she murmured. "They brought you back to me safe." She pulled away, and Percy felt the chill of the air between them. She stood so still, so alone. He could change that. Indeed, he felt the rightness of it in his soul.

"And if I were to ask you to marry me again," he said, "how would you answer this time?"

Her lips trembled, and Percy waited, feeling as if he faced a firing squad and a promotion board at the same time. He willed her to say yes, to banish the darkness that surrounded him even on Christmas, to let in the light for them both.

But the voice he heard was his sister's. The word rose to a wail and was accompanied by the pounding of running feet.

"Percy!"

She burst into the room and passed Ellie as if Ellie were not more than a piece of statuary. Amelia held out a note, blue eyes wide.

"A courier just delivered this. It's from the War Office!"

Ellie stepped back. His sister must have noticed the movement, for Amelia glanced at Ellie with a frown, as if wondering how she'd gotten there.

Percy broke the seal and scanned the contents, pulse hammering harder with each word. "It's from Wellington. He's been asked to join the Congress of Vienna, and he's offering me a place at his side."

"Oh, Vienna!" Amelia clasped her hands. "Such a charming place, and you won't have any trouble traveling now that you've put down that horrid Napoleon."

She made it sound as if he were about to take a pleasure trip. He knew the truth of the minefield Wellington was about to enter. Yet something inside him quickened at the thought.

Lord, help me! I'm tempted just by the idea! I thought You brought Ellie back to me because You wanted me to have peace.

Percy folded the note and laid it on the desk to be answered in the morning. "I'll decline," he told his sister. "The congress has little chance of success. Our allies and our enemies will be packed together and each determined on the outcome. The negotiations will be challenging, to say the least."

"But not impossible," Ellie put in, meeting his gaze, "for a man of your skills."

Percy frowned. Surely she understood the ramifications. Did she want him to leave?

His sister evidently did, for she snapped a nod before turning for the door. "Of course you'll go. I'll have your things packed immediately: winter cloak, galoshes, your best coats." She paused to tap a finger against her chin. "I wonder what's in fashion in Vienna now."

Percy shook his head as she drifted out the door. "And now I'm her project. She doesn't seem to be happy without one."

"And neither are you," Ellie reminded him, returning to his side. "You want to go, Percy. Admit it."

There was danger in admitting it, in hearing the words said aloud. He could very well lose himself in the intricate negotiations. Worse, he would lose Ellie again.

"It matters not," he assured her, clasping her hands and cradling them against his chest. "I have more important matters to attend to. I asked your opinion on such a matter, madam. I have not had an answer from you. Eleanor Grasland, will you marry me?"

How was she to answer? He still had the ability to hold her heart in his capable hands, yet those hands were needed hundreds of miles away to settle far larger matters. She'd refused to follow once. Yet in the six years since he'd last asked her, she'd learned something about the world and about herself. Whatever happened, she had Someone who would look out for her. She didn't have to be afraid.

"I will give you an answer, Major," she said, pulling her hands free. She stood at attention the way her father had taught her and held her fingers to her forehead in salute. "I will do my duty and follow my husband to Vienna and anywhere else he might need to go."

Percy stared at her as if he could not believe her. Then he pulled her close and sealed the promise with a kiss that set her to trembling anew.

"You're sure?" he pressed when at last he raised his head. "I don't need to go. I can finish the book, make us a home here at Night's Court."

Ellie shook her head. "You said you wanted a way to make the war right. This is your chance. I cannot ask you to give it up for me. I want you to succeed, for everyone's sake!"

He touched her cheek again, sending a shiver through her. "This will mean big changes, for both of us."

"Changes for the better," she insisted, smiling up at him, more sure than she'd ever been.

"There you are!"

Ellie glanced back to see Harriet standing in the doorway, with Edmund, James, and Amelia just behind her. All of them were staring at her in Percy's arms. The only one who looked dismayed was her cousin's wife.

"Wish us happy," Percy said to them. "Eleanor has agreed to be my wife and join me in Vienna with Wellington."

The men grinned, and Amelia clapped her hands. Harriet clutched her chest.

"Salts!" she cried, wavering on her feet.

Ellie was too busy kissing Percy to respond.

"Don't fret, Harry," she heard Amelia say as if from a great distance. "It's Christmas. We have to expect surprises like this on such a day. Come downstairs with me. I want to put a candle in the window. Mother always said it guided the Christ child to our door."

It had taken more than a candle to guide Percy back to her, but Ellie knew she would never let him go again.

"Happy Christmas," she murmured against his lips.

"With you, Ellie," he answered, "every day is Christmas."

For nearly 20 years, readers have been turning to award-winning author **Regina Scott** for warm and witty inspirational historical romance. Literary critics have called her more than 25 stories "quietly compelling," "sweetly romantic," and "impeccably written." Her books have been translated into many languages and issued in hardcover. The mother of two grown sons, she lives in Washington State with her husband and an overactive Irish terrier.

www.reginascott.com

COMING HOME

JOAN JOHNSTON

New York Times Bestseller

"I'M NOT GOING OUT with him. And that's final."

"Even if Luke's innocent? Even if he never did what they said?"

Savannah Whitelaw eyed her older sister sideways. "Don't give me that look, Christy. No means no."

"Come on, Savannah," Christy urged. "You, of all people, know what it means for someone to give you a second chance."

Savannah grimaced as she met her sister's imploring gaze. Savannah had been adopted into the Whitelaw family when she was nine, and she had both emotional and physical scars from the years she'd spent in the foster care system. Christy, who was two years older, was a "real" Whitelaw. Savannah had learned over the years that it was foolish not to call herself a "real" Whitelaw, because she was loved every bit as dearly by her parents, Jake and Hope, as any of the children Hope had borne.

Based on Christy's description of the events surrounding Luke's downfall, Savannah was inclined to give him the benefit of the doubt. But she was an FBI agent home on medical leave, and dating convicted felons was definitely not approved behavior. Savannah had left a class at Quantico to donate bone marrow to a younger brother she hadn't known existed, and she was still reeling from meeting her biological parents and the child they'd had together many years after she'd been given up for adoption.

She was staying with her adoptive parents at their ranch in northwest Texas, Hawk's Way, while she waited for the next Behavioral Science class at Quantico to start. Her parents were on a cattle-buying trip and wouldn't be back for a few days.

Savannah shook her head at the thought of dating a man who'd spent time in prison. Forget her own misgivings. What would her parents think? "It sounds like a bad idea, Christy."

"Luke's been completely exonerated, his record expunged, if that's what you're worried about."

Savannah sighed. "You know me too well." She put herself in Luke's place and imagined how she would feel if her reputation had been tainted forever by a false accusation. She knew from personal experience how it felt to have someone believe in you when everyone else had given up on you. Her life had been transformed because the Whitelaws had enfolded a troubled child in their arms.

"Dad gave Luke a job here at Hawk's Way while he tries to put his life back together. He deserves a chance for a normal existence, don't you think?"

"I don't know how you talk me into these things, Christy, but you always do. Fine. I'll go on a double date with Luke and you and Harve. But you'd better not leave me alone with that man. I don't care if Luke Winters is pure as the driven snow, he's been in jail for six years. Heaven knows what that did to his psyche. I don't want to end up in a wrestling match with him."

"Why not?" Christy said with a grin. "You'd probably win."

Savannah smiled wryly. She'd learned a great deal about self-defense during her FBI training, but she had no wish to put that knowledge to the test on a date. "I wouldn't have a chance if he looks anything like he did on the football field in college."

Savannah was tall, five foot eleven in her stocking feet, but Luke was a good six inches taller. While she was fit, she had definite feminine curves. Luke had been all muscle and bone.

Christy sat down beside Savannah on the studded leather couch in their parents' living room and pulled a cowhide pillow to her chest. "Honestly, I hardly recognized Luke when I saw him after he got out of prison."

Savannah frowned. "He got fat? Lost all his hair? What?"

Christy shrugged. "I think you were closer to the mark when you mentioned his psyche."

"He looked wild-eyed? Ready to pounce?"

"The opposite, actually," Christy said. "As I recall, in college he was pretty cocky. You know, football quarterback with looks like a Greek god, girls falling all over themselves to go out with him. He's still as attractive as ever, but he seems ... subdued."

No wonder, Savannah thought, after what he'd been through. She'd been a freshman at the University of Texas at Austin when Luke was a senior. He'd been broad-shouldered and lean-waisted, blond-haired and blue-eyed, a perfect specimen of the All-American Male.

Then he'd been accused of raping a girl on the quad near the college library. Luke had argued that the sex was consensual. The girl's parents had sued the university for failure to provide proper security for their daughter, and with UT's zero-tolerance policy for misbehavior by athletes, they'd thrown Luke to the lions. The university had agreed to a multimillion-dollar settlement with the girl's parents to avoid the public relations nightmare of a civil suit, and based on the girl's convincing testimony in the criminal trial, Luke had ended up in prison.

The story of Luke's release six months ago had made national headlines. Apparently, the girl who'd accused him had come to visit him in prison and apologized for wrongly accusing him of rape. She'd explained that her parents had needed the money they'd gotten from the settlement, and she'd been afraid that if she admitted the truth, they'd have to give it back.

Luke had managed to get the girl to repeat her story to a friend of his on the outside who'd been wired. It had taken the courts a while to consider her testimony, to arrange to have his record expunged, and for him to be released. He was a free man, but his reputation had been forever smirched. There would always be folks, especially in the small Texas town where he'd grown up, and which he'd left without a backward wave when he'd gone off to college, who'd believe he was guilty.

Which was why Savannah wasn't crazy about the idea of being

seen on a date with Luke Winters. She had a reputation of her own to protect, especially where the FBI was concerned.

She reminded herself that Luke was innocent. She reminded herself that he deserved a chance to prove himself to be the absolute gentleman Christy said he was.

"I didn't bring anything with me to wear," Savannah said. "Every dress I own is back in Virginia." It was a weak excuse, but she was running out of them.

"I've got something that should fit you."

Savannah laughed as she eyed her shorter, much less curvy sister. "We're not remotely the same size."

"Have you looked at yourself lately in the mirror?"

Savannah glanced down at the ragged jeans and cutoff T-shirt that revealed long, slender legs and trim abs and asked, "What am I supposed to see?"

"All that physical training you've been doing at Quantico has slimmed you down. Just in case you said yes, I brought along something for you to wear. I hung it in the guest room closet."

"I think I'd be more comfortable in something of my own," Savannah said.

"I'd rather see you dressed like a girl. I suspect Luke would, too."

Savannah was surprised into laughter. "What does that mean?"

"It means no FBI clothes," Christy said firmly. "No navy blue suit. No trousers. When Harve and I arrive here with Luke at seven to pick you up, I want to see you wearing something that shows off your figure."

"Isn't that a bit like setting raw meat before a slavering wolf?"

Christy grinned. "Now there's an image to make a girl's heart beat a little faster." She rose and leaned over to give Savannah a hug. "Just go for it! See you at seven," she said over her shoulder as she headed for the door.

Christy found it amusing that Savannah always wore severely tailored suits, but as far as Savannah was concerned, showing up anywhere in a dress was no laughing matter. She'd inherited her biological mother's hourglass figure, and in any kind of form-fitting outfit, she looked too much like Jessica Rabbit to be taken seriously as an FBI agent. Her sun-streaked chestnut hair and piercing green eyes only added to her allure. When Savannah "dressed like a girl," she was a knockout. The last thing she wanted to do was engage Luke's libido.

On the other hand, if he made an unwelcome move on her, she could end the date and head home early. She wasn't interested in starting a relationship with anyone, let alone someone who lived in Texas, since she was headed back to Virginia in a couple of weeks. Besides, she had enough problems of her own without getting involved with someone who'd had as much trouble in his life as Luke Winters had.

Savannah wasn't quite ready when Christy returned with Harve and Luke at seven. She was standing before the mirror in the guest bedroom staring at the leaf-green, low-cut, snug-fitting dress, wondering what her sister could possibly have been thinking. The dress was the wrong size. Savannah wore an eight. This was a six.

She wished it had been impossible to zip, because then she could have told her sister it didn't fit and put on the navy blue pants suit hanging in her closet. But Christy must have been right about all that physical training Savannah had done at Quantico, because the dress zipped right up, conforming to every curve she'd worked so hard to hide from her fellow agents.

"This is the wrong dress to wear for a date with a man who's been stuck in prison for six years," she muttered, trying without success to adjust the bodice to make it more concealing. "Way too much cleavage."

She pointed a toe, surveying the black strappy heels she'd found in the bottom of the closet with a note from Christy stating that they were to be worn with the dress. "Who knew bare feet could make you feel half naked?" she said as she surveyed herself in the mirror. The dressy shoes were only a couple of inches high, but they were open at both toe and heel. Savannah was used to sensible footwear that allowed her to run full tilt after a "perp," which was what she'd learned to call the bad guys.

"What's holding you up in there?" Christy said as she knocked and then shoved open the guest room door. "It's time to go!" She took a step inside and closed the door behind her, leaning back against it. "Oh, my God."

"What is it?" Savannah asked anxiously, taking a step toward her sister.

"You're gorgeous! Your hair. All those curls really soften your sharp cheekbones. Your makeup. Those false eyelashes and that dark eye shadow make your green eyes look huge. I thought the dress might look nice on you. But holy cow!"

Savannah felt herself blushing, but her feelings of pleasure were mixed with embarrassment at her sister's over-the-top compliments. "It's the wrong size. I usually wear—"

"You usually wear your clothes a size too big," Christy interrupted.

Savannah tugged at the silky green fabric that clung to her body like a second skin. "Don't you think it's a little ... snug?"

"It's absolute perfection," Christy replied. "Luke is going to love it. Come on. My favorite country band is playing at the local bar, and we're going to miss the opening set if we don't hurry up and get to the restaurant."

Savannah was halfway to the door when she pulled up short. "Restaurant? I thought we were going dancing."

"Sure. After we have dinner."

"I don't want Luke Winters buying me supper," Savannah protested.

"It's no big deal. We're just going to the cafe in town."

Savannah glanced down at her visible cleavage and said, "I'm way overdressed." Or underdressed, depending on how you looked at it.

Christy got behind her and herded her toward the door, then reached out, opened the door, and shoved Savannah through it. "Stop being silly. You look amazing."

Savannah was still resisting Christy's gentle shove when she found herself in the living room facing Christy's boyfriend, Harve Stevens, and her date, Luke Winters.

Savannah thanked her FBI training for keeping her from actually gasping when she got a look at Luke up close. He was even taller than she remembered, towering over her even in her heels.

His emotionless face looked carved from stone, but the sculptor had obviously loved his model, because the high cheekbones, sharp nose, and square chin were in perfect proportion. Wide-set, ice-blue eyes stared back at her, and Savannah felt herself shiver.

She swallowed over the sudden knot in her throat and said, "I need a sweater." What she needed was to cover herself up. It wasn't Luke's ice-blue eyes that had made her shiver, it was the heat she'd felt at his appraising glance.

She turned to leave the room, but Christy grabbed her hand and said, "Savannah Whitelaw, I'd like you to meet Luke Winters."

She was caught. Like a mouse in a trap. She reached out and found her fingertips enfolded by a warm, callused hand.

"Nice to meet you, Miss Whitelaw," he said in a gruff, Tex-as-accented voice. "Your dad speaks very highly of you."

She forced herself to meet Luke's gaze and said, "Call me Savannah, please." She smiled ruefully and added, "My dad speaks highly of all his children."

Her parents had adopted several children, and Savannah was the last in a long line of lost waifs who'd found themselves part of the Whitelaw clan. In fact, when she thought about it, she shouldn't have been surprised that her father had hired Luke Winters. Most of the children her parents had adopted and loved had come to them with problems.

Luke's blond hair was still wet, as though he'd just gotten out of the shower. The sleeves of his wrinkled western shirt were folded up to reveal sinewy forearms, and the faded plaid cotton was tucked into worn jeans that led to scuffed brown cowboy boots.

Luke saw her staring at his face and rubbed a hand over the stubble that shadowed his cheeks and chin. "Your dad has me on a job that kept me working late. Sorry I didn't have time to shave."

"I should go change," she said, aware of how mismatched the two of them looked.

"Don't." Only the one word, spoken in a gravelly voice. Not an order. A request. "You look stunning."

Savannah resisted the urge to protest. As an FBI agent who wore a gun on her hip, it wasn't often that a man looked at her as a woman. She met Luke's gaze, flustered, and mumbled, "Thank you."

"We should get going," Christy said, grabbing Harve by the elbow and heading toward the front door. "You guys coming?"

Savannah edged away as Luke reached for her elbow and walked ahead of him to the door. She realized she was being rude and dropped back to walk beside him. His cheeks were flushed, and she knew he'd recognized the snub for what it was.

"It's not you," she said. "It's me. I'm not used to asking for help from anyone."

He eyed her for a long moment, as though deciding whether she was telling the truth.

"I don't date much." She hesitated, then admitted, "Actually, I don't date, period."

His lips curved in a wry smile. "Haven't been out myself much lately, either, but I have an excuse. What's yours?" he asked as he held the front screen door open for her.

"My job, mostly. It's too hard being 'one of the guys' if you're trying to be 'one of the girls.'"

"Your dad told me you're an FBI agent."

She turned to look him in the eye and said, "My dad seems to have said a great deal about me."

Luke shrugged. "He's been worried about you. I mean, about you finding out that your biological parents gave you away and then had another child that they kept."

"That's private," Savannah said sharply, feeling the ache in her chest that hadn't yet gone away in the short time since she'd learned that truth. "Dad shouldn't have shared that with you."

"I guess he thought I'd understand," Luke said quietly. "I mean, about how it feels to be rejected because of something that wasn't your fault."

Savannah stared at him, realizing that Luke must feel an ache in his throat every time he thought of what might have been, if only he hadn't been falsely accused, and what his life most likely would end up being with a constant shadow of guilt hanging over him.

They'd reached Harve's extended-cab pickup, and Luke opened the truck's back door and waited for her to get in. Savannah realized there was no way she could climb into the high cab without hiking her fitted skirt halfway up her thighs.

"Can I help?" Luke asked.

"I could use a hand," she conceded.

Instead of taking her elbow and assisting her, Luke set his hands on either side of her waist and lifted her onto the seat as though she weighed no more than a bag of feed. Savannah's flesh felt hot where his hands had been, and she quickly scooted across the seat to make room for him.

There should have been plenty of room on the backseat for the two of them to sit apart, but Harve used his truck for work, and he hadn't cleaned out the backseat. A pile of junk on the seat to her left meant Savannah had to sit thigh-to-thigh with Luke. She was aware of the heat of his leg and the ripple of muscles beneath his jeans.

"I didn't realize Harve had left all that stuff on the seat," he said. "We all three sat in the front coming over."

"I'm used to it," she replied.

"Be careful you don't snag your dress on that wire," he said as he leaned across her and moved a small roll of barbed wire out of her way.

His arm brushed against her breast and Savannah gasped.

He dropped the barbed wire and leaned back into his seat. "Sorry about that."

He looked as uncomfortable as Savannah felt. "This was a bad idea," he muttered.

"Hey, you two," Christy called to them from the front seat. "We're so late, what would you think about just grabbing something to eat at the bar where the band's playing?"

"Fine with me," Luke said.

"Me, too," Savannah agreed. The sooner this date was over, the better. Luke was as jumpy as a bullfrog on a hot skillet, and his discomfort was making her uncomfortable.

The jukebox was blaring a Carrie Underwood tune as they entered the bar. Harve grabbed a booth near the sawdusted dance floor as a couple of cowboys got up and left, and the four of them sat down. Getting a booth necessarily meant that she and Luke ended up sitting next to each other, but Savannah put an extra few inches between them to be certain they weren't touching.

Unfortunately, the music was so loud it was impossible to hear, so Luke had to lean in close to ask, "What would you like to drink?"

"*Dos Equis*," she said.

"Coming right up," Luke said as he left the booth with Harve on his heels.

Christy got out of her side of the booth and came around to sit next to Savannah. "What do you think of Luke?"

"I don't think he wanted to do this any more than I did," Savannah replied.

"Harve had to talk him into it," Christy admitted. "But I think you and Luke have a lot in common."

"What are you talking about?"

"I mean, you've both been betrayed by someone."

There it was again. The suggestion that they were both emotionally damaged goods. Savannah wanted to protest that her biological parents hadn't "betrayed" her, they'd "abandoned" her and then gone on to get married to each other and have another child. But it was hard to deny that what she'd experienced with her biological parents felt a great deal like betrayal.

Before she could argue the point with Christy, Luke returned with her drink. Christy jumped up and returned to her side of the booth as Luke set Savannah's beer on the table in front of her. He sat down beside her, then lifted his beer to clink it with hers. "To better times."

"I'll drink to that." Her beer was cold and refreshing, and she drank it in small sips to make it last. She had no intention of having more than one. She wasn't about to let down her guard with someone she found so physically attractive.

"The band's here early!" Christy said as the musicians began setting up on the stage.

Someone unplugged the jukebox, and a woebegone cowboy abruptly stopped singing. The silence was jarring.

"I'm going to order some food from the bar," Harve said. "What would you like, Christy?"

"A burger and fries." She glanced toward Savannah and Luke and asked, "How about you two? Same thing?"

"Sounds fine," Luke and Savannah said almost in unison.

"I'll come wait with you, Harve, and help you carry everything," Christy volunteered as she leapt out of her seat.

Before Savannah could protest, the other couple was gone, and she was alone with Luke. Well, not precisely *alone*. They were sitting in a crowded bar decorated with Christmas tree lights, with a live rattlesnake in an aquarium behind the bar. Deer heads were mounted several places along the wooden walls, and an eight-foot-wide set of longhorns had a place of honor above the stage.

Savannah watched Luke peel at the label on his beer bottle with his thumb, his eyes focused on his hands. She knew she ought to say something, but she had no idea what.

"I'm no good at this dating thing," she said at last.

He turned his head to meet her gaze and said, "I used to be great at it. Not too many women are interested in going out with me now."

She heard the sarcasm in his voice and felt way more sympathy for him than she thought she should. "What happened to you was a travesty and a shame."

"What happened to me was my own damn fault."

Savannah was shocked into blurting, "You mean you did it?"

"Hell, no! I mean I didn't give a damn who I dated. I didn't care whether there was any substance behind the pretty face. I wanted only one thing from the girls I went out with, and I usually got it."

He looked at her directly, so Savannah was in no doubt that the only thing he'd wanted from his dates was sex and that he'd been successful in getting it.

"I chose the wrong girl, and I got burned," he said. "I'd like to think I learned my lesson and that I'll make better choices in the future."

"I'm a better choice?" Savannah asked skeptically.

"You're smart. You have a career. Most importantly, you're a survivor."

He didn't add, "Like me," but Savannah heard the words anyway.

"If you're referring to the fact that I'm adopted and turned out to be a good human being, Jake and Hope deserve all the credit for that. How about you? Have your parents been supportive?"

"My mother never believed a word that girl said. My father died when I was ten."

"I'm sorry. That must have been tough on you and your mom."

"We managed. I was hoping for an NFL contract that would let me buy her a new house, but that ended with the rape conviction." He shrugged. "I send her what I can, but even with the political science degree I finished in prison, there aren't many businessmen who'd consider hiring me, despite having my record cleared."

"So you settled for working as a ranch hand for my father," Savannah concluded.

Luke's lips quirked. "I'm still exploring my options. Politics is definitely out."

"I thought your plan was to play professional football."

"Football only lasts until you reach your thirties. I intended to pursue a career in public service afterward."

"And that's out of the question now?"

He pursed his lips. "You tell me. Would you elect a man with my reputation?"

"I guess you're right. What do you want to do?" she asked.

"I've been considering law enforcement."

"That's an option?"

"As far as the justice system is concerned, I'm an innocent man. I think I'd make a good lawman. Eventually, I'd like to become a Texas Ranger."

The Rangers were an elite force of Texas lawmen, lone wolves who worked on their own to solve crimes and keep the peace. Savannah could see why the job might appeal to Luke.

"Why did you become an FBI agent?" he asked.

Savannah shrugged. She kept her gaze focused on the bottle of beer in her hands, unwilling to reveal what had sent her into the field of law enforcement.

"Out with it," Luke said.

"If you must know, a friend of mine was raped."

Luke's face paled. "Oh."

"It wasn't date rape or anything like that. This man was a serial rapist attacking women across South Texas." She met Luke's stricken gaze and said, "He's still out there. He's never been caught. And now he's killing the women he rapes."

A furrow appeared between Luke's brows. "That's why you were taking that special FBI class, the one you had to leave to donate bone marrow to your brother?"

Savannah nodded, because her throat was too swollen with emotion to speak. "My friend was devastated by that attack. She's never been the same. She hardly leaves her home. She's become a recluse. I keep thinking if I can figure out enough about how this guy thinks to find him, maybe, someday, she'll feel safe enough to leave her home again."

Luke met her gaze and said, "You're pretty amazing, you know that?"

Savannah felt self-conscious again. "I just want to help."

"I know what you mean. I have this feeling that if I were a lawman, I'd be able to tell the good guys from the bad guys better than the cops who arrested me."

Savannah opened her mouth to speak, but he held up his hand to silence her and continued, "Yeah, I know it's naïve and improbable."

"It's noble and worthy," Savannah countered. "And naïve and improbable," she agreed with a smile. "But where would we be without a little idealism in our lives?"

Savannah hadn't realized the band had begun to play until Luke said, "Would you like to dance?"

Savannah wondered what had happened to Christy and Harve. As she looked toward where they'd disappeared, she said, "The bartender must have had to butcher the beef for those hamburgers."

"Is that a no?" Luke said.

Savannah realized she wanted to dance with Luke. She wanted to be held in his arms. She wanted to feel the heat of his body next to hers. Which she would, since there wasn't much material in the dress she was wearing to separate her flesh from his. Nothing covering her bare chest and back, her bare arms and shoulders, or her bare legs.

"I need a bigger dress," she muttered under her breath.

He leaned in close and asked, "Was that a yes?"

Dress. Yes. He'd heard wrong, but why fight the inevitable? "Sure," she said. "Why not?"

There were plenty of reasons why not. She was headed back to Quantico. She didn't want to get involved. He was a man with problems. She had problems of her own.

A moment later, Savannah was being held in Luke's arms, and they were moving slowly around the dance floor. Why couldn't the band have started with a lively Texas two-step, which would have had her twirling around the dance floor at arm's length? Or even with a waltz, where she could have kept her distance? Instead, it was a slow tune with wailing violins and a lonely guitar.

Luke carefully slid his arm around her waist and pulled her close. To her surprise, he kept a half inch between their bodies from breast to hips, but their faces were so close she could feel his breath on her cheek.

The dance floor was soon crowded with couples, until the distance between them had decreased to almost nothing. Savannah heard Luke inhale sharply as a couple bumped into them from behind. Savannah's breasts were suddenly pillowed against Luke's muscular chest, and his hips cradled hers. For a brief moment, she felt the hard length of him against her belly.

Savannah realized he was trying to separate their bodies, but he was bumped from behind again, and their bodies were pressed firmly together, leaving no doubt of his arousal.

She met his gaze and saw a myriad of emotions. Defiance and resignation. Shame and longing. Apology and desire.

What surprised her were the answering emotions she felt that must be equally apparent to him. Embarrassment and arousal. Longing and shame. White-hot desire.

How could she be feeling so much for someone she barely knew? Wanting Luke Winters was strictly a matter of animal lust, she told herself. She should be slaking her body's purely physical thirst for sex now and again with an appropriate man so she wouldn't feel such a powerful attraction to such an unsuitable partner.

Savannah felt Luke's hand slide up her naked back until his callused fingers caught on her nape. She shivered as he angled her head back so he could look more directly into her eyes.

"You feel it, too." His voice was guttural, and she could feel the tautness in his body.

"It would be foolish to deny it," she answered in an equally coarse voice.

His eyes narrowed slightly as he surveyed her features. She wondered if he was looking for signs of a betrayal to come. She wondered if he was hoping she would stop him before he did what she knew he was going to do.

They were no longer dancing but stood perfectly still surrounded by other couples whose bodies were entwined and who moved languidly around them.

She saw his lips move as though he was uttering an oath, but she wasn't able to decipher what he said before his mouth covered hers. His kiss was surprisingly gentle, almost tentative, seeking permission rather than demanding what she knew he wanted.

She was the hungry one. She opened her mouth and felt him take what she'd known he wanted, tasting her, uplifting her, and making her feel exultant.

"Hey, you two!" a female voice interrupted. "Get a room."

Savannah broke the kiss and stared into Luke's eyes, alarmed to realize that her hand was caught in his hair. She lowered her hand to his shoulder, feeling embarrassed at her forwardness. She felt tongue-tied, unable to speak, which was a good thing, because she had no idea how to explain her behavior.

Her other hand was still enfolded in his and rested against his chest. Without a word, he began dancing again, moving them out of the crowd toward the edge of the room.

"What are you doing?"

"Our hamburgers are getting cold," he said.

"Oh."

He chuckled. "You thought maybe I was on my way to get a room?"

She cocked a brow. "It occurred to me."

"I'm no longer interested in casual sex."

But he was interested in her. She lowered her lids to avoid the avidity in his eyes.

He pressed her body against his so she could have no doubt about his arousal. "I've wanted you from the moment I laid eyes on you tonight in that dress. But when I was in prison, I made a vow to myself that I was going to change. That I was going to be more discriminating in my choice of sexual partners."

"What does that mean?" she asked as he ushered her into the booth they'd left and then slid in after her.

"That I want to like the person, to start with," he said with a self-deprecating smile. "And that she has to like me."

Savannah thought about what Luke had said and realized that what seemed like a pretty low threshold for sex wasn't that at all. "Do you like me?" she asked.

"I like the fact that you were willing to help your brother, despite the fact that your biological parents decided to give you away. I like the fact that you've planned a career that will enable you to help a friend. I like the fact that you put on that killer dress for me, even though you knew I was a former convict. And I like the fact that you kissed me in full view of all your friends and neighbors, despite who I am."

Savannah flushed. She'd been so captivated by the man holding her in his arms that she'd been totally unaware of her friends and neighbors.

He surprised her by asking, "Do you like me?"

"I don't know you," she blurted. She responded to the disappointment on Luke's face by saying, "I'm glad that you like me, and I'm pleased at the reasons you gave for liking me."

"That's it?"

Savannah realized there were several things she knew about Luke that she appreciated. "I like the fact that you finished your degree, even though you were in prison. I like the fact that you have ambitions for your future that include law enforcement." She smiled and added, "And I like the fact that you plan to be more discriminating about who you choose as your sexual partners in the future."

"I guess that's a pretty good place to start," Luke said with a grin. "Come on. Eat up. Your hamburger's getting cold."

"That's it? No more questions?" Savannah said as she picked up her burger.

"One more," he said, meeting her gaze. "I've been accepted for the next class at Quantico. When I'm there, will you go out with me?"

Savannah dropped her burger back in the basket. "Luke! Congratulations! When were you going to tell me this?"

"I just told you. And you haven't answered my question."

Savannah laid a hand on his whiskered cheek. She leaned forward until their lips were close but not touching and said, "I'd be glad to go out with you."

Savannah saw the gleam of tears in his eyes before she had to close her own as he leaned in to kiss her.

"Hey, you two!" a female voice said. "Get a room."

Savannah broke the kiss and turned to smile at Christy and Harve. "You get a room!" she shot back. She grinned in Luke's direction and said, "We plan to eat our burgers and then dance the rest of the night away."

"Could've fooled me," Christy said as she plopped onto the bench seat opposite them and then scooted over so Harve could join her. "You seemed pretty involved with one another on the dance floor."

Luke smiled at Savannah, then took her hand in his and said, "That was just two people deciding they'd like to get to know each other better."

Savannah smiled back as she felt the ache in her heart ease. The world suddenly seemed like a nicer place. And the future seemed filled with possibility. "Yeah. Luke and I have decided we'd like to be friends."

"Friends," Christy said, her face falling in disappointment. "Is that all?"

Savannah looked into Luke's blue eyes and felt the warmth of his gaze all the way to her toes. She smiled and said, "It's a pretty good place to start."

Luke leaned in and whispered, "Be sure to take that dress with you when you head back to Washington. I'm looking forward to seeing you in it again." The gleam in his eyes said he was even more interested in seeing her *out* of it.

Savannah smiled and said, "I will."

Joan Johnston is the top ten *New York Times* and *USA Today* bestselling author of 55 novels and novellas with more than 15 million copies of her books in print. She has been a director of theatre, drama critic, newspaper editor, college professor, and attorney on her way to becoming a full-time writer. You can find out more about Joan at her website, www.joanjohnston.com, or www.facebook.com/joanjohnstonauthor, or twitter.com/joanjohnston.

THE POET

T. L. COSTA

I FIRST REALIZED I was doomed when I Googled my name-sake. I was twelve. I stared at the screen of the iPad, eyes wide, my brain sorting data like Uncle Frank scans channels.

"Mom?" I called from my perch on the couch-of-many-quilts.

"Yes, Wyatt?" She marched up the stairs from her "zen-den" running her hand through her tangle of grayish curls.

iPad trembling, I asked, "Did you seriously name me after a *poet*?"

"Sir Thomas Wyatt, yes."

"What? Why did you do that? I thought I was named after Wyatt Earp or somebody cool, not some dead guy in a lacy collar."

"He's credited with inventing the sonnet ..."

"It says here that he was in love with Anne Boleyn. You know, queen of England, wife of Henry the Eighth, *executed*." My throat was tightening, strangled by the weight of some over-starched fancy collar that probably itched. Itched *a lot*.

"Yes." Mom walked *away* from me and into the kitchen, grab-bing a bottle of water like it was no big deal. "Pretty romantic, huh?"

"It's not romantic if he watched her get *beheaded*, Mom. Why would you *do* that to me?"

She shrugged, her shoulders lifting in a wicked slant like a bat about to suck all the juice out of some poor, unsuspecting mango. "When you were born, I looked into your eyes, and I saw a gentle soul, a romantic soul. The soul of a poet. And I just knew it was right."

This is why I now play football.

Offensive line. Me and my poet's soul can kick some major ass on the field. What can I say?

I compensate where I can.

Jimmy Tsao rams into me, and my shoulders ache as I dig my feet into the turf. I push back with every ounce of strength. He moves left and I block, biceps burning.

The whistle blows. I stop, panting.

He laughs, "Great play, man. Getting tired. You?"

"Yeah." The sun has disappeared, leaving only a smudge of orange on the horizon. "Coach has to call it soon."

But he doesn't. Coach yells at the other guys on the line for not making their blocks, for leaving our quarterback, Derek Smith, defenseless. My mind wanders to the poem I have to write for Mom for her birthday on Friday.

The problem the coach isn't addressing, of course, is that even when we give the guy time to throw the ball, he never makes the play. Ever. Poor guy can't throw to save his life. How he ended up being the quarterback I'll never know, but if he's the best we got, then, well, it's going to be a long, miserable season.

Personally, though, Derek is a pretty nice guy, even if I disapprove of his throws and his hair.

He has this hair that, well, it *flounces*. Yes, I mean *flounce*. I'm a pretty open-minded guy and all, but dudes just shouldn't have hair that does that. It's long and wavy and constantly looks like it's been blowing in the wind.

Coach blows the whistle, and we get back on the line. Derek calls the play, and just as I start to pump myself up to block Jimmy, I look up at the bleachers.

My throat goes dry.

Hannah Smith is in the stands.

Concentrate, Wyatt, focus on the game or—

Jimmy Tsao slams into my side, and I slip and crash to the ground. Shoulder exploding in pain. No! I reach out to grab at least an ankle or something, but it's too late. Jimmy sacks Derek, and now Coach is screaming for real.

At me.

"Thomas Wyatt Hershowitz that was the worst freaking play I've ever seen! Where was your head?" He stands over me, flecks of spit landing on my helmet. "Everyone else can hit the lockers. Wyatt's going to stay here and give me a hundred push-ups. And none of that girly-knee crap. Get to it."

I lay flat on my back for a minute as the sneakers of my team-mates rush by me.

I'm cursed. Yes, I mean cursed. I've had a crush on Hannah Smith for as long as I've known that girls grow boobs.

So, um, for a while now. Like, for years and years.

You wouldn't think that this would automatically equal eternal damnation, I know. But for me, the problem is that she's all I think about, the only girl I ever see myself wanting to be with, and, well, I can't speak to her.

Not like I stammer or start to drool when she's around, or even that the words come out like a slush of slow-motion pathetic-ness.

I actually can't speak.

Nothing.

Not a squeak or a chirp.

Nothing.

Everything, all sound, dries up in my throat, and I end up just standing there, mouth moronically ajar, looking like some kind of large, mute, gorilla-man-boy.

Watching the stars blink into view in the chill of the darkening sky, I pull off my helmet and turn over, eyes automatically rising to the bleachers as I start my push-ups.

Hannah's at the base of the bleachers, talking to her brother. She's always here. She's at every game, every practice. She never miss-es any chance she has to support her brother in his valiant efforts to, you know, make an actual pass. Every day before practice, I tell myself to not get all distracted when I see her, but that's like telling a frog to run and not hop. I'm just wired to go on the fritz around Hannah.

Push-ups suck. Have I mentioned this? Well, they do. As I hit number ten, I look at Hannah's hair, how the moonlight sort of gets trapped in its waves, how it falls over the curves of her—

Enough of that. I need to get these push-ups done so I can go home. Talk to Juliet about what to do for Mom's birthday.

But as my fingers dig into the cold earth, Hannah's laugh carries across the empty field, riding over the waves of chirping crickets and the distant sounds of traffic from Main Street. My insides quiver. That's right, *quiver*. I've tried to think of a manlier adjective to describe the feeling, but nothing covers it quite like *quiver*.

Love can either hit like lightning or burn slow and low like a … well, a really good barbeque sauce, I guess. And Hannah is definitely the lightning type of girl.

It started my first day of sixth grade.

She ran across the playground, and she was the most beautiful girl I had ever seen. Black, wavy hair, torn jeans, and a Metallica T-shirt. She could kick a ball to the moon and then race around the bases so fast that no one could catch her. I was in awe. But then, as she was up for her third kickball at bat, Billy Flannigan called her something. I couldn't hear what from where I was standing on the pitcher's mound, but her face—full of light and determination and the urge to dominate the field—fell flat.

He turned out the light, the glow behind her smile. He kept talking, and her face got darker and darker, her glorious eyes wet with pools of unshed tears.

I'm not a violent person by nature, though I realize that may sound strange coming from a guy who plays on the offensive line, but that day, well, that day, standing there on the pitcher's mound, large, round, rubber instrument of violence already in my young, trembling hands, I'd never hated anyone the way I hated Billy Flannigan. So I looked at Hannah, her eyes cast at the ground, and at the round, reddish face of Billy.

And I pitched the ball, hitting Billy square in the stomach, knocking him to the ground.

This, of course, wasn't cool.

The teachers all rushed to Billy's aid, and I lost my recess for, like, a week afterwards, but Hannah, well, Hannah rushed the mound just as Billy's cries from the ground lit up the schoolyard. She grabbed me by the shoulders and said, "Thanks."

And she kissed me on the cheek. Things went all slow-motion at that point. Her lips were soft and her breath cool against the skin of my cheek, and I felt like maybe my head just up and floated off the top of my body.

I've been a goner ever since.

Pathetic? Yup.

But hey, when lightning strikes, it leaves a burn.

Hannah's not in the bleachers when I hit the showers.

She never is.

Mom's birthday lands with all the subtlety of a hurricane. Ever since Dad died, my sister, Juliet, and I have tried really hard to keep Mom's cheer up. Her birthday is hard, though, because Dad first asked Mom out on her birthday. She's told us the story maybe a hundred times, my crazed father sneaking into the courtyard outside of her dorm, reciting love poems through a megaphone in the middle of the night.

Things didn't go exactly as he planned, though. Campus police arrested him before Mom was able to find her shoes and get into the courtyard to accept his invitation to dinner or whatever. She did, however, bail him out of jail, and, penniless and now a hardened criminal, he read her all the poems he had been writing for her since they'd first met in organic chemistry months beforehand, and they wandered around UCONN's moonlit campus for the rest of the night.

Juliet and I try to keep the tradition alive, but there's always some point in the day where Mom's eyes go all distant and she clutches the locket that holds Dad's picture where it hangs around her neck, her cheeks wet and her voice breaking.

This year's poem is going to be the best yet. I just have to finish writing it. And time is running out. I want to text it to Mom before school gets out, so that way, even though she's going to hit that dance class of hers after work, she'll have that mid-afternoon pick-me-up to keep her going until we all get home.

Juliet made her some Eggo waffles this morning, so she's covered, but me? I need to get this poem done and out the door.

Which is difficult because now I'm in Spanish. So is Hannah, which means, well, *no hablo bueno*, that's for sure. Hard to focus on conjugated verbs or Mom's poem when the freaking sun sits right across the room from you.

Her dark hair's pulled back off her neck, and she's wearing these dangly earrings that, well, *dangle*. They skim the creamy flesh of her neck, and my fingers ache to trace the lines of her neck, to feel the weight of the earring heavy and delicate in the center of my palm.

The teacher flips on the SMART Board, and the class shuffles into note-taking mode. Finally some inspiration comes to me, and I work out a few lines for Mom. The bell sounds, and I jot down my homework and rush out of the door and down the hall. The hall smells like kids and sneakers and gum and whatever lemon-scented cleaner they use to scrub the floors.

Study hall is next, which would be great, but Mrs. Frick keeps the class quiet. And I mean quiet. If anyone so much as coughs, she raises her slow, vicious eyes like a dragon, lifting them from her grading to shame her prey into submission.

I throw my books onto my desk with one minute left before the bell rings. "Hi, Mrs. Frick, aren't you looking lovely this afternoon," I say and draw suspicious stares from the other kids. Hey, a little buttering up never hurt anyone, so let them think what they will.

Mrs. Frick gives me a foul, low-toned growl thing in response and turns back to her grading.

About three seconds before the bell, Hannah slides in, robbing the room of its oxygen. I swallow as she glides into the desk beside me, her body visibly relaxing as her eyes graze the clock and she realizes she's made it on time. Her shoulders unwind and she stretches. Her arms reach up behind her head as she arches her back, and close to three hundred thousand firecrackers go off under my skin at the same time.

Don't look, Wyatt, just don't—

But the bottom of her sweater rides up just a bit, exposing a thin line of a stomach that looks soft and smooth and—

My cheeks burn as I force my eyes to the desk. I cross my ankles. Uncross. Cross them again.

This is so bad. Thank God it's last period. Notebook. Look at your notebook. The poem for your mom. Your mother. Don't notice the legs in the desk next to you. Do not stare at the jeans that look like they were stitched into place, hugging those calves, those—

Mom. Think about your mom. Right. Mom. Got it. My hand flies as I throw myself into the poem. The hour flies by, and by the end, I think what I have is pretty good, actually. So I start typing it into the phone to send to Mom.

That's when I feel it.

A slight brush at my hand. A slip of paper, folded in half. I look up. Hannah's holding the paper out to me. Shaking the paper, in fact.

Oh, my God, oh, my God, oh, my God. Hannah. Holding a note out.

To me.

I stare at the note, and the blood rushes out of my face in shock. My stomach clenches and no! Don't! No!

But it does. My mouth.

It gapes.

Falls open.

I can't close it. My jaw just hangs there like a lead bar.

Please don't drool. Don't drool.

Just don't drool.

Hannah's brows rise like I'm some caveman, which, it seems, I totally am. I will my body into action: jaw—close now! Now! Please close now!

Nope, not working. She shakes the paper again and glances over at the grading dragon.

Now! Jaw, close now!

Yes! Finally. I swallow, since it's all my throat can do at the moment. Speaking clearly isn't an option for so, so many reasons. I grab the paper and Hannah smiles.

That's right. Pulls her full lips back into a smile, and it's like jumping into a pool on a hot summer's day. Every muscle in my body, every sound, every thought, goes still. All I see, all I know, is that smile.

"Read it," she whispers.

She *whispers*. To *me*.

My thoughts and my nerves tornado, and I grip the edge of the desk with one hand so I don't pass out. That's right, *pass out*.

You know, like guys do.

I am the biggest loser.

Ever.

They'd throw me off the team if they knew.

She giggles and shakes her head.

My stomach feels like I ate a whole bag of Pop Rocks, and I lose my bottom jaw again. *Boom*, right to the center of the earth.

I need to surrender my man card right now.

The bell rings, and Hannah gives me another smile, and it wipes my hard drive clean. Reboots everything. I glance down at the note.

> Missed the Spanish homework.
> Can u text it to me? 5558675309

Hannah gave me her number. My throat dries. Hannah gave me her number. My thoughts crackerjack around in my head. Her number. I have her number.

Everyone leaves class. Running for the buses.

Which is great, because that way no one but the dragon sees my hands shaking or hears the thunder going on behind my ears.

Spanish homework. Yes, I have that. I can do this. I can send it to Hannah, who gave me her *phone number*.

Moving my fingers over the keys of the phone feels like trying to perform neurosurgery with a sock puppet, but slowly, slowly, I add Hannah's number to my contacts.

Should I say hi first? Or something more conversational? Like, should I say something like, *Hey, thanks for asking me for the homework,* or *I hate vocab lists, but that's what for homework,* or *Conjugating verbs sucks, pages 23-24?*

Rubbing my palm against my forehead, I grimace. Why is this so hard?

I don't have to be in the weight room for another, like, half an hour, so I have time. Sort of. The dragon shuffles and chuffs behind her desk, but she doesn't try and hustle me out, which is great, because I really need to *not* mess this up.

Okay, so, there's her number. In *my phone.* Her name staring at me from my backlit screen.

I close my eyes. Open them again. Yup. Still there. Still matches the number on the paper. Good. This is good.

Flipping over to the poem I wrote for Mom, I read:

> There is no one in the world like you.
> Kind and beautiful and warm
> You make me smile when I'm down
> I will love you even when you get really old.

Mom totally should have read a couple of these birthday poems first before naming me after a poet. Well, naming me after a *good* poet, anyway.

I should send that first, get that done, and then I'll work out how I should send Hannah the homework. I click the button that will convert the note file into a text and—

The Dragon stands up, legs of her metal chair scraping across the tile, her voice like talons. "You going to stay here all day, Wyatt?"

"No, ma'am." I stand up, tucking my phone into my pocket, and shove my books into my pack. "Sorry."

She emits this low, guttural sound that I can assume means that she is either harrumphing at me or she's preparing to belch fire.

Either way, I need to go.

Swinging my bag up onto my shoulder, I hit the mostly empty hallway. It's funny how quickly kids scatter once that last bell of the day rings. Grabbing the stuff I need for homework out of the locker, I pull out the phone and make my way to the weight room. I don't *have* to hit the weights today, but on days like today when we get to choose between cardio or weights, I always—

What?

What sent?

I hit the screen of the phone. Hannah?

I sent something to Hannah?

I blink. Heat dribbles out of my cheeks.

Oh, no.

My stomach leaps and twists and then drops straight to the floor. No.

I reach a hand out to grasp onto the wall.

No. No, no, no, no.

There's no way.

But I blink, and my blood rushes into my head, and the message is still there.

Mom's poem.

I sent Hannah Mom's poem.

I squeeze my eyes shut, taking in a long, deep breath. It's okay. I'm going to open my eyes again and see that the phone says *Mom* at the top of the poem and not *Hannah*.

Opening my eyes, again, I shout, "No!"

Still sent to Hannah.

This can't be happening.

I bend over, hand across my middle, my head whirling.

The girl asked me for a homework assignment, and I send her a freaking poem? And oh, my God, what a poem. I mean, *I will love you even after you get really old*?

I'm going to vomit.

Like, everywhere.

Right now.

This can't be. I can delete it, right? I mean, she hasn't necessarily seen it yet, so if I can just …

But the phone. The text, it has those little bubble things. Like she's responding.

The police. She's going to call the police, right? I mean, she asked me for a homework assignment, and I go and get all Shakespeare on her?

She's never going to talk to me again. Ever, any chance, any hope I ever had of actually, like, holding a conversation with her is over.

As in: game over.

No-rematch kind of over.

I have to think. I have to figure this out. There has to be a way to explain. I can just tell her that I meant the text to go to Mom and then she'll … what?

Not believe me?

Wonder what kind of a freak writes poems to his mom?

And this is assuming I'll actually be able to *speak* when I see her.

This is bad. This is so, so bad.

Something hits my shoulder, and I hear, "Hey, bro, you going to hit the weights?"

Bro? Only one person on the team speaks eighties like that: Derek. Hannah's brother. This must be a sign. Picking my consciousness up out of the doom-spitting vortex that's taken hold of my head, I say, "Derek! Your sister!"

Derek freezes, his expression going dark and hard like some chocolate-candy-shell ice cream topping. "What about Hannah?"

"Nothing! I mean, she's fine, I just, it's just—"

"You better tell me what you're talking about right now or—"

"Shut up and listen." I stand up tall so that he knows exactly why I'm on the offensive line and he's not. I am large. Like *large* large. Fat, no, but I've got a good foot and at least sixty pounds on Derek. He needs to listen, and *now*. "Look, man, Hannah asked me for our Spanish homework, and I texted it to her, but instead, I texted something else and—"

"You didn't text her a picture of your—"

"Hell, no, would you shut up and listen? I texted her a poem I wrote for my mom. It's her birthday, and I always write her these poems, and now Hannah's going to think I'm some kind of freak, and she's not ever going to speak to me. Do you know where she is? If maybe I can talk to her—"

"You wrote a poem for your mom?" Derek's beefy eyebrows rise a bit.

"Yeah, it's her birthday. Where's Hannah?"

"Isn't that a little girlie for you, bro?" He smirks like a twelve-year-old who just discovered the Victoria's Secret catalog.

"Do you know where she is, Derek?"

"You gonna try and delete the text or something?"

"Or something."

"'Cause you might actually have to, you know, *speak* to her."

I stop, staring at Derek and his terrible, perfectly styled hair. I hate him, just a little. Why does his hair always look so good and mine just looks, well, curly? "How do you know I can't talk to Hannah?"

"Dude, you've been crushing on my sister since, like, forever. Just use your girlie-ass poem as an icebreaker. She's gonna laugh, I promise. If I tell you where she is, you're going to, like, open your mouth and actually talk to her."

I shake my head, his words sort of burning my cheeks. Man, does everybody know I'm into Hannah? That's awkward. "Yeah, I'll try."

"She's at Zumba. She teaches a class at the YMCA after school. If you hurry, you can catch her before class starts."

Zumba? What the hell is Zumba? Guess I'm going to find out. "Hey, man, tell Coach—"

"That you're catching your cardio at the Y? Yeah, I'm all over it. Remember, you have to talk to her." He grabs me by the shoulders, and I blink at the speed he never shows on the field. "*Just* talk, got me?"

"Zumba. Y. Talk. Delete poem. Got it."

He lets go, and I race out of the building, hoping to hit the Y before her class starts. I check my phone. If she's changing to teach her class and setting up the music or whatever, then maybe I still have a chance to catch her before she sees the poem.

Maybe.

"What do you mean, I'm not dressed appropriately?" I stare at the woman behind the counter, her hair all blueish and jagged, her face pinched tight like a vulture. I don't have time for this. I have to get into Zumba *now*.

"I can let you take one class as a sample, but the waiver is only good if you are wearing the proper clothes." Her words are snipped, and I stare down at my baggy jeans and sneakers.

I take a deep breath. "What, exactly, would be considered proper Zumba attire?"

Her eyes roll over my body, like she's sizing me up for different cuts of meat. I shiver. "Well, the T-shirt's okay, but the jeans have to go."

"Please, ma'am, I have to take this Zumba class—"

"You're already missing the warm-up—"

"I don't care. I have to get in there today, please. What if I change?"

"Do you have anything to change into?"

"No, my workout clothes are at school." This is bad. I have to get to Hannah, and quick.

A man clears his throat behind me, waiting to click his card at the scanner to let him into the gym. The woman behind the desk looks at him and says, "Bill, this young man wants to try Zumba, but he doesn't have any sweats. What do you think?"

Bill gives me the once-over, and I try my best to look like a man in desperate need of a Zumba fix.

Well, maybe just desperate.

Bill, all six feet two inches of solid muscle topped off by a mop of gray hair and a fuzzy yellow headband, nods and says, "I have an extra pair of shorts in my bag." He reaches into his gym bag and pulls out a pair of red shorts. "Just leave them here with Cheryl when you're done."

"Oh, my God, thank you. You're a lifesaver." I take the shorts and bolt toward the locker room. My stomach drops as I think about convincing Hannah to delete the poem. I'm going to have to talk to her to do that.

Whatever. Time to man up, Wyatt. Now put on your fire-engine-red shorts and—

Oh, no. I pull on the shorts, suddenly aware that there is waaay too much air hitting my legs.

No.

I step in front of the full-length mirror. Bill, Bill, what have you done? My throat swells in horror. Did I say fire-engine red? Because that's wrong. They are more like candy-apple red, bright and sickeningly sweet. But that's not the problem; the problem is that there is not nearly enough of that candy-apple-red cloth to go around.

Running my hands through my hair, I try and get control over my quick, frantic gasps for air.

I'm in short shorts.

Hot pants, as it were.

Shoot me. Please, somebody, Bill, anyone, just shoot me now. I have to face down Hannah and ask her to delete my message wearing these? I look like, like, well, I don't know what I look like, because I've never seen a dude wearing hot pants before.

I'm going to be lucky if Hannah doesn't take my picture with that phone of hers and ruin me for life.

No.

No. Hannah wouldn't do that. And I only need to stay in Zumba long enough to delete the message and talk to Hannah. I can do this.

No one will care. It's not like I know anyone other than Hannah who takes Zumba anyway …

I hope.

Music blasts through the door. The wood door is practically pulsing with it. My hand slides over the handle. I can do this. I can do this. I mean, girls like short shorts, right? Why can't a guy wear them? Talk about sexist. I mean, I work out, my legs should look good, if a bit, you know, hairy.

I open the door and walk straight to the back of the room, trying to dodge the mass of ladies moving back and forth across the floor.

There, in the back of the room, standing behind a woman roughly the age of my grandmother who is wearing sweatpants with *shake it, baby* written across the butt in neon letters, Hannah turns and meets my eye.

Suddenly I go from the large, confident boy bound and determined to at last speak to the girl he's had a crush on for a thousand
years, and I become *Wyatt, the mute werewolf in the lollipop-red hot
pants, the only person in the room not, um, Zumba-ing.*

But then Hannah curls her lips up into a smile, and she waves.
Waves. At me. She walks toward me like she's going to come and
say hi, but then a lady in the front row pushes a button, and the
music starts.

My chest tightens, and I barely hear her as she tells everyone to
get ready to go. Grandma with the neon-ass-pants pulls me into a
line and tells me, "Watch sweet Hannah, and do your best to keep
up. The key is to keep moving."

And then, with a quick sweep of her eye, she checks me out.
Not kidding.

Well, at least *Grandma* over here is diggin' the hot pants.

Maybe I should just go.

But then the music picks up, and Hannah turns so that she's
facing the wall and shakes her hips. The class is off. First we move
to the left, one leg having to somehow move behind the other, and
it brings you sideways, then back and forth with these little moves.

I look up to get the moves, but I find myself lost in the movements of Hannah's butt, and I don't want to be staring at the ass of
the girl I'm trying to impress, so I look down and—

"Watch out!" Two huge breasts whip in my direction as another older lady with a mass of curly gray and blond hair pushes me
back into my line. "You have to watch Hannah," she huffs. Then
she directs her eyes straight at Hannah's ass.

Oh, my God. This is awful. Am I *really* supposed to watch
Hannah's butt? That seems sort of rude.

Bill, tall, happy-looking Bill, who thinks that giving me short
shorts is, you know, an okay thing for one dude to do for another,
muscles his way beside me. "C'mon, kid, it's not that hard."

He starts calling out English translations for the bizarre language
that Hannah is speaking into her microphone. She'll say, "Salsa!" or
"Mambo," and Bill says, "Up for two, now back one ..."

Bill, no surprise here, I don't think is from the States. His accent is off. He does something different with his vowels, to the point that I think he might originally be from Russia or somewhere.

Being European would totally explain his taste in clothes. Slowly we make our way through the first song. It ends. Great, now maybe I can—

The second song starts, and this one's even faster. Oh, no. Bill points to Hannah and says, "Watch her." But I notice Bill's eyes aren't on Hannah at all but rather on this woman next to Hannah, dancing in the front row.

The woman has a mass of gray hair and is thin and really seems to know what she's doing. Something about her looks familiar—

"Now left," Bill hisses, and we move, but before I can get all the way left, Hannah yells, "Shimmy."

I'm still moving left, but the lady on my left has stopped, and I bump into her. I hold out my hands so I won't hurt her, but she's already pushing me into the line in front of us, and I get sent flying directly into the woman with the breasts the size of small continents, who is mid-shimmy.

Now I'm headfirst in a pair of massive breasts that are shaking violently from side to side, my head a Ping-Pong ball in the Grand Canyon. "Bill, help!" I cry, but no one hears.

Hands push me away, and the woman screams, "Cheeky thing!"

At me. "No, ma'am, I'm sorry, I'm not cheeky, I promise—"

But now the class is moving again, and the woman slaps me on the ass. Through the hot pants.

Now, let me explain.

I am used to getting slapped on the ass. I play football, so my butt gets more hits than a baseball team, but not by some woman older than my mom. My stomach turns. Please let Hannah not have seen.

Bill winks and pats me on the back with a hearty laugh.

Don't laugh at me, Bill. Put me out of my misery, maybe, but don't laugh.

Hannah turns to see the woman slap me on the ass, and I notice that the woman next to her turns and—

Mom. Oh, my God, it's Mom.

Bill! Bill's been staring at my mom during the whole class, and when she turns around, he blushes.

Blushes.

Mom stops mid-step. "Wyatt?"

I can't hear her so much as feel the words. Then her eyes do this quick one-two sort of thing, and she takes in my outfit and the old lady who's *still* checking me out.

I wave.

Because, seriously, what else can I do?

The rest of class is a nightmare. I stumble into everyone. Bill and the lady next to me are probably going to have bruises on the tops of their feet. Just when I feel like I can't do any more without accidentally hospitalizing the people on either side of me, the class is over.

We stretch. I watch Hannah's ass. I don't mean to, but hey, all the ladies are, so ...

After the stretching, Hannah stands up and claps. "Great class, you guys."

Okay. So ... now what?

Now I have to do this. I have to take my sweaty, hairy, hot-pants-rocking self up to the front of the room and talk to her.

And, well, to Mom.

I put one foot out, then the other, my breath heavy and hot, and oh, my God, I don't think I can do this. No, I have to. One foot, good, now the other and—

"Hey, Wyatt," Hannah says.

Thump, thump, thump.

My heart's the loudest thing in the room. Words stick to the back of my throat. "Hey."

Awesome. Lyrical, actually. Hey? That's the best I can do? But her dark eyes soften, and I feel like I'm drowning in a sea of goodness and—

"I really like your poem," she says, and she bumps my hip with hers.

Mom, watching the whole thing, steps back a few feet, and I see that Bill pulls her into conversation.

Have to deal with Bill later.

Hannah steps in closer, and I think I've lost all feeling in my toes. "You liked it?"

"Yeah, it was sweet."

"But I forgot to send the homework. You only wanted the—"

"I've only wanted you to ask me out for, what, like, four years now?"

Holy what? I grasp my head in my hands so it doesn't fly right off my shoulders. She's wanted ... Four years ... *What* ... ? Thoughts swirl and my stomach trembles, and I don't know what to do, so I grab her hand, bring it up to my lips, and I kiss it. She gasps, and it's electric, and I smile so big that my face may get stretched out permanently.

"I still have your homework assignment if you want it," I say. Can I? Can I ask her out? To what? I have, like, no money, and what if she doesn't like movies, or should I ask her to a park, maybe, like, for a walk, or would that seem creepy? My heart jackhammers in my chest, and I feel all my senses draining, blanching—

"Hey, Wyatt, Hannah." Mom. It's Mom, her voice strong and sweet and steady.

Please, Mom, help, help, I can't, I don't know what to do, I need—

"Bill offered to take me out for ice cream for my birthday. Would you guys like to join us?" Mom's smile is comforting, and Bill looks so proud you'd think he, like, bagged a deer or something. Definitely going to have to talk to Bill about his eyes on my mom.

Hannah leans in, whispers in my ear, sending fireworks bursting all the way through to my fingertips. "I love ice cream."

Then it's settled. "That'd be great, Mom, happy birthday." I give Mom a hug and tell her, "Thanks."

As we're all walking out of the room, I stop in front of the locker room, "Hey, you guys think I have time to change before we hit the ice cream shop?"

Hannah's the first to respond. "I don't know, those shorts are totally you, Wyatt." She winks. *Winks.*

And then she checks out my legs.

My face burns and air singes my lungs.

Oh, yeah, today's definitely the best day ever.

T. L. Costa is a graduate of Bryn Mawr College and has a Masters of Teaching from Quinnipiac University. Her debut, *Playing Tyler*, won the 2014 Nautilus Silver Winner in Young Adult (YA) Fiction, won the 2013 USA BEST BOOK AWARD for Young Adult Fiction and was a finalist in the Booksellers Best Awards and the 2014 Silver Falchion Awards. She taught high school for five years before becoming a full-time mom and writer. She has lived in Texas, New York, New Jersey and Spain. Currently, she lives in Connecticut with her husband and two children.

DEAD WRONG

CINDY GERARD

New York Times Bestseller, RITA® Winner

THE MOODS OF THE lake suited her. The water was either placid or full of fury. As blue as a cloudless sky or as murky as a sinner's soul. Today, it raged, liquid steel, hammering against the shore.

There was no halfway here, Erin thought. And she needed absolutes these days. Needed the black and the white of it after living for months in either blistering Technicolor or prison-gray walls.

Across the bay, autumn painted the birch and ash swaying along the rock-strewn shoreline in burnt umber and gold. Brilliant pops of magenta from the sugar maples mixed in with the rustling pine.

Erin sat at the edge of a rock outcropping, ten yards above the water, her grandfather's cabin several yards behind her, her lightweight flannel jacket wrapped tightly around her lean frame, and watched the steel-gray water at war. Frothy rollers slammed the dock anchored to the lakebed by a cedar crib filled with stone. The wind's relentless push and pull stung her cheeks and whipped her short, dark hair around her face. Beneath her worn jeans, the flat rock was hard and cold. Unforgiving. Much like life. Much like her life of late, at any rate.

She let out a long breath. That was why she'd come here. To get away from that life. To hide away from the accusing stares of neighbors, the microphones the news crews shoved under her nose, the sympathetic but increasingly uncertain glances from friends, the worried looks from her family. And she'd come here to feel safe. Ryan's father couldn't find her here. He didn't know about this place. Only her mother knew where she was. No one would know to look for her here. The gun tucked in her pocket assured her that if, on the off chance someone did, she'd at least have a fighting chance.

"You'll pay!" Clayton Livingston snarled when she'd been unable to avoid him in the crowded hallway outside the courtroom after the trial. "You killed him. You killed my son! Those little-girl-lost eyes may have fooled that jury of fools, but I know the truth. And you will pay for what you took from me."

She shook off the memory of the fury in his words and the hate in his eyes and looked out over the water. As a child, the lake had been her playground. Now it was her escape. Here, she didn't have to deal with the past or the pain or the fear of Livingston's threat. She could watch the shifting water and listen to the wind and the wild sounds of the forest and lose herself in the beauty and the pulsing rhythms that mired her in the best part of her past.

That helped somehow. It helped to know that, in the overall scheme of things, the fact that she'd been tried and acquitted of murdering her husband mattered little to the world within this sanctuary. She'd been a second-page story at best on the global scene but had been the topic of sensationalized and brutal headlines in the Minneapolis press for months.

It was time to put it behind her.

The low-hanging sun broke through the rolling cover of clouds, touched her face, reminding her of another of life's constants. The lake swelled, the wind blew, the sun shone. She lay back and closed her eyes.

Constants.

Comforts.

Yes. It was good that she'd come here. She'd needed a sense of peace. Peace, after all, was what she'd sought when she'd left Minneapolis a week ago against the advice of the MPD detective still working the case on his own time.

"Livingston is not going to give you a pass on this," Josh McKenna warned when she'd told him she was leaving town. "He'll come after you. Running's not going to solve anything."

She knew McKenna was right. Running wouldn't solve a thing. Ryan's father wanted his pound of flesh, and if his threats were to be believed, he would stop at nothing to make sure he got it.

And there, she thought as she sat up, pulled her knees to her chest, and wrapped her arms around her legs, was the serpent in paradise. She could escape here for a little while, but eventually, she had to return and face Clayton Livingston's wrath.

Suddenly realizing that she was chilled to the bone, she checked her watch. Five fifteen. She'd been out here almost two hours. The sun had begun to set. She rose stiffly, shoved her hands deep in the pockets of her jacket, and felt the Smith & Wesson .38 Special inside. McKenna had insisted she needed to be armed. He'd taken her shopping for the revolver. Then he'd marched her out to a shooting range and taught her more than she'd ever wanted to know before making her fire so many rounds her palm had blistered.

She stood for a moment longer, needing one last look at the lake, then hunched her shoulders and turned back to the cabin.

The rocky ground beneath her hiking boots was covered in needles from the ancient white pines towering above her; the path back to the cabin was uphill and steep. From years of summers spent here, she knew every niche and gnarled tree root by heart, but she kept her head down as she climbed.

It wasn't until she'd reached the moss-covered stone walkway that she realized she wasn't alone.

CHAPTER TWO

ERIN STOPPED, HER HEART pounding, ready to run, ready to hide, flight taking precedence over fight. Still, she wrapped her fingers around the gun and remembered McKenna's words.

Aim for center mass. Ride the recoil and keep on firing. Get him before he gets you.

Filled with an impending sense of doom, she forced a steadying breath and looked up.

A man, enveloped by forest and shadowed by a darkening sky, loomed at the top of the path. Silent, he stared down at her. Hands loose at his sides—huge, menacing. A threat.

She gripped the S&W tighter, wondered if she could possibly fire even one of the five rounds if it came to that. She tried to make out his features in the waning light—couldn't see his face.

Then he said her name.

"Erin."

She flinched, then gasped when she recognized the voice … and the pressure inside her chest unfurled like a sail in the wind.

Jed. Oh, my God.

She hadn't thought she had it in her to smile, but she did.

She hadn't thought she had any tears left to shed; wrong again.

And she hadn't thought that her heart could still react—as it had the first time Jed Rafferty had kissed her what now seemed like a lifetime ago.

"Thought you might want some company." His deep, coffee-warm voice brought back memories of carefree summers here at the lake.

Until this moment, she hadn't realized how badly she'd missed him. Or how grateful she was to her mother, who had evidently trusted Jed and told him where she was.

"I'm so sorry, Erin." He walked down the path to meet her. "I'm sorry I couldn't get here sooner."

"You're here now." She walked into the arms he opened to her.

"You're here now," she murmured again against the broad expanse of a chest covered in soft, supple leather.

The strength of his arms was a gift; the weight of his chin on the top of her head and the leather-and-woods scent of him wrapped around her like a blanket. Warm, protective, and familiar.

Constant.

Comfortable.

For the first time in longer than she could recall, it felt safe to remember who she was. She was Erin Marie James. She was her grandfather's little water fish. She was her mother's spitting image. She was Jed Rafferty's first big crush, pure of heart and free of spirit, and the world and a bright future lay at her feet.

She was not the thirty-year-old woman who'd been tried and acquitted of the murder of her husband. She was not an outcast of suspicion in her community nor a victim of the press. She was not hunted by an angry father bent on revenge for the loss of his son.

In Jed's arms, she was just Erin. She was sheltered. She was loved. Unconditionally.

"I've needed you," she confessed, just this moment admitting it to herself.

"It's okay. Come on." He set her gently away from him—just far enough for her to look into his eyes and know that, behind them, he was still the boy who'd turned into the man that a girl had once fallen hopelessly in love with.

Time had been more than kind to him. His eyes were still the deepest, darkest brown. Steady and true. They were older, yes. Wiser, undoubtedly. Most important, the deep grooves that crinkled the tanned skin at their corners told her he was still her friend.

"I took some liberties and put on a pot of coffee." He linked his arm through hers and urged her up the path. "Hope you don't mind."

"How did you get in? I swear I locked the cabin."

"You did."

She heard the smile in his voice and remembered how he used to sneak into her bedroom at night. The boy had had a way with locked windows and doors—apparently the man did, too.

"Now let's go have that coffee."

"At least you don't have to worry about being seen with me," she said as they neared the cabin. "There's no one else here." She'd meant it to sound teasing. Instead, it came out a little desperate, a lot angry, a little bit afraid.

True, the north woods were isolated, but even the wilderness had eyes. The James cabin—the one her grandfather had built—was one of ten cabins on Lake Point at the southeast end of Legend Lake. Total, there were no more than fifty cabins on the entire two-hundred-thousand-acre glacial lake that, on a cloudless day, nestled against the boundary waters like a sapphire sparkling in the sun.

This time of year, only the diehards stayed to brave the chill autumn weather and the moods of the lake. Even so, Erin had seen lights on and off in two of the cabins last week, but everyone had pulled out yesterday. She was completely alone on the Point.

"If I remember," Jed said, accomplishing what she hadn't—to tease with humor and no remorse, "there was a time you wouldn't be caught dead being seen with me."

A laugh, on the edge and needing release, burst out before she could police it. "Well, you were cramping my style back then. And you were hanging around on purpose, just to tick me off," she said in her own defense.

He made a sound that was more grunt than acknowledgement. "All those guys were jerks," he said, referring to the townies and tourists who used to take her out on dates. "You just couldn't see it. Until you finally got old enough to appreciate a good thing."

She laughed again and let herself remember. Jed was right. She couldn't see it. Not back then. She couldn't see a lot of things. Like how bad Jed's crush on her was—not until she turned seventeen. Then she'd felt the same fire, and they'd ended up spending every minute that he could sneak away from his job as dock boy for the resort across the bay together. They'd paddle their kayaks out to Echo Island and away from the prying eyes of her family, where they'd make out for hours. They'd never "gone all the way," but there'd been a lot of heavy make-out sessions that had tested both of them to the limit.

But that was then. She sobered. "Yeah, well, I seem to have a history of picking the wrong men. And being in the wrong place at the wrong time."

"Hey, hey." He gave her a bracing hug. "Let's not go there just yet. Let's get you warm, get some coffee in you, then you can tell me all about it."

CHAPTER THREE

THERE WERE A LOT of things Jed was sorry about when it came to Erin. The worst was the way she looked right now. He watched her across the pine-paneled kitchen in the open-floor-plan cabin as he filled their coffee mugs. She'd huddled up on the sofa under a red wool blanket in front of the fire he'd built in the old stone fireplace. Her eyes were fixed on a place—or a time—in the distance. The thousand-mile stare. He'd seen it often enough on the faces of the young soldiers under his command in Afghanistan. On a cold winter night or a blistering summer day when they'd been too many miles from home, with too many threats to sleep, that stare had become as common as the sight of chocks of Black Hawks scooting across the Afghan sky.

"The stew was great." He returned to her side on the over-stuffed sofa and handed her the coffee.

Since it was close to dinnertime and she had made a huge pot of beef and vegetable stew earlier in the day, she'd offered to feed him the minute they'd walked into the cabin. He hadn't eaten since the bagel he'd grabbed at the Atlanta airport earlier this morning. By the time his connecting flight had landed in Minneapolis and he'd booked his rental car, then made contact with Erin's mother, it was after noon. And all he'd wanted to do was get to Erin. So he'd set out on the five-hour drive and headed straight for the cabin. He hadn't thought about eating. He'd simply wanted to get to her.

The scent of the stew reminded him just how hungry he was.

So they'd eaten. He'd eaten a lot. She'd mostly played with her spoon. So much that he was worried about her.

"Does the cabin get much use these days?" he asked after taking a sip from his mug.

"Not like it used to." She'd wrapped her hands around the mug, warming them. "Mom rarely comes up since Dad died. And this past year ... well, I was a little tied up." She gave him a feeble smile. "It's probably been three years since anyone was here. Anyway, it seemed like there was at least three years of dust on everything when I got here.

"So," she said, infusing a brightness in her voice that didn't match the weary look in her eyes. "Tell me about you. I want to know everything. Where you've been. How you've been. What you're doing now."

"You're that bored?"

She gave him a gentle elbow. "I'm that interested."

"Oh, well then, let's see. After you broke my heart, I moped around for a while."

She grinned at him. "I did not break your heart. You broke mine. Or life did. We both had plans that took us in opposite directions. Besides, word was you recovered just fine."

He should have recovered. He'd even convinced himself he had. But seeing her again, even after all these years, told him he'd be fooling both of them if he said yes. She still had the most beautiful green eyes, the softest hair, the sweetest, sexiest smile. And she still had the ability to make his heart rate go haywire. Yeah. Damn him for a fool, he still had it bad for Erin James. Correction, Erin Livingston.

He smiled and lied. "Yeah. I recovered. Barely."

"Skip forward a few years," she said after a curious look. "Let's get to college and all the co-eds who threw themselves at your feet and helped heal that poor heart of yours."

"Well, there *was* a lot of healing going on," he conceded because he knew it would make her smile and because there *had* been a lot of co-eds. Problem was, none of them had been her. "Minnesota State. But only my freshman year before the West Point appointment came through. Then officer's school. Soon after that, my first deployment. Then another. Pretty tame stuff."

She sank deeper into the sofa, and he sensed she was relaxing a bit. "*Three* tours in Afghanistan? Doesn't sound tame to me."

"How do you know I was in Afghanistan?"

"I don't live in a complete vacuum, Jed. Jena and I keep in touch."

He knew that Erin and his sister, Jena, had remained friends long after those carefree summers had given way to the reality of growing up—which meant college and internships and real jobs that didn't allow for their summers at the lake.

"I would have kept in touch with you if you'd answered my emails," she said, sounding melancholy. "I even wrote you a couple of letters. But you never answered."

He still had those letters in a box somewhere. Hell. Who was he kidding? He knew exactly where they were. Just like he'd always known where she was and what she was doing. University of Minnesota, graduate degree in literature, professor soon to have tenure in a small private school north of the Twin Cities. And somewhere in there, she'd fallen in love, gotten married, and gotten indicted for killing her husband.

CHAPTER FOUR

"WHY DIDN'T YOU EVER settle down with someone special?" Erin asked sleepily when Jed rose to add more wood to the fire.

He couldn't tell her it was because of her. It would sound pathetic. Because it was pathetic.

So he shrugged. "Married to the army."

"How did you manage to get time away to see me?"

He could see she was touched by his actions. "I'm just off deployment. I have a lot of leave," he said with a smile. "So don't start feeling guilty."

She looked away. "Guilty. Now there's a word."

He let her have a moment, knew she was back there again, thinking about the trial. It had been over a year since her husband's death. He wondered if she mourned him—or if she simply felt relieved it was finally over.

"Want to tell me about it?"

"What? You don't read a newspaper?" She wasn't smiling now. She looked down into her mug, then toward the fire. That thousand-mile stare again.

"I want to hear it from you."

She made a frustrated sound. "I don't even know where to start."

"Why don't you pick up where we left off," he suggested gently.

Silence, then a heavy breath. "College, like you. Got my masters. A position at ECU."

He watched her as she sipped her coffee and worked over-hard at avoiding his eyes. "Where you met Mr. Right?"

She looked so weary. "Where I met Mr. Wrong. He was a big donor at the university. Him and his father. I met them when I was forced to attend a fund-raiser and had the bad luck to be seated at their table."

"It must not have felt like bad luck at the time."

"No. Ryan was quite charming. Both father and son were. And I was pretty gullible. Six months later, Ryan and I were married."

"So what happened?"

"Am I limited to one answer?"

"You're not limited to anything. Not here. Not with me."

"Well, we could start with the cheating. Ryan had a thing for the cute little co-eds. But I didn't find that out until later—even though the press was determined to make 'a woman scorned' the motive and the headline."

She stared at her coffee, deep in thought, before taking a sip. "He was controlling. Manipulative. Selfish. If ... if he hadn't been murdered, I would have filed for divorce. In fact, I was about to do just that when I stumbled across something I wasn't supposed to see."

"What kind of something?"

"A document Ryan had not intended to be left open on his computer. A ledger, actually. It was filled with names of contractors—plumbers, carpenters, electricians, dry-wallers, painters, you name it—all of whom I recognized as the beneficiaries of plum contracts related to the college."

"Kickbacks?"

"Yeah. He and his father were on the take from all of the businesses listed in the ledger to insure jobs were sent their way. Because they were such big donors to the college, all they had to do was suggest a company and it was done. Need a new athletic field? The Livingstons had your man. Need new administrative office suites? The Livingstons' palms got greased, and the contractor was a sure thing."

"Not exactly ethical but not unheard of."

"Still, it wasn't something either of them wanted exposed. When I confronted Ryan about it, his true nature jumped front and center. He threatened me."

Jed's chest tightened. "He hurt you?"

Her eyes grew hard. "Only once. I started packing my bags before my cheek quit stinging. Of course, he went into full damage-control mode and begged me to stay and let him explain himself."

"Tell me you got the hell out of there right then."

She nodded once. "I did. With him alternately threatening me if I left and pleading with me to stay. Ryan was used to having his way."

"But you left anyway."

She nodded again.

"And yet you went back to the house."

"That's where the wrong time, wrong place came in. The next day I went back to get some more of my things. He had a standing lunch date at the country club with his father at noon every Wednesday—that's when I went to the house."

"Only he didn't keep his date that day."

"You have been following in the newspaper." Her voice had gotten thready as she relived that day.

"What happened, Erin?" he prompted gently.

She braced herself with a breath. "I ... I used my key to get in. As I opened the door, I heard the clock in the foyer chime twelve times. The pure, ringing chime in the middle of that big empty house made me shiver. For some reason, it felt like an omen. That something was wrong. That it was the very wrong hour to be there. Turns out, it was."

She stopped again, and he covered her hand with his. Her fingers were so fine and cold even though she'd tried to warm them on the coffee mug.

"I wanted to get in and out, so I ran upstairs and into our bedroom. And found him there. On the floor. Blood pooling around his body. I can't ... I still can't get that deep red blood saturating the white carpet out of my mind."

She shook her head sharply, then went on. "I ran over to him, dropped to my knees, and pressed my ear against his chest to see if there was a heartbeat. Maybe it was wishful thinking, maybe it was panic, but I swore he was alive, so I ripped his shirt open to see if I could find the source of the bleeding and stop it."

He squeezed her hand and urged her to continue—if for no other reason than to get it out of her head and maybe give her some release.

"I could see it then. A knife. Buried deep in his ribs, under his arm. I ... I didn't know what to do. I didn't want to be married to him anymore, but I didn't want him dead, either. So I tried to pull it out, but it ... it must have been buried in bone. By then, I knew he was dead. And I was as covered in blood as he was."

She let her head fall against the back of the sofa. Closed her eyes, clearly exhausted from months of tension and pressure and regret. "That's how Ryan's father found me. I was arrested an hour later."

Jed looked away from her toward the fire and gave her some time to rest. He had no doubt that reliving how she'd found Livingston had been akin to a PTSD episode for her. She'd no longer loved her husband, but the trauma of finding someone killed that violently took a toll. Just as the trial had taken a toll.

He'd been deployed at the time, but he'd been able to get the local news online, and he'd followed every detail. The rest of the story had played out plainly in the papers. The only DNA found at the scene was Erin's and Ryan's and his father's. No one had seen anyone enter or leave the house. No mysterious cars had driven away. No matter how many times Erin had pled innocence and insisted she hadn't killed him, the physical and circumstantial evidence all pointed to her as the killer. The knife was from their kitchen. Her prints were all over it, just as Ryan's blood was all over her hands and her clothes. And the stories of Ryan's infidelity had surfaced.

A crime of passion. That's how the police saw it going down—all but Josh McKenna, who was the one dissenting voice in a police department convinced that she was guilty. And when all of the students linked to Ryan had alibis, that left only one suspect. Erin.

The only reason she'd been acquitted was because someone in the forensics department had bungled the DNA tests, which ended up thrown out of evidence. That left only a circumstantial case against her. Her testimony had apparently been compelling enough that juror number seven had held out for an innocent verdict. In the eyes of the media and the general public, however, she was still a guilty woman.

Jed turned back to ask her if she had any thoughts about who killed Livingston and realized if she wasn't asleep, she was close to it. So he sat beside her, silent, letting her rest until her fingers grew lax and he nabbed the half-empty coffee mug before it dropped to the floor.

He waited a few minutes more to make sure she was sleeping, then eased to his feet.

The plan had been to bunk on her sofa—if you could call that a plan. He had no intension of leaving her. Not with Livingston throwing around threats like stones. Maybe it was all bluster. Maybe it was a father's heartbreak. But a threat was a threat, and until the real killer was found, Erin was a target.

Until that target was taken off her back, he wasn't going anywhere.

CHAPTER FIVE

ERIN WOKE UP SLOWLY, then lay for a while, wondering why she could see the fire from her bedroom. It took a while longer for the cobwebs to clear enough to realize she wasn't *in* her bedroom. She was on the sofa, a pillow from the bed tucked under her head and a quilt tucked around her body keeping her toasty warm.

Jed.

She'd fallen asleep on him, which was a little hard to believe because sleep wasn't something she did a lot of lately. She'd been living on the sharp edge of a blade for over a year, and just because the trial was over—and yes, she felt relief because she'd been acquitted—it didn't mean life was back to normal. Life would never be back to normal.

Jed Rafferty showing up out of the blue was proof of that. Wonderful, positive proof and the best thing to happen to her in a very long time.

Speaking of Jed ... she lay quietly and listened, then smiled when she realized the unfamiliar sound she heard was Jed snoring softly nearby. She sat up, looked around, then down. And there he was. Asleep, wrapped in a thin blanket on the floor. The only concession he'd made toward comfort was the extra pillow from her bed.

When the comforter inched down around her hips, she realized how cold the cabin had become. The fire had burned down to embers. Jed had to be freezing.

Quietly, so as not to wake him, she eased off the sofa, stepped carefully around him, then as silently as possible fed the warm coals two pieces of wood. She watched until they caught fire, added a couple more, then turned—to find him awake and watching her.

For a long moment, neither of them spoke. Their gazes caught and held, and in those electric moments, Erin felt awareness of every sensory detail surrounding her. The pleasant scent of the fire, the flickering light dancing off the walls and in his eyes. The size of him, the maleness of him, the dark edge of desire that emanated off his big body. And suddenly she felt the way she'd felt when she'd been seventeen and Jed would sneak into her room at night, smelling of summer sun and soap as he burrowed under the covers and proceeded to warm them both up beyond a heat she had ever imagined.

She dropped to her knees beside him, barely aware that she'd done it, achingly aware of the pull that the memories and the magnitude of his physical presence had on her. He was solid and strong. A safe haven. And she felt such desire for him that she shook with it.

He held out a hand. She reached for it like a child for candy, wanting it badly, afraid something would take it away. And then she was in his arms, pressed as tightly against him as was physically possible as he rolled to his back and let her use his body as a cushion and as heat against the cold, hard floor.

"Bed," she whispered against his lips when he tried to kiss her.

"In a minute. I need this now." He forked his big hand through the hair at her nape and brought her mouth down to his.

And oh, oh, how she'd missed his mouth. The boy had stolen tender kisses. The man demanded, with a man's need, a man's hunger.

He framed her face in his hands and, on a growl, lifted her head and searched her eyes. "Don't let this be a mistake. In the morning. Do not make this into a mistake."

"I've made mistakes," she whispered as he stood, then picked her up and carried her into the bedroom. "This isn't one of them. *You*," she murmured against his open mouth and another breath-stealing kiss, "could never be a mistake."

Much later, when she'd recovered enough to breathe, Erin pressed her lips against the heartbeat pounding against Jed's throat. "What are you thinking?"

The sky had cleared during the night, and the moon, as full and luminous as she felt, shone in through the window and limed his chest with smoky gold.

He dragged her on top of him, brought her down for a long, wet, and sinfully wicked kiss. "I'm thinking I'd like to do that again."

She laughed and, pressing kisses against his jaw, his neck, across the expanse of his chest, then lower, murmured against his skin. "Hold that thought."

He clutched her hair in his hands and groaned when her lips brushed against his belly, then forayed lower. "You think ... that ... I could possibly have a thought?"

He groaned again when she barely skimmed her tongue over the tip of his erection.

"What I think is that there's too much thinking going on. You just lie still while I do something about that."

Then she took him in her mouth ... and neither one of them thought about anything but what she did to him for a very long time.

CHAPTER SIX

JED SAT IN FRONT of the fire the next night, exhausted yet feeling more rested than he had in years. They'd made love on and off all night the night before. Sometimes tender. Sometimes rough. All the time with a dawning and growing revelation that something amazing was happening here. He knew it. She knew it. They just hadn't gotten around to talking about it yet.

But they would. He'd walked away from this woman once—granted, they'd both been little more than kids—but even then, his heart had known the truth. This time, there'd be no walking away.

"You're moving a little slow there, sunshine," he teased when she joined him on the sofa.

"And you're gloating." She snuggled in close and nestled her head beneath his chin.

"I was referring to being stiff from today's hike. What were you talking about?"

She pinched him through his shirt, which made him yelp, then laugh. "You know exactly what I was talking about ... and it wasn't hiking."

"No? Then whatever could it be?" He shifted her, then lifted her until she straddled his lap, her knees digging into the soft cushions at either side of his hips. The smile on her face was a little shy, a little wanton, and a lot woman.

"It's all those big-boy muscles you're sporting ... sport."

He sobered abruptly, horrified that he might have actually hurt her. "Was I too rough?"

She leaned in and kissed him softly. "You were perfect. And I loved it. I just used a few muscles I don't think I've ever used before."

Oh, God, that look in her eyes. Invitation and love and lust. He'd never get tired of it. "Wanna tell me exactly where it hurts? I'll kiss it and make it better."

She pressed her forehead to his. "Kissing is what got me in this shape, if I remember right."

"I can always sleep on the sofa tonight," he offered.

"Over my sore body."

He laughed and hugged her hard, daring to look forward to years ahead of lovemaking and playing and planning with her.

Outside, the night was ink-black and wet. They'd gotten back from their walk before dinner when the low, heavy clouds that had threatened all day let loose. Rain peppered steadily against the cabin as a north wind rattled the old windows.

"If it's dry enough, I'll caulk those tomorrow," he said when a chill skittered through the room.

Erin sat up abruptly and looked toward the window facing the drive. "I could swear I just saw a quick flash of headlights. But there's nothing now."

Jed had seen it, too. "No one else is on the Point, right?"

"Right. Maybe it was lightning." But her eyes had grown wide and wary.

He could feel the suddenly rapid beat of her heart as he set her away from him and shot off the sofa. It hadn't been lightning. Definitely car or truck lights. Flashed on, then quickly off. Like someone didn't want to make his or her presence known but was unfamiliar with the terrain and risked the lights to get their bearings.

"Turn out the lights," he said and moved to a window, flattened his back against the wall, and peeked outside.

Before she had a chance to hit a switch, the cabin went dark.

"Sonofabitch," Jed swore under his breath.

"It could be the storm took the electricity out."

"Then how do we explain the security light that's still on at the cabin down the road?"

"Oh, God." She sprang to her feet. "Someone's out there."

He headed for the bedroom, dug his handgun out of his duffel, then quickly retrieved her .38 from her nightstand drawer.

"You know how to use it?" He handed her the S&W, then rushed from window to window, jerking the curtains closed.

She nodded, her eyes wide and a little wild in the firelight. "You think it's Livingston?"

"What I think is that there's no good reason for anyone to drive out to the middle of nowhere on a night like this. But he or they are the ones in trouble. I'll handle it. You got a flashlight?"

With only the fire to light the cabin, she rushed to the kitchen and pulled one out of a drawer. "It's got fresh batteries."

"Good girl. I'm going to go out and look around. I want you in the bathroom. Wedge yourself into the corner of the shower with your gun and be ready. I'll ID myself the moment I come back inside, so if you hear or see anyone come in there, shoot."

She rushed to his side. "Don't go out there. Please. It's too dangerous."

He grabbed her and kissed her hard and quick. "Nothing's happening to me, sunshine. Now I've got to go. Better I get the jump on him than the other way around. Promise me you'll shoot."

"I promise." She looked scared for him but resolute. "Be careful."

"Lock the door behind me."

Then he carefully opened the door, looked around outside, then squeezed out and into the rain.

CHAPTER SEVEN

JED HAD SPENT A lot of wet, cold nights in Afghanistan. He figured he had the advantage. This was home turf. He knew this point like the back of his hand. But he'd still give his left nut for a pair of Night Vision goggles right about now.

Braced against the wind and rain and aiming his gun ahead of him, he inched around the corner of the cabin closest to the driveway. He didn't see a vehicle, but he'd known he wouldn't. It was likely parked down the hill out of sight.

Wind whipped through the trees, and he tread softly to keep from making any sound on the wet carpet of leaves and pine needles, always watchful for a movement out of sync and time with the forest.

He reached the breaker box, huddled over it to block the light, and flicked on the flashlight. Wires had been cut. Quickly shutting down the flashlight, he moved on. He didn't know who he was facing or how many. But when he turned the corner closest to the lake, where the sounds of thrashing water and frenzied wind were the loudest, he spotted a lone man in a guard position behind a tree and knew he was dealing with more than one.

Years of training and muscle memory kicked in. He swung wide and crept soundlessly up behind the guard. Before he knew he'd been had, Jed clamped a forearm around his throat, cutting off his breath. He held tight and hard. The man quit struggling after two minutes. He went completely limp after three. Jed lowered him to the forest floor, snagged the fallen man's assault rifle, stuffed his own .45 in his waistband, and continued the hunt.

He was the predator now. And he always got his prey. This was going to be over soon.

Then he rounded the last corner—and saw the cabin door standing wide open.

Erin. They were going after Erin.

Adrenaline fired through his blood like rocket fuel. He sprinted for the door, made himself stop short just outside and listen. Nothing. Just the wind and the rain and the relentless roar of the water pounding the shore below.

He eased inside—and saw a man, rifle shouldered as he crept across the floor and headed directly for the bathroom.

"Stop right there," Jed commanded and knew the moment he'd said it that the gunman had chosen this day to die.

He swung around firing. Jed dropped to a knee and squeezed the trigger, firing a three-round burst, all direct hits in the center of the gunman's chest.

He was dead before he hit the ground.

Jed raced across the cabin, leapt over his body, and ran straight to the bathroom.

"It's me. It's me, Erin. Don't fire." She ran out and met him in the kitchen, flying into his arms and hitting him so hard she almost knocked him backward. He set the rifle on the table and drew her against him, relieved beyond words that she was safe.

"Is it over?" she whispered against his throat.

"No," a voice said from behind them. "It's not quite over."

They both turned to see Clayton Livingston standing in the doorway, soaking wet, an insane look in his eyes and a pistol in his hand.

Jed shoved Erin behind him.

"How touching." Livingston's voice was eerily calm, in complete juxtaposition to the look in his eyes. "I'll kill you, too, whoever you are. I don't care. But she will be dead before I leave here."

"She didn't kill your son, Livingston. You've got the wrong person." Jed tried to stall, to come up with a plan to distract Livingston. All he needed was a split second to shove Erin out of the line of fire so he could drop, roll, and reach for the rifle.

Livingston merely shook his head and lifted the pistol.

A shot rang out, and Jed waited for the pain. Felt nothing but a loud ringing in his ears.

Livingston lowered the gun; he looked confused. He staggered. Touched his chest. Drew his hand away covered in blood. Then crumpled slowly to the floor.

Jed spun around … and there was Erin. Both hands gripped around her .38. A horrified look on her face.

"Baby," he whispered and drew her trembling body against his.

"Did I … did I kill him? Please, please go see if I killed him."

He carefully removed the gun from her hand, sat her down on a kitchen chair, then knelt and pressed his fingertips to Livingston's carotid artery. There was a pulse. Weak but steady.

"Is he dead?" she all but cried.

"No. He's alive."

She did cry then. In relief. "Thank God. Thank God."

Jed found his cell phone and dialed 911, then held pressure on Livingston's wound until the police and the ambulance arrived.

CHAPTER EIGHT

8 months later

ERIN STRETCHED OUT ON her back on an inflatable raft and let the gentle breeze rock her in the water of the bay. It was a glorious summer day at the lake. Above, the sky was a pristine, perfect blue, the water a mirror of that perfection with hardly a ripple to disturb her nap.

Jed was off somewhere, doing man stuff. Chopping wood or caulking windows. Who knew the kinds of things that man could find to keep himself busy.

At least that's where she thought he was until she felt a slight ripple of water around her and heard the distinct sound of his voice mirroring the *dadum, dadum, dadum* cadence from *Jaws*.

"Just couldn't handle not checking on me, could you?" She opened her eyes to see his dark, wet head as he surfaced right beside her. "Practicing your submarine maneuvers?"

He liked to do that. To slip into the water, swim below the surface, then pop up beside her raft when she least expected it and scare the stuffing out of her.

"You're not screaming anymore. It's kind of taking the fun out of it."

She caressed his beautiful face, then pressed her hand on the top of his head and dunked him.

He surfaced again, smiling. "Hello, wife."

She smiled back, loving the look of the sun glistening on the water droplets clinging to his eyelashes. For such a macho man, he sure was pretty. And silly sometimes, and she loved all those parts of him. "Hello, husband."

They'd gotten married in January, right after McKenna had found Ryan's killer. One of the co-ed's alibis ended up having some crater-sized holes in it, and when McKenna pushed hard enough, she'd tearfully confessed that Livingston wanted to break off their affair, so rather than lose him, she'd killed him. The press had been right about a "crime of passion." Just wrong about the true murderer.

The burden that confession had lifted from Erin's shoulders could not be measured. Neither could the fact that Clayton Livingston had lived to stand trial for attempted murder. She hadn't wanted to carry the guilt of his death, either, but she'd shoot him again if Jed's life were at stake.

"How do you feel about Tokyo?" Jed asked, crossing his arms on the side of her raft and floating along beside her.

"Will Godzilla be there?"

He pushed up out of the water and kissed her. "'Fraid not, sunshine. It'll only be for a couple of years, then I can request a stateside assignment."

"Have you not yet figured out that whither thou goest, I will go?"

He smiled again. "Was there subtext in your use of the word wither? The water's cold, after all. You know that's not a myth about shrinkage."

She laughed and pulled him back for another kiss. "Men. You have such fragile little egos."

"As long as I have you, I can wither any storm."

She rolled her eyes.

"I can keep 'em coming if you want me to."

She dunked him again. And thought about how grand life could really be.

New York Times, Publishers Weekly and *USA Today* bestseller, **Cindy Gerard**, is a six-time RITA® finalist and is proud to display two RITAs in her office. Cindy writes fast, sexy, action-adventure romantic suspense featuring former Spec Ops warriors and is proud to count many military families among her readers.

Catch up on Cindy's news at www.cindygerard.com.

THE FALLOUT

HARPER ST. GEORGE

NOBODY GETS MARRIED AT eighteen.

Elena took a deep breath to steel herself against the sudden pain that stabbed through her chest before opening her eyes to look at the divorce papers in front of her. Nobody gets married at eighteen and *stays* married, she quickly amended. The proof was in front of her in black and white. A half-inch thick legal document with her name emblazoned on the top page. It seemed like an excessive amount of paper to dissolve a marriage that had been more of a whim than a solid commitment, but when you were being divorced by Dexter Thomas Harrington, she guessed it was reasonable to expect a lot of paperwork.

"Mrs. Harrington?"

She dragged her gaze from Dexter's name typed right there near hers to look at the attorney perched in the chair across her cluttered desk. "Black. I never changed my name."

His mouth turned up in a curt smile, as if he couldn't bother himself to care about the intricacies of her domestic life. He was probably angry that he'd had to deliver the papers to her in person; given his age and the quality of his suit, she expected he had lackeys to do this sort of thing. "Of course, right. Ms. Black, if you could just sign on the last page, I can leave you to finish …" His voice drifted off as he threw a disdainful glance around the lab. "Whatever you were working on."

She took offense at his tone. Sure, the lab was dingy and needed a new paint job, but the equipment was state of the art. She'd worked hard to get the upgrades they needed and had succeeded because her work was being noticed. With only a year of her post-graduate study left, she hoped to be offered a full-fledged research position. This was her second home.

"If you think I'm just going to sign this without having my lawyer review it, you're crazy." She didn't have a lawyer, but it sounded better than the Internet searching she planned to do.

But he smiled as if he knew, he was indulging a petulant child. "Ms. Black, I don't think I need to explain to you the confidentiality required in dealing with this matter. It would behoove no one to have this brought to the attention of the press before everything is settled. If you could—" Something started vibrating. He paused to reach into the hidden breast pocket of his coat and pulled his phone out, pressing a button that stopped the interruption without looking at the screen. "If you could just sign, everything will be done, and we can all get on with our lives. If it would make you feel better, I'd be happy to review every page with you."

He didn't look like that would make him happy at all. He looked like he wanted to grab her hand and force the signature. There was no way she could sign this tonight. It was all so sudden. Sure, it had been over four years since she'd even spoken to Dex, but that didn't mean she could so easily wipe it all away with a stroke of her pen—and without wine, plenty of wine.

"Thank you." The phone vibrated again, so she waited in respectful silence while he quieted it. "That's a very generous offer, but I'm sure you can understand my reluctance to not have someone else look it over. You would never counsel your clients to sign something like this without your first reviewing it, would you?"

His jaw clenched. "Come into my office Monday. I'll have another attorney review it with you."

His blatant attempt to manipulate her was starting to make her angry. Before either of them could say anything else, the phone buzzed again, prompting him to pick it up and finally look at the display. Elena watched in amazement as his expression went from almost hostile to anxious. He held up a long, manicured finger to her and brought the phone to his ear. "Yes, sir?"

Her eyebrows went up at the respectful greeting, and she had to force herself to not listen to the angry male voice coming from the phone. The attorney's words she couldn't help but hear, and they came out as a broken string of subordination. "I understand … but you said … yes, yes, of course … Jonathan must have misunderstood … right. My apologies, sir."

He dropped the hand holding the phone to his lap and closed his eyes. If she weren't so convinced that he wasn't in possession of a soul, she'd have thought he was trying to find his center. When he opened his eyes, he was back to business and tucked the phone back into his pocket before picking up his leather satchel. "I'll be in touch, Ms. Black." He flicked a glance to t..e papers as he turned and left.

For the next five minutes, she had a very difficult time drawing air into her lungs or taking her eyes from the top page of the divorce papers. Every time she tried to breathe in, a fresh wave of pain would threaten to send her into hyperventilation. So she forced herself to sit calmly and swallow down the thick lump that had formed in her throat.

It wasn't like she'd never thought this day was coming. Of course it had been coming. No one like Dex married someone like her—a nobody from a desert town who had nothing but a pile of student loans, a flaky mother, and no father. The Harringtons had money that could be traced for centuries, and a pedigree like that demanded a certain type of wife.

Just because the blow had been expected didn't mean it didn't hurt. It hurt like hell. Elena closed her eyes and remembered the first time she'd seen him. He'd been under the hood of his cousin's car and had just leaned back to wipe his brow with his discarded shirt. His dark brown hair curled where it touched his neck, wet with sweat. Her attraction had been immediate, and she'd been unable to look away in time before he caught her and smiled back. She and her roommate had spent the rest of the day stealing glances at him and his cousin from the window of their new apartment.

But Dex had turned out to be more than a great body. He'd become her other half, and that wonderful, disastrous summer had ended with their marriage in Las Vegas. Despite what had happened, thinking of that day still made her smile. She'd loved him so much. Still did.

"Elena? You okay?"

Her eyes flew open to see Ron standing in the doorway. No! She'd forgotten about their date, forgotten about everything the minute that attorney had walked into her lab. She looked down and, realizing that the papers were blatantly visible on her desk, quickly grabbed them and stuffed them into the messenger bag hanging on the back of her chair. No one knew she was married, and she wanted to keep it that way.

"I'm fine ... I just forgot—" She bit her lip to stop the confession. Ronald was sweet and a fellow post-graduate student. They'd worked on a research paper together and had kept up the friendship. When he'd started to press for more, she'd had a hard time coming up with excuses, so she'd agreed to a few dates. This was to be their third, but it was the last thing she wanted to do right now. He didn't deserve to be hurt by her personal crisis. "I forgot about the time. I'm sorry."

He walked in and stopped in front of her desk. "Are you sure you're fine? You look really pale."

"Actually, no, I'm not fine. I just started feeling ... strange. Would you mind if we postponed?" He looked crestfallen. "I'm sorry to do this, Ron."

"It's okay. I just want you to feel better. I'll take you home."

"No, you don't have to do that. I can catch the bus." But she wanted to be home, and taking the bus would add half an hour to the trip, so when he pressed, she agreed.

The ride was more awkward than she could have anticipated. He kept asking questions, and she got the feeling he didn't buy that she was sick. He knew something was up, but there was no way she was going into the details of her marriage and soon-to-be divorce with him when she was still reeling from the news herself. All she could think about were the divorce papers burning a hole in her bag.

When they arrived at her complex, he insisted on parking and walking her to her door. Elena knew he wanted her to invite him in and was already working out a response in her mind when he surprised her and grabbed her arm to pull her around to face him. He'd never been remotely aggressive, so the move surprised her. But when she looked up at him, he was smiling.

"Look, I know you're not sick, but I also know something's troubling you. You obviously don't want to share, and that's okay. But I'm here when you decide that you do."

The warmth in his soft blue eyes caused the lump to return to her throat and her chest to shudder with a suppressed sob. Before she could stop herself, she leaned in and gave him a hug. His arms came around her and held her close for a moment, but then he stiffened. She looked up at him, but he was looking behind her.

"Who is that?"

Her heart dropped to her stomach. Without even looking, she knew who it was, but she made herself look anyway just to be sure. Dex had stepped out of the shadow of the overhang at her door. His hair was messed like he'd been running his fingers through it, and his untucked shirt was unbuttoned near the top. But those were his only vulnerable attributes. He looked pissed.

CHAPTER TWO

"DEX!" HER STOMACH FLOPPED over on itself.

His gaze traveled over them both before settling on her face in the meager light from the pathway lamp. "We need to talk." His voice was calm and cold.

No, no, no! Not now. She agreed they needed to talk but not tonight. Not when the bombshell had just been dropped.

"Who is this, Elena?" Ron's voice reminded her that she was standing too close to him, so she moved back a step. But then an image of one of the latest tabloid pictures of Dex in the Caribbean with a bikini-clad blonde draped across his lap made her reconsider. He'd crossed that line long before she was even capable of thinking about it.

"I'll see you Monday, Ron. Thanks for the ride home." She didn't want to answer him and draw him further into her drama.

"I'm not sure I should leave you." His brow furrowed as he looked at Dex again and then back to her. She had to agree that Dex looked formidable in his current state. Of course, she'd seen pictures of him, but nothing had prepared her for the man he'd grown into. His height was the same, but he somehow seemed bigger. Stronger.

"I'll be fine." She tried to force lightness into her tone but failed.

"Elena—" Ron looked like he wanted to say more, but the second he paused, Dex's voice cut through the moment.

"Good-bye, Ron."

She gasped and looked over to see Dex smiling that arrogant smile he seemed to have perfected in the time they'd been apart. He'd never had that look when he was hers. "I'm sorry. I'll explain things later." She brushed Ron's hand with hers but couldn't bring herself to do more than that. After he nodded and walked away, giving her one last backward glance, she stood for a moment trying to get her thoughts in order. But Dex wouldn't let that happen. He was there beside her. Too close to allow any rational thought. He'd always had that effect on her.

"Why don't you have a car?"

"The lab's not far, so I don't need one. I usually take the bus, but—" No! She would not explain Ron giving her a ride home. It was none of his business. "What are you doing here?"

"We need to talk."

"Yes, your lawyer came by to see me at the lab." The shock was giving way to anger, but she refused to look at him and let it flare. Instead, she dug in her bag for her keys, but the damned things didn't want to be found.

"I know. I came over to apologize for that. He was never supposed to come to your work." He actually managed to sound contrite. At least the coldness was gone from his voice.

"Oh, well, you apologized. Are we done?" She checked the back pocket of the messenger bag with still no sign of her keys.

Dex reached out to touch her shoulder. "Elly, I'm sorry." The nickname made her stiffen. No one called her that but him, and it had been so long since she'd heard it. "This isn't how I meant for this all to happen." His fingers lingered a minute to touch a lock of her shoulder-length brown hair before dropping back to his side.

It was on the tip of her tongue to ask if he meant the divorce or the marriage, but it didn't matter. They would both be over soon enough, so she went back to looking for her keys.

"Let me get it."

She didn't know what he meant until she heard the click and looked up to see that he'd unlocked her door with a key from his key ring.

"You never changed the lock." He offered a partial smile.

No, almost everything was exactly the same as it had been when he'd lived there with her. Pathetically the same. She stopped her search and dropped the bag back over her shoulder but couldn't manage to smile back at him or even address the question in that statement. "Thanks," she muttered and stepped inside.

"Let me start over. I didn't mean to start like that." He gestured to where Ron had disappeared. "I'd like to come in and talk."

He stepped forward so that he was framed in the doorway, and she couldn't have closed the door on him if she'd wanted to, which she very much did. She really didn't want a conversation with him tonight. Anytime, actually, but especially tonight, when she was so angry and hurt and vulnerable.

"I'm not sure tonight is good. Can't we schedule something? Get coffee?" Go somewhere with no memories of their time together.

"I'm heading back to New York on Sunday. I'll be back in two weeks, but I'd rather get this over with. Tomorrow I have meetings and a dinner. I'm actually supposed to be somewhere now, but ... I thought this was more important."

The excuses touched on why it hadn't worked out between them. There was always something else that needed to be done. A meeting, a dinner, a cocktail party ... always something more important. But it was the phrase "get this over with" that made her agree. He was obviously eager, after six years of marriage, to end things. She should be just as eager. She supposed, on some level, she was. "So why now? If you don't have time to deal with it now, why do this?"

"I only meant for the paperwork to get started. I thought we'd talk when I came back in two weeks. It never occurred to me that the paperwork was already there, waiting. Look, I'm coming in. We can talk about it."

She had no choice but to back up as he walked into the living room and shut the door. With the full light on him, he took her breath away. Another effect he'd always had on her. His dark hair and olive skin made his greenish-hazel eyes seem even lighter.

"I can give you half an hour." She gestured him to the couch. "Just give me a minute to get settled." Somehow she'd convinced herself that if she stayed professional and upbeat, it wouldn't hurt as much. She forced herself to not run to her bedroom, but once there, she closed the door and hurried to her bathroom to splash water on her face. The cold barely registered with her. Everything seemed surreal, like it was happening to someone else. Dex wasn't really here in her apartment.

But he was. Somehow she could still smell him. He didn't wear cologne; he didn't need to. His body wash and his own unique scent blended to create a fragrance more intoxicating than any cologne. She hated that he affected her.

Her shoes landed in the closet with a thud that was much harder than was necessary. She debated changing but decided her jeans and sweater would do. Now she realized why these things were normally done in a conference room somewhere with both parties in suits. The suits were armor. She'd feel much better prepared facing him in the one that she owned.

Finally, she pulled the folder from her bag and marched back to the living room. He was standing at the window looking out but turned when he heard her.

"I'm gonna make tea. Do you want something?"

"I'm fine, thanks."

She put the folder on the breakfast bar and then went through the motions of heating water and grabbing a cup, all the while wondering how he could be so calm. He'd clearly moved on. Every picture in every magazine she'd ever seen of him showed her how easily he'd moved on. If only it had been so easy for her.

"I'm not signing anything tonight. I'd like to have someone look it over first." She crossed her arms and eyed the folder.

"I wouldn't expect you to. I thought we could talk about what's in there. Have you read it?"

She shook her head. The damned lump had returned to make her throat ache.

"I think you'll find it's a fair settlement. But let me know if you don't. My father had it drawn up years ago. I glanced through it but ..." His voice trailed off, and his fingers raked through his hair.

Dex's father would certainly have made sure his only son's interests were protected, so there'd been no need for him to read it. However bitter her thoughts were about the man, she still had been sorry to hear about his death two years ago. "I was sorry to hear about your father." It was the last time she had attempted to call him.

"Thanks. I wasn't sure you'd heard." She didn't miss the cutting look in his eyes before he was back to calm again.

"Of course I heard." The man had run a multibillion-dollar company. His sudden death by heart attack had been all over the news.

The silence that descended was only cut by the whistling of the kettle on the stove. Elena busied herself with making her tea, but all too soon, that task was complete, so she made her way to stand at the breakfast bar. He stood on the other side, the folder between them. She blew gently on the dark liquid and took a sip before nodding to the papers.

"So ... anything in particular in there you want to talk about?" When he didn't answer right away, she looked back at him. His eyes were glued to the folder. While he'd waited for her, he'd rolled up the sleeves of his shirt. The bottom of a tattoo peeked out of the sleeve. Further testament that his life had gone on without her. She let her eyes move over him, taking in his broader shoulders in the black shirt and the way the charcoal pinstriped pants clung to his hips. He seemed foreign to her now but somehow achingly familiar. If she held him, would he even feel the same?

"I meant it, Elly. I never wanted this to happen." When he looked up at her, the pain in his eyes made her heart clench. God knows she never wanted this to happen, either. The day she'd married him had been the happiest day of her life. No, the day he'd proposed to her had been the happiest day of her life. It had been the day she'd finally been sure that he really meant it when he said he loved her. That she wasn't a summer fling. The day she married him had just been icing on the cake.

It was never supposed to end in divorce. She'd honestly thought what they had was the real thing, that nothing could come between them. But she'd been young and stupid. Dex had just graduated college that summer and was in Southern California to have one last summer of fun with his cousin before starting at his father's company. She'd just finished her freshman year and hadn't really been looking for love. She wasn't one of those girls who went to college to have a social life. Her scholarship had demanded total devotion to her studies. But she'd never imagined meeting someone like Dex.

They'd been together from that first day he had caught her and Sara peeking out at them and he'd knocked on their door. Pretty soon, far sooner than she'd have thought possible, he was spending every day with her and every night in her bed. He'd become her best friend, the other part of her soul. He got every corny joke she made and knew exactly what to say to make her happy. But the summer came to an end. His flight was scheduled for her nineteenth birthday, so the four of them had planned a trip to Vegas to celebrate early. On the first night there, he'd asked her to marry him. She'd said yes without a second thought.

He'd still had to leave on her birthday, but it was so much easier knowing they were bound together. They talked daily, and he flew out for some weekends. His parents hated that he'd gotten married, and it was decided that it wouldn't be announced. That should've been her first clue that it wouldn't last. More demands were placed on him at work until they were lucky to see each other once every two months. Then he wanted her to move to New York to resume her studies there and became angry when she refused. He'd told her she didn't need a scholarship when she had the Harrington money to pay for her tuition. But he'd never understood that she couldn't give up her scholarship because she wouldn't be reduced to living on his charity. Her mother had spent her life living from man to man, and Elena could not let him support her like that. The idea had been inconceivable to her.

Finally, just over a year after their first anniversary, they'd had a huge argument, and she'd told him to never come back. It was too heart-wrenching to have so little of him. She'd told herself it was better to just stop it before it got worse, but she'd been wrong. There had never been any part of her that didn't love him. It didn't get worse than that.

Soon after, he'd begun popping up in magazines and tabloids. The media attention had exploded after his father's death and he'd taken the helm. They probably should've taken care of the divorce long ago, but it had been easy to go on without doing anything.

If she could stay angry, then it wouldn't hurt as much, so she used one of the models he'd been spotted with against him. "Why now, then? Planning to propose to Brunhilda or whatever her name is?"

"You kicked me out, Elly." He wasn't accusing her. The same pain that had shown in his eyes was in his voice. "I fucking loved you."

That was an accusation.

CHAPTER THREE

THE WORDS SENT A shard of pain slicing through her. Loved. Past tense. Why had she agreed to this conversation? It would do nothing but destroy her. Her hands shook so badly she put her cup down on the bar, afraid she'd spill tea everywhere. "I loved you, too."

"Obviously not enough." His hands gripped the edge of the bar so tightly his knuckles turned white.

She sucked in a deep breath, but her voice shook anyway. "That's not fair, Dex. We tried to make it work. It just wouldn't. It wasn't meant to work."

"You could have come to New York."

"Dex"—she closed her eyes against the pain—"I couldn't leave here just like that. Besides, what would've been waiting for me in New York? A scrap of your time on the rare occasions work let you come home? You could have moved here."

"You know I couldn't leave."

"Neither of us could leave, so it never should've happened. It was a stupid idea to get married in the first place."

He was silent, but she could feel the weight of his eyes on her. The scrutiny lasted so long she had to stop herself from fidgeting or walking away to the living room. She couldn't look at him, though. Couldn't bear to face his rejection again.

"It wasn't stupid. We were in love and desperate to hold on to it. I can't deny that the challenges we faced were more than most people have to overcome, but it wasn't stupid, Elly. And those challenges weren't insurmountable to the girl I knew, to the girl I married. What happened to her?"

"I don't know what you mean." But she did.

"Bullshit." His jaw was clenched, and his eyes blazed in anger.

"This is pointless. What does it matter, anyway? You obviously want it over; the papers are right there."

"I don't know why it matters, but it does. You stopped talking to me, remember? Every time I came home, there was another wall between us. I just want to know what I did to make you turn away from me and move on. I think I deserve that."

"Move on?" She could feel her control slipping, and her voice rose on that. "How can you say that? You're the one out with a new woman every night. You're the one taking vacations with them. I still live in the same apartment. The only man I've dated is Ron and he's ..." She sucked in a breath and made one last effort to control her anger.

"There aren't as many as you think, Elly. There was never anyone until I was sure I'd lost you." His voice was low and measured.

Even one was enough to break her heart. "It doesn't matter. I'm not doing this with you again. You've made your feelings clear. I'll have someone read over the papers and get them back to you when I can." The tears were starting to well in her eyes, so she moved past him, hoping to reach the bathroom before they started.

"Don't run away again. Talk to me. I really don't know how you feel. You'd never tell me." When she showed no sign of stopping, he followed. She'd almost made it to her bedroom by the time he grabbed her arm. "Please, Elly."

It was the catch in his voice that made her look back. The pain was clear on his face, and she wondered if maybe he did still feel something. Something that would make this confrontation important to him. She couldn't even begin to hide the tears in her eyes, didn't even try. When she closed them, a tear fell down each cheek. She pressed her palms to the wall at her back and leaned into it for strength. "What do you want me to say? I said everything there was to say ... I poured out my heart in that voice mail. You never called me back. What can I say after that?"

His thumb rubbed a tear from her cheek, and she heard him breathe in deeply. "What voice mail?" His breath whispered across her face. He was standing so close to her the heat from his body warmed her, and it was intoxicating.

She'd hoped to avoid reliving the embarrassment of that phone call. It had always been hard for her to open up, but to be rejected after that had been a harsh blow to take. She opened her eyes to refuse him, but when she met his fierce hazel gaze, she was lost. Looking back at her was the Dex she'd married. "After our fight. I don't know, maybe a few weeks. I'd gotten a new phone because you wouldn't stop calling me. But I missed you, so I called and left you a message. When you didn't call back, I knew you were angry, so I called again and apologized." It had been more than an apology. She'd asked for another chance. "You never called me back, so I took that as your answer."

He closed his eyes as his hand cupped her cheek. "What did you say, Elly?"

A part of her wanted to play it off, to pretend she couldn't remember, but she was done hiding. If it was over, then it would be over without her shrouding her feelings. "I said I loved you. That you were the most important thing in the world to me and I didn't want to imagine my life without you in it. I asked if I could come to New York to see you so we could talk about it, make a plan for staying together. I wanted to do whatever it took to be with you." The words threatened to stick in her throat, but she forced them out. Though by the time she finished, they were scarcely more than a whisper. "Surely you remember that."

But he was shaking his head, and her chest tightened because she knew what he was going to say. "I never got it. I swear to you I never got that message."

"How is that possible?"

"I never got it," he repeated.

"But I'd called you before ..." But her voice trailed off when she remembered she'd thrown her old phone out. She'd dialed his number from memory when she usually only pressed his name to call him. Was it possible she'd gotten it wrong? "You didn't get my message when I called about your dad?"

He shook his head and held her face cupped between his hands. "Don't you think I would have come back to you as soon as I heard you say you wanted me?" His lips were so close they almost brushed hers as he spoke. "You're all I ever wanted, Elly. It's always been you. It almost killed me when I thought you didn't want me."

The sob escaped before she could hold it back. "No, Dex, I

never stopped wanting you. Never!" One hand rested on his cheek, the light stubble abrading her fingertips. "I was just so afraid of becoming dependent on you, of becoming my mother, I couldn't— I didn't know how to have a relationship, how to be a wife to you." She did cry then, and his arms immediately went around her.

"Don't cry. Please don't cry. I don't ever want you to cry." His lips brushed her ear.

She buried herself against his chest, and it felt so good to be there after all these years. But even that wasn't enough. "I love you, Dex."

She turned her head until her mouth met his. He groaned, and his tongue slipped past her lips to brush hers. The touch ignited a spark in her that begged to be flamed. She needed him, needed to touch him, hold him, have him inside her. Her hands moved under his shirt, seeking the heat of his chest. When the fabric pulled tight, he yanked it apart, sending buttons flying, to give her total access. Her fingers savored his warm skin, and she marveled at how solid he felt.

Strong, eager hands went down to cup her bottom, urging her up against him. She complied and wrapped her legs around him, feeling him hard and thick against her center. He moved his hips, grinding against her, causing her body to pulse in need. It had always been like this, her need for him so heady and overwhelming. The absence of him from her life had only intensified that need. She had to have him now, so she pushed his shirt down over his shoulders and shamelessly rubbed herself against his chest.

"Jesus, Elly," he groaned, and his hands tightened on her as he walked them to the bedroom.

He followed her down on the bed, but his eyes were solemn and full of tenderness as he rose to look at her. Anxious for him, she tugged him back down, but he refused to budge. "I want you to know that you're the only one I've ever been with without protection, and I haven't been with anyone in a very long time." He took in a deep breath and brushed a strand of hair from her cheek. His throat worked as he swallowed. "I want to take you without anything between us …" The unspoken question hung heavy in the air.

She blinked back the sudden ache of tears and touched the

beloved features of his face. If they were to move forward, then everything in the past had to be put behind them. The idea of not having him bare inside her was unacceptable. "I don't want anything between us, either. I'm still on the pill."

He smiled and kissed her gently before moving back to undress. She watched, greedy for the sight of him, appreciating every bit of masculinity he unwrapped for her pleasure. His body was sculpted to flawlessness. The pictures in the magazines hadn't done him justice. They couldn't compare to the perfection in front of her. The sight of him standing there fully aroused, his penis hard and silken, his eyes hungry and fierce, sent a flood of heat to her core.

"My turn." He grinned as he knelt on the bed and reached for her sweater.

It occurred to her then that she should be self-conscious. Her body in no way compared to his, but it didn't matter. This was Dex, and she needed him inside her now. He pulled the sweater off over her head, and she was already unbuttoning her jeans so that he pulled them down, too, and off her legs. Then he was on top of her, the weight of his body feeling so welcome as it pinned her down and pressed her thighs open.

His mouth took hers almost savagely, and his hands seemed to be everywhere. On her waist, kneading her breasts through her bra, on her bottom, squeezing as he pressed his erection against her. She moaned when the heat of his cock scalded her through her panties. She needed that barrier gone, needed him.

He rained hot kisses along her jaw and down her neck to her breast. Taking it first through the thin lace of her bra and then hastily pulling the cup down so his mouth could feast on her bare nipple. The spasm of pleasure that shot to her middle when he drew it deep into his mouth was her undoing.

"Now, Dex!" she cried.

He pulled back, and before she realized what he meant to do, he'd pushed the thin barrier of her panties aside, and his tongue licked the length of her slit. She shuddered at the intense wave of pleasure that washed through her. But he wasn't done, and his lips closed over her clit, sucking the swollen nub into his mouth.

"Please. I need you." She thought it might be possible to die from the need.

He pulled the white panties off and rose above her. The head of his hot erection notched at her entrance just before his hard length pushed into her. It had been so long since he'd been there, her passage was too tight. She closed her eyes and forced her muscles to relax, and he pushed forward, sinking into her until he was completely seated within her warmth. They both cried out with the pleasure.

Her fingers clenched in his hair as she arched under him, feet pressed on the bed to hold herself open for him. This was what she'd been missing, the feel of him pulsing inside her, wrapped in her intimate embrace.

"I love you." The words were whispered as he brushed kisses on her cheek, her brow, her lips. "I've always loved you. I'll always love you."

Elena smiled as she looked into his eyes. He smiled, too, as he began to move inside her. Softly at first, but then his hands went to her bottom, pulling her cheeks apart as he pushed into her, and his pace became harder, wilder.

She pushed her knees wider, wanting to be open to him, wanting to be split apart by the force of him driving into her. Soon their rhythm was too violent to sustain eye contact any longer, and he buried his face in her neck. The hitch of his breath with each pounding thrust, harsh and uneven against her skin, was her undoing.

Her orgasm washed over her in wracking waves of pleasure, and he kept pounding, drawing it out until she was sure she couldn't take any more. Then he groaned, and she felt the warm spray of his release inside her, but neither of them wanted it to end, and he kept moving until the spasms stopped.

They gasped for breath, wrung out from their pleasure.

Finally, he laced his fingers with hers and held himself above her to look down into her eyes. "You're mine, Elly. I want you in my life. We'll make it work this time, whatever we have to do."

She smiled as she saw all her secret hopes for a future with him within reach. It would be different this time because she was different. She'd learned from her mistakes. Loving him wouldn't make her like her mother. Loving him could only make her stronger. "This time, whatever we have to do. I love you, Dex. You're everything that's important to me. Marry me again?"

"God, yes!" He rolled to his side and took her with him, his arms wrapped around her as if he never wanted to let her go. She loved the way he looked at her. Loved that he was hers.

Harper St. George was raised in the rural backwoods of Alabama and along the tranquil coast of northwest Florida. It was a setting filled with stories of the old days that instilled in her a love of history, romance, and adventure. By high school, she had discovered the historical romance novel, which combined all of those elements into one perfect package. She has been hooked ever since.

She currently lives in Atlanta, GA, with her family and loves to connect with readers. She would love to hear from you. Please visit her website at www.harperstgeorge.com or connect with her on Facebook www.facebook.com/harperstgeorge.

HARD TO BREATHE

SYLVIA DAY

#1 *New York Times* Bestseller, RITA® Finalist

THE CAPTAIN HAS AN unholy temper, I remind myself as Rebecca frowns.

Her narrowed gray eyes glance up from the transfer request lying on the ruthlessly barren desktop. "I'll be honest, Annalise. The chances of my approving this are practically nonexistent. You are one of the most naturally gifted aviatrixes I've ever seen, which is why I was so pleased that you ended up in Commander Gareth's squadron."

I resist the urge to squirm in my chair, holding my wings tightly to my back to avoid betraying my nerves. "I'm grateful for your belief in me, Captain. Really, I am. And being assigned to Commander Gareth is a huge honor, I know—"

"He speaks very highly of you," Rebecca interjects, her slender fingers drumming silently and impatiently against the dark wood. Behind her and through the window, I see other cadets going through drills, their slender bodies launching from the tarmac in powerful vertical lifts. The afternoon sky is streaked with multi-hued wings as unique to their owners as human fingerprints. "He says you're at the top of your class."

A soft shiver of pleasure ruffles my feathers to hear Gareth's praise, even secondhand. It is the least of the myriad reactions the warrior angel inspires in me. I would do anything short of grounding myself to feel nothing but respect and admiration for the instructor who is teaching me aerial combat. But Gareth stirs far more dangerous emotions. Longing and desire. Possessiveness and hunger. All of which are strictly forbidden between trainers and their students.

So many squadrons, so many instructors … What were the odds that I would be randomly selected for Gareth's?

Rubbing my damp palms over my knees, I press on. "It makes me feel proud to hear that, of course. But I'd still like to train under Commander Sarah instead. I think she'd be a better fit and that I'd excel under her guidance."

Rebecca heaves out a long-suffering sigh. With an impatient hand, she ruffles her cap of graying curls. "You are *not* in love with him, Annalise."

I blink, startled by her piercing insight. "Excuse me, ma'am?"

"And even if you were, it wouldn't matter. The commander isn't interested in fledglings."

"I'm not a fledgling!" I protest. In fact, I'm the oldest recruit in my rotation, having taken far longer than most angels to decide which caste to join. That's due to Gareth, of course. Watching my brother, Samuel, blossom under his guidance changed the course of my life.

"To him, you might as well be. His experience is as vast as yours is nonexistent."

I debate the wisdom of denying the captain's assessment of the situation, but in the end, I sag in my seat, defeated. "I just want to focus on my training."

If only that were possible. Instead, I'm too often mesmerized by the way sunlight glints off the inky darkness of Gareth's hair, reflecting an indigo glimmer that perfectly matches the sapphire filaments in his wickedly cool black wings. His eyes are the same lush blue, framed by thick lashes and boldly slashed brows. He is far too masculine to be beautiful, but he's gorgeous nonetheless, and so damned accomplished and confident in the sexiest of ways.

I've fallen so hard for him. I think about him constantly. Gareth is the inspiration for both daydreams and impossibly carnal fantasies. When he stands in front of the class in his instructor's sleeveless black tunic and slacks, demonstrating proper form with his muscles flexing beneath golden skin and his wings snapping open with crisp precision, I find it hard to breathe.

I'd wanted him to see me from afar, to watch me blossom un-der another's tutelage, to maybe entertain the thought of pursuing me at some point in the future …

Which he can never do as my instructor.

"I expected better from you," Rebecca scolds. "With all of your talent, I couldn't be more disappointed that you'd be distract-ed by a handsome face. I would think—"

"There's more to him than his looks! And I'm disappointed in *you* if you can't see that."

The captain pauses with her mouth open, startled at my crit-icism. It shuts abruptly, and she straightens, her gaze lifting past my shoulder.

A tingle races down my spine, telling me who's standing be-hind me before his smoky voice drifts into the office.

"Is there a problem with my cadet?" Gareth asks.

My fingers curl into my palms, and I beg Rebecca for mercy with my eyes. If Gareth ever finds out how I feel about him, I will die of mortification. Because one thing has become abundantly clear: He doesn't feel anything deep or hot for me.

"No, Commander," she replies after shooting a glance at me. "We have things in hand."

But Gareth strides in and catches up the transfer request with a quick swipe of his hand. He reads it, then turns that icy blue gaze onto me.

I squirm under the intensity of his scowl.

He glances at Rebecca. "Did you agree to this?"

"I did not."

"Good." He flicks the request back onto the desktop. "Come with me, cadet."

He's gone before I manage to rise to my feet, his footfalls nearly silent despite his sturdy combat boots and the heavy weight of his wings. With my stomach knotted, I give a quick salute to Rebecca. "Thank you for not saying anything, ma'am."

Her hard look offers no sympathy. "I don't have to tell him, Annalise. You do."

CHAPTER TWO

MY PULSE IS RACING as I scramble after Gareth, bolting through the hangar door to the tarmac with my wings ruffling behind me. Although his ever-present stern expression hasn't changed, I can sense his irritation. Does he think I don't value his guidance? Surely he doesn't suspect what my true motivation is … ?

Unlike me, Gareth marches into the wind without a single ripple marring the lines of his wings. His spine is rigidly straight, his posture militarily precise. The wind twists lovingly through his hair, riffling through the dark strands the way my fingers itch to. Heads turn to follow him, his dark presence drawing every eye. I chase after him like an overeager puppy, desperate to please him and wishing for any sign or scrap of real affection.

I don't let him see it, though. When he pauses on the edge of the tarmac and clasps his hands beneath his wings, I pull myself together, lifting my chin and standing at attention.

"What is your objection to being in my squadron, cadet?" he asks, turning and nearly knocking me back with the sheer force of his full attention. His chiseled face is impossible perfection. The wind forces me to appreciate that flawlessness by whipping the tips of his hair along those sculpted cheekbones and lips.

It really isn't fair. How am I expected to get over him when I have to see him every single day? Leaving his class is the only hope I have.

I suck in a deep breath, struggling to ignore the butterflies in my stomach. It's physically painful to keep the few feet of distance between us. I can't explain it, have never fully understood it. Something inside me I can't ignore screams *mine, mine, mine.* "My request is personal, sir."

His arms cross, causing his biceps to thicken in a way that makes my mouth water. The leather straps securing his blade to his back are unadorned by the medals and commendations he's rightfully earned, symbols of accomplishment that all the other

instructors wear with pride. Gareth doesn't need the embellish-
ments. He's stunning enough all on his own.

"It won't go beyond me," he says. "Explain."

My thoughts tumble, searching for an answer that won't stray
too far from the truth. "I have inappropriate feelings for someone."

"Inappropriate feelings," he repeats.

"Yes."

"Of what nature?"

"Uh ... romantic?" I don't mean for the reply to come out like
a question, but I'm not good at lying. There are a lot of words I can
use to describe how I feel about Gareth. Lustful and greedy. Awed.
But romantic is a little too soft for such a strong creature.

Gareth is silent for a long time, his gaze assessing. Then he
poses a question in return. "For who?"

You! I want to shout. *Can't you see how much I love you? How
long I've worshipped you?*

Over his shoulder, a flash of emerald catches my eye—the
distinctive green of my best friend's wings. "Josiah," I blurt out.

"Josiah?"

"Yes."

"I see."

My attention's caught by the purr in Gareth's voice, a rough
sound of indulgent amusement I've never heard from him before.
His powerful frame visibly relaxes.

I feel my cheeks flush. Could he be any more obvious that he's
relieved I'm not crushing on *him?*

"I think it would be best if Josiah and I were separated until
after graduation," I say tightly. "I don't want any distractions."

Gareth nods. "That's a reasonable request."

Blinking, it takes me a second to grasp that I've gotten what I
want. Regret pierces me, but I hold back the small sound of pain.
"Thank you for understanding."

"You should've come to me earlier."

Perhaps. But I was stupidly clinging to fantasies, choosing to
believe Gareth and I were meant to be ... until I saw him with
another woman in the hours just before dawn.

I'd woken early to practice, hoping to please him and show him that I was worthy of a warrior of his skill and renown. Instead, I'd seen him with one of the female instructors, standing in the shadows cast by the side of the main hangar, his head bent over her as they spoke, their body language too intimate and familiar. The gentle morning good-byes of a man and his lover.

"I'll see that Josiah is transferred to another squadron by morning."

Gareth's words hit me like a rush of chilled water.

"*What?*" I break my pose. "I'm the one who should be reassigned! It's my problem."

"But losing you would become my problem," he counters reasonably, the words sparking hope in me, which he quickly dashes. "Josiah isn't nearly the flyer you are."

Oh, God. This can't be happening. "He shouldn't be punished because of me!"

"It's not a punishment. It's a transfer."

I take an involuntary step closer. "None of the other commanders are as good as you are. Giving him to someone else is a step down no matter how you want to look at it!"

Those brilliantly blue irises of his warm slightly. It is the closest I've ever seen him come to a smile. "Thank you, Annalise. But your evaluation is incorrect. Every instructor at the academy is similarly accomplished."

"You're missing the point! *I'm* the one who should transfer."

"The matter is resolved, cadet." His arms drop to his sides, and he walks past me, heading toward the barracks.

"The hell it is." I run after him.

"Say that again," he says, pivoting abruptly, a move that has his wings flaring like a cape.

"If you transfer him, I'll wash out."

"Oh, no, you won't," he says silkily, advancing. "I would have to approve your discharge, and I guarantee that's never going to happen."

I feel invisible walls closing in, caging me. I can't let Josiah pay for my mistake. He'd never forgive me. I'd never forgive myself. "Never mind, sir. I can deal with him. Leave him be."

"After all the trouble you've gone to?" Gareth comes to a stop mere inches from me. I can feel the heat of his body, smell the scent of his leathers and his skin. "Filing the transfer request. Talking with the captain. This display of insubordination. Suddenly, you can train with the cadet you've worked so hard to be separated from? I'm doubtful, Annalise."

My hands fist at my sides, and his gaze drops to take that defiance in. "It's not Josiah," I amend between clenched teeth.

"No?" he queries, his gaze following the crisscrossing knife sheath straps that frame my breasts, before gliding up my throat and coming to rest on my mouth. He is strung taut again, as if awaiting the most unpleasant news.

I'm happy to give it to him, since he's pushed me into a corner. "It's you, Gareth. I'm in love with *you.*"

CHAPTER THREE

"AGAIN, CADET," GARETH SNAPS, glaring at me as I slowly—
and painfully—get to my hands and knees.

The sky is cloudless above us and the ground precariously
rocky beneath our feet. We're training on the Precipice, a narrow
jut of land surrounded by a steep drop.

"Jesus," Josiah says under his breath as he bends down to offer
me a hand up. "What the fuck is his problem?"

My teeth clench against the pity I see in his eyes, the same pity
I see in everyone's eyes lately. In the week since I told Gareth how
I feel about him, he's done his worst to push me away.

"Let her stand on her own two feet," he tells Josiah, swinging
the long staff in his hand so that it whistles through the air. We've
been sparring for nearly an hour, far longer than any of the other
cadets in our squadron.

Bethany steps forward. "I'm ready for a shot, sir."

"Not yet," he says curtly, watching me as I release Josiah's hand
and stand.

When I draw a deep breath, a sharp pain arrows through my
side, forcing me to bend over and hold my knees.

Gareth's gaze hardens. "We're all waiting for Cadet Annalise to
decide whether or not she's joining us for training today."

The sneer in his voice is the final straw.

I tackle him with a shoulder to his midsection before I even
know what I'm doing, my left wing curling around and under him
to knock his footing loose. We hurtle past the edge of the cliff and
fall, spinning in a flurry of wings as the wide canyon rushes up
on either side of us, swallowing us like a gaping mouth. His body
flexes against mine, big and hard and powerful, and I shove him
away, hating my unwelcome physical reaction.

The craving is still there, an unappeased hunger that gnaws.

My wings flare wide to slow my descent, but the force of the wind is too great, and the angle I'm falling is wrong. My wings bend back too far, shooting agony along my spine. I tuck and roll, my teeth grinding against the pain.

"Annalise!" he shouts, diving toward me in an ebony rush.

I plummet on my back; my wings wrap along my biceps and point upward, my hair whipping free of the ponytail that usually contains it. The air roars over my ears with hurricane force, screaming at me to slow down.

"Stay away from me!" I yell at Gareth, kicking out when he reaches for me.

"Damn it! Let me help you."

Twisting, I change direction, tucking my wings in and racing toward a small ledge that bleeds into a cave. There's scarcely enough room to land with the best of conditions, but I go for it anyway. Anything to get away from the angel who is slowly but surely driving me crazy.

As the rock-strewn outcropping rushes toward me, I force my body to relax, knowing I need to hit the ground with bent knees, followed by a quick rolling tumble. I am nearly there, my breath catching in anticipation ...

Gareth slams into me from behind, crushing my back to his chest just before his booted feet hit the earth, and we tumble into the hole in the side of the canyon.

We flip end over end. Wrapped in his wings, I'm cocooned against the impact until we hit the wall with bone-jarring force, knocking the air from my lungs. I lie dazed and wounded, shielded in soft inky down.

He groans and pulls me closer. For a moment, I let him hold me, too shaken to resist the comfort of his embrace.

Then he opens his mouth.

"Stupid girl," he mutters, his lips moving against my throat.

I stiffen. "Let me go."

He ignores me, his wings tightening as his hands slide over my belly. "Are you hurt?"

Goose bumps sweep over my skin despite the warmth of his body. "I'm fine."

"Bullshit. I heard something snap when you tried to fly."

His words make me feel the burn in my right wing. "Get off me."

"Don't be so damn stubborn. Tell me where you're hurt."

"Where *don't* I hurt? You've been kicking my ass all week!"

His grip eases. "Annalise—"

I break free, but when my lame wing bumps his, I cry out and recoil.

"For chrissakes," he bites out, hauling us both to our feet with his hands at my waist. He pins me to the wall, my breasts pressed to the cool stone. His hips arch into the small of my back as his hands sweep over the upper curves of my wings, searching for injury.

His touch, so strong and warm, is heavenly. The soft brushes of his palms ... the gently seeking fingers ... the delicate pressure ...

To my horror, a low moan of pleasure escapes me.

Gareth freezes.

My eyes close in embarrassment. How can he affect me so strongly without even trying? "Please," I whisper. "Let me go."

He doesn't move for a long moment. Then his lips touch the nape of my neck. "Tell me where you're hurt," he murmurs, his breath warm and soft through the disheveled strands of my hair.

My fingers curl into my palms. "Right wing."

His hands move along my primaries, prodding carefully. I whimper when he finds the spot that throbs like a bitch.

"A ruptured tendon," he says quietly.

My head bows. I won't be able to fly for months. I won't graduate with my class. Hot tears slide down my face.

"Sweetheart." His hands go to my hips, and he nuzzles against me. "I'm sorry."

"Don't." I can't bear his sympathy. "Just go away."

"I have to take you back."

"Send someone else."

His fingertips dig into my flesh. "As if I'd let anyone else carry you."

I absorb that, try to process it. But it's impossible to think with him surrounding me, his chest heaving against my wings. "Gareth ...?"

He makes a low, soft noise. "You shouldn't say my name."

The rebuke goads me to push back against him. He groans and leans harder into me.

I feel him then, thick and hard against the small of my back. His arousal startles a gasp from me.

"Give me a minute," he says hoarsely.

Confused, I try to turn my head and look at him.

"Stop wriggling!"

I stare out the opening of the cave, at the world beyond the cliffside. A world in which Gareth looked at me coldly when I told him I loved him and said, *Do us both a favor; keep that to yourself.*

"You have *got* to be kidding me," I complain.

"Shut up, Annalise."

"When did this happen? Just now?"

He begins to pull away. "We're not talking about this."

"The hell we're not." I turn the moment I can and find myself facing the same hard-faced instructor I know so well. "Do you want me, Gareth? Or do you always get a hard-on when you fall off cliffs?"

"Don't forget your place, cadet." He straightens, his composure restored as if it'd never been shaken. "You need to report to the infirmary."

"They'll cycle me," I tell him quickly, needing to reach him again before we return to the world that keeps us apart. "You won't be my instructor anymore. I could rejoin another squadron—"

"You'll still be a cadet." Gareth shakes off his splendid wings, sending dust billowing into the air.

"At least I won't be *your* cadet."

"Oh, yes, you will."

"You don't know that!"

"I'll ensure it," he says harshly.

"Why?" Tears of frustration burn the back of my throat. "I don't understand you! Why are you fighting this so badly? We could have—"

It hits me then. Those odds of ending up in his squadron. The process of standing with the other recruits and awaiting the random selection of squadron number.

"You cheated the system!" I accuse. "You did something to get me assigned to you. And all this time I've been so angry at fate for giving me the wrong squadron number, and it was *you!* You've put the legion between us!"

His words lash out like a whip. "You're too gifted, Annalise. They'll exploit you to the fullest extent. You need to be better than you think you can be. Tougher, more lethal. You need to be as ready as it's possible to be."

The burn spreads to my chest. "You said the other instructors were equal to you," I remind him. "But you don't trust them with me, do you? I'm too important to you."

"You're important to the legion as a whole."

I step toward him, my hands extended imploringly. "Why won't you say it? Would it be so terrible to admit that you care about me?"

"*That's enough!*"

Gareth and I jerk in guilty surprise as Rebecca lands on the outcropping and strides into the cave, her silver wings reflecting light in brilliant spots along the dark rock walls. Her glare is so fierce it glows eerily, causing my stomach to knot.

"This," the captain growls, "stops now."

CHAPTER FOUR

"IT'S A GOOD THING you're nearly cleared to fly again," my brother says, throwing himself on my bed in a sprawl of orange-red wings that resemble flame. "There are rumors war is coming."

I look up from my book with a frown. The sun's rays warm me in my favorite window seat in my bedroom, the place that has become my refuge from Gareth's painful silence. I've been recuperating at home for nearly three months and have heard nothing from him the whole time.

"Who's talking about war?" I ask, setting my tablet aside on a mirrored end table. A tingle of unease ripples down my spine. When angels go to war, the whole world is scoured by their fury.

"All the cadets at the academy." Samuel shoves one of my decorative pillows under his head, making himself comfortable. His hair is the same color as mine, the dark gold strands framing a strong face and soft green eyes. "The new rotation started this week, but Commander Gareth isn't teaching. Can you think of any other reason why they wouldn't have their best instructor training new recruits? He's got to be preparing for something bigger."

I sit up. *Or he's being punished. Because of me.*

"Is he at court?" I fear for him if he is. Everyone knows that the archangels' court is deadlier than a battlefield.

"That's what I heard. I'm seriously thinking about heading in to the capitol to get the scoop for myself. You're going to be cleared for duty in the next week or so, and then my leave will be over. I've got to go now if I'm going at all."

"I'll go with you."

He grins. "Fat chance. You're only authorized to be home. No way Mom's going to let you leave."

"So we won't tell her."

"Ha!" Samuel sits up. "I'm not getting in trouble for you.

Besides, you don't want to risk a relapse. Flying long-distance now could set you back to square one."

"If we're going to war, I'll need to be airborne sooner rather than later," I argue. "Anyway, you're only on leave to be with me."

He pushes to his feet. "Guilt trips won't work. Let me find out what's going on before you get all worked up. I'll call you when I have news."

"Samuel." I stand, too. "I *need* to go."

I need to talk to Gareth. I need him to tell me what's going on.

My brother shrugs. "Fine. You get Mom to give the okay, and we'll go together."

"Deal."

Samuel takes off first thing in the morning. I stand beside our mother while he ascends powerfully and gracefully into the sky, my wings twitching with the need to stretch and lift me along with him.

Unfortunately, my mother couldn't be swayed, even after I confided in her. It isn't right for me to chase after the commander, she says. When and if he's ever ready, Gareth will come to me.

My brother waves before darting away, leaving me standing alone after my mother retreats inside. Unable to bear another moment trapped within the walls of my bedroom, I turn my back to the house and stalk off through the garden, heading toward the untamed land beyond.

Our home sits on a seaside cliff, bordered by billowing grasses and endless views. In centuries past, smugglers used the caves at the shoreline to secrete contraband into the country. Now, the coast is entrusted to my mother and policed by those who serve under her command.

Reaching the edge, I close my eyes and feel the salt-tinged breeze tug at me. If he's lost his command, will Gareth ever forgive me? He's given his whole life to the legion, even sacrificing whatever feelings he has for me.

"I won't always be around to catch you, Annalise."

My eyes fly open. Gareth hovers over the drop, his massive

wings beating in rhythmic silence. He's dressed in jeans and a white T-shirt, and I stare greedily, never having seen him in anything other than a uniform. My heart begins to ache, bleeding from the image of him so casual and at ease. I want this side of him. I want all of him.

"And that's the problem, isn't it?" I step back. "That's the reason you won't be with me."

He lands in the space I create for him, folding his wings. He stands majestically before me, so tall and dark, a commanding presence. Awareness thrums in my blood, a visceral reaction to the sexual magnetism he projects so effortlessly. I remember the feel of him against my back, so hot and hard. His steely control only makes his innate sensuality all the more compelling.

I look at Gareth and want sex. He makes me crave the darkest and most decadent pleasures.

"I'd heard you were at court," I say.

"Obviously not."

My feathers ruffle with irritation and his gaze darkens.

"Why are you here, Gareth?"

"I live here. Just around the inlet."

Surprise has me blinking. "Since when?" My mother would've known, but she said nothing.

"This will be my fifth summer." He watches me like a hawk as that information sinks in. "I visited once and found a reason to stay."

Me. He has to be talking about me. It was five years ago that he came to visit Samuel. Five years since I first realized that Gareth is everything I want.

I stumble back from the blow, my eyes stinging. Then I turn away and rush toward the house.

"Annalise!" he calls after me.

"No!" I round on him. "I've *pined* for you! Cried over you. Prayed for you to notice me. And now you tell me you've wanted me this whole time!"

He catches me by the elbows and yanks me close. "Your mother is a legend. Your father was, too. Samuel graduated at the top of his class. There was no way you weren't going to be drafted, whether you realized it or not."

Tears burn the backs of my eyes. "Go away!"

"When I accepted your mother's invitation to scout you, I expected to find the next generation of a great lineage of warriors. Instead, I found my mate. And the one woman I couldn't claim as my own. Too many people wanted a piece of you."

"And the legion's needs always come first," I say bitterly. "Don't they?"

Gareth shakes me. "I'm here, aren't I? I resigned my commission."

I freeze. "*What?*"

"I was going to push through until you graduated, but I realized in that damned cave that you were suffering without me, and I couldn't stand it."

My brain scrambles to grasp what he's saying. "I assumed you got in trouble ..."

"For what? I did nothing wrong, Annalise. The captain knows that. She knows me."

My wings sag, the ends settling on the ground. "I went to the academy *for you*. If you'd told me how you felt five years ago—"

"You need the legion as much as it needs you. It's in your blood." He tucks a windblown strand of hair behind my ear, his touch achingly gentle. "And you were too young. You needed time."

"It's been three months since that day in the cave." I can't hide the accusation in my voice.

"I was still an instructor. I couldn't reach out to you until I was free to."

I push away and he lets me go. Gareth needs the legion, too. But he's given it up. For love. "I need to think."

His jaw tightens, but he nods. "This could be our beginning, Annalise."

The words are spoken as a statement, but his gaze searches mine for confirmation.

It breaks my heart that I can't give it to him.

CHAPTER FIVE

MOONLIGHT ILLUMINATES THE SHORT flight from my family's home to the one I've learned is Gareth's. Before seeking him out, I spent the afternoon pacing the grounds, mentally searching for a way to have everything and to have it now. But the truth is obvious and, eventually, unavoidable.

Our paths are meant to crisscross, weaving through and around the legion. He is meant to lead, to teach. Someday, maybe I'll be able to join him. But not for many years and at least one war.

His home glows with golden light in the semidarkness. It juts out from the cliffside in three wide tiers, protected on every side but the front. Modern and sleek, it isn't what I would've picked for him, and yet it fits him perfectly.

I land on the highest deck and find myself staring directly into his bedroom. A large bed waits on the right, while a massive TV screen hangs on the natural rock wall on the left. Two passageways are dug into the earth; one leads to a just-visible bathroom and the other to the top of a staircase.

I've never seen anything like it, and awe fills me as I pass through the opening in the glass, a sliding partition that was left ajar. My gaze goes to the bed, my mind imagining being tangled with Gareth there.

"Annalise."

I look toward the sound of his voice as he enters the room from the stairway. My pulse quickens at the sight of him shirtless and barefooted, his long legs covered in the jeans he'd worn earlier. My gaze slides over the hard ridges of his abdomen and up to the powerful definition of his pectorals. Dark hair dusts his chest and arrows below the denim waistband, teasing me by drawing my eye to the thick heft of his cock beneath his button fly.

He studies me as thoroughly. I see when he comprehends the significance of the unsubstantial wrap dress I'm wearing on such a cool night. I can be naked in a moment, bared to his hands. His mouth. His cock.

"Your home is amazing," I say as the tension builds between us. His gaze is hot like flame, his lips parted with breaths that are nearly as quick as mine.

"I had it built for you. For us."

A sharp pain twists in my chest. How unfair that he's saying everything I've dreamed of at the very moment I have to say good-bye. I suddenly want to know how the plumbing works, and the power; how he looks cooking at the stove and sprawled on the couch. All the little and big details that would make the home—and him—feel like mine.

"You were very sure of me."

"No." He keeps his distance, waiting. "I was sure of how *I* felt."

"You forced me to confess my love at the academy."

He shoves his hands in his pockets. "You wanted to transfer away from me and said you loved another man. I understood why but still ..."

"You slept with Commander Jessica."

Gareth's brows rise. "Long ago."

Jealousy eats at me. "Not that long ago."

"Before you. There's been no one since."

"I saw you together. At the academy."

"Did you?" A soft smile curves his lips and makes my heartbeat skip. "Is that why you requested the transfer?"

I say nothing, irritated that he won't admit to the crime I've judged him guilty of.

"You saw one old friend telling another that the nature of their relationship will never be what it once was."

I study him, believing him, just as I always have. I love him for so many reasons. His integrity is just one of them. I acknowledge the truth with a nod. "I suppose you're not home very often."

"We'll make time, Annalise," he says, understanding what I'm thinking.

My wings flex with agitation, and it affects him. I see his eyes darken and his body harden, thick veins coursing between tense muscles and golden skin. He looks primal and dangerous. I feel the need radiating from him. He's a sexual creature, one hundred percent pure male, and he's saved himself for me for five long years.

I can't fully grasp the how and why, but I'm grateful.

"Have you decided I'm not worth the effort?" he asks quietly.

"Gareth, you're worth the world. But you've proven that you won't let me give it up for you. And I won't let you give up your career. So what's left?"

"This." He steps toward me. "Whatever hours and days we can spare. They're worth a thousand years I could spend with anyone else."

My vision grows misty. "We've wasted so much time."

"Not wasted. You've grown. Changed. I could've held you back if I loved you less, but I want you to soar, Annalise. When you land and catch your breath, I just want to be your refuge. That's all."

My hand lifts to my heart, which hurts. "That's everything."

I'm in his arms before I know it, my fingers in his silky black hair—finally—and my mouth on his. He takes over instantly. His hand grips my nape, his palm cups the curve of my buttock, lifting me into the grind of his hips. His tongue licks inside me, stroking, demanding. I'm possessed. Captured. *Claimed.*

I grow wet between my legs and ache with emptiness. I hook one leg around his lean hips, and he understands, pulling me up so that I'm wrapped around him and the hardness of his erection is pressed against me. Shameless, I rub my sex against his cock, moaning into his ravenous kiss, swallowing the rough growls that rumble through his chest.

Gareth starts carrying me toward the bed. Pulling back, I look at him. His face is hard with lust, his jaw tight with determination. I can see questions in his gaze, but they're not going to stop him from taking me. I've waited so long for him to want me despite everything that says he shouldn't.

Seeing that obstinacy is proof enough for me to damn the consequences. For the moment, he's mine. No one has any claim on him; no rules restrict him. I'm going to drain him, slake his hunger and indulge my own, even though tomorrow is even more uncertain than today.

The trailing edges of my wings touch the sapphire silk of his bedspread just before he lays me down like the most fragile of treasures. His lips brush across mine, then he whispers, "It'll hurt the first time. You'll be sore all the times after that. Forgive me in advance, Annalise. I can't promise I'll always be gentle. I can only promise to try."

My feathers ripple with anticipation. My fantasies of Gareth have never been girlish. I know him too well and love the reality of him, not an ideal. I know he's a hard man, one who sees the world in black and white. I know how fierce he is, how dangerous. Lethal. And I know that he will love and desire a woman with that same no-holds-barred intensity.

"Don't try too hard," I whisper, wanting him to rise with the sun with no regrets.

"Sweetheart." His eyes close as he takes a deep breath. His callused fingers go to the fly of his jeans, and he rips it open, revealing that he wears nothing underneath.

I swallow hard as my mouth waters, my mind etching into memory the sight of his leanly muscled body bared to me, his rigid erection thrusting upward between the opened halves of his jeans. He's brutally hard there, too, thick and long and as heavily veined as he is everywhere. His body is a machine, honed by hard use and dedication.

I can't wait to feel him against me. Inside me.

Shoving his pants down, he steps out of them and sets one knee on the bed, then the other, crawling over me. I spread my wings, opening space on either side of my hips.

"I cleave to you," he says hoarsely. "I will love you and protect you. I will lead and I will follow. I will fly with you and to you, now and forever."

Tears run down my temples and into my hair. I've dreamed of him saying the binding vows to me but gave that dream up only hours ago.

"I accept you," I tell him as he straddles me and sits back on his heels, his hands untying all the slender ribbons that fasten my dress.

He pushes the loosened edges out of his way. "Say the rest."

"Gareth ..." There's a plea in my voice I can't hide. How can I promise a future I can't picture?

"There will never be anyone else for you." His hands cup the lower curves of my breasts, his thumbs stroking over the hardened tips. "You'll vow that, Annalise. I'll hear you say it."

He's right. Whether we're together or not, he's the only man I could bind myself to. I can assure him of that, and I do. "I will love you and honor you. I will stand and fight beside you. I will fly with you and to you, now and forever."

With splayed hands, he pins my wings like a butterfly's on display, his knees sliding downward along the silk beneath me until his erection lays along the seam of my sex. I'm wet with desire, and he feels it, his tongue tracing the curve of his lower lip as he thrusts, the length of his cock stroking over the hard knot of my clit.

I writhe in pleasure, my hands going to his waist. I want to spread my legs, but he's holding me closed, forcing me to settle for his slow, rhythmic rubbing. Forcing me to watch the erotic play of his body over mine, his power and seductive beauty as his muscles flex from head to toe. A visual promise of his intent to drive me out of my mind.

Raking my nails over his skin, I grip the bunching curves of his gorgeous ass and urge him against me. His skin is feverishly warm and damp with sweat, flushed in a way it never gets while exerting himself in training. I know it's because of me that his blood runs so hot, and I'm awed by that, amazed that I could affect him so deeply.

"Yes," he hisses as I fight to move him in the way I need. "Show me how you want it."

"Gareth." I arch and moan as he massages my sex with his, the tension building in my core. "Inside me."

His lips curve. "Not until you come for me."

My eyes squeeze shut in protest, my hips rolling and shifting. The decadent smell of him fills me with every hurried breath, the scent of the wind and hunger and hard-working male.

"You're so beautiful," he whispers, his lips against my ear. "I've dreamed of you like this, fisted my cock imagining it until I came. Over and over again."

My mind is seared by the image of him pleasuring himself to thoughts of me. He rocks against me and captures a nipple between his teeth. It's too much.

With a long, low moan, I come for him, my sex clenching in demanding ripples that echo the pull of his mouth on my breast. His cheeks hollow as he tugs, the suction reverberating through me. I go wild beneath him, scratching and bucking, and he takes me then, shoving the steely length of his cock into the grasping depths of my core.

I cry out as he pierces me, stiffening against the sudden shock of pain. He groans my name and buries his hot face in my throat, shuddering violently.

"Annalise," he says brokenly, tucking his arms and legs tighter around mine. "I'm sorry."

Blinking through tears, I stare at the rough-hewn rock of the ceiling and absorb the feel of him inside me. My legs are held closed, his penetration only deep enough to claim me. I can't imagine him deeper, but I want him completely. I tighten around him and he gasps. His cock flexes, then spurts hotly.

He curses and comes, grinding into me, which sets me off again. I'm climaxing as he empties himself, milking the broad tip of his cock as it pumps thick washes of semen. It's a raw, swift orgasm, and I'm lost in it, in him, in the sounds he makes as the pleasure rocks him. He groans my name again and again, his sweat coating my skin, his lips pressing kisses against my violently throbbing pulse.

I grip his waist and sob with joy and sorrow, so desperately in love that I find it hard to breathe.

CHAPTER SIX

THE SUN ANGLES ACROSS the bed as Gareth rides me hard. I'm sprawled across tangled sheets, my legs shoved wide by the spread of his thighs, my fingers whitened by the grip of his hands linked with mine.

I can't hold back the moans of delight spilling from me. His cock plunges deep into my slick sex, his chest heaving against my back as he drives us both to orgasm. The rhythmic pumping of his penis through sensitive tissues is delicious. I'm addicted to the feel of it. Addicted to him.

The slap of his testicles against my swollen clit is maddening, the pounding of the headboard marking the desperate need between us. As the hours pass, we've grown greedier. He woke me twice with pleasure, once with his tongue and again with coaxing fingers. I woke him once with the ravenous pull of my mouth, taking him over the edge before he could deny me the taste of him.

"I'm coming," I gasp, my sex spasming in ecstasy.

Gareth growls like an animal and fucks harder, his cock thickening as I ripple along his length, begging for his climax. I'm drenched with him and still want more, but he holds back until I'm limp and unresisting, too drunk with pleasure to do more than lie there and take him.

I feel him stiffen and arch. His wings spread wide, flaring in passionate abandon, the iridescent feathers shutting out the world. He explodes inside me in a heated rush. His hands tighten painfully on mine, and he shoves deep, over and over, massaging the farthest reaches of my sex with the broad crest of his magnificent cock. I tremble in bliss, my mouth open in a silent cry, my heart bleeding from the breadth of love he's shown me. From the basest pleasures to the loftiest of emotions, I am all things to him, and he gives his all to me.

When he's drained, he rolls to the side and takes me with him, our bodies still joined and his wings a silky cocoon. I've learned he can't stop touching me. He's held me throughout the long night, whispering love words and sex words, telling me how good it feels inside me and how he's felt being with me. I can't reconcile the lover with the teacher; they're two different men. One so remote as to be unreachable and the other so intimate I can't tell where he ends and I begin.

"This is only the beginning," he insists with his hand clasped over my wildly racing heart.

"I can't keep you."

"You don't have a choice. I'm already yours."

I stare out the massive windows and dream of waking every morning just like this. I should have gone home before sunrise, before I'd be missed. But I don't regret the hours I've stolen, knowing how few and how precious they will be.

"Annalise," he prods, rubbing his cheek against the curve of my wing. "Can you live without this? I can't."

"You'll have to," I say flatly. "You'll wake up alone more often than not, until you resent me enough to take another woman to bed."

"I don't need to fuck. I need you."

"I don't know why."

I feel his smile. "And that's why you're afraid. You don't see how you inspire me. I'd reached the point where I believed violence and death were my only reasons for existing. And then I found you, and I knew what I was created for. Didn't you feel it when you first saw me? Didn't something tell you that I belonged to you?"

Turning in his arms, I face him. The evidence of his pleasure seeps from me, a primitive claiming that even now could be creating a new life. Had he thought of that during the night? Had he hoped?

I brush the sweat-slicked hair back from his proud forehead, reveling in my right to touch him so intimately. "Yes, I felt it."

His brilliant eyes glow with satisfaction. "So we'll make it work."

"How?"

"If the archangels want us badly enough, they'll take us on our terms."

Fear chills my skin. There is only one set of rules, and the archangels write them.

"You have to trust me, sweetheart." He rubs the tip of his nose against mine. "I'll never do anything that puts you at risk."

Chimes ring out and I jerk in surprise. "What's that?"

"A visitor." His chest expands slowly, and I watch a change come over him, the lover giving way to the warrior. "Sooner than expected, but I'm not sorry about that."

"Gareth—" Of course he'd be pursued. He was too valuable to just walk away.

He slides from my arms, pressing kisses over my heart, tummy, and the pout of my sex before he leaves the bed. I watch him pull on his jeans, his skin still glistening with sweat. He smells like sex and me, and doesn't care. The pride in his bearing is obvious, his eyes hard with determination.

I realize he'd take on the world for me.

He pauses at the foot of the bed. "Stay here."

The next moment, I'm alone and he's gone downstairs. I hear voices as I dress quickly, his low and deep and another that's higher pitched and clearly female. I'm heading down before I can think better of it, my bare feet silent on the cold stone floor.

"She'll have to graduate before I can turn this coast over to her. You know that."

I stumble to a halt as I recognize my mother's voice.

"I'm not holding her back," Gareth replies. "When it's time for her to return to the academy, I'll see her there myself."

"And what about you? Will you return to duty with her?"

"I could be persuaded."

Peeking around the corner, I see my mother standing just inside the sliding glass partition leading outside to the second landing tier. She's dressed in her uniform, the gold stripes of her rank not too dissimilar from the color of her wings. Her blond hair is pulled back in a neat chignon, and her sea-colored eyes remain fixed on the angel who holds my heart in his hands.

"What do you want, Commander?" she asks.

"As I told you years ago, I want your daughter. And she wants me nearby. If she's going to be here, here is where I need to be."

My knees weaken. I sink down to sit on the step. There's been speculation for years about my mother. She's in a prime position for advancement, has been long overdue for one. But she'd have to serve some time at court, and to do that, she needed a second to hold her interests here.

"This coast will be defended by my children," my mother says icily. "Binding with my daughter won't secure it for you."

I push to my feet.

"He wants to train here," I interject, entering the room. My eyes are only on him. "That's what you're suggesting, isn't it, Gareth? A satellite academy."

The fierce look of love he gives me tells me I'm right. "It's a prime location for marine aerial training."

My mother glares at me while she takes in my ravished appearance, but there's love there, too. "I expected a binding first, Annalise."

"He gave me his vows."

"And you gave him everything."

I glance at Gareth and see warm amusement in his eyes. He is cocky and shameless, and I fall a little more in love with him. "Did you know what my mother wanted?"

He must have suspected I'd be assigned a tour of duty here. I hadn't factored in my mother's career—and influence—but he would have. Gareth was, after all, a widely admired strategist.

He shrugs. "I hoped. Planned to make the suggestion, if necessary."

My mother makes an exasperated noise. "There's no guarantee my requests will be honored."

"You're overdue many favors, General," Gareth says, coming to my side. "I think you'll manage well when you call them in."

"And your terms," she queries, "are nonnegotiable?"

I take his hand and smile. "They are."

Sylvia Day is the #1 *New York Times* and #1 international bestselling author of over 20 award-winning novels sold in more than 40 countries. She is a #1 bestselling author in 23 countries, with tens of millions of copies of her books in print. Her Crossfire series has been optioned for television by Lionsgate, and she has been honored with multiple nominations for Romance Writers of America's prestigious RITA® Award.

www.sylviaday.com

ALL I WANT

ERICA RIDLEY

USA Today Bestseller

ANOTHER ELEGANT SOIRÉE, ANOTHER flesh-crawling pro-
posal from a money-hungry suitor old enough to be Matilda's father.

Despite her heeled slippers, Lady Matilda Kingsley fairly sprinted to the gaming parlor. She wanted nothing more than to run
home and forget her troubles in the comfort of a good book. But to
get there, she needed Cousin Egbert. She'd been his ward for most
of her life.

He'd been a wastrel for all of his. He was a fixture at every gaming table and gambling hell across the city. Worst of all, he had the
devil's own luck. He wouldn't leave a table until everyone else's coin
clinked inside his pockets, which sometimes took well past dawn.

Matilda's footsteps slowed. Was that Cousin Egbert, swathed in
cigar smoke and wrinkled linen, standing with one foot inside the
gaming parlor and one foot out? Was he motioning her *forward*?

She stopped walking. Usually *she* was the one found hovering at
a doorway, vainly trying to signal him she was ready to leave, without letting her toes cross the thin threshold from proper ballroom to
scandalous gaming parlor. To do so would be to court scandal. And
yet, here he was—beckoning her to join him. Something was very
peculiar. Her neck tingled. All her senses were on high alert.

She ventured only as far as the doorjamb and laid her hand on
her cousin's arm.

"I want to go home," she murmured. "Please, cousin. It's been a long night."

Their unspoken arrangement was that if she managed to catch his attention, he was obliged to take her back to the townhouse. But this time, he shook his head. His eyes were cold and hard, his easy smile distorted and mean. Her stomach twisted. She hadn't seen that expression on his face in years, but she well knew what it meant: there'd be no talking him out of whatever trouble he was brewing. And he meant to involve her in the thick of it.

"*Please*," she repeated, though she knew it was useless. His eyes were too glassy. But she had to try. "The music is over. Can we not go home?"

"Of course," he said, but his harsh smile only widened. "I'm just finishing a game of chance. If you'll play my last hand, we can be on our way."

Her heartbeat stuttered, then sped to new heights. What could he mean? If crossing the threshold was scandalous, gambling would be ruinous. It could only be a trick. But why? And on whom?

"You ... wish for me to wager?" Her throat was too dry to swallow properly.

He smiled. "Just play one hand. Then I'll take you home. I promise." He gripped her by the wrist and pulled her into the candlelit parlor.

Her muscles locked up. She shouldn't be anywhere near this room. Or these men.

Smoke rose from the fingers and mouths of every gentleman present, making the air thick and sickly sweet from the fumes of their cigars. A gaggle of dandies encircled what she assumed to be a gaming table. Two dozen sotted spectators in linen superfine and buckskin breeches surrounded the whole.

They parted to let her through.

The table was small, round, and empty, save for a folded slip of paper and a set of playing cards stacked to one side. A soldier sat at one of the two wooden chairs, his back to Matilda. His broad shoulders and defined muscles filled out his pristine red coat. Golden epaulets and matching stars marked him as an officer. She jerked her gaze toward her cousin. His vicious smile etched deeper into his face as he hauled her in plain sight of the soldier's face.

Owen Turner.

The roiling in her stomach bubbled over into nausea. She reached out to steady herself. Someone shoved her into the empty chair. She tried not to look, not to stare, but her eyes had hungered for the merest glimpse of him for so, so long …

He was beautiful. The first friend she'd ever made. The only boy she'd ever loved. A good four years older since last she saw him, his heartrendingly familiar face now belonged to a man she no longer knew.

The dark brown curls that had once fluttered in the morning wind and stuck to his forehead when caught in a sudden shower were now neatly clipped at the ears and nape, as befitting an officer. No. Not an officer. A *major*.

Clear blue eyes that had once sparkled merrily as they raced across moors or jumped into the river—those beloved blue eyes were now stormy and shadowed, no trace of merriment in their depths or etched at the corners. And why would there be? He'd fought Napoleon's army for four long years only to find himself battling her cousin Egbert in a gilded parlor.

Her throat tightened. It had been Owen who taught her to skip rocks and climb trees, but for all his comparative world-liness, neither one of them had ever expected him to step foot outside North Yorkshire's borders. Above all, she'd never thought he'd leave her. To see him here, a grown man, a celebrated soldier, even more dashing in the flesh than the stories upon everyone's tongues …

Ah, the gossip.

She wasn't the only one he'd dazzled. If half the rumors were true, those hard, beautiful lips had kissed every willing mouth between here and Paris. If it didn't make her violently ill just thinking about it, she might appreciate the irony that the boy Society had once considered beneath them was now the primary reason smelling salts were in higher demand than breakfast tea.

He was known for giving pleasure to everyone and his heart to no one, vie as women might to catch the uncatchable. But there was no hope of corralling a force of nature. Owen was a tempest, not a summer rain. He was passion and power, a storm in the soul ... and just as quickly gone.

She should know.

Other than keeping his piercing eyes focused on hers, he hadn't moved since she'd sat down. Hadn't smiled. Hadn't offered his hand. Hadn't even spoken her name. By all appearances, he neither recognized her nor cared for an introduction.

She knew better.

His very stillness was as telltale as other men's nervous tics. Whenever he was on edge, a life in the shadows had taught him to go silent and still. Not like a deer or a rabbit. Like a lion. Eyeing his prey. Preparing to strike.

Whatever was going on here, she wanted no part of it. She pushed to her feet.

Egbert stopped her with one hand atop her shoulder. A cold sweat broke out beneath her stays.

"What's this about?" Her voice trembled as she eased back into the seat.

"A gentleman's wager." Egbert waved his hand toward the table. "Except this *gentleman* dared question my integrity. Rather than meet him at dawn and sully a bullet with his blood, I have chosen to let an impartial stand-in play the final hand. *You.*"

Her jaw clenched so tight her teeth hurt. "I am scarcely impartial."

Owen's voice was smooth velvet, smothering as it caressed. "Whose side might you be on?"

"My own," she snapped. Or meant to snap. She had loved him for so long and he had broken her heart so carelessly that his mere presence was enough to twist her into a knot of hate and desire.

"I see." His shoulders relaxed infinitesimally. "I trust you."

That slight movement twisted her heart. He *did* trust her, damn him. If only she could say the same. "What is the game?"

His eyes softened. "*Vingt-et-un.*"

Twenty-one. She took a deep breath.

One of the dandies elbowed his way forward. "That's French for—"

"She speaks French, you ninny." A different blackguard raised his voice. "I'd be a richer man if Lady Matilda would cease translating Parisian fashion plates to my sister. Now, if one of you gents would like to *explain* the game instead of translating the—"

"She already knows." Owen's voice was quiet but laced with a thread of danger that silenced the entire room.

Matilda's breathing slowed. He'd taught her to play as a jest and regretted the decision when she took an immediate fancy. He hated games of chance. Which meant an exceptional turn of events must have driven him to this table.

She rubbed the back of her neck. "What are the stakes?"

Owen's voice was even, his face impassive. "Addington bet five thousand pounds."

She pinched her lips together. A pittance for Cousin Egbert, but unspeakable riches to Owen. "And you? What did you wager?"

"His *cottage*," spat one of the onlooking Corinthians with disdain. "He hasn't anything else."

His companions rolled their eyes in agreement. "I can't fathom why Addington would even want it."

Matilda could.

The little cottage would mean nothing to a wealthy peer, but it was everything to Owen. A gift from his father to his mother. It was all he owned. His sole link to his heritage. The only place he could call home.

Her nails bit into her palms. This had nothing to do with money, then. At least not for her cousin. This was a continuation of a four-year-old brawl, in an arena where Egbert held the upper hand. She could not stop them. But since she was at the root of their animosity, she would not contribute to Egbert's cruel games.

She made her decision. "I'm in. But if I play, I play for keeps. Any spoils I win belong to me."

The crowd roared with delight. "Already counting how many gowns she can purchase with five thousand pounds, is she? Her modiste is going to be richer than I am."

"Gowns?" Egbert scoffed. "More like *novels*. While the lot of you are queuing up for a spot on her dance card, I'm dragging her out of the library by her bluestockinged feet. This chit would rather spend her nights with gothic melodrama than be twirled about by *you* pups."

More laughter erupted. "You're the marquess. Sell off the library so she has more time for her lovesick swains."

"Sorry, lads. You'll have to win her on your own." Egbert grinned down at her. "Of course, cousin. Anything you win is yours."

Matilda's shoulders tightened. Her cousin's teasing comments had been delivered with obvious affection, but she could not forgive him. Not for this farce he'd dragged her into unawares. And not for the devastation he'd wrought four long years ago.

She turned to face Owen, whose body was perfectly still.

Cousin Egbert reached for the cards. "Shall we begin?"

CHAPTER TWO

"STOP." THE QUIET STEEL in Major Owen Turner's voice belied the torment churning within him.

Addington's ungloved hand paused above the set of cards. Silence engulfed the room. The only movement came from plumes of smoke fleeing expensive cigars and the fluttering pulse point upon the neck of the only woman who had ever cracked Owen's armor.

"I have to deal the cards for you to play, *Major*." Addington spat the word as if it left ash upon his tongue. "My cousin wishes to retire. We cannot stay here all night."

Owen didn't bother to acknowledge this last. Addington was in no hurry to escort his cousin anywhere. He was too eager to deny Owen something he wanted.

Again.

"I don't trust you to deal honestly." Owen's words ricocheted through the hushed room. For Addington, they would hold a double meaning.

Shock and a touch of eagerness widened the onlookers' eyes, but no one stepped backward to make room for a mill. Not here. These were "gentlemen." Peers didn't solve problems person-to-person, a flurry of fists followed by a handshake. They preferred dueling pistols at twenty paces. One shot, straight to the heart.

Addington's fingers curled, but he crossed his arms beneath the frosty white of his cravat before his hands could become fists. "*You* certainly won't be touching the cards, *Major*."

Ah. There it was. Owen almost smiled. By the nervous titter elsewhere in the room, he was not the only one who knew precisely what Addington meant every time he spat the word "major." For most people, the soldiers who fought Napoleon were heroes. Never Owen. No military title, no heroics or self-sacrifice, no amount of medals could ever erase the blight cast upon him at the moment of his conception.

Nothing he could ever do or achieve would stop him from being gutter-bred Owen Turner. Bastard of a duke. Son of a whore.

"Not me." Owen inclined his head toward the other end of the small table. "Her."

Her. Although he still hadn't brought himself to speak her name aloud, it had never been far from his thoughts. Or his soul.

Lady Matilda Kingsley. He'd met her when he was ten and she was eight. Her pinafore had cost more than all his clothes combined. She'd escaped her sleeping nanny and was deep in the back garden in search of adventure. He'd been crouched on her side of the property line, peering through the fence at the adjacent estate in hopes of glimpsing his father.

He'd found something much better.

"Very well." Lady Matilda's voice was smoother than he remembered. More refined, like everything else about her.

She was no longer the lonesome sixteen-year-old he'd left behind, but a grown woman who captured the eye of every gentleman who crossed her path.

Like right now.

She was removing her gloves. Inch by bollocks-tightening inch, the rolling crimson silk revealed ever more of her perfect, creamy skin. Those fingers might be oft employed in the flipping of pages, but every man in the room was imagining them doing something very, very different.

The first glove fell to the table in a pool of red silk. She turned her attention to the second glove. They *all* turned their attention to the second glove. Its unveiling was even more deliberate, more sensuous than the first. Her lashes lowered. She held every eye transfixed ... and knew it.

His lips tightened. This seductress was not the fresh-faced innocent he'd left behind. That girl was gone. The Lady Matilda seated across from him was a stranger.

And yet he was here because of her.

"*Vingt-et-un,*" Addington reminded her the moment the second glove hit the table.

She leveled him with a freezing look. "I haven't forgotten."

Owen glanced away as she shuffled the cards. He could not risk catching her eye and seeing indifference reflected back at him. Not if he wished to walk away with his heart intact. He let out a slow breath and fought to keep up his spirits.

His evening had wanted only this.

He'd been stationed all over France and was finally back in England on a two-week leave. He'd gone straight to North Yorkshire, straight to Selby, straight to her.

She wasn't there, of course. She was already in London for the Season. But rather than continue on to his empty cottage, he'd first swung by the baker's to retrieve his dog. He'd found Ribbit the same day he'd met Lady Matilda. He'd been able to keep Ribbit. When he'd enlisted in the army, he'd entrusted his half basset hound, half lump of molasses to Mrs. Jenkins and sent considerable funds for Ribbit's safekeeping.

But Mrs. Jenkins had lost the dog within days of Owen leaving.

As if it could possibly make up for it, she had presented him with a coin purse containing every penny he had ever sent. He'd brought the money back to London, intending to throw it away on whiskey and women until it was time to sail back to France. But he'd found himself rubbing shoulders with the very people who had never before noticed his existence. People who now included Lady Matilda.

Tonight, when he'd seen her a-swirl in another man's arms, he'd been struck with a yearning so sharp and so deep he'd had to force himself not to yank her into his own embrace. A mad scheme had tumbled into his head. He'd hurried to the gaming parlor, intent on turning the funds he'd meant for his dog into a gift for his lady. If he won enough coin, perhaps then he would be worthy of her affection.

But instead of luck, all he'd found in the gambling parlor was Lord Addington, who was all too eager to divest Owen of his money. Addington's eyes were as cold as Owen remembered, his nose as crooked as Owen had left it four years ago. Addington hadn't forgiven Owen the slight. Owen hadn't forgiven Addington the reason behind it.

Lady Matilda placed the set of playing cards in the center of the table. She lifted a palm toward Owen, then folded her hands back into her lap.

He divided the stack into three piles, then placed them back together. His entire body was on edge. He'd led troops, faced down enemy squadrons, taken a bullet in the thigh, and he was never more nervous than when in her presence. It'd been thus since the day they met.

She'd introduced herself as Lady Matilda. She'd dipped a curtsy, then taken him to task when he didn't bow. Why should he? He'd never been taught to bow. Or been curtsied to. He'd been mortified by his failure to please her. From that day forward, his dream no longer was to be acknowledged by the father he'd never met but to meet with approval in the eyes of Lady Matilda Kingsley.

For a short time, he'd even succeeded.

"Ready?" Her fingers hovered just above the stack of playing cards.

No. He would never be ready. If he hadn't been willing to lose the game to Addington, he certainly wasn't eager to risk losing in front of the woman he most wished to impress.

"Ready." He hoped his grimace counted as a smile.

She turned over the first card and placed it before him.

One-eyed jack. Spades, not hearts. Ten points. Owen rubbed his damp palms down the soft buckskin of his breeches. So far, so good. He held his breath. The next card was hers.

Eight of diamonds.

Not splendid, but not terrible. He rolled his shoulders back. His score might be closer to twenty-one at the moment, but he wasn't closer to winning. He needed to be closest to twenty-one without going over.

"Bets?" Addington called out. His mocking eyes cut to Owen.

Owen cast him a level stare. The blackguard *knew* Owen didn't have anything left to bet. He'd already bet it all. Addington just wanted to parade Owen's unsuitability in front of Lady Matilda.

She was the first to reply, her voice firm. "No more bets. The stakes are high enough."

Owen's spine went rigid. She'd saved him. But she shouldn't have needed to. A sour taste filled his mouth. Addington had been right after all. Owen *wasn't* good enough for her. Yet the truth didn't stop him from wanting her. Or wanting her to know how he felt. His heart clenched. When he won the game, he would buy her what she desired most. And then ... he would file onto a boat and sail back off to war.

She lifted the next card and placed it next to his jack of spades.

Eight of clubs. Not bad. He was up to eighteen. He would stand here. Taking a hit with anything higher than seventeen was to risk losing it all.

Her next card was the ace of spades.

His lungs froze. The ace was either one or eleven, which meant she now had nineteen points. She was winning. His skin went clammy. Gambling was a rich man's pleasure and a poor man's folly. Never had it been more apparent that he didn't belong here. His throat was too thick to swallow. But like it or not, he would have to take another hit.

He inclined his head toward the stack of cards. He did not trust his finger to point at them without shaking.

He needed a three. Dear Lord, let him have a three. Surely Fate wouldn't strip him of his pet, his home, his dignity, and his last moments with his lost love all on the same day.

Lady Matilda turned over the final card.

Even though his eyes were open, even though he was staring right at it, the image did not immediately register in Owen's mind.

It didn't have to. Addington's crow of delight and sputtering laughter was proof enough.

Owen blinked at the card until it swam into focus. Five of hearts. Wrong number.

He had lost.

Lady Matilda reached across the table. "Owen—"

He leapt to his feet before her bare fingers could scald his. Or worse. Her cousin wasn't the only witness to her familiar use of Owen's given name, and he'd be damned if he ruined her on top of being a disappointment.

He gripped the back of his chair. "If I leave now, I can have the cottage clear within a week."

Addington pealed with laughter. "What possessions can you possibly own that would need to be cleared out? That dilapidated shack is only fit to be razed to the ground."

"I'll do no such thing!" Lady Matilda glared at him.

Her cousin was, in all fairness, likely correct. Owen didn't see his childhood home as a dilapidated shack because he'd remodeled every inch with his bare hands. To a marquess, however, the cottage would be nothing short of laughable. And to Lady Matilda—

"*Ciao.*" Addington wiggled his fingers at Owen. "Long walk ahead, since you haven't any coin for a hack."

The crowd tittered.

Owen bowed instead of replying, which he knew would rile Addington the most. The marquess was obviously trying to egg him into saying or doing something rash. But Owen had spent four dark years serving his country. Self-control was one of the first things he'd learned.

Not that it mattered overmuch. He'd never see Addington or Lady Matilda again. Instead, in another week's time, he'd go back to battle. Just another soldier who no longer had any home or anyone to return to.

He turned his gaze toward Lady Matilda one last time.

She glanced away.

He was not even to have eye contact, then. Very well. Owen stood straighter. He'd been foolish to think he could ever be worthy of her, for even a moment. Had he won instead of lost, had it been five million pounds instead of five thousand, it still wouldn't have changed the essence of who and what they were. She was a lady. He was a bastard. They would never be equals.

She could never be his.

CHAPTER THREE

LADY MATILDA DIDN'T WAIT until the weekend, nor for her cousin's approval. She needed to speak to Owen before she lost the chance forever. Last time, he had not bothered to say good-bye before disappearing. This time, he would not be so lucky. She might not merit his love, but she certainly deserved an explanation.

Before first light, she arranged for a carriage and tore out of London toward North Yorkshire. With luck, Cousin Egbert would be too involved in his gentlemanly pursuits to note her absence until at least the morrow. All the posting houses had known her family for years and would do what they could to speed her along, but their country home in Selby was still two and a half days' journey.

When she arrived at Owen's small cottage in the poorest section of town, she asked the driver to return in an hour's time. Despite her being the daughter of a duke—or perhaps because of it—he refused to leave. The carriage would remain out front, and that was final.

Matilda had no choice but to acquiesce.

Whether the driver feared for her life or her reputation, she couldn't say. But Owen was only fearsome in battle, and as for her reputation ... Well, she was unlikely to run into anyone of her social circle on a street such as this. And even should she find herself immortalized in gossip rags, there was no scandal powerful enough to undo the allure of marrying a young lady with a thirty-thousand-pound dowry.

She held no illusions about her appeal. Her name and her money were the only reasons any eligible bachelor took an interest. Were it not for her fortune and bloodline, she would be just another plain-faced wallflower, with no friends save the ones she found in books. That was the way the world worked.

Owen was the only one who had ever treated her like something more than a title and a purse. All he saw in her was a friend. During every one of her nanny's afternoon naps, Matilda had shot straight out the servants' exit to the secret meeting place in the backwoods. Owen taught her to whistle and trounced her at chess. She taught him his sums and read to him from books nicked from her father's library.

Until he disappeared without a word.

She needed to know why.

But now that she was here, standing atop the stoop she'd only visited once before in her life—right after his disappearance—she couldn't quite bring herself to lift the brass knocker. Last time, her call had gone unanswered because he'd joined the army without so much as a fare-thee-well. And this time ... What if he stood on the other side of the plain wooden door and still didn't care enough to answer her knock? How would she go on?

She lowered her hand.

The door flew open.

"What the *devil* are you doing here?" Owen. Furious and handsome beyond words.

Her body tingled all the way to her fingertips. He was not what one might call pleased to see her, but at least he wouldn't be leaving without saying good-bye. "Good afternoon to you, too."

She elbowed past him. Or tried to. He was a fortress, tall and unmovable. He filled the doorway. His strong arms locked around her torso, preventing her from entering.

Or leaving.

She closed her eyes and breathed in deeply. When Owen was a boy, he'd been too poor to smell like anything other than soap and sunshine, but now the clean red wool of his military jacket bore the faint scent of cologne. Something rich and spicy.

A long moment later, he still hadn't moved. Nor did she wish to. She was pinned too well to wrap her arms about him as she wished. Instead, she laid her cheek against his chest and listened for the beat of his heart. But the thick wool blocked the sound. Even trapped in his arms, she still could not reach him.

He released her abruptly.

"I suppose you've come to have a look at the goods. And why not? It's yours." He didn't bother to hide the bitterness from his voice.

She hitched up her chin. She hadn't forced him to wager his childhood home on the turn of a card. Her shoulders sagged. Nor had he forced her to take a stance against him. She bit her lip. She'd only wished to prevent her cousin from having something else to lord over Owen, but all she'd managed to accomplish was to drive a wedge further between them.

"A tour, madam? Your mansion awaits." He brandished his arm as if he were escorting her into a royal palace. Both his tone and his grandiose movements dripped with sarcasm.

His anger was well placed. Nor could she blame him for being displeased with her unexpected appearance. But she had no choice. This was the last time she would ever see him. If she did not take his arm now, the opportunity to touch him, to stand by his side, would not present itself again.

She curved her fingers against the crook of his elbow before she could change her mind.

He tensed, his entire body still as stone.

She stared straight ahead without blinking. If his expression betrayed displeasure at her touch, she had no wish to see it. "Ready."

Without another word, he led her down the hall. He seemed to be avoiding her gaze as assiduously as she avoided his. The muscles of his arm had not relaxed. But although he controlled his steps with the precision of a soldier, his stride was nonetheless graceful.

He was comfortable with his body in a way he'd never been as a boy, she realized with a jolt of awareness. Back then, he had been awkward and carefree. Now, he moved with the confidence of a tiger. Lean and strong and devastating. Her heartbeat thundered. No wonder ladies everywhere swooned in his presence. The aura of controlled danger was irresistible. This was a man who knew what he wanted and took as he pleased. It would be heady indeed to be the object of such single-focused passion.

It would be her darkest desire come true.

She tugged his arm closer. "Let's make a new wager."

He stopped walking. "A new wager for what?"

"This. Everything." She rolled back her shoulders. "All or nothing."

His eyebrows arched. "You already have everything. What more would I have to offer?"

His heart. His soul. His love. She fumbled in her reticule and pulled out a stack of playing cards. His lip curled. She forged ahead. "One shuffle. Highest card takes all. If you win, you keep your house *and* the money you would've earned last night."

His eyes narrowed. "And if you win?"

"I'll tell you after." If she won, she would give it back anyway.

"No deal." He leaned away from her. "I don't gamble without knowing what I've wagered."

"What if we both do?"

His head jerked up. "Wager blind? Are you mad?"

"We can write down what we wish to receive if we win, and seal the bets with wax. Completely fair."

A laugh startled out of him. "The loser has no option to say no, regardless of the winner's choice of spoils, and you call that fair?"

She could see he had no intention of agreeing to something so risky. "Is that a no?"

He nodded. "It's a yes."

She blinked. "What?"

"I've paper at my escritoire. Come this way. We may as well start the tour with my bedchamber." Heat flashed in his eyes before he turned and strode down the corridor.

The shiver that raced down her spine was half panic, half desire. She rushed after him. She had just wished to return what was rightfully his in the one way he would feel honorable about accepting. What if she'd risked more than she was prepared to give?

She hurried through the open doorway.

He was already at his escritoire, dipping his pen in ink. A small bed stood to one side, a humble wardrobe at the other. The room was otherwise empty.

She crept forward, trying not stare too obviously at the bed, with its twin white pillows and one corner of a chestnut-colored blanket turned smartly down. It was simple but inviting, and she shouldn't have been able to see it. Much less wish to lie upon it in his embrace.

He dripped wax atop a folded scrap of paper, then rose to offer her the chair. "Your wager, my lady."

She slid a narrow-eyed glare in his direction but this time could find no trace of irony in his words or mien. Her stomach fluttered. With a final glance over her shoulder at the open doorway, she straightened her spine and crossed the last few feet to the waiting chair.

Owen leaned against the corner of his bed. He was too far away to touch, yet his gaze upon her stripped her as bare as if his rough hands were undressing her.

Her fingers shook as she reached for the pen. Somehow she managed to dip the nub in black ink and scratch out a few fairly legible words. When she blew on the paper to dry the ink, she caught his dark gaze out of the corner of her eye. He wasn't staring at the parchment but rather the pucker of her lips. His slow, arrogant smile melted her like honey in a kettle.

She folded the paper as quickly as her trembling fingers allowed and sealed the edge with candle wax.

"Here." She thrust the small square toward him without waiting for the wax to harden. "My wager."

He shook the wax dry, then rose to his feet. Her wager disappeared into his pocket along with his own folded square. He held out his arm. "Care to see the rest of the cottage? Or do you prefer we remain in the bedchamber?"

She leapt up from the escritoire and flew out into the corridor without accepting his proffered arm.

His low chuckle sent heat down her flesh. He followed her into the corridor and placed her fingers upon his sleeve before lowering his mouth to her ear. "A scoundrel can hope."

She glared at him. At least, she meant to. The problem was, she was less shocked by his scandalous suggestion and more disappointed that he hadn't meant it. Her cheeks burned. She'd waited almost one-and-twenty years for someone to kiss her, and thus far, no one had ever tried. She smiled bitterly. A spinster could hope.

He led her to the next chamber, hesitating only slightly before flinging open the door.

The room was completely empty.

She glanced up at him, a question surely writ upon her face.

"My mother's room." He didn't meet her eyes.

Her heart squeezed. "You must miss her terribly."

"She was my mother," he said simply.

No other words need be spoken. Matilda well knew the pain of losing a parent. She'd believed it the worst possible hell when she lost both her parents at a young age. Poor Owen. His father still lived but had never once acknowledged him. His mother was all he'd ever had. Losing her meant losing everything.

She held his arm a little closer to her side. "Must you go back to the army?"

He snorted softly. "What other choice is there?"

She plucked at the folds of her gown. "You could sell your commission."

"With no home to return to? Come. There are only two rooms left to show. First, the kitchen." He turned to look at her, his eyes hopeful. "Might you stay for luncheon?"

She shook her head. "I shan't put you to any trouble. I've a carriage out front, and—"

"Sit." He pushed her onto one of two battered stools flanking a scarred wooden table. "I learned to simmer broth and boil potatoes at my mother's knee, but I learned to *cook* in France." He stoked the fire beneath the stove, then shot her a mischievous grin. "I also learned ribald drinking songs, but I'm guessing you would appreciate the food more."

She stared in disbelief as he chopped and diced seemingly at random, tossing handfuls of ingredients into a sizzling skillet until the resulting aroma made her mouth water and her stomach clench in anticipation of a delicious meal.

It didn't disappoint.

"Anyone would hire you as a chef," she said once she'd eaten the last bite.

He wrinkled his nose. "Chefs don't get invited to nearly as many dinner parties as soldiers do."

She grinned despite herself. "A salient point."

He cleared the table and submerged the dishes into a basin to soak. "Ready for the last room?"

She nodded and allowed him to help her down off the stool.

He curled her fingers back on his arm—odd how much they felt like they belonged there—and led her into the corridor toward the final doorway. Like the other chambers, the door was closed tight. But unlike the others, he made no move to open it.

He turned to face her, his expression serious and his eyes unreadable. She had to force herself not to babble to fill the heavy silence. He took her hands in his, then dropped them just as quickly. She held her breath and waited.

"Lady Matilda …" He shoved his hands in his pockets for the briefest of seconds before reaching forward to take her hands once more. "Before I left, I called upon your cousin."

She nodded. "I know. You broke his nose."

"Yes, well, I …" Owen gripped her fingers harder. "What you don't know is *why*. I didn't drop by that day to fight with Addington. I came to ask for your hand. In marriage."

She nodded again. "I know. He told me."

"But then Addington said— What?" Owen dropped her hands in disbelief. "He told you I wanted to marry you?"

She folded her arms across her chest. "We're cousins. He keeps no secrets from me. That night, he sat me down and explained that any man who asked for my hand was actually asking for my money. He said a smart woman would exploit her wealth in exchange for the highest title her dowry could buy."

Owen's jaw dropped. "That's exactly what that halfwit said to *me*. That's why I punched him."

"But he's right." Matilda's voice was flat. "Every suitor I've ever had has been in want of more coin. They've made no attempt to hide it."

Owen grabbed her upper arms. "That doesn't mean it's the sole reason they court you."

Of course it was. But she lifted a shoulder and tried to hide how much the truth had always hurt. "What other reason is there?"

"Love, for one." He cupped her cheek. "Passion, for another."

He drew the pad of his thumb over her lower lip, and she shivered. "P-passion for me?"

"Only for you." He slid his fingers into her hair, his strong hands cradling her face. He lowered his lips until they touched just beside hers. "I've wanted you from before I even knew what that meant. I've spent years dreaming of you every night. Imagining your touch on my skin. Your lips beneath mine. Our bodies locked together."

She gasped. Or possibly panted. Her insides had melted, and she had to grip him tight just to stay upright. She leaned closer.

His lower lip was now low enough to graze the edge of her jaw as he spoke. "Lady Matilda, if you don't strike me across the face right this second, I'm going to kiss you senseless."

She gripped his waistcoat. "It's about bloody time."

Desire flashed hot in his eyes, and then his mouth was finally on hers.

Molten heat streaked inside her as his lips parted hers. His soft kisses became harder and more insistent as her body cleaved to his.

His fingers sank deep into her hair as he held her to him. He suckled her lower lip and then swept his tongue inside her mouth to claim her as his own.

She tightened her grip on his hips and yanked him closer. She loved the feel of his hands in her hair, his mouth mating with hers, the hardness of his body flush against her belly. She loved *him*.

They stumbled backward until her shoulders hit solid wood. A door. The fourth room. One which ideally contained a bed, and if not, at least a floor. Without lifting her mouth from his, she reached behind her back for the handle and twisted it open.

The door flew inward. They would have toppled over had Owen not caught her at the last second and swung her upright. His eyes were no longer clouded with passion. He looked ... embarrassed?

Reluctantly, she pulled out of his embrace and glanced about. Her mouth fell open in surprise.

Two lonesome wingback chairs constituted the entirety of the room's furniture. But the walls—the walls! Custom floor-to-ceiling pine bookshelves lined every inch of the room. They were empty, save for a handful of books lying in the far corner.

She walked the perimeter in awe, pausing when she reached the small pile of books. One was *The Old English Baron*, the last book she'd loaned him before his disappearance. The second was her favorite out of all Ann Radcliffe's novels. The third was a well-worn book of French poetry. She clutched all three to her chest, then spun to face him.

"Did you do this?" she demanded, unable to tear her eyes from his. "Did you build a library?"

He nodded hesitantly. "I knew you wouldn't accept anyone who wouldn't open his arms to your books as well as you. They're just as big a part of you as ... as *you* are. That's why I was in the gaming parlor, risking my last penny. How could I offer you an empty library? I thought, maybe if I stocked it full of the things you loved best ... If I came to *you* with a dowry, something you couldn't resist ..."

The room seemed to disappear. All she saw was him. *He loved her.* Or at least, he had. Once. Her breath hitched and her legs wobbled. She tried to smile. "We never played our last hand."

"I want no games between us." Owen stepped forward, a determined set to his jaw. "We can throw the wagers in the fire, or we can open them together."

"Together." She linked her arm through his so that she stood by his side. Where she intended to be for the rest of her life. But whatever he'd written, he'd written before he'd known how she felt about him. How would she live with herself if he wanted nothing more than to have his cottage back? If he'd rather head off to war than face a future with her? She took a deep breath. Her legs remained unsteady. "Ready?"

He nodded.

They broke the seals together. The parchment unfolded. Her throat clogged when she read the same five words printed on both scraps of paper:

ALL I WANT IS YOU.

And so it was.

Erica Ridley learned to read when she was three, which was about the same time she decided to be a writer when she grew up. Now, she's a *USA Today* best-selling author of historical romance novels. Her latest series, *The Dukes of War*, features peers and war heroes who return from battle only to be thrust into the splendor and madness of Regency England. When not reading or writing romances, Erica can be found riding camels in Africa, zip-lining through rainforests in Costa Rica, or getting hopelessly lost in the middle of Budapest.

COVERING HER SKIN

LAURA KAYE

New York Times Bestseller

AS EMERY MORGAN PARKED her car in front of Kane Brothers Tattoo, she hoped she wasn't making the biggest mistake of her life. Or, at least, the *third* biggest mistake, since falling in love with professional football quarterback Hunter Jameson and getting a tattoo of his team logo and jersey number had the top two spots locked up tight.

The dark doors of the red-brick tattoo shop taunted her, tempted her, *dared* her to enter. Just as she had a little over a year ago, when she'd gone in to get a special and very personal wedding present for her then fiancé.

Enough, Em. This will be different.

Yeah, it would. Because *that* ink she'd done for Hunter. *This* ink she was doing for herself.

A year was more than long enough to spend grieving and wondering how it all had gone bad—and why she hadn't noticed until Hunter looked at the tattoo, told her he wished she hadn't done that, and ended their five-year relationship. Today, Emery should've been celebrating her first wedding anniversary. Instead, she was starting over by getting rid of the last reminder of those mistakes. Because the number seven had not turned out to be lucky for her; it had turned out to be unlucky, painful, and very, very wrong.

Clutching her scarf around her throat, Emery jogged to the

doors and into the wide foyer of the shop, hurrying so she didn't have time to overthink her plan and chicken out. Compared to the frigid chill of Pittsburgh's winter outside, the warmth inside combined with the sultry strains of a southern rock song to make her feel welcomed. Or maybe that was just because she'd been to Kane Brothers so many times—not for her own ink, because she only had the one, but with Hunter, who used Ronan Kane exclusively for all of his tattoos.

Ronan Kane. As her gaze scanned a wall of vibrant designs, Emery's stomach flipped at the thought of the man who had drawn her wedding gift to Hunter permanently on her skin. When she'd come up with the idea of the tattoo, she'd known Ronan was the only one to do it. Many times, she'd gone with Hunter and watched as Ronan carefully put needle to skin and made something beautiful appear that had never existed before. Saying Ronan was talented was like saying Pittsburgh's fanatic fans kinda liked football. Ronan was a master, an artist, a god with a tattoo gun in his hand. So he'd been the only one for her.

How ironic that she'd put her trust in the right man with her skin—because Ronan had managed to take the hard lines of Hunter's number and the masculine team logo and make it pretty and feminine on her shoulder—while blowing it so spectacularly in trusting the wrong man with her heart.

Footsteps offered all the warning she had of a presence behind the counter. "Can I help y— Emery?"

Oh, that voice. Fine whiskey on a cold winter's night. Emery turned slowly, hesitant to see the expression on Ronan's face. Would Ronan find her naïve, presumptuous, pathetic? Or *D: All of the above*? After all, she was no one compared to Pittsburgh's hometown hero—after Hunter had dumped her, the gossip rags had made *that* crystal clear even as they'd fawned all over Tiffany Ames, his new actress girlfriend. And since Hunter was a celebrity client who brought business and notoriety to the shop, no doubt the tattooist would feel the same.

"Hi, Ronan," she said, approaching the counter. Her gaze dragged up the black button-down stretched taut across his chest to the surprised expression on his rugged face. "Any chance you have time to see me today?"

"Uh, yeah. What about?" he asked, bracing his hands against the counter. The position drew her gaze to the abstract black design that covered his skin from cuffed sleeve to fingertips on his right arm.

Emery was glad for the distraction, because she didn't miss the note of wariness in his voice. It made her want to shrink into her thick down coat. "I was hoping ..." She burrowed her hands in her pockets and stared out the frosty front window. *You can do this, Em. You* need *this.* "I was hoping you could do a new tattoo for me." She forced her gaze back to Ronan's deep brown eyes and shrugged. "To, um, cover the one I have."

Ronan's brows rose the slightest bit. "You want me to cover Hunter's jersey number?"

She nodded as her stomach began a steady fall to the floor. "Yeah?" Emery really hadn't intended the upward lilt in her voice that turned the declaration into a question, but the man's expression was part incredulity and part ... something she couldn't name.

And then it hit her—had she offended him? Did tattoo artists find it offensive to be asked to cover their own work?

"I'm sorry," she blurted. "I wasn't trying to offend you. I just figured the person who did the original work would have the best sense of how to design something new over it." Not to mention that Ronan was the only artist she could trust not to expose the existence of the tattoo. How embarrassing it would be if the tabloids found out. Luckily, Hunter had kept his mouth shut about it, but she couldn't count on a stranger to do so, too.

"I'm not offended, Emery. And I'm free for the next two hours, so I'm all yours."

Butterflies tore through Em's belly at the words. Which was ridiculous, since she was nursing a broken heart and he was simply offering his services. But with his dark eyes and brown hair worn a little longer on top and his miles of ink and his perpetual facial scruff, possessing Ronan would be anyone's dream come true.

Emery blinked the errant thoughts away. "Oh, okay. Great. So..."

He nodded to the side. "So, come on back."

Ronan Kane wouldn't have been more surprised if the Abominable Snowman had walked through the front door.

Emery Morgan, with her startlingly blue eyes, light brown hair with golden highlights, and petite, curvy body, was literally the last person Ronan thought he'd ever again see.

Not after he'd failed her so horribly.

Thoughts whirling, Ronan led her through the lounge, past his brother Aidan's and cousin Ethan's tattoo rooms, and finally to his own room at the back of the long, narrow space.

Goddamn, but the moment he'd realized who it was, his gaze had zeroed in on her right shoulder. And though layers of clothing covered the soft, warm skin beneath, Ronan was intimately familiar with what was there—the tattoo *he'd* done of her quarterback fiancé's jersey number and team logo. Ex-fiancé now.

What a freaking disaster.

"Have a seat," he said, gesturing to the black vinyl chair in the center of the room. "Take your coat?"

"Sure," she said, not quite meeting his gaze. She unzipped the thick winter number and slid out of it, then unwrapped the scarf from around her neck. Ronan's heart tripped over itself, and his mouth went dry. Because his memory hadn't nearly done justice to this woman—not to the curves just meant for gripping, nor to the round fullness of her breasts, perfectly sized for her small frame, nor to the pert little ass hugged so sweetly by those tight, dark jeans.

He hung her belongings on a hook on the back of the door and pushed it mostly shut, nerves making him tug at the top of his hair as he took a seat at his desk. "Tell me what you're thinking," he said, settling his gaze on her pretty face.

Emery took a deep breath. "I don't want the number tattoo anymore." She unfolded a sheet she'd pulled from her coat pocket and handed it to him. "Some things that inspired me," she said.

Ronan dragged his gaze away from Emery and studied the page. Six images, all tied together by a common theme. Butterflies.

Symbolic of transformation and profound changes of the soul. A boulder parked itself on his chest.

So many times, Ronan had wished he could go back to the night last December when Emery had walked into his shop and shyly asked him to do her first ink. And, man, he'd been thrilled that she'd come to him ... right up until she'd told him what she wanted. Even as his needle had marked her, Ronan's gut had worried that Hunter wouldn't go the distance with Emery and then she's be stuck—literally—with his number on her skin. Forever.

Be honest, asshole. You did more than worry. You suspected.

Yeah, he had. From things he'd overheard from other players on the team—about a half dozen of whom came to him or Aidan for their ink—Ronan knew Hunter's eyes wandered and suspected the man's hands did, too.

But aside from a casual *Are you sure?*, Ronan hadn't done anything to try to dissuade her.

Because he'd been afraid his motivation stemmed less from legitimate concerns about Hunter's fidelity and more from the crush Ronan had had on Emery since the first time she'd walked through the doors of Kane Brothers so many years ago.

But seeing her sitting here now, so obviously uncomfortable, and knowing how the media had dragged the breakup through the mud ... yeah, he wished he could go back and do it all over again.

Ronan settled the paper on the desk. "I can definitely work up something along these lines, but covering a tattoo requires some planning." Emery's full, pink lips slipped into a frown. Leaning forward, he placed his hand on her knee. "Hang on now. It requires planning so the camouflage is effective. It's not a problem," he said, trying to reassure her. He couldn't imagine how hurtful it must've been to wear Hunter's number on her skin for a whole year after the man had broken up with her and quickly flaunted a new girlfriend around town. Last thing Ronan wanted to do was add in any way to Emery's discomfort.

"Okay," she said, her gaze flickering from his hand to his eyes. He wished he knew what to say or do to put her at ease, especially as what he needed to say next was definitely *not* going to do so. "I need to see your tattoo."

After a moment, Emery slid the thick ivory sweater she wore over her head and folded it over her lap. Her long, wavy hair curled around her face and over her shoulders. For a split second, it was possible Ronan's heart came to a full stop, because the thin navy blue tank she wore left *nothing* to the imagination and sucker-punched him with how freaking gorgeous this woman truly was.

Hunter Jameson was an asshole to have treated you the way he did. The thought sat on the tip of Ronan's tongue, but he knew expressing it would only escalate her discomfort.

Forcing his gaze away from the enticing dip of Emery's cleavage, Ronan grabbed a sheet of tracing paper and a Sharpie. "Okay, a quick trace and I can start building a new design."

"Great," she said, finally giving him a small smile.

And, man, if he'd thought her attractive before, she was a total knockout with a little happiness shaping her face. Whenever she'd come to the shop with Hunter, she'd always been so happy and talkative. That was part of what attracted Ronan to her. Now, he wanted to do whatever he could to make her smile again and again.

"Hold still," he said, stepping behind her.

And there it was.

A circular tattoo with Hunter's number seven highlighted and positioned at nine o'clock and the yellow, red, and blue diamonds of the team's logo at the twelve, three, and six positions respectively. To make the design more feminine, Ronan had surrounded the logo with scrollwork and placed two dark pink roses on either side, as if growing around the scrolls.

Emery's face had been absolutely radiant when she'd first seen it. She'd loved it, and had been so sure Hunter would, too.

Shoving the memory away, Ronan pushed the silk of her hair over her far shoulder and laid the paper over her ink. The warmth of her skin taunted him through the thin sheet as the scents of vanilla and oranges filled his nose. As he carefully traced his creation, he had to restrain himself from leaning in and drinking her down.

But damn if he didn't want to put his nose, his mouth, his tongue against the long line of her throat. For starters.

"Done," he said a few minutes later, returning to his desk. "Next step is to draw your new design. Should I draw while you're here? Do you want to come back when I have something worked up?"

Her eyes went wide. "I'd like to stay, please."

Exactly what he'd hoped she'd say. "Did you want to start new ink today?"

Emery hugged herself, inadvertently plumping her cleavage. "Yes. But by start, do you mean we won't finish?"

Ronan tried not to look at her breasts. He really did. "No, we won't finish today. This will take at least two sessions."

"Oh," she said, her hands falling into her lap.

"Hey," he said. "Don't worry. It's going to be awesome when we're done."

She nodded. "I know."

"Come tell me what you think as I'm drawing," he said, nodding her over to the light table as he sat. He laid the page with the old tattoo in the center and taped it down, then placed a new sheet overtop and secured it the same way.

For the next twenty minutes, Ronan worked up a design that made use of the existing lines of the tattoo so as to best camouflage them. A tattoo could never truly be covered. Instead, the ink from the new tattoo mixed with the pigment from the first. The team's logo became a big open-faced flower, and the scrollwork became leaves extending on both sides. Above, butterflies fluttered. Some smaller, some bigger. Some fully opened and others with wings folded mid-flight. He extended the leaves and added a stem of unopened buds to the flowers, connecting the disparate parts into one flowing image. He could see this coming to life on her skin, and goddamn, he just knew it would be feminine and colorful and sexy. Like Emery. "How's this?" he asked, lifting his gaze to hers.

And damn. She was so close it wouldn't have taken anything to close the gap and press his lips to hers.

A smile played around Emery's lips. "Beautiful," she said. "That's right. Exactly what I wanted." Her smile widened as she studied the image. "You really are the best."

Satisfaction filled Ronan's gut. At her compliment. At getting to touch her again. At getting to right this wrong. "If we start now, I can get the outlining done today," Ronan said.

Emery nodded. "That's the best news I've heard in a while," she said. "Let's do it."

"Almost done outlining," Ronan said a while later, voice deep and full of concentration.

Straddling the tattoo chair so her back faced him, Emery gave a small nod. And it was all she could do. Between the bite of the needle over her skin, Ronan's big hands and warm breath on her bare shoulder, and hammering this final nail into her life with Hunter, she was a little overwhelmed.

She'd met Hunter in college, before he'd even been noticed by the NFL. A huge fan of football since her childhood, she'd known who Hunter Jameson was the moment she'd met him and was instantly infatuated—he had that effect on people. But he was *Hunter Jameson*, and she was just a museum studies major who enjoyed researching old objects. It was only after Hunter had come to the opening of the museum exhibit she'd interned on that she'd believed his interest was genuine.

Five years. That's how long they'd been together before he'd stared at his number on her skin and shaken his head.

Enough. She was done mourning. It was time for a change. And this was the perfect way to start.

"I'd like to do one last thing if it's okay with you," he finally said.

She heaved a shaky breath. "What's that?" she managed, caught up in the memories.

Ronan leaned back and stared at her for a long moment. "You okay?"

"Yep." She met his gaze so he'd believe her.

He nodded. "I've got just enough time to put some white ink

over the parts of the old tattoo not incorporated into the lines. It'll make the color blend better."

"Great," she said. "Thank you." Moments later, the needle returned to her skin, this time concentrating in small areas instead of drawing long lines. She sucked in a breath at the burn but relished it, too. The pain made it easier to stay focused on the present.

"Done," he finally said. Ronan handed her a mirror. "You'll still see the old tattoo. For now. The color will get rid of it next time."

She nodded, bracing as she peered at her reflection.

The butterflies and flowers that climbed up her shoulder and just wrapped over the top of it were beautifully done, but the open-faced flower and leaves covering and surrounding Hunter's number seven were a jumble of the two designs. Neither Hunter's old mark nor her new one. A work in progress. Just like her.

"Looks great," she said while reminding herself to be patient. "Thank you, Ronan."

He bandaged the ink, and she got dressed, and then she followed him through the shop. Damn, but Ronan Kade did all kinds of justice to a pair of jeans.

The thought made her look at this man anew.

No question she'd always found Ronan attractive. How could she not? His rugged good looks, dark intensity, and incredible talent had been appealing even when Hunter represented everything she'd ever thought she wanted in a happily ever after. But before today, she'd never let herself look at him as a man she might like. Or want.

"In two weeks, we'll color it in," he said as they entered the area behind the reception counter. He flipped open the schedule book and leafed through the pages. "Should leave at least three hours, so … I've got the eighteenth at four or the twenty-first at three."

Emery pushed the ridiculous thoughts away. This man was intimately familiar with just how deep her naïveté and humiliation extended—into her very *skin*. No way he'd find *that* attractive. Because sometimes it made *her* want to scream. "Let's do the eighteenth." She tied her scarf around her throat as his pencil paused against the page. "Last name's Morgan," she added.

Eyebrow cocked, he cast her a sideways glance. "My ink is in your skin, Emery. I know your name. Trust me." His intense gaze latched onto hers and refused to let go.

Emery's pulse spiked. "Right. Sorry," she said.

Ronan dropped the pencil and stepped so tightly into her space she had to tilt her head to look into his absolutely blazing eyes. Her back came up against the counter. Trapped. "Don't apologize to me. Not for this. And not after I—" He shook his head, and agitation poured off his big body.

His heat against her breasts. His scent, all clean, male spice. His gaze, lighting on her face until she couldn't decide whether to flee or beg for a kiss. A kiss. Definitely. She licked her lips. "After you what?" she whispered.

"Yo, Ro," a deep voice called from the direction they'd just come. His brother or cousin, she guessed. The intensity binding her and Ronan together popped like a balloon.

Ronan jerked back, his gaze skittering to the hallway. "Just a sec," he called.

That was her cue to go. Heart in her throat, Emery jerked her coat on and rounded the counter, placing wood and glass and metal between him and a host of desires she *really* didn't need to be feeling right now. To touch him. To taste him. To take him in. God, what was wrong with her? "I won't keep you, Ronan. Thanks for everything."

She made for the door and could almost swear she felt the weight of his gaze on her back.

"Emery," he said in a low voice. Hand on the knob, she froze. "See you soon." A promise. A threat. Whatever had just happened between them, it wasn't over.

Her belly flipped. "Yeah, see you soon," she said, and pushed out the door.

Emery's voice echoed in his ears. *I won't keep you, Ronan.*

And all he'd wanted to do was march across the room, pull her into his arms, and beg for her to do just that.

Jesus. He'd known the woman for nearly four years, and what

he'd always thought was a crush had developed pretty much from the start. He could still remember their first meeting—Emery had been talkative, happy, and totally fascinated by Ronan's work, peppering him with a thousand questions. But she'd also so clearly adored the man he'd been inking that Ronan had known he didn't stand a chance. And, of course, it didn't help Ronan's cause that her guy was a professional football player. And the quarterback, at that, for fuck's sake. So he'd kept his interest to himself, ignored the pang that always hit his chest just left of center each time she left the shop on Hunter's arm, and went about the 24-7 of life. The day she'd come for that first tattoo, Ronan had forced himself to say a silent good-bye to those feelings once and for all because she'd been on the verge of forever with another man.

But now, knowing she was alone? And touching her skin again? And laying his eyes on her, in the flesh?

Goddamnit all to hell, but those feelings had come roaring back so forcefully that his brain had him stripping her down, lifting her on top of the counter, and burying himself deep while he confessed just how long—and how much—he'd wanted her, cared for her.

"Ronan?" a voice said from behind him.

Ronan blinked and cut his gaze to his older brother Aidan, standing in the doorway to the back of the shop. "What?"

Aidan arched a brow. "Emery Morgan, huh?"

Rolling his eyes, Ronan pushed by him and headed to the back. "Did you need something?"

Footsteps followed right behind. "Yeah. To talk about Emery Morgan."

Stopping outside Aidan's door, Ronan turned. "She came for a tattoo. End of."

Aidan shook his dark hair out of his face, exposing the thin black lines of the tribal that curved around his right eye, and crossed his sleeved arms. "Doesn't have to be, now that she's single."

Like Ronan needed the fucking encouragement. But Emery didn't know that Ronan had suspected Hunter's infidelity all along and *still* let her mark herself with the man's jersey number. "Don't need your advice here, A."

Aidan's eyes narrowed. "Maybe. But it's not every day a man has the thing he's always wanted but thought he couldn't have dropped right in his lap."

The words—and the sexy image they unleashed in Ronan's imagination—scrambled his brain for a long moment. Jesus. Ronan shook his head. "I appreciate the concern, man. I do. But it's more complicated than that."

"Only if you let it be," Aidan said, clapping him on the shoulder and disappearing inside his room. A buzzer sounded out front, probably Ronan's next client, given the time. And he was glad. Art and ink had always served as the best forms of distraction and escape for him. Right now, he needed that, badly, or the next two weeks were going to drag like a mofo.

Because, as it was, he could barely wait to see—and touch— Emery Morgan again.

Sometimes Ronan hated being right, like about the fact that time was going to crawl until Emery's followup appointment. It had damn near gone backward. But today was finally the day. When she got here, he was going to finish her tat, come clean about what he'd suspected, and—provided she was still talking to him—ask her out.

Because, on *rare* occasion, Aidan was right, too. And after overthinking the hell out of his brother's advice regarding Emery, Ronan had finally admitted to himself that this was one of those times.

Ronan *needed* to see if Emery was open to something with him, or he'd always wonder *what if*.

Fuck that. Life was too short. Besides, nothing risked, nothing gained.

Buzzzzz.

Finally.

The sound hauled Ronan out of his seat, across the lounge, and into the small space behind the front counter. He'd moved so fast that Emery was still stomping snow off her boots by the door. "Hi, Emery," he said.

Her gaze cut to his. "Oh, hi. I didn't see you there." She smiled, and the easy openness of it reached into Ronan's chest and tugged at his heart. The discomfort he'd sensed from the previous appointment appeared to be gone, and he was glad. Now he just hoped what he had to tell her later didn't bring it back. And then some.

"Ready?" he asked, his gaze trailing over the flush in her cheeks from the cold outside. So damn pretty.

"Definitely. Let's do it." She rounded the counter.

The words were totally innocent, but that didn't keep his body from wishing she was talking about something else. Something that involved the two of them alone in a dark room with a big bed and a whole lot of free time. Damnit.

As they walked to his room, Ronan's hands itched to touch her. "Any questions before we get started?" he managed.

She shook her head as they stepped through his door. "Nope." This time, she didn't wait for his invitation or command. Emery slid out of her coat and hung it on the hook herself, then tugged her red sweater over her head and tossed it onto a chair.

For a long moment, a sliver of skin above Emery's waistband showed as the hem of her tank slid up, utterly captivating Ronan's gaze and sending his heart into a driving beat. He swallowed hard and forced his gaze upward, only to get caught on the outline of the red bra visible through the cream-colored tank. "Um." He turned toward his desk and raked his hand through his hair. "Have a seat, like last time." Ronan listened for her to get settled before turning back. "Still good with the colors I sketched out?" he said, finally allowing himself to look again.

"Yes. It's exactly what I want," she said, her arms and breasts resting against the back of the chair. As he watched, she slowly dragged the cream and red straps of her tank and bra down her right arm, out of the way of where he needed to work.

It was the sexiest fucking thing he'd seen in a long time.

"Okay," he said, his voice a raw scrape. "Let's see how you've healed."

She rested her face against her folded arms and peered over her shoulder at him. "I'm healing good, I think," she said.

Something about the tone of her voice made him think she

was talking about more than just her skin. Ronan would've sworn it. Whatever happened between them after today, he hoped with everything he was that it was true. For her sake. Running his fingers over the smooth skin of her shoulder, he nodded. "Yeah, I'd say you are." She shivered under his touch, and his eyes flashed to hers. Emery didn't look away, didn't blush, didn't hide from him at all. His body flooded with heat and hope.

But before he could entertain anything else, Emery deserved all his attention and energy on her tattoo. Because he couldn't tolerate it if she found herself regretting his ink on her skin a second time. He prepped his tools, his supplies, and her skin. And then he was ready.

"Here we go," he said, using a bright blue ink on the wings of a butterfly high on her shoulder. The bones there were close to the surface, so he wanted to get what were likely to be the most sensitive areas done first. "Okay?"

The smile was small but easy, striking him again with how much more relaxed she seemed this visit. "Yeah, I'm good."

No, Emery, you're amazing. But first the ink, and then he'd give her these words. And so many more.

Assuming he hadn't fucked it all up before he had the chance.

One by one, he colored the butterflies in shades of blue, purple, yellow, and orange. The only sounds were the buzz of the tattoo gun and the music playing out in the lounge. Every once in a while, he'd check in to make sure she was still okay, and she'd reply with that same confident smile.

From the direction of the lounge, laughter rang out and then the sound of voices trading jokes and jabs. Ronan stretched behind him to shut the door the rest of the way. The quiet between them had been comfortable, and Ronan wanted to keep it that way.

"Mind if we take a break?" Emery asked a few minutes later. "I need to use the restroom."

"Absolutely," Ronan said, securing his gun. "Up the hall just before the lounge."

She smiled as she pushed off the chair. "I remember. How's it looking?"

"Great, if I can say so myself." He winked, and her laughter was the sweetest reward.

"You can. Be right back," she said. And then she slipped out the door.

Emery felt better than she had in a long time. She'd survived the breakup, the long year alone, and the anniversary of her never-happened wedding. At work, she'd just landed a big grant that would allow her to start a new research project at the museum in the new year. And she would *finally* be able to look in the mirror and *not* see that awful number seven on her shoulder.

Add to all that the fact that Ronan had been looking at her like he could eat her, and Emery was about floating on cloud nine, the feeling amplified after being down for so long.

As she stepped out of Ronan's room, boisterous laughter sounded from the lounge. She pulled the straps on her bra and tank up a little higher on her arm to make sure she was decent but hoped she'd be able to skirt into the bathroom without being noticed at all.

She'd nearly reached the bathroom when she heard a voice she recognized. Her stomach plummeted to the floor. There it was again. As she stood glued to the spot, she had absolutely no doubt that Hunter's best friend and running back teammate, Jake Ashton, was in the next room. *Shit.* Was Hunter here, too?

As she eavesdropped on the conversation, prickles of nervousness broke out across Emery's skin, freezing her in place. All year, she'd gone out of her way to avoid Hunter and his whole crowd. She just hadn't been ready to confront the man and the life she'd always thought she wanted. And since very few of "their friends" had reached out to her after the breakup, Emery had always thought avoidance the best way to go. Who needed their false, fair-weather friendship anyway? Not her, that was for sure.

Then again, was she really going to chicken out and hide if Hunter *was* here? Pittsburgh wasn't that big of a town. Inevitably, they were going to run into each other. Maybe it was better to get it over with now than spend forever dreading the moment.

COVERING HER SKIN   263

Besides, as hurt as she'd been, Hunter's actions and the year apart had done at least one good thing: made Emery realize she was better off without him. If she couldn't trust him to be honest and faithful, he didn't deserve her. At her lowest lows, that was sometimes easier said than believed, but in her heart of hearts, she knew it was true.

I can do this. I have to do this.

Emery took a step forward, belatedly remembering that her shoulder was bare and her unfinished tattoo visible. She froze again. *No way* was she seeing Hunter for the first time half-dressed and with the shame of his number on her shoulder. Her bravery only extended so far.

Maybe Ronan could cover the tat so she could put her sweater back on. And then she could say a quick, breezy *hi, how are you?* and then get back to doing what mattered—moving on with her life. Which started with getting Hunter's number off her skin once and for all.

"Let's head back," Aidan said from the lounge.

Oh no! She hurried, almost to the turn in the hallway that led to Ro—

"Emery?" a voice said.

Everything inside her said to keep going and just pretend she hadn't heard Jake saying her name. But she refused to give in to her inner chickenshit. Pulling up her mental big-girl panties, she turned and smiled. "Jake? Hi." She peered around him but didn't see anyone else ... namely, Hunter.

Jake's smile was genuine, and that eased her nerves a bit. "How are you?" he asked as he walked toward her.

It's just a regular, normal, polite question. Right. "Great. How are you?" she managed.

"Good, good. Season's going good. My knee's been behaving. Can't complain," he said, gaze dragging over her bare shoulder.

She forced herself not to fidget. *And* not to wonder if he'd seen the remains of Hunter's number and their team's logo on her shoulder. "I'm glad to hear it. So, uh, you here alone?"

"Oh, yeah. Just me. A's doing a new piece for me. Hunter doesn't come here anymore, so don't worry," he said, kindness in his gray eyes.

Hunter doesn't come here anymore? Oh, geez, had she cost Ronan the business of probably his biggest-named client? "Oh, okay. Well, I hope you have a Merry Christmas, Jake. I should get back," she said, gesturing behind her.

"Yeah, yeah, you, too," he said, raking a hand through his blond hair.

Emery stepped backward, not wanting to show him her tattoo.

"Hey, Em?" Jake said, coming closer.

"Yeah?" she said, ignoring the prickles on her neck.

"Listen," he said. "I just wanted to apologize for the way everything went down. Not just with you and Hunter, but I'm sorry, too, that I never reached out to see how you were doing."

The tension melted from Emery's shoulders. Jake could be a big goof, but he was never meanspirited. "Thanks. But you're his best friend, so ..." She shrugged.

"I know, but still, it's never felt right. Someone should've said something to you sooner and saved you from going through all that. I told him—"

"Wait. What?" Emery frowned, unable to tease meaning from what he'd said. "Said something sooner to me about what?"

"Oh." Jake frowned and scratched his jaw. "I, uh, thought you knew."

She swallowed around a knot in her throat. "You've lost me."

"Tiffany," he said, almost wincing as the word came out of his mouth.

The actress girlfriend? "What about ..." The question died on her lips as realization hit. Hard. "Oh." She nodded and struggled to act like learning of her fiancé's infidelity didn't hurt like hell. "Right. Of course. Who *didn't* know about that?" she said in an Oscar-worthy performance.

Jake gave a small, uncertain smile. But he finally said, "Yeah, exactly. Well, I just wanted to apologize for not having been a better friend. I love Hunter like a brother, but that doesn't mean he treated you right."

Was there any oxygen in this hallway? Emery suspected not as spots danced at the edge of her vision. "Thanks, Jake," she managed. "Take care."

She bolted, not giving him a chance to say another word, and pushed through Ronan's door so fast she nearly crashed into his hard chest.

Arms crossed, head down, he said, "You okay?"

"Yeah. Sorry." She hugged herself. And though her heart was racing and her mind was spinning over this new betrayal, what she didn't do was cry. Because, really, this news changed nothing. It simply confirmed the whole situation had worked out in her best interest and that she was too damn good for Hunter Jameson. Emery forced a deep breath and met Ronan's eyes.

"I knew." Ronan shook his head. "Or, at least, I suspected. I'm so sorry."

The words came to her as if traveling through a long tunnel. "What?" she asked, stepping backward.

Ronan gestured to the chair. "I was going to tell you all this when we were done, but I'll do it now if you prefer."

Emery's feet moved without her telling them to, and then she sat and stared at the man she'd spent the last two weeks fantasizing about touching her. "Tell me," she managed, trying to keep an open mind.

He pulled a chair so close all that separated them was her defensiveness. Looking into her eyes, he said, "Hunter's teammates would sometimes talk when they were here. Things they said made me question Hunter's faithfulness, but they never said anything so blatant that I could be certain. When you came to get the tattoo, I wanted to tell you. But I couldn't bring myself to interfere in your relationship without proof."

"Oh," she said, heart beating hard against her chest. Emery sifted through his words, evaluating them for sincerity and finding it. Besides, it wasn't Ronan's place to tell her that her fiancé was a cheating loser. "I don't know if I would've believed you anyway. I loved him. I had faith in him 'til the end."

Ronan winced. "I know."

"I'm just sorry your business got caught in the middle of this, Ronan. Jake said Hunter doesn't come here anymore."

A storm rolled in across Ronan's expression. "That's because *I* refused to work on *him*."

Emery gasped. "What? Why?"

He shook his head, brown eyes blazing. "I've regretted keeping my mouth shut the whole past year, regretted that I did something I knew in my *gut* I shouldn't have done." The passion in his words set her to trembling. "No way I was going to compound those mistakes by taking money from the man who hurt the woman I—"

"What?"

He closed the gap between them, taking her hands in his and sending her heart into a sprint. "I was really into you." He cleared his throat. "I *am* really into you. It's part of why I didn't say something then. I feared I was letting my emotions cloud my judgment where he was concerned. Because I wanted you for myself."

Heat tingled over Emery's skin in a fast rush. "Wanted?"

Ronan flicked his tongue over his bottom lip. "Want."

"Oh," she said, Ronan's words sending a wave of excitement through her that made her smile. Inside her, Ronan's words and desire covered the pain of Hunter's betrayal in the same way his ink was covering her skin. Both gave her the chance for a fresh start.

"Oh?" Ronan pressed in closer, so close his knees slid between hers. "Emery, throw a man a rope because I'm dying over here."

Without letting herself overthink it, she leaned in and did something she'd been dying to do since she'd seen Ronan again two weeks ago. She kissed him. "How's that?" she whispered.

He answered by burying his hands in her hair and kissing her until she was dizzy and giddy and filled with a red-hot desire she'd never felt before. Not with Hunter. Not with any man. Ronan's lips moved and his tongue explored and the most incredibly urgent sounds spilled from the back of his throat, drawing Emery to thread her hands around his neck and pull him closer.

On a groan, Ronan tugged her body into his lap so that she straddled him. The body-to-body contact was maddening and fascinating and absolutely thrilling. The kiss might've gone on for minutes or hours, Emery couldn't tell. What she *did* know was that she didn't want it to end. Not tonight. Maybe not ever. But there'd be plenty of time to figure that out.

Ronan finally pulled away. "Jesus," he rasped. "You're amazing,

Emery. I've always thought so." A soft press of his lips against hers that made her smile. "Can you forgive me?"

She stroked her fingers through his hair. "Nothing to forgive. You had to keep your clients' confidence, and you had no proof. It sucks, but I'm okay, Ronan. All that's in the past." She shrugged her bare shoulder and glanced at the hint of the butterfly's wing she could just make out. "Well, almost."

"Amazing," he murmured, kissing her again. "Let's get it all in the past, then. Right now. Because I'd like to talk to you about the future. Namely, whether you'll go out with me tonight."

She laughed. Really, truly laughed. "Yeah?"

Ronan nodded and heat slid into his gaze. "Hell, yeah."

"I'd love to." She smiled, amazed at how the whole evening had turned around. Thanks to Ronan. Emery slipped off his lap, immediately missing his hard heat, and straddled the tattoo chair one last time. "But first, you gotta finish what we started."

"Yeah," he said, settling in behind her again.

And as the needle bit into her skin one last time, Emery couldn't help but smile, because sometimes doing something wrong led to something so right.

Laura Kaye is the *New York Times* and *USA Today* best-selling author of over twenty books in contemporary and paranormal romance and romantic suspense, including the Hard Ink, Heroes, and Raven Riders series. Laura grew up amid family lore involving angels, ghosts, and evil-eye curses, cementing her life-long fascination with storytelling and the supernatural. Laura lives in Maryland with her husband, two daughters, and cute-but-bad dog, and appreciates her view of the Chesapeake Bay every day.

THE LONG WAY HOME

KATY REGNERY

CLARISSA'S HEART FELL WHEN she realized there was only one seat left on the packed bus. She took a long look at the co-occupant of said seat, at his bowed head of thick, chestnut-colored hair. Her fingers twitched. *Ford McInerney. Damn my bad luck.*

"Going with us or not?" the driver asked her, his hand on the door lever, clearly irritated by her eleventh-hour arrival.

Ford looked up when the driver barked at her, and his warm hazel eyes held hers for a split second, registering surprise, as his lips turned up in that old teasing grin. Her heart beat the crap out of her chest, and she twisted the leather handle of her duffel bag in her sweaty hands.

Clarissa scanned the other seats carefully, wishing a free spot would magically appear. The other passengers on the bus were already sleeping, reading, or looking out the window. No one noticed the uneasiness in Clarissa's searching eyes.

No one except Ford, the grinning fool.

"Missy, we ain't got all night," the driver said, his voice ratcheting up a notch. "Are you staying on or—"

"Staying," she muttered, and the door shut behind her.

She stared at the floor, unwilling to look at Ford or give him the satisfaction of seeing her irritation. She wished there was another way to get home, but she'd used the last of her money on this bus ticket.

When she got to the row where he was sitting, she raised her chin. Familiar eyes that she'd known all her life slammed into hers.

"Why, Clarey Calhoun," Ford drawled in his thickest West Virginia accent. "Fancy seein' you here."

Her first thought was that his eyelashes were still much longer than any man's had a right to be, especially on such a masculine face. They framed the hazel eyes that were, at that very moment, sweeping down her body lazily before returning her gaze. He held on to his amused grin, knowing full and well she'd rather be anywhere on earth than trapped sitting next to a McInerney. Should have known he'd be heading home, too. His brother, Dodge, was marrying Clarissa's best friend, Myrna.

She hefted her bag up and over the mesh barrier into the overhead luggage rack, feeling her T-shirt pull free from the waistband of her jeans as she stretched her arms upward. She made sure her bag was nestled safely, then quickly pulled the T-shirt back down.

When she looked down at Ford, his eyes were locked on her now-covered tummy.

"Can't go 'til you take a seat, miss!" The driver was definitely running out of patience now.

"Move over," Clarissa said in a tight, low voice.

"Nope," he replied, readjusting himself so he took up most of the two seats with his muscular, football-player's body. One lip quirked up in a teasing smirk as he crossed his arms over his chest. "You didn't ask nice. I know you got better manners than that, Clarey Calhoun."

"Will. You. *Please*. Move. Over?" She gave him a plastic, sour smile that passed just as well for a grimace.

"Well, since you asked so sweet and all …" He shifted his body as close to the aisle as possible, freeing up the seat beside the window.

She looked at the free seat, then back at his eyes, which danced merrily over her obvious discomfort. She couldn't think of anything she'd like less than riding from Boulder, Colorado, to Charleston, West Virginia, sandwiched snugly between Ford McInerney and a window, but if she didn't want to get kicked off the bus, it didn't look like she had much of a choice.

She took a sideways step toward the empty seat, but he didn't pull his knees up, which meant that her knees rubbed against his as she sidled by him, her breasts practically brushing his nose. She didn't want to put her butt in his face, so she twisted toward the window, then finally sat down, squishing as close as possible to the window. Still, her shoulder rested flush up against Ford's in the compact space, and there was nothing she could do about it.

"I *did* shower today," Ford teased, nudging her knee with his.

Clarissa had a sudden, unwelcome image of Ford in the shower and quickly looked down at their legs to distract herself. They both wore jeans, but his were old and light from wear, probably super soft and warm if she touched the hard thigh beside her. Hers were newer, darker, Old Navy skinny jeans that seemed fussy next to his.

She looked up, turning to catch his eyes in the dim light as the bus started moving east.

"Is hygiene new for you?"

His eyes narrowed briefly before he shrugged, ignoring her question. "Headed back for Dodge's wedding?"

She didn't answer. They might have to ride together, but they didn't have to talk, did they?

He waited a few seconds before continuing. "That's where I'm headed." She felt him glance over at her as she kept her attention riveted on the grimy knob that kept the tray upright on the seat back in front of her. "This is the only bus that'd get me to the wedding in time."

Clarissa rolled her eyes.

He raised his voice a little, drawing the attention of the woman across the aisle when he asked, "That where you're headed, too, Clarey?"

She sighed loudly, assuming—scratch that, *knowing*—he'd make some embarrassing scene to force her into talking to him if she continued to ignore him.

"*Myrna's* wedding. Yep."

"Myrna McGovern, my future sister-in-law. Hey! That's right," he said, lowering his voice again, now that she'd answered him. "Weren't you two best friends?"

She huffed, wishing he'd shut up. Everyone in Big Chimney,

West Virginia, knew that Clarissa Calhoun and Myrna McGovern were practically joined at the hip from infancy through high school. And everyone—especially Ford McInerney—knew that while Myrna had dated Dodge McInerney, Clarissa had dated his other older brother, Lincoln.

"You the maid of honor? 'Cause I'm the best man," he said, patting his knees through his jeans. "Guess we'll be walking down the aisle together."

She crossed her arms over her chest and glared at him as if to say, *Are you done?*

He paused for a moment, all traces of teasing disappearing. "By the way, Linc's comin' home, too."

Clarissa clenched her jaw and turned to look out the window at the darkness. Catching the shininess of her glistening eyes in the reflection, she closed them, leaning her forehead against the glass and praying that Ford would just stop talking.

Man, it must have taken guts for her to get on this bus to go home, but Clarey Calhoun always had a mess of guts. She was way too good for his brother Lincoln. Always had been. Always would be.

Ford McInerney couldn't remember a day of his life when he hadn't been madly in love with Clarissa Calhoun, the blond-haired, blue-eyed girl next door. Two years his senior, Clarey had started dating his older brother Lincoln when they were in the eleventh grade and Ford was still a scrawny little freshman. He'd suffered through walking in on the amorous couple making out more than once, wishing it were him kissing Clarey's soft lips instead of Linc. He'd pretend not to notice as he walked through the basement den, headed out to the garage to get his bike and meet friends at the park. Sometimes he'd walk extra slow, though, watching them on the couch, watching Linc's hands run up and down her back, listening for that small moaning sound she sometimes made in the back of her throat. Even now, remembering, he could hear the sound in his head, and it made his blood rush south.

He shifted in his seat, looking away from her. He'd be lying if he said he'd decided to go to the University of Colorado for any reason other than following Clarey Calhoun, but dang it if Linc hadn't screwed things up and good. After what had happened, she didn't want anything to do with *any* McInerney, including Ford.

She took a deep breath beside him, and he felt her shudder lightly. He was pretty sure she was trying not to cry. Now, it was one thing to tease her a little, but he didn't want her to cry. He tried to think of a way to distract her.

"Hey, Clarey," he said, nudging her waist with his elbow, his voice light and playful. She kept her forehead against the window. "Clarey Calhoun." He nudged her again, and this time she turned to him slightly, grudgingly. His heart clutched, seeing the tears in her eyes, but he forced himself not to react. "Remember when we were kids and we all used to play Super Spies? And if we had to stop the game to go into dinner, we'd call a truce? How about we do that now? Call a truce. Just like when we were kids."

"If memory serves, the McInerneys always cheated on truces. Shared information with the enemy. Kept secrets. Took advantage."

"Not all of us," he said softly. "You're remembering wrong."

"Am I?" she asked, her eyes glassy and blazing at once.

"Listen, it's seven thirty-five now, and this is a thirty-five-hour ride," he said, trying a different tack. A wisp of blond hair had escaped from her braid, and Ford wished he could tuck it gently back behind her ear. "You can go back to hating me on hour thirty-six."

"Nope. On hour thirty-five and one minute," she countered with a hard gaze, her lips a tight line.

He looked into her aqua eyes and felt his face softening. A truce meant they'd have the whole ride together. *Who knows what could happen? If she would only get to know him, only let him—*

He shouldn't let his hopes run away with him. Oh, he was all sorts of a fool for this woman, and he knew it, but she didn't need to know. He forced his face into a look of mild amusement, giving away nothing he felt for her deep in his heart.

"Deal," he said. For one second, he thought she might turn away in a huff as she stared at his proffered hand.

"Deal," she finally replied, shaking it.

His hand was warm and calloused, likely from all the hours he'd spent weight-training during the recent football season. As soon as she touched him, her heart kicked into a gallop, the wild hammering almost making her breathless in the seat beside him.

Since when did Ford McInerney make her feel anything special? She'd been Linc's girl, for heaven's sake! Well, except for that night, that one night …

She'd purposely glossed over the details of *that night* in her head. She insisted on forgetting the way she'd fallen into Ford's waiting arms. She wanted to hate him for offering her kindness and comfort when he'd been the one who'd confirmed the terrible rumor. She'd tried to make herself believe that he had taken advantage of the situation—of her suddenly broken heart, her lightly inebriated state, her need to hate one McInerney brother by loving another. Damn it, he was Linc's brother! He'd had no business reaching for her, comforting her the way he had that night.

But, truth be told, she knew it wasn't all his fault. She'd willfully fallen into Ford. She'd wanted him to hold her. She'd wanted his lips on hers. Almost as if she had *always* wanted—

His thumb moving lightly over her skin jarred her from her thoughts, and she released his hand as if it were on fire, quickly crossing her arms over her heaving chest. She looked out the window again into the pitch night.

Damn Ford, anyway, five ways to Sunday! She didn't care about him like that, certainly didn't want to.

He shifted beside her, and she could feel the heat of his hip pressed against hers, his shoulder grazing hers. Lord, the man was big. And warm. And distracting.

"So … a truce," she murmured.

"Yep. We shook on it. Can't welch now."

"Calhouns don't welch."

"McInerneys, either."

What crap, she thought, thinking about Linc, about his vows of love, about how much he'd promised her once upon a time.

She scoffed, tightening her grip around her middle, hating that Linc's betrayal still hurt. It'd been months since it had happened, and she was mostly over it. But then, she'd been at school all fall, keeping her distance from any reminders, including Ford.

"Okay," he amended, sighing. "Not *this* McInerney."

His voice was soft and gentle, and when she looked over at him, she was surprised to find his eyes warm and worried.

"Sometimes I still can't believe it ..." she started, but the rest of the words wouldn't come. She bit her bottom lip, wishing away the lump in the bottom of her throat, unable to bear the shame of crying all over Lincoln's younger brother. Again.

"Me, neither," he said. "Sorry for it. Hated like hell to be the one to tell you it was true."

"Hated like hell to be told it was true," she whispered.

"But," he said, pausing for a beat before continuing. "Wasn't sorry for what came after, Clarey. I'm not sorry about what happened that night. Between you and me."

She stared into his eyes, at those beautiful damn eyelashes that had shown up in more than one of her dreams, waking her up all twisted in sweaty sheets, hot and cold at once.

She didn't think before she spoke. If she had, she'd never have allowed the words to roll off her tongue.

"Me, neither."

His eyes widened, and his tongue darted out to wet his lips as he stared at her, shocked by her confession.

She felt the heat in her face, scorching and sharp, and pressed her cool fingers against her cheeks. Where in the world had those words come from? Damn it, she couldn't take them back now. She stumbled to fix things. "I—I mean, the news was so ... um, upsetting, and you were just trying to—to be nice, and I, well, I ..."

"Hey, Clarey," he said, taking one of her hands and drawing it away from her face. He brought the knuckles to his lips and kissed them, lingering for a moment before looking up at her. "Want to play some cards?"

Bless you, Ford McInerney, she thought, feeling the tension leave her shoulders, trying to ignore the way his lips had felt on the back of her hand.

She gave him a small, relieved smile and nodded.

They played cards for two hours before the bus stopped in Burlington, Colorado, at nine forty-five p.m. Clarey got off to use the ladies' room, promising to bring them both back a snack. Ford leaned over to watch her out the window, the way her hips moved as she walked away from the bus, into the truck stop, as a light snow gathered on the shoulders of her leather shearling jacket. He forced himself not to follow her so he could stare down every man in that Qwick-Sip who was about to get a look at the prettiest girl walking the earth.

Taking a deep breath, he sat back in his seat, trying to get a hold of his feelings, and of course his thoughts returned to that night—the night he'd confirmed the rumors about Linc for Clarey. The night his brother had broken her heart, and she'd come to Ford for the truth.

He'd run into her a few times on campus during orientation and their first few weeks of school in August—the only two students from a small town in West Virginia were sure to bump into each other, especially when they'd grown up together. Clarey had always treated him like her boyfriend's little brother, an old friend from home. She'd offer a fond smile at the Commons, a warm hello from across the Quad. They'd shared coffee once or twice and even danced together at a few frat parties. But mostly Clarey lived her life with her other junior friends as Ford found his way around as a new freshman.

She'd certainly never sought him out. Not on purpose. Not until that night.

Clarey had found him at a frat party the second weekend in September. He'd seen her arrive, purposefully walking through the door and scanning the massive crowd on the dance floor with deliberate intent but wild eyes. At first, he hadn't realized that she was looking for him. But when her eyes had finally slammed into his, she had beelined across the dance floor, pulling on his shirt sleeve without a word, until he followed her outside.

"Tell me the truth, Ford," she demanded, looking up at him. The pain in her eyes made him wince. She was out of breath, her cheeks blazing red.

He hadn't been sure what she was talking about at first. Had she somehow found out how he felt about her? Did she want him to confess his feelings?

He hedged. "Wh-what are you—"

"Lincoln and Bettina!" she screamed. "Tell me if it's true!"

His heart had dropped. "Clarey—"

"Myrna says Bettina's pregnant. Says it's Linc's. Tell me if it's true. Tell me. Say it, Ford. Say your brother's a lying, cheating sack of shit who got Bettina Bray pregnant last summer while he was still dating me! Say it, Ford. Just say it." By the end, tears were streaming down her pretty face and her voice had broken. He watched as her legs buckled and she stumbled forward.

Without thinking, he'd pulled Clarey into his arms, holding her against him, wishing he could absorb her sorrow into his body, feel it for her, take it away.

"Oh, Clarey. Oh, God, Clarey, I'm so sorry. I'm so damn sorry."

She'd wilted against him like a ragdoll, crying, her shoulders shaking with quiet sobs. He'd picked her up into his arms and carried her back to his dorm room, laying her gently on his bed, taking off her shoes, brushing her hair off her face as she wept.

"Lie with me," she said softly, and at first he pretended he hadn't heard her. But she said it again, "Lie with me, Ford."

He kicked off his shoes and got into bed behind her, wrapping his arms around her, just wanting to offer comfort to this unspeakably sad girl of his dreams. When she turned in his arms, pressing her body up against his and leaning forward to touch her lips to his, he knew he should have pushed her away. Some part of him knew it was wrong to return her kiss, knew she was a wounded thing who needed comfort, not complication. But he'd waited his whole life to be with Clarissa Calhoun, and here she was, in bed, with him.

They hadn't ended up having sex, only making out for a while before Clarey turned back around in his arms and fell asleep pressed against him. She'd been gone when he woke up the next morning and had avoided him like the plague ever since.

Although he had always hoped—even prayed—for something to happen between them, he'd never wanted for their first experience to be so mired in brokenness. In fact, when he'd confirmed Linc's affair with Bettina Bray in the dim light outside of the Delta Phi frat house, he'd expected Clarey to haul off and hit him, if for no other reason than he was Linc's little brother. He certainly hadn't expected for her to end up in his bed asking him to hold her. He couldn't have seen it coming. But, truth be told, even if he had, he probably wouldn't have gotten out of the way.

When the bus jolted over a bump, Clarissa's eyes opened, and she was momentarily confused about where she was. She was leaned up against the window, covered by a blanket with something warm and heavy draped over her shoulders and something even warmer—and hairier—pressed against her neck. She took a deep breath and sighed. Soap and cotton and Ford.

Oh, right. Mmmm.

It was Ford's arm around her, his head on her shoulder, his soft and wavy chestnut hair warming the smooth hollow of her neck, and his breath on her chest every time he exhaled. He was fast asleep.

She shivered, more from the deliciousness of the contact than from the chill inside the late-night bus. She wiggled her wrist out from under the blankets, tilting it to catch the light. Three twenty a.m. They'd only been asleep for three hours, and they'd be pulling into Topeka, Kansas, in about twenty-five minutes if the bus was on time. They still had a long day of travel ahead, including a midnight transfer in Columbus, Ohio.

After two hours of gin rummy, Clarissa had gotten off the bus at the rest stop, grabbing them Cokes and snacks, and when she returned, the cards had been put away. She'd smiled as she sat back down and he asked about her major.

"So," he'd started. "English and Studio Art, huh? What're you planning to do with your degree after you finish?"

"How do you know my majors?"

"I keep track of you," he said, grinning at her.

"Well, I still have another year. I don't know yet." She shrugged, wondering about Ford, wondering why she'd never considered him. She'd been so blinded by Linc she had never really noticed his younger brother. In addition to being hard-bodied with deep eyes and beautiful lashes, Ford was kind to her—he'd *always* been kind to her. He had always listened when she talked. He always had a smile for her. And, of course, there was that night ...

She shook her head as if to clear it. *What were they talking about?* Oh, yes. Her plans. She knew, of course, what she wanted to do after graduation, but she'd never told anyone, not even Lincoln.

"Come on," he said, nudging her gently with bright, interested eyes. "I bet you know exactly what you want to do."

She smiled, feeling herself blush. "Well, there is this one thing ..."

"Which is?"

"Don't laugh."

"I promise." He crossed his finger over his chest.

"Seriously. I've never told anyone except my academic advisor."

"I won't laugh, Clarey." His grin faded as he held her eyes.

"I want to ... write children's books." She swallowed, hoping her dreams would be safe with him. "The English is for the writing. The Studio Art is so I can do my own illustrations." She searched his blank face, feeling worried. "What do you think?"

"I think you're perfect," he whispered, reaching up to tuck a stray wisp of blonde hair behind her ear.

"You mean my plan," she murmured. "*It's* perfect."

"No, Clarey. I mean *you.*"

He had asked her more about the books she wanted to write, and she'd told him about this idea she had about two pennies named VinCENT and MilliCENT who start their lives at the U.S. Mint and travel the country together. He'd laughed at all the right places, holding her eyes, nodding and smiling, and making her feel like all of her dreams would someday come true.

But, if she were honest, the whole time, all she'd heard were the words *No, Clarey. I mean you.*

He adjusted in his sleep, the hand on her shoulder pulling her closer to his chest, his face burrowed into her neck. Her body heated up from the contact, her blood racing, pumping faster, as she became aware of every place his body was touching hers. She wanted ... She *wanted*—

As the bus rumbled over another pothole, the bump caused his lips to momentarily graze her skin, stealing her breath away. She swallowed, trembling, wanting more, wanting Ford to kiss her again as he had that night several months ago.

Oh, good Lord! I can't be falling for Ford McInerney, can I?

She wanted to sort out her thoughts, but the light in the bus was so soft, and the motion rocked her to sleep in her warm cocoon. Before she could wrap her mind around the daunting, inconvenient question, her heavy eyes had closed again, and she fell back to sleep.

They slept through the three stops in Kansas, finally waking up when the bus rolled into Kansas City, Missouri, at seven fifteen, for breakfast.

Ford woke up first, his eyes opening slowly against the glare of sunlight streaming in through the tinted window. He was warm. And hard. And the reason was clear.

Clarey Calhoun's cheek was nestled under his neck, and she was curled into him, her breasts pressed up against his chest. As she breathed deeply in her sleep, they pushed into his chest, then back, into him, then back. He groaned, flicking the blanket off his body with his free hand, then gingerly sliding his other arm from around her body and urging her back gently. She murmured in her sleep, resting her head on his shoulder. He was glad she didn't wake up. He didn't want her to see the naked lust on his face. The want. The love.

He forced himself to think of his last football game, the play that had led to the final touchdown, and he felt his body relax. Faking a yawn as she stirred beside him, he smiled as she opened her eyes slowly, blinking twice in surprise as she looked up at him, recognizing him.

"Ford," she breathed in a drowsy, half-asleep voice, licking her lips and pressing them together.

"Morning, Clarey," he whispered, his lips a breath away from hers.

She tilted her chin up, just a fraction of an inch, and, closing his eyes, he lowered his lips to hers. It was just a touch, a brush, a grounding gesture, to be sure she was real beside him, to be certain he wasn't dreaming. He drew back from her, his heart thumping madly and his breath catching as she opened her eyes wide and sat up, pressing her fingers to her mouth.

"It's like that?" she asked him.

"It's always been like that."

She swallowed and nodded once, looking down, but he tipped her chin back up so she would look at him.

"Hungry?" he asked. "Can I take you to breakfast?"

She grinned, the uncertainty fleeing from her face like a passing cloud.

"Starved."

He stood, offering her his hand, and he couldn't be sure if it was butterflies or hunger rattling around in his stomach when she took it.

By late afternoon, they'd reminisced about elementary school, middle school, and Sunday school, with Clarey laughing to the point of a snort when Ford confirmed that he, Lincoln, and Dodge had been the culprits who'd managed to hoist a shopping cart from the Pathmark onto the top of the water tower. It had been the anonymous prank of the century and had all of Big Chimney up in arms for weeks, trying to figure out how it had gotten there and how to get it down.

"My favorite," he said, eyes twinkling, "was when old man Thoroughgood suggested that a rogue tornado had ripped the cart from the Pathmark parking lot in the middle of the night and gently placed it atop the tower without a bit of damage to any other part of town!"

"That was the popular theory for at least two weeks!" she said, wiping her eyes. "How in the world did you do it?"

"That's a McInerney family secret," he said, pretending to lock his lips and throw away the key. He mumbled through closed lips, "I'll never tell."

"You still ticklish?" she asked, lunging toward him.

He chortled as her fingers wiggled over the hard lines of his stomach. Finally, he clamped his hands around her wrists, pulling them away.

"Quit it now," he said.

"If we needed information," she said, grinning at him, "that was always your biggest weakness."

"Not even close," he murmured, his body throwing off heat and his eyes full of longing as he studied her.

"Then what was?" she asked, even though she knew the answer. She wanted to hear him say it.

"You."

He pulled her wrists toward him, wrapping them around his neck, then lowered his head to kiss her.

He sensed that she had something to say to him as they sat side by side on a bench in the Columbus, Ohio, bus depot, waiting to board the transfer that would take them the rest of the way home. He had his arm around her, unable to resist the opportunity to touch her, to hold her, to continue to ride the wave of awesome that had started as a result of their thirty-five-hour truce.

Anyway, it was almost two o'clock in the morning, and he knew she was tired. He ran his hand distractedly up and down her spine.

"Ford," she said softly, not looking up at him, "I gotta say something."

"Okay," he answered, not sure where she was going.

"I think I owe you an apology."

"I don't know what for."

"I was real angry at you back in September. When I walked into that party after getting off the phone with Myrna. I mighta blamed you a little bit for what Lincoln did. But it wasn't your fault. I'm sorry I blamed you. I'm sorry I avoided you … after."

"I probably should have pushed you away that night, Clarey."

She paused before answering in a small voice. "I'm glad you didn't."

"Yeah?" He leaned back from her, tilting her chin up with his free hand so he could look into her eyes.

"Made me see there was more to you than just being Lincoln's little brother."

"Man, I hated being Lincoln's little brother when I found out what he was doing behind your back. Broke his nose when—"

"Wait. What do you mean, when you found out what he was doing? Nobody knew he was cheating on me until Bettina announced she was pregnant." Her eyes widened as she stared up at him, her mouth dropping open. He could see the wheels in her head spinning. "Oh, God. Did you know? You knew he was cheating on me?"

He wanted to deny it, but he knew his eyes had already given him away.

"You knew. You knew Linc was sleeping with her behind my back, didn't you? You knew last summer. You knew when we rode the bus out here in August. All those weeks at the beginning of school when you'd see me around campus. You knew. I must have looked like such a fool to you. Stupid Clarey Calhoun, doesn't even know her boyfriend's cheating on her. Stupid little …" Her voice trailed off as her eyes filled with tears, broken, but not because of Linc this time. Because of him. She scooted back from him on the bench, still holding his eyes, hurt and wary.

"Clarey," he said, reaching for her hands. "I woulda died before hurting you."

"But you didn't die." She pulled her hands away. "And I am hurtin'."

"I *couldn't* tell you," he whispered. "I couldn't—I didn't want to be the one who—"

"You chose your brother instead of me." She looked down,

swiping at a tear that trickled down her face. She reached down for her bag, standing up. "I'm going to go get a seat by myself."

"Clarey, please—"

"No! You knew!"

"Please let me explain—"

"No, Ford McInerney. You leave me be," she said, her voice thready with disgust and betrayal as tears flooded her eyes, wetting her eyelashes before they tumbled down her face. "You made your choice."

She walked away from him, out the wooden doors, stepping on board the waiting bus outside, leaving him alone.

Damn Linc! Damn him! Ford strode across the depot, watching from the windows as she found a seat next to someone else on the new bus. She bowed her head, and he knew she was crying. *Damn it. Damn, damn, damn you, Lincoln!*

He clenched his jaw painfully, remembering the day he'd found out about Linc cheating on Clarey. He'd stopped by Linc's place unannounced in late August to say good-bye before leaving for school, shocked to find a half-naked Bettina riding Linc like a rodeo bronc in the center of his brother's bed.

"Get the fuck out!" Linc had shouted to Ford in the doorway.

Bettina, mistaking his meaning, had scrambled off his lap, grabbing her panties and skirt off the floor before scurrying from the room to leave the brothers facing each other alone.

Ford stood at the foot of the bed with crossed arms, staring at Lincoln, who had laced his hands behind his head, his face annoyed, shameless with his slick erection still in plain view.

"What the hell, Linc!" Ford whipped the bedspread over his brother's lap, then ran a hand through his hair, processing the scene in an instant. His thoughts led him to one place: to the prettiest, sweetest girl in Big Chimney, who had no idea her boyfriend was a cheating scumbag.

"What?" asked Linc, shrugging. "You're telling me you'd say no if Bettina Bray offered you a ride? Bullshit."

"I'd say *hell no* if I had a girl like Clarissa Calhoun in my life." Ford spit the words, hating that he shared the same blood as his asshole brother. "You're a bastard."

"You don't *fuck* girls like Clarey," explained Linc, as though speaking to a moron. "You *marry* them. You want to do kinky stuff, you need a friend like Bettina."

Ford sneered. "You make me sick."

"Ain't your concern no how, pup."

"Screw you, Lincoln. You don't deserve her."

Lincoln jumped out of bed, pulling on his jeans and zipping them before approaching Ford. Ford was big, but Lincoln, who had dropped out of junior college to work in the coal mines, was bigger.

"Keep your nose out of it, little brother. Always knew you had a thing for my girl. Always knew you wished it was you—"

Ford drew back his fist, and it connected, sending Lincoln's head reeling as his nose erupted in a bloody mess.

"Fuck, Ford, you dumb shit! You mighta broke my nose."

Lincoln turned and stalked to the bathroom, returning a moment later with a wet washcloth pressed up against his face. When he spoke, his tone was laced with menace.

"You try a stunt like that again? I'll take you down. That's a promise." He drew the washcloth back to look at the blood, then pressed it back up against his nose. "Stay the fuck out of it."

Ford had considered going straight to Clarey, telling her everything. But when he'd consulted his older brother, Dodge, he'd decided against it. Not only was Dodge the smartest guy Ford knew, teaching math and science at the local high school, he was also full of good advice.

"You're headed to the same college she's at, Ford. Don't be the messenger of bad news. She and Linc will end things soon enough. Trust me."

A week later, he'd sat next to Clarey on the bus that had taken them from home out to college in Colorado, keeping his awful secret hidden from her. Maybe, being so far from home together, he could make her see *him* for the first time. Maybe he could find a way to connect with her without telling her about Lincoln and Bettina. Maybe he'd find a way to make her *his*.

And maybe pigs would fly out of his ass.

Ford twisted his neck to look back at her, at her blond head against the headrest five rows back, at her slender neck and closed eyes. They'd been riding for four hours since Columbus. They'd be pulling into Huntington, West Virginia, soon—the last stop before Charleston. Ford felt a dire need to resolve things with Clarey before they got home. Like if they didn't, they never would.

Desperation, raw and insistent, bubbled up from inside of him. He loved Clarissa Calhoun. All he had left was the truth, and it was time to tell her exactly how he felt about her. It was time for her to know.

"Huntington, West Virginia, folks. Five-minute stop to drop off and pick up."

Clarissa roused herself, stretching lightly as the driver's voice bit into her unhappy dreams. She'd been kissing Linc, who'd turned into Ford and stayed Ford. Her eyes felt puffy from too much crying and too little sleep. She reached into the seat pocket for her bottle of water, and her hand brushed against a crisply folded paper sticking up, bearing her name: Clarey.

She took a deep breath and peeked over the seats to find Ford's wavy brown hair five seats in front of her, exactly where he'd been when the bus had rolled out of Columbus.

A letter. From Ford.

She took a sip of water, then put the bottle away and unfolded the paper.

> Dear Clarey,
>
> I have a few things I want to say, and I know you don't want to listen to me, but maybe you'll be willing to read instead.

I found out about Linc and Bettina back in August. I walked in on them a week before we left for school. I hated keeping it from you, but I didn't want to hurt you. I didn't want to see your eyes when you found out what a bastard my brother is. I should've told you. I'm sorry. I'll never keep anything from you again, Clarissa Calhoun. That's a promise I intend to keep, which means I need to come clean about something else...

I've been in love with you for as long as I can remember-with the blond-haired, blue-eyed girl who lived next door. My childhood friend. My teenage crush. My brother's girlfriend. I feel like I waited all my life to kiss you, to tell you I love you. Heck, I only applied to Boulder because that's where you were going, too. And all I ever wanted, in my entire life, was to be close to you.

I understand if you never want to talk to me again. I get it. But if you'd give me a chance, I'd never hurt you again, Clarey. I would love you every day of my life. The way you deserve to be loved.

Ford

As tears coursed down her face, she read the letter four more times, feeling her heart surge with love for Ford McInerney, who was offering her his heart—his whole heart—after a lifetime of waiting for her.

When the bus pulled into Charleston, she waited until everyone got off. Even the driver got off to take the luggage out from the compartment underneath the bus, leaving Clarissa and Ford the only two people on board. For all that it mattered, the only two people in the world.

She took her bag down and made her way up the aisle. He stood as she approached, turning into the aisle to face her, worry and hope fighting for dominion on his face as his hazel eyes searched hers. She stood before him, returning his gaze, her swelling heart brimming with love.

"It's not a thirty-five-hour ride," she finally said, wetting her lips and pressing them together.

"It's not a thirty-five-hour ride," she said again, letting her bag drop to the floor and taking a step to close the space between them. Her breasts brushed up against his chest, and her hands trembled at her sides. "You got it wrong."

"Is that right?" he asked, slipping an arm around her waist.

"Uh-huh." She laced her fingers behind his neck. "It's a thirty-six-hour ride."

"So what?" he said, trying to think straight, trying not to hope too much even though it would be unbearable if she walked away from him now, after he had bared his heart to her.

"So according to our original truce," she said, "I should've gone back to hating you fifty-nine minutes ago."

"Haven't you been hating me since Columbus?"

She shook her head, flicking her glance to his lips, then back to his eyes.

"No, I haven't." She smiled at him—a smile that reached her eyes and softened her face and made him feel like heaven had just opened up, letting loose one perfect angel. "I've been fallin' in love with you instead."

"Clarey," he breathed, his eyes filling with tears, undone and overcome as he pulled her up against him, wrapping her in his arms, resting his face in the soft, warm hollow of her neck. "Finally."

"That letter …"

He leaned back to search her eyes. "I meant every word. I'll never hurt you again, and I'll love you forever. I promise you, Clarey Calhoun."

"Ford," she breathed, her eyes filling with tears, too. "I just wish you'd told me sooner. I got distracted by the wrong brother for a while. Sorry it took me so long to see you."

She moved her fingers from the back of his neck to cup his jaw and cheeks, giving him a tender smile. "Make up for lost time?"

He closed his eyes, tilting his head and leaning down to press his lips to hers. She sighed into his mouth, offering him the perfect opening to sweep his tongue past her lips, claiming hers, stroking it, loving it. After a lifetime of waiting, Clarey Calhoun belonged to Ford McInerney, and the thought was so sweet, so unbelievable, so mind-blowing he drew back to look in her eyes. Just to make sure it was true.

And it was.

"We're here, Clarey," he said, smiling at his girl. He reached down for her bag, then took her hand in his, lacing their fingers together, pulling her off the bus, into the fresh air of a brand new day. "We're home, darlin'. We're finally home."

Katy Regnery, Amazon bestselling author, has always loved telling a good story, and credits her mother with making funny, heartwarming tales come alive throughout her child-hood. A lifelong devotee of all romance writing, from Edwardian to present-day, it was just a matter of time before Katy tried her hand at writing a love story of her own.

As it turned out, one love story turned into a series of six Heart of Montana romances, following the love lives of the Yellowstone-based Lindstrom siblings. When Katy's fans asked her to turn up the heat, she wrote *Playing for Love at Deep Haven*, a sexy standalone story about second chances. Over the Summer of 2014, Katy was pleased to offer another stand-alone romance, *The Vixen and the Vet*, which was an Amazon bestseller She also launched The English Brothers, a contemporary romance series about five wealthy brothers looking for love.

Katy lives in the relative wilds of northern Fairfield County, Connecticut, where her writing room looks out at the woods, and her husband, two young children, and two dogs create just enough cheerful chaos to remind her that the very best love stories of all begin at home.

THEIR NIGHT OFF

ALLISON BRENNAN

New York Times Bestseller, RITA® Finalist

FBI SPECIAL AGENT SUZANNE Madeaux walked into Roberta's in Brooklyn, the garlic and herbs and tomatoes and cheese blending together to make her mouth water and her stomach growl. She spotted Joe immediately, sitting at the table in the corner, where both of them could put their back to the wall. Her stomach did another flip, this time at how damn *gorgeous* this man was. All six-foot-tall Italian perfection.

Damn, she'd missed him. She was hooked *again.* She didn't want to be. Her heart told her Joe was *the one,* but there were so many complications and obstacles that her head told her *steer clear.*

Just because the sex is amazing doesn't mean this is going to work.

Joe saw her a beat later and got that cocky *I know I'm good-looking and you want me* grin on his face. Then he held up two beers and she laughed. This was why she loved him. Arrogant and thoughtful; sexy and kind. He knew her well.

She sidled over to the small table and slid in right next to Joe, taking the beer in one hand and putting her other hand on his thigh. She smiled as she leaned in. "It's been nearly two weeks since we've seen each other and you want pizza instead of sex?"

That half grin on his face always did her in. "You'll need to store up energy for tonight, Suzi."

He was the only one she let call her Suzi, and only when they were alone. He kissed her, meaning it to be quick and light, but Suzanne wasn't having light. Between their jobs and Joe's demanding ex-wife, they hadn't seen each other—touched each other—in twelve days.

She wrapped her hand on the back of his neck and kept his lips on hers. That briefest moment of resistance melted, and their mouths exploded in the fire that was uniquely theirs. A groan of lust and sheer joy escaped her throat, and Joe's lips turned into a smile even as they devoured hers.

She pulled back, raised a single eyebrow, and said, "You like that I'm horny, don't you?"

"Is that a trick question?" He tugged on her long, straight blond hair, then wrapped it around his hands until he pulled her back to him. He teased her lips with his, then rested his forehead on hers. "I've missed you, Suzi."

"Right back at ya, Detective."

It wasn't that they were trying to keep their relationship secret—their closest friends knew they'd gotten back together after they'd worked a multi-jurisdictional case back in October, six months ago. But Suzanne was the FBI liaison to the NYPD, and Joe DeLucca was a detective out in Queens. That alone made their relationship a bit sticky. But until she knew they were going to make it, Suzanne didn't want to create problems for Joe with his psycho ex-wife, Stephanie, who used their nine-year-old son as a pawn to keep Joe close to home and celibate.

Obviously, the celibate part didn't last long. But seeing each other on the down low made it easier to explore the relationship without the additional pressure. Suzanne had walked away once before because she'd been falling in love and known it wasn't going to end well with all the drama Joe's ex kicked up. But now, maybe she'd grown up. Life was messy. They'd make it work, just taking it one day at a time.

"You're all quiet," Joe said, taking a long drink of his beer. "That scares me."

She smiled as if she had a secret. "Maybe you should be scared."

The waitress brought over the pie, with added mushrooms and sausage. Joe motioned for two more beers.

"I'm starving," Suzanne said. She carefully pulled out a hot slice and dropped it on her plate, shaking her fingers to cool them. "Heaven is pizza."

They ate in silence for several minutes. One of the things she loved about Joe was that he got her. She loved pizza and beer, and she could be just as happy sitting quietly eating and enjoying the eye candy that was her boyfriend as she could be going to the Mets game and screaming her lungs out.

She nibbled at her third slice, now that the painful edge of hunger had abated.

"Is all well on the ex-home front?" she asked, trying to keep it light even though Joe had grown increasingly frustrated with Stephanie's games.

"Same as usual, which I consider a blessing," he said. "Thanks for the Mets tickets. Tyler had a blast last night."

"Well, you owe me one. Make it two." She smiled. "I'll collect tonight. And tomorrow."

"Close your case?"

She rolled her eyes but nodded and popped a stray piece of sausage in her mouth. "For a stupid criminal, Dusty Gaines had a run of good luck. I still have paperwork up to my ass, but that'll wait until tomorrow. Four days tracking that bastard all over the five boroughs was enough to make me want a desk job."

Dusty Gaines was a common thief who had hit on the FBI radar when he'd broken into the apartment of Dina Carr, the ex-wife of Assistant Director Frank Carr of the NY-FBI. Left his prints behind, but he must have known he'd screwed up, because he'd rabbited, hiding out in every hole and sewer he could find. In the course of the investigation, they'd tied him to a series of break-ins all over Manhattan—some that hadn't been reported because the victims didn't know anything had been taken. The only reason the police had been tipped off was because Dusty—the common, stupid thief that he was—had dropped his phone while being chased. The data inside was all dates, times, and locations—of his scores.

"I take it back," she said. "I would slit my throat if I had to sit at a desk all day. But when I watched the interview, I couldn't help but think Dusty Gaines was a fucking idiot and how on earth did he get away with robbing one apartment let alone the eighteen he had in his records? He kept everything on his phone. Everything." She shook her head, took a small bite of pizza. "Listening in to the interview, he just didn't seem smart enough to pull this off for so long. Except, he did ask for his lawyer pretty quick."

"Was he working with someone?"

"That's what I thought—we played that angle, but he wasn't talking. I guess even stupid criminals get lucky sometimes."

"Until they break into the apartment of the former wife of the number two guy in the FBI."

"Exactly." She paused, drained the last of her beer. "You know what I think?" Before Joe could answer, she finished. "I think he had a partner who was smart—smarter—than Dusty. That they've been doing this for a long time and targeting people less likely to report the crime. Or taking something that wouldn't be noticed. Like information. Account numbers. Passwords. They had a falling out, or Dusty got greedy and took his show on the road," she speculated. "That's how we were able to get so close."

Damn, now she was thinking about work again. The case had been bothering her all day; ever since she'd left headquarters, she'd kept running the facts through her head. Dusty Gaines wasn't the sharpest tack in the box.

She glared at Joe. "I *was* horny; now my mind is working overtime. Your fault, babe."

He edged closer and grinned, his hand moving up her thigh, to her waist, until his fingers pulled her T-shirt from her slacks. All it took was his touch on her bare skin to make her shiver. "Okay, that's good," she said. "Pay the bill, Detective, and maybe I'll let you kiss me good-night."

He kissed her neck, his mouth hot and open. "Just one kiss?"

His hand moved up to just under her demi-bra, and she stopped him. "DeLucca, I'm going to arrest you for indecent exposure if that hand moves a half inch more."

"That's a local crime, not federal," he whispered in her ear. "And I don't have my handcuffs on me."

"You don't? There goes the night I had planned."

He kissed her ear. "We'll use yours."

"Your place or mine?"

"Mine's closer." He dropped his hand and glanced at the bill, then swore under his breath. "They gave us the wrong bill." He motioned to the waitress, who came over surprisingly quickly considering the place was packed.

"Sorry," she said and immediately swapped out his bill for another. "I realized I'd made a mistake."

"No problem," he said with his award-winning grin that made everyone—man, woman, or child—feel like they were the center of his universe. But loyalty was Joe's strength, and Suzanne trusted him with her life, and her heart. That was why this time, she was going to fight to make them work.

What had changed? Was it just her? Willing to risk her heart for someone else? She'd become so lonely over the last two years. She'd seen what she could have with Joe, and she'd walked away—and no one since had come close.

"Hey," Joe said and touched her cheek. "You look sad."

She shook her head, gave him a smile. "I'm good."

"You're lying." He kissed her nose. "I'll get it out of you. You know I can."

"Woo hoo, you scare me," she teased, needing to lighten the mood. She and Joe would talk about it—they'd have to—but not tonight. After nearly two weeks of work keeping them apart, tonight was for them to reconnect.

"You're impossible." Joe paid the bill and left a healthy tip. He drained the rest of his beer and stood, pulling Suzanne from her seat. "I finally moved from my studio to the unit upstairs. It has a bedroom, a bigger bath and kitchen. Even a balcony, and a view of Manhattan if you stand in the far corner and stretch your neck."

She laughed as they walked toward the subway station. "I can't wait to christen the place."

"Four rooms," he said. "It's going to take some time."

"Four?"

"Kitchen. Bedroom. Living room. Bathroom. Five if we count the closet."

"You might not have to work tomorrow, but I do."

"Then we'd better get started." He wrapped his right arm around her waist. "You know, the best thing about this relationship is that you're right-handed and I'm left-handed."

"That's better than the sex? You're weird, DeLucca."

He pushed her against his right side. "If I were right-handed, you'd get the butt of my gun jammed into your ribs."

She laughed. The tension of the hunt for the moron Dusty Gaines and her personal worries about her and Joe and where they were going was finally gone. A couple beers, a delicious pie, the sexy man she loved ... it just didn't get any better.

Dusty's whiny voice cut through her euphoria.

But I didn't *break into an FBI agent's house.*

Not an FBI Agent. The assistant director's ex-wife.

No, no, no. I didn't do it. I swear.

"You're thinking about work again," Joe said. "If you really want to work, I have a foot-high stack of unsolved homicides on my desk."

"Something Dusty said. No," she corrected. "It's more than that. Shit."

She stopped walking as they reached the entrance to the subway. "Hold on, one sec," she said and pulled out her phone.

Joe sighed. "I have a feeling neither of us is going to be satisfied tonight."

She kissed him hard on the lips. "Yes, we will. But just a ... minute."

She had a copy of the thief's records, the same records they'd found on his phone when he'd dropped it during the pursuit. The records that gave them the list of addresses he'd robbed.

"Dammit! I can't believe I missed this!"

"Missed what?"

She turned her phone toward Joe. "This. In his log, all these numbers are dates and times, and these are abbreviations of the addresses he hit."

"And?"

"Just like you got the wrong check, he got the wrong apartment."

"He went into the wrong apartment?"

"Dina lives in number 350. He kept saying he wasn't in that apartment. I think he got the apartments wrong."

"Like he was supposed to be in the apartment next door?"

"Like he was supposed to be in apartment 530. Damn bastard must be dyslexic or just has a piss-poor memory." She shook her head, and they walked through the turnstile toward the train platform. "All weekend, as we were going through the list of his targets, I kept thinking that Dina didn't fit the profile. She's an interior decorator. She works part-time for a nonprofit educational foundation. All the other targets are professionals. Lawyers. Doctors. Wall Street executives. People who make a lot more money than Dina."

"Stop." Joe spun her around. They were in the middle of the subway station. Two stops, then a quick transfer would put them at Joe's apartment. They could walk there; it was less than two miles, just inside Queens. Or they could take the L straight into Manhattan—FBI headquarters, Suzanne's apartment ... and Dina Carr's apartment.

"I know that look in your eye," Joe said.

"Okay, let me explain. Remember we talked about Dusty having a partner?"

"Yes, it was only five minutes ago. I only drank two beers."

"Go with me on this, okay? In all the follow-up, I'm thinking, this guy, Dusty Gaines, just isn't smart enough to pull off all these jobs. So he has some tech skills. He had a B&E bust awhile back. But these are bigger, smarter jobs. What if it's his partner, or rather, someone hires Dusty to go in, look for something specific?"

"And I gather Dusty the dumb thief didn't give up anyone."

"No. NYPD started to press, and he lawyered up. But he could be scared of the guy, so what if they weren't partners so much as Dusty is working for him?" That felt right to her. She pictured the lowlife sweating. Nervous. He was more worried about what was waiting for him outside than being arrested by the cops. "What if Dina was a mistake? Whoops, wrong apartment, why don't I grab these pretty diamond earrings? See? Totally out of character. Every robbery we tracked down from the list on Dusty's phone had cash or bonds or a specific document taken. The burglar didn't go after jewelry; he was only after cash and information—and we always knew there were victims who didn't call it in."

"Blackmail," Joe said flatly.

"Bingo. And Dina wouldn't have a lot of cash in her apartment; she wasn't being blackmailed. It's an outlier. No one thought of it, or if they did, they don't care because we have him. He simply went to the wrong apartment."

The train pulled up to the platform and they boarded. It was Sunday evening, and the train was less than half full.

"Call it in," Joe suggested. "Have the detectives push on this angle. He'll crack if he's the idiot you think he is."

"Dusty Gaines will crack eventually—but I'd put good money on the partner/boss/head honcho hitting the *right* apartment tonight. Before we break the weak link. My guess? It's number 530."

Joe rubbed his eyes. Suzanne knew that expression—he was exasperated.

"Say I agree with you. You can't know that he's going to attack tonight, or which apartment."

"Assuming there is a partner, and my gut tells me there is, he's going to know Dusty will eventually spill everything. And he knows now, or will know soon enough, that we have Dusty in custody. So he has to act tonight. And he's going to make this hit and then disappear, so if Dusty does give him up tonight, he's not going to be home, anyway."

"Okay. That makes sense, in a convoluted way. You're lucky I understand how you think, Mad Dog."

She hit him—hard—on his arm. He winced. "I told you *never* to call me that."

"You get a bone, you don't let go. It's a compliment."

"Like hell."

Years ago, she'd been dubbed Mad Dog Madeaux by the press when she'd worked a kidnapping case that'd hit her hard. She'd gone after the media for endangering the lives of not only the FBI agents working the case but the kid who had been taken. That incident had earned her a lot of praise, as well as a lot of criticism. Fortunately, she had also developed a good relationship with NYPD, which had since been parlayed into the FBI liaison position.

Joe kissed her cheek. "Sorry, Suzanne. I love you."

She looked up at him and saw it. Maybe she'd seen it before, but not this raw, not this exposed. He'd teased her, he hadn't meant to hurt her feelings, but he also knew her and knew about the case that had torn her apart, the case that had resulted in the nickname she hated.

"I know," she said. Then she smiled and said, "I love you, too, DeLucca."

The subway stopped where they needed to transfer to the G train to get to Joe's apartment. Suzanne made no move to get off. "You can go home; I'll call in a team."

Joe took her by both arms and pulled her into a kiss. Hard, fast, angry. "Hell, no," he whispered. "You promised me a night of hot sex, and if we have to catch this bad guy before you'll get naked with me, that's what we're going to do."

She smiled.

He didn't.

"Joe—thanks. I mean it."

He sighed and shook his head. "You're impossible."

"So I've been told."

He had a thoughtful expression. He thought she was right, too, and that pleased her. "You said apartment 530?"

"It makes sense. You could have been right—it could have been the next-door neighbor—but I think he just mixed up the numbers when he was typing them into his phone. But we'll check both."

She pulled out her smartphone to call her office and get the stats on apartment 530, plus call in a team for backup. "Damn, we're in the tunnel."

"Patience."

She stared at him. "*You* telling *me* to be patient?"

"I'm remarkably patient. You're not naked, are you?"

"You have a one-track mind."

"Damn straight. I've been thinking about you and me being horizontal all day." He put his arm over her shoulder and kissed her.

She tilted up her chin and raised her eyebrows. "Wait—have you been thinking about us doing the dirty all day, or spending all day horizontal?"

"Both," he said, practically growling. "You're not getting out of this. We're going to get this guy, and then we're going to have sex. Got it?"

"What makes you think I want to get out of anything except these clothes?" she whispered in his ear, then playfully bit it.

"You do that again, and the poor mark in apartment 530 is going to be robbed, because I'll be taking you back to your apartment, kicking and screaming if I have to."

She laughed. "I'd like to see you try."

"Don't tempt me."

But Joe had on his thinking face, and she knew he was just as interested in her theory as she was.

"This all depends on whether apartment 530 has something the perp wants," Joe said. "I assume it's a nice building."

She nodded. "Tenant-owned apartments, doorman, expensive. Dina got it in the divorce, but both she and Frank come from a bit of money. East Twenty-Second and Park Avenue, north of Gramercy Park. Quiet building, not a lot of kids. People of means, mostly white collar."

She stared at her phone. No bars. When were they going to be out of the damn tunnel?

"What does Dina do? Nonprofit, you said?"

"Some education foundation. She also does interior design part-time, and apparently makes a shitload of money catering to the hoity-toity." Suzanne rolled her eyes. "It's amazing what people will pay good money for."

"Some people would argue that you waste too much money on baseball tickets."

"Bite your tongue, DeLucca. It's my only vice."

Now he laughed out loud. "Oh, Suzi, you have far worse vices than baseball."

"Watch yourself, or you won't be able to enjoy any of them tonight. Yes! Got a signal."

She called Frank Carr. Technically, he wasn't her direct supervisor; he was her boss's boss. But he was taking an interest in this case because his ex-wife was a victim, and he'd told Suzanne to contact him if there was any news.

"Director Carr, this is Agent Suzanne Madeaux. I told you earlier that NYPD caught the burglar."

"I remember. It was only four hours ago."

What was it with sarcastic men tonight? "I think he has a partner or was hired by someone to break in. I don't think Dina was the target; I think Gaines got the wrong apartment. But I need to talk to her. Can you call her and tell her to expect me? I want to ask her about one of her neighbors."

While she was talking to Carr, Joe was talking to the sergeant from the Gramercy Park Precinct, the closest cop shop to the building. She heard him say, "Backup only, we don't want to spook him."

She and Joe didn't work together often, but she enjoyed when they did. She didn't have solid evidence about Dusty working with anyone, but her gut told her there was something to the theory. That Joe trusted her gut meant everything to her. She'd do the same for him, because he was a damn good cop. It was one of the things that attracted her to him.

Cops were also her vice, but right now she only had eyes for the hot Italian cop standing in front of her.

"Do you need backup?" Carr asked her.

"I have a detective with me, and he's talking to the local precinct. We want to do this quietly. If we're right, we don't want to chase him off. If we're wrong, I don't want to get anyone's panties in a wad."

"Understood. Keep me informed."

Three minutes later, Suzanne and Joe got off the subway at Union Square. They could have taken another subway up Park Avenue, but it was faster to walk the eight blocks than wait for a train. It was a beautiful spring evening—cool, but clear. After the rain of the last two weeks, she was grateful for the break.

She scrolled through the messages on her phone as Joe steered her through the thin Sunday-evening crowds. "I'm amazed you don't get yourself killed stepping in front of a bus."

She ignored him and read Dina's text message.

"Plan?"

"I'm working on it. Dina just sent me info about who's in Apartment 530. Owned by Kathryn Jones, an attorney for a big civil litigator. She works long hours and is rarely home except to sleep."

"Okay, devil's advocate here. This guy has been off our radar because he doesn't go in when people are home, until he breaks into Dina Carr's house and she just happens to be downstairs in the gym and catches him coming out of her apartment. He does his research. He sneaks in, sneaks out. Has a good grasp of security systems. Is a safe cracker. All of which can point to the guy you have in custody."

"True, but I'd question the research portion. I think the partner does the research and Dusty does the legwork. Dusty's a safe cracker, but I'm doubting he's an electronics guy. Some of these security systems are high-end." She pocketed her phone. "I just sent Dina a message asking if she has contact information for Jones. If it's not tonight, it'll be tomorrow. But it's tonight."

"You want to bet on it?"

"I'm not betting my Mets tickets." She glanced at him. "But you can come with me if you're not working."

"I'll be there, because I know if the Mets win, I can have my way with you." He smiled. "And if they lose, I'll need to console you with lots of sex to keep your mind off the loss."

"Damn, you have a one-track mind," she said.

"It's been twelve days, Suz. But let's bet anyway. Who's on top."

"That's a win-win."

"Exactly."

Suzanne was laughing as she turned the corner at East Twenty-Second. The door into the building was locked. "Shit."

Joe read the small sign in the door. "There's a doorman here Monday through Saturday six a.m. until midnight. On Sunday, only until six p.m."

It was half past nine. She called Dina. "Ms. Carr, I need to get into the building, then I'll come up and explain what's going on."

Dina Carr buzzed them in immediately. Suzanne took a moment to survey the spacious lobby. She explained the layout to Joe. "Mail room is in the back—needs a card key to get in. Desk there, for the doorman. Manager is on two, somewhat of a jackass, but I ran him, and he doesn't have a record."

"No crime in being a jackass," Joe noted.

She ignored Joe's wisecracks. "Down that hall is the laundry, stair access to the garage, a large but windowless gym, and access into the adjoining building, which is closed to the public on weekends."

"Still—that's a security issue."

"Yeah. We checked surveillance, and those cameras weren't messed with. Ditto for the garage access. There's an emergency door that goes to the alley—that's where he jammed the security feed, but he had a key."

"Did you find the key on him?"

"Yep. Seems one of the maintenance guys lost his but didn't report it. It's apparently a pain in the ass to get new locks installed."

"Dusty picked his pocket."

"My guess, too." Suzanne looked around a last time before heading to the elevator bank. "Very easy for someone to access this building, in hindsight. It's a quiet street. Alley access. Adjoining public building. Good, not great, security."

"Did you find Dusty's jammer?"

"NYPD searched his apartment. It wasn't there, and it wasn't on him when he was arrested."

"If I were a criminal mastermind, I'd set everything up and find a dufus to do the dirty work. If he's caught, I'm walking away fast."

"Isn't society lucky that most cops aren't moonlighting as criminal masterminds?"

She hit the elevator button, and the doors immediately popped open. "No card keys required."

"You're nervous. Why?"

"Because I should have figured this out before," she said, irritated more at herself than anyone else. "I've been a cop for thirteen years; I should have known."

"Technically, you're not a cop. You're a federal agent."

"Screw you."

He grinned. He loved pushing her buttons; she shouldn't give him the satisfaction of a reaction.

They exited on the third floor, and Suzanne rapped on Dina Carr's door.

Dina opened immediately. She was fifty, attractive, with light mocha skin and hazel eyes. "Agent Madeaux, please come in," she said graciously.

Suzanne introduced Joe as Dina closed the door behind them. "Detective DeLucca didn't work the original case, but I brought him up to speed," she said.

"May I get you something to drink? Water? Iced tea?"

"We're good, thank you," Suzanne said. "I tried the number you gave me for the attorney, Jones, and she's not there."

"I called the apartment manager," Dina replied. "She's out of town until tomorrow morning, has him holding her mail for her."

"When did she leave town?"

"Thursday, he said. It was a planned vacation."

She glanced at Joe and he nodded. The thief knew. That was the only explanation. He'd known Kathryn Jones was going to be out of town and sent Dusty Gaines in to rob her. Tonight was the last night he could get what he wanted out of her place. And if he knew that Dusty was in jail, it was the best time to go after it.

Whatever *it* was.

Joe said to Suzanne, "I'm going to contact your NYPD counterpart and see if they can lean on Gaines more tonight, get anything we can use to nail this guy."

Suzanne nodded. While Joe stepped aside to make his call, she asked Dina, "Do you know Ms. Jones?"

"A bit. I've been here for fifteen years; Kathryn moved in three years ago. She's very career-minded."

"Do you know what type of cases she works?"

"No—" Dina hesitated. "Well, she came to me once last year because she knew I worked in interior design—I redesigned her kitchen for her; it was original to the building and needed a lot of work—and asked questions that made me think she did civil fraud cases. She works for one of the most respected civil litigation firms in the city."

"I checked into them while walking over here. I'm going to talk to the manager, get him to let us into her place."

"You really think the man who broke in here wasn't working alone?"

"It's a hunch."

Dina smiled. "I was married to a federal agent for nearly twenty years; I would definitely trust your hunch."

Idly, Suzanne wondered why Frank and Dina had split in the first place. Frank was a good cop, dedicated, maybe too serious about everything, but Suzanne had always respected him. And what she knew about Dina, the woman was attractive, pleasant, and intelligent. These two people should have been able to make their marriage of twenty years work, right? What did that mean for people like her and Joe, who were both more flawed and stubborn to a fault?

She shook her head. What the hell was she thinking? *Marriage?* She didn't want to get married, not anytime soon. Maybe moving in together. Except for the issue of Stephanie the psycho ex-wife, they probably would have done it by now.

"You're thinking," Joe said.

"Always," she snapped. She certainly didn't want him to know she was thinking about *him*. His ego was big enough as it was. "What'd your sergeant say?"

"They have two cars waiting for my call. Out of sight. Two foot patrol sitting in the Starbucks at the corner pretending to be on break. It closes at ten, so they'll be walking at that point, will stay in the area."

"Okay. Let's call the manager and have him let us into Jones's apartment."

The manager balked. He refused without permission from Kathryn Jones or a warrant. Suzanne probably couldn't blame him ... except she did.

"Give me her contact information," Suzanne told the manager over the phone.

He said, "I'll call her myself."

"I'd like to speak with her," Suzanne said.

Dina slipped over her cell phone. She'd brought up a contact, Kathryn Jones.

"I could kiss you," Suzanne said to the woman.

"Excuse me?" the manager said.

Suzanne almost hung up on him but said, "I'll call you right back."

She used Dina's phone to call Ms. Jones. She answered on the third ring, Suzanne identified herself, explained her relationship to Ms. Carr, and asked for permission to access her apartment because she suspected it would be robbed tonight. Ms. Jones asked to speak to Dina.

Dina confirmed everything, then handed the phone back to Suzanne. "All right," Jones said, "I'll call the manager and give permission for you to enter. But why would anyone break into my place? I don't keep cash around; I don't have a lot of jewelry."

"Is there anything in your apartment that's confidential? Maybe information that would be valuable to a competitor? Or your opposition in court?"

"I—I suppose. My computer. But to access my work files, they'd need my password."

Suzanne knew that a good computer hacker could get in—especially if they were using a terminal that regularly accessed an outside network. She had a friend who made his living finding holes in corporate computer security; she knew now that most systems weren't secure from someone who had the skill, means, and desire.

"Paper files?"

"Maybe. Notes, depositions I'm reviewing, contact information on my clients."

"Hmm," Suzanne said out loud.

"Do you know who this is?"

"No, but I'm getting an idea. Please call the manager." She hung up.

"I know what you're thinking," Joe said. "You think that Dusty and whoever he's working with are hired."

"Something like that."

"Like a dirty PI."

She smiled. "Yeah. Someone who gets information. What better way than go to the source? But he contracted out to the idiot Dusty, who broke into the wrong place."

"Then why steal cash and bonds?"

"To throw people off the real reason for the break-ins. If you don't know someone accessed your private information, you don't know to change codes, warn clients, prepare for court. Information is worth more than money to some people."

The lights flickered, just for a moment.

Dina's eyes widened. "That happened on Thursday, when I was in the gym. The night that man broke in here."

Joe said, "He could have interrupted the circuit when he broke into the building."

"He's inside." Suzanne turned to Dina. "Stay here, keep your doors locked. I don't think you're in danger, but let's be safe." She turned to Joe. "Upstairs?"

They stepped out into the hall. Joe said, "You take the elevator, I'll take the stairs. I'm going to go up to six and watch the landing from above. We have to catch him in the act."

"Agreed."

"Watch your back."

Suzanne pressed the button and bounced on her feet while Joe walked down the hall and toward the staircase. How much time did they have? If they didn't catch the guy in the act, they'd have no cause to arrest him. They might be able to come up with a reason to search him—find an illegal jammer, find lock-picking tools—but without a crime being committed, they wouldn't be able to hold him for long.

The doors opened, and a wiry old man who looked like a skinny Grumpy stood there. The manager. "I remember you," he scowled.

She stepped inside, pressed the fifth-floor button, and flashed her badge. "We don't have a lot of time. Give me the key and go back down."

He wanted to argue, she could see it in his mousy eyes, but

instead, he handed her the key. "If anything happens to the apartment, I'm taking it up with your boss," he said.

"You do that," Suzanne snapped and exited on five—after pressing the ground-floor button for the manager.

No one was in the hallway. She didn't see Joe, either—she hoped he was already in place.

She unlocked the door to Kathryn Jones's apartment and slipped inside. Listened. She heard the tick of an old-fashioned clock. The low hum of a refrigerator. A light above the stove was on, and another night-light coming from the bathroom, both casting odd shadows across the high-ceilinged, turn-of-the-century building. Big place for a single woman, but then again, Suzanne was a federal agent on a civil servant salary, and Kathryn Jones was a high-priced civil litigator.

She closed and locked the door. She sent Joe a text message.

I'm in. Will hide.

The front door opened into a small hall, then a large living room. The kitchen and eating area were to the left, two small bedrooms straight ahead. An oversized bathroom had a washer and dryer where a linen closet had once been. Now Suzanne was jealous. She didn't care about the space—Suzanne was rarely home anyway—but she'd kill for her own washer and dryer. She just had no place for it in her one-room studio.

Jones used the smaller of two bedrooms as her office. This was likely where the thief would come. There was no place to hide— the closet had been converted to shelves with a printer, file cabinet, and supplies.

Her phone vibrated. It was Joe.

White male wearing dark hoodie exited stairs on five.

It was time.

She slipped into the bedroom and stood flat against the wall. Waited, gun in hand. Dusty Gaines didn't carry a weapon, but that didn't mean his partner behaved the same.

She heard nothing. Maybe it was a false alarm. She glanced at her phone, but Joe hadn't sent another message.

Suzanne looked through the crack in the door. She didn't hear the thief pick the lock—or use a key, if that's what it had—but she saw the swath of light from the hall cut across the apartment before he closed the door and locked it behind him.

Terrific. Suzanne was on her own for the time being.

She couldn't see the suspect's face. It was concealed in shadow from the lack of light and the hood. He stopped just inside the door, just as she'd done. Listening. There was a television on in another apartment, so faint that either the walls were thick or it was several units away. Street traffic from Park Avenue, but again, the soundproofing was good, and it sounded like they were twenty floors up instead of five.

He started down the hall, toward the bedrooms. Did he know where he was going? He hesitated outside each opening, looked, listened.

Then the thief turned into the den and clicked on a flashlight. She didn't hear him boot up the computer, but instead he pulled out a drawer and started going through papers. Slowly, carefully, as if he had all the time in the world.

Suzanne had two options. Confront him now, or try to walk past the open den door and let Joe in the front.

He'd see her. There was no way around it. She had to confront him while he was trapped in Jones's office.

She stepped away from behind the bedroom door. The floor creaked. Just a little sound, but she froze.

No more rustling in the office.

Shit. The office door was only a few feet down the hall. She walked quickly, gun out, and immediately identified herself.

"Federal agent! Put your hands where I can see them!"

She sensed the gun in his hand more than she saw it. He fired at the same time as she stepped away. Her blood rushed through her body as the adrenaline kicked in, beating in her ears. No, that was Joe breaking down the door.

The suspect had the window open and was climbing onto the fire escape. She didn't dare shoot out into the dark night, not without a clear target. If she missed, the bullet could hit an innocent in the apartment across the road.

She spared a glance into the office. The burglar was on the fire escape and fired two more shots at her, which both missed.

The front door burst open, and Suzanne shouted at Joe, "He's on the fire escape! Call backup and go down the stairs!"

"You good?" he called.

"Yes—hurry!"

Joe turned and ran back out.

Suzanne looked again into the room. Shit, he was gone. She ran to the window. He was only one floor down. She aimed at his right arm, which held his gun, and fired, hitting him. He dropped the weapon, and it skittered down a flight of metal stairs.

Now or never. She jumped out on the narrow escape and pursued him. "Federal agent!" she shouted at him. "FBI!"

He practically slid down the stairs. She saw blood, and he was holding his right arm, but he kept moving.

She was gaining on him, slowly, and it was only five flights. By the time he got to the second floor, he tried to release the ladder, but it didn't immediately drop down. He climbed over the railing, hung for a second, then dropped. He fell on his ass, scrambled up, and started running east.

If he got too far down the block, they could lose him in an alley or subway station. She jumped from the third level to the second, then leapt over the railing into a controlled roll on the cement. Damn, it hurt, but she got up and ran after him, angry and motivated to catch the bastard.

The two beat cops who'd been at Starbucks stood on the corner. The suspect saw them and immediately turned to run back the way he'd come. He spotted Suzanne.

She had her gun pointed at his chest. "Down! Now!"

He was obviously considering his options, looking for a place to bolt, but both she and the uniformed cops were closing in. From the alley, Joe ran out. He must have flown down the staircase to get out here this fast. He, too, had his gun out and trained on the suspect.

"Down!" Joe shouted. "Hands where I can see them." He glanced at Suzanne. "You good, Suz?"

"Good."

The thief realized he had no place to go but on his knees. "I need a doctor! The bitch shot me!"

"That's Special Agent Bitch to you," Suzanne said. She holstered her gun and took out her handcuffs. "And you really pissed me off. Do you know the mountain of paperwork I'm going to have to fill out for discharging my weapon?"

She cuffed him, and two patrol cars came down the street, lights flashing. Joe knew several of the cops, talked to them while Suzanne let the beat cop read the prick his rights. "Better call him an ambulance," she muttered, "though it's hardly worth a Band-Aid."

"I'm bleeding everywhere!" the suspect said.

"What's your name?" Suzanne asked him.

"I'm not talking. I want a lawyer."

"Then exercise your right to remain silent and stop complaining about a flesh wound."

Joe walked over to her. "Well, I guess our night just got a whole lot busier."

"I'm sorry." She frowned, glancing at the suspect. "I should have known if I were right and we caught the guy, we'd both be working until dawn."

Joe shook his head, but he was smiling. "You did great."

And she was pleased that she'd been right.

Joe continued. "I'm sure you'll have a shitload of paperwork to do tomorrow, but my guys will take him in, process him. He already asked for his lawyer. Go give your statement, turn your gun over for ballistics, and then we're going to your place."

"I thought we were going to your place tonight?"

"Your place is now closer." He ran his hands up and down her arms and kissed her. Fast, hard, possessive. "You won. You can be on top."

"Maybe I want you on top."

"That can be arranged."

"Let's do it both ways."

"I'm agreeable to that."

She laughed. "I'll bet you are."

"And honestly? There's nothing hotter than a kick-ass chick with a gun."

She grinned, melting under his dark, seductive gaze. "What a pair we are."

"Yes, we are. I wouldn't have it any other way, Mad Dog."

Her heart skipped a beat, expecting anger at the nickname, but she only felt warm and loved. Instead, she warned in a low voice, "You're going to pay for calling me that."

"I can hardly wait for my punishment."

Allison Brennan is a *New York Times* and *USA Today* bestselling author of more than two dozen romantic thrillers and numerous short stories. Lisa Gardner says, "Brennan knows how to deliver," and *RT Book Reviews* says, "Brennan is a master of suspense."

She's currently writing the Lucy Kincaid/Sean Rogan romantic suspense series about a young FBI agent and her private investigator boyfriend, as well as a mystery/thriller series featuring independently wealthy investigative reporter Maxine Revere. *Compulsion*, the second book in the Max Revere series, will be out in April 2015. For more information about Allison and her books, visit her website http://allisonbrennan.com

FLYING IN THE FACE OF CONVENTION

LEX VALENTINE

THE MAILBOX BULGED. WELL, not really, but the edge of a couple of envelopes peeped out of the bottom of the box's door giving away its full status. Trey grimaced as he stuck his key in the lock. Junk mail, most likely. That's about all he got since he'd gone paperless on every bill and paid them all online. He didn't even get letters. No one resorted to snail mail when they had email.

The mailbox door opened, and a cascade of junk mail spewed out, some into Trey's waiting hands and the rest onto the floor. Gathering it all up, Trey moved over to the lobby's trash can and began to sort through papers, dumping the junk mail into the trash. At the bottom of a stack of letters from political candidates, he found two identical square envelopes, one with his name and address and one with someone else's name and address on the front.

Tossing the rest of the junk mail into the trash bin, Trey looked at his envelope. The thickness denoted some sort of card inside. He opened it and found an invitation to a wedding. His friend Casey Peters had met the woman of his dreams and was trading in his bachelor pad for a house in the suburbs of Seattle.

Trey smiled. Casey had sown his wild oats in college, but he'd turned out to be a family man at heart. Trey thought that if a beer-bong-loving guy like Casey could find his one and only, anyone could. He'd enjoy going to the wedding.

Tucking the envelope into his pocket, he looked at the second envelope. It was identical to his except for the name. He turned the envelope over in his hands before returning his gaze to the address. It had his address but not his condo number. His number was 405, at the top of the complex. The address on the envelope was 415. Same floor, but the opposite side of the building from him.

He stared incredulously at the mail. Obviously, the mailman had mixed up the mailbox numbers somehow, but that wasn't what held him spellbound, staring at the envelope. It was the name of the resident in unit 415 that had him suddenly trembling and a little shaken. Years of fantasies and the memory of a crush that wouldn't die flickered in his head.

Jordan Smithson.

Trey remembered the last time he'd seen Jordan. Graduation day at the University of Washington. Jordan had come out of the dorm room bathroom across from Trey's room wearing only a towel, laughing, excited, talking with his roommate, Alex Rodriquez, as the two headed down the hall to their room. Trey had stood in his doorway, shaken by the sight of all that gleaming gold skin covering the expanse of muscle and bone that made up the hottest man on campus. And his heart had ached because he'd known he would never see Jordan again.

Trey had taken his shower, jacking off as usual to thoughts of Jordan, but not with his usual enthusiasm. That day his heart had been heavy because Jordan was graduating and leaving. For three years, Trey had idolized the older man, crushing on him as he'd never crushed before. They had a couple of friends in common, but mostly, the thing that had kept Jordan on Trey's radar from freshman to junior year was football. They both played, and being on the team together had been both torture and heaven for a smitten Trey.

But Jordan had graduated and left for a job in California. Trey had finished his senior year and gone on to grad school in Seattle. He'd put Jordan out of his thoughts and moved on with his life. Six years had passed since the day he'd last seen Jordan. Men had come and gone from his life. No one had touched his emotions in the way Jordan had, and his career path had consumed him to the point that he hadn't cared about anything else. But now, they apparently lived in the same building, on the same floor, and were invited to the same wedding. *That* Trey cared about.

He shook his head, marveling at Fate. Why the hell would she —he was convinced Fate must be female—move the only man he'd ever wanted a relationship with into the same condo complex as him? Why would she put him on the same floor as Trey? And most of all, why would she have the mailman put Jordan's mail in the wrong mailbox? In the year Trey had lived there, he'd never received anyone else's mail. Now, he had Jordan Smithson's.

As he took the elevator to his floor, Trey thought about taking the envelope straight to Jordan's condo and sticking it under the door or in the doorframe. He thought about knocking and saying, "Hi, here's your mail. The mailman got the mailbox numbers wrong. Your envelope was in my mailbox." He wondered briefly if he could get away with pretending he didn't remember Jordan.

None of those options appealed. In truth, he wanted to see Jordan. Wanted to see if he still felt that buzz of arousal in his balls when he looked at the guy. He wanted to know if all the years since he'd last seen Jordan had made any real difference to the feelings he'd once had.

When the elevator doors opened, his feet carried him to his own condo, not Jordan's. Inside, he tossed the invitations on his coffee table and headed for the shower. If he had to knock on Jordan Smithson's door and face the guy, he'd do so in clean clothes, not the end-of-the-day-limp suit he currently wore.

For the first time since he'd set eyes on Jordan, the thought of the man didn't make him want to jerk off in the shower. Nerves kept his cock flaccid, and Trey thought maybe he really could do this. Maybe he could really face Jordan and not feel anything but friendship for him.

Yeah, right.

He dried off and dressed in faded jeans and a T-shirt advertising the coffeehouse a block over. He flirted with the idea of dinner for a few minutes and finally decided he couldn't eat until he'd gotten the whole Jordan thing dealt with. Scooping up the invitation, his cell phone, and keys, he left his condo and walked to the opposite side of the building.

CHAPTER TWO

TREY OWNED ONE OF sixteen condos on the fourth floor of the building. All of the condos at that level were large two-bedroom units complete with a separate study, the largest units in the building. Trey had purchased his when the building was brand new, and he'd had his choice of units. He'd chosen one in the corner, facing the morning sun. He enjoyed morning coffee on his deck in the spring, summer, and fall, even when it rained.

Jordan's unit faced the wooded hillside behind the complex rather than toward the city lights. Trey figured since the building kept a pretty high occupancy rate, Jordan had been lucky to even get a unit on the fourth floor. The demand for their exclusive complex exceeded the supply of available units.

As he neared unit 415, Trey's feet lagged a little. Jordan had once claimed Trey had the most nimble feet on the football team, but that didn't seem to be true any longer. Trey had the sense that he walked in quicksand, getting slower and sinking faster the closer he came to Jordan's condo.

When he finally stood in front of the man's door, panic set in. What if Jordan was married? What if he lived with someone? *Oh, God.*

Trey shuddered and shook off his panicked thoughts. Way too overly dramatic, Trey Beaumont, he told himself sternly. Pull yourself together! What does it matter if he's married or involved with someone? He's straight and he's not interested in *you*. So get over it already!

Pushing his panic aside, he firmly pushed the bell. He could hear movement inside the condo. When the door swung open, Trey found himself speechless.

Jordan Smithson hadn't changed. Much. Still tall, dark, and handsome. Still muscular. Still with an expanse of golden skin that instantly called to Trey's libido. His former teammate stood before him, shirtless, wearing nothing but a pair of cut-off sweats. His chest heaved, and perspiration gleamed on his shoulders, chest, and face.

"Can I help—?" Jordan broke off, and a frown pulled his dark brows down. Then he broke into an ecstatic grin. "Trey!"

He reached out as if to give Trey one of those manly pat-on-the-back hugs that teammates exchanged before he seemed to re-call his state of dishabille. He pulled back and made a face.

"I'm a little stinky right now. You caught me in the middle of a workout."

Trey smiled self-consciously. "It's okay. I only stopped by to bring this over and welcome you to the neighborhood." He hand-ed Jordan the wedding invitation. "It was in my mailbox along with my invitation to the wedding. Either the mailman screwed up or the person who sorts the mail got the mailbox numbers wrong."

Jordan glanced at the invitation. "Huh. That's weird. You liv-ing in the same building and on the same floor as me. How long has it been since we've seen each other? Five years?"

"Six." Trey could have kicked himself. He shouldn't have shown that he'd counted!

A chuckle escaped Jordan. "You were always the smartest guy on the team." He grinned happily and stood back, pulling his door wide. "C'mon in. I can't believe you're here. Only Alex and Casey know I've moved back, and Casey only knows because Alex told him where to send the invite."

Stepping into Jordan's condo, Trey could see that the floor plan was somewhat different than his but just as spacious. The door shut with a thud, and then Jordan cleared some space on his sectional sofa by setting several half-empty boxes on the floor. Trey sat, and Jordan perched on the oak coffee table, elbows on knees, a smile brightening his handsome face. Trey's stomach tightened.

"So you've only just moved in?" he asked and could have kicked himself for asking the obvious.

"Yeah. I got here a week ago, and the furniture showed up four days later. Settling in is taking more of my energy than I thought it would. It hasn't left me much time to unpack or reconnect with old friends." Jordan grimaced and wiped his face with a T-shirt that hung from the arm of the sofa. "Ugh. I need a shower."

He stood, and Trey looked up at him, unable to take his eyes off the man's gorgeous body. "I should probably …" He trailed off as disappointment flashed in Jordan's eyes.

"Do you have somewhere to be? I'd love to talk and catch up. I can make dinner or order a pizza if you haven't eaten."

A hint of uncertainty colored Jordan's words, and suddenly, Trey didn't feel quite so self-conscious. He smiled and relief flooded Jordan's expression.

"No, I've nowhere I need to be, and I haven't eaten yet." Trey's smile widened. "I'd love to have dinner with you."

"Great!" Jordan jumped to his feet. "Let me grab a quick shower, and then we can order a pizza."

"Tell you what, I'll order us some dinner while you're showering." Trey plucked at the front of his T-shirt. "The coffeehouse a block down will deliver here, and their café has great food."

"Awesome. I'm not a picky eater. Order me whatever you think is their best dish."

Flashing another grin, Jordan disappeared down the hall. Trey pulled his cell phone out of his pocket and called to order a couple of subs and soup from The Leaky Bucket. Amy, the waitress who took his to-go order, knew him pretty well and commented on the fact that he ordered two of everything.

"Someone's got company!" she crowed in his ear. "Is it a date? Is he cute?"

"No, I don't have company nor am I on a date. I'm at a friend's house. He just happens to live in the same building as me," Trey corrected her. "He just moved in, so tell Mikey to make sure he brings the food to 415 not 405."

Trey hung up and scrolled through his email. He might not be on duty, but in his head, he was always working. He'd never been good at leaving his work at the office, another reason he didn't have a boyfriend. Well, his gun always seemed to turn them off, too. He steered clear of the guys who got excited over his gun and badge. Just a little too kinky for him.

"Hey!"

Jordan's voice calling out to him startled him into reaching for his weapon, but, of course, it wasn't there. He'd locked it in his gun safe when he got home. He turned sheepish eyes on the other man. Jordan stood in the doorway wearing nothing but a towel. Trey swallowed hard, mesmerized by the vision of his former crush half-naked.

"Sorry. Didn't mean to startle you," Jordan apologized with a smile.

"It's okay. Occupational hazard, I'm afraid. I'm always a little jumpy." Trey smiled back at his friend, trying to relax but finding it difficult when Jordan wore only a skimpy towel that left very little to Trey's imagination.

"Occupational? What do you do?" One dark brow winged up curiously.

Trey's throat threatened to close up on him before he let out any words that might chase Jordan away. He swallowed hard for a second time. "I'm an FBI agent."

Jordan's eyes widened incredulously. "You're kidding, right?"

Shaking his head, Trey said, "Afraid not. They recruited me while I was in grad school."

"Wow. Casey told Alex you'd come back to Seattle not long ago, that you'd been gone almost two years. I was going to ask him how to contact you once I got settled in."

The odd expression on Jordan's face unnerved Trey, but he tried to keep his expression calm and not show his emotions. "I left for twenty weeks of training at Quantico and then my first posting, which lasted about eighteen months."

Hitching the towel tighter with one hand, Jordan tipped his head to one side, his face filled with curiosity. "Where was that?"

"Los Angeles."

The curiosity on Jordan's face turned to outright astonishment. "Holy shit! You were in California and I didn't know? Why didn't you tell Casey to get my number? I would have come down to meet you! We could have hung out or something."

Uneasiness settled in Trey's gut. He and Jordan hadn't been that close in college. They had friends and teammates in common, but other than the football team or dorm events, they'd never hung out together. It seemed odd that Jordan would be surprised that he hadn't sought him out while he'd been in Los Angeles.

"Where'd you move to, anyway? All I knew was that you went back to California because you had a job lined up there. It's a big state. I had no idea where you might be," Trey stalled, not wanting to answer Jordan's question.

A frown replaced the surprise on Jordan's face. "Hang on a sec. Let me throw some clothes on."

Jordan disappeared down the hallway, and Trey let out a sigh. He liked his life neat and predictable. His job could be hugely chaotic on occasion, so he really liked his personal life to be on an even keel. Seeing Jordan again had shattered his peace, and he didn't know what he'd have to do to regain it.

Why the fuck had the mailman put Jordan's mail in the wrong box? Sure, he'd have run into Jordan sooner or later since they now lived in the same building on the same floor and would be going to the same wedding. But either of those situations would have been in public, around other people, most likely. This reunion, if you could call it that, had become something more than bumping into an old teammate on the street. And that scared the crap out of Trey.

Jordan returned wearing jeans that fit like a second skin and a threadbare University of Washington T-shirt. Trey's mouth went drier than it had when Jordan appeared in the towel. Now, the older man looked almost exactly like he had when they were in college, when Trey's crush on him had been at its height. Jordan plopped down next to Trey on the couch, a slight frown marring his handsome face.

"Were you not at the big dorm party my senior year? The one at the end of the year?" he asked, his voice rough and almost demanding.

Trey tried to remember if he had been. All he really remembered about the end of Jordan's senior year was the depression that enveloped him at the thought of not seeing him anymore. "Maybe. I'm not sure," he replied honestly.

A huge sigh escaped Jordan. "So you never heard me tell everyone I'd been accepted to the Police Academy in San Francisco?"

Blinking in utter confusion, Trey mumbled, "Police Academy? San Francisco?"

Jordan turned bright green eyes on him. "My whole life, I dreamed of being a cop. I went to college and played football because my parents asked me to. They told me to take the football scholarship and get an education. Afterward, if I wanted to be a cop, then I could go to the Academy with their blessing. So that's what I did. I turned down the recruiters who were interested in drafting me and applied to SFPD."

The fact that Jordan had ended up in law enforcement just as he had didn't shock Trey nearly as much as where Jordan had been living for the past few years.

"Why San Francisco? Your parents don't live there, do they?"

Jordan shook his head, a lock of damp chocolate-colored hair falling onto his forehead. "No. They live in Sacramento." He paused, took a deep breath that expanded his chest, and caught Trey's gaze, holding it intently. "Trey, I'm gay."

CHAPTER THREE

EVERYTHING TREY HAD BELIEVED for nearly ten years shattered. His chest hurt and his ears rang. It took him a moment to figure out he was holding his breath. Letting it out in a whoosh of air, he suddenly smiled. *Damn.* Life was stranger than he'd thought.

"Trey?" Jordan's voice held a note of caution, and the skin between his brows furrowed.

A weight seemed to lift from Trey's heart, leaving him feeling more alive than ever before. His smile widened. "Jordan, I'm gay, too. I thought you knew."

The other man's eyes rounded a little in surprise, and he shook his head. "I thought … I hoped … I mean, I wondered if you were but I …" He broke off on a self-conscious little laugh. "What I mean is that I always hoped you were."

"You did? Why?"

A slight flush stained Jordan's cheekbones. "Because I had a crush on you."

The beat of Trey's heart took on a sledgehammer-hard thumping. "Holy fuck. I had a crush on you, too." The words tumbled from his mouth of their own volition.

Silence reigned as they stared at each other in shock. Trey had the sense that the expression on Jordan's face matched his own. Stunned. Pleased. And seriously horny. Before they could say or do anything, the doorbell rang.

Vaguely, Trey recalled that he'd ordered food. With a sigh, he got up and answered Jordan's door. The freckle-faced young man on the other side grinned at him and held up two large bags.

"Hey, Mikey," Trey greeted the delivery guy. "Thanks for bringing this over."

"No problem, Trey. Did your friend just move in?" Mikey handed over the bags and then shoved his hands into his pockets, his hazel eyes bright with curiosity. "Is he in the FBI, too?"

Jordan appeared at Trey's shoulder and took one of the bags. "No, I'm a cop. Jordan Smithson." He held out his hand, and Mikey shook it.

"Mikey here is the son of The Leaky Bucket's owner, Kevin O'Reilly, who used to be Seattle PD," Trey told Jordan. "They only deliver to a handful of privileged people in the neighborhood. Since you're a cop, that makes you privileged."

Jordan grinned at the young man. "I'm honored, Mikey. It's good to meet you."

"Same here, Jordan. If you ever need something to eat, just give us a call. My sister, Amy, will take your order, and I'll bring it over. You can run a tab like Trey."

"I'm sure I'll take you up on your generous offer. It's been a long time since I lived here, and I'm still finding my way around. So much has changed."

When Mikey left, Trey and Jordan sat at the small dining table and pulled out the two subs and two cartons of soup. While they ate, they talked about mutual friends from college, where they were, and what they'd done with their lives thus far. Both of them ignored the elephant in the room throughout the meal, although Trey had the distinct sense that not talking about their confessions wouldn't last. Every now and again, he'd catch Jordan's gaze on him and recognized the confident, predatory gleam in the deep green depths. No doubt about it. In the quietest, most understated manner imaginable, without a single word that gave it away, Jordan was flirting with him.

It had been a long time since Trey had been cruised, and never had it happened in such a low-key manner. Usually, men waltzed up to him and asked to suck his dick. Or asked him to suck theirs. No-nonsense, right to the point. They didn't usually go the scenic route and exchange long looks with him, nudge his knee with theirs, rub their foot alongside his, let their fingers brush his as they reached for the pepper ...

Trey could hardly believe it, but it seemed that Jordan's crush, like his, had never died. Unleashed from their shared past, acknowledged aloud for the first time, the force of their attraction to each other sizzled hot as it finally saw the light of day. Denying he had feelings for the man across the table from him wasn't possible. Naturally reticent, Trey discovered that knowing Jordan felt as he did freed his inhibitions. And so, for the first time ever, Trey found himself flirting.

"You're really cute when you let go of that conservative persona you hide behind."

Jordan stood and gathered the trash from their dinner, taking it into the kitchen to toss in the garbage. He glanced over his shoulder at Trey and winked. The crotch of Trey's jeans tightened.

"I'm not conservative," Trey protested. "And I don't hide behind anything. What you see is what you get."

A rude noise escaped Jordan as he returned to the table and stood, hands on hips, gazing down at Trey.

"That's only partially true. You really do hide the best parts of your personality behind a cool, conservative, conventional storefront. You always have. When we were playing football, the other team never knew what you would do."

"I'm not conservative or conventional," Trey huffed at Jordan's words. "I'm a gay man. How the hell could I be conventional?"

A long, low laugh escaped the older man. He held his hand out, and Trey hesitated before he put his own in the strong palm. Jordan tugged and Trey stood. Walking backwards, Jordan pulled Trey toward the couch. He fell backward onto it and pulled Trey down on top of him.

Gasping in shock, Trey tried to lever himself off Jordan, but two strong hands gripped his buttocks, holding him tightly to Jordan's body. He squirmed a little but stilled as the hands began to caress him through the worn denim of his jeans.

"You are. You're the most conventional man I've ever met," Jordan whispered. "I bet you're running a thousand scenarios inside your head right now, trying to come up with the one that feels right, the conventional, conservative response to me holding you like this when I haven't seen you in five years."

"Six," muttered Trey, unable to stop himself.

Jordan's sexy laugh held a note of genuine humor. "After the first couple of years crushing on you, I stopped counting. You want to know why?"

The word *no* balanced on the tip of his tongue for a moment before he swallowed it. "Why?"

The smile that curved Jordan's lips held a breathtaking beauty that made Trey's heart stumble and his breath stutter. Sliding one hand up Trey's spine, beneath his T-shirt, Jordan pressed him down.

Lips grazing the edge of Trey's ear, Jordan whispered, "Because I knew counting wouldn't matter. I was always going to feel that way about you."

Time stood still as Jordan's words sank in and filled Trey with a heat that seared him from the inside out. He trembled in Jordan's arms as every emotion he'd ever had for the man beneath him grew a thousandfold. Like a flower seeking the sun, his body arched against Jordan's, hips rubbing first seductively, then more urgently as the hard ridge of his denim-covered erection found a matching swelling in Jordan's jeans.

"Fly in the face of convention, Trey."

Jordan's low growl filled Trey's ears, causing him to shiver and vibrate like a tuning fork. The scent of the other man filled his nostrils, and the rough silk of his skin heated Trey's palms where they rested against Jordan's ribs.

"I know we haven't seen each other in years, but in my heart, I've always wanted you, always had very deep feelings for you. You were the one dream I could never give up. Being a cop was a dream I could've given up. I could've done something else and probably been content, but I couldn't give you up. It's why I moved back here."

Stunned once more by the man beneath him, Trey raised his head, and their gazes met. Jordan's expression held a gravity Trey couldn't ignore.

"It's true. Casey told Alex you'd moved back. Alex called me, and I started hunting for a job here the moment I hung up the phone. It took months, but they finally offered me a job at Seattle PD as part of the SWAT Team. I haven't even checked in yet. They're expecting me on Monday."

Jordan touched Trey's cheek with the back of one hand, and

Trey leaned into it, unable to deny his feelings for the man whose touch lit a fire in him like none he'd ever experienced.

"What do you mean about flying in the face of convention?" he asked, noticing how breathless and excited he sounded despite trying his damnedest to be cool and in control.

"Let go. Of your inhibitions, your caution, your skepticism."

Jordan's soft words, accompanied by the fiercely passionate expression in his eyes, held Trey riveted.

"Just believe, Trey. Believe that I want you. Believe that your feelings are reciprocated. Believe that a crush that lasts this many years has got to be something more."

Mesmerized by Jordan's words and touch, Trey knew he wouldn't be able to resist the man. Whatever Jordan wanted of him, he would give without reservation.

"What do you want from me?" he whispered.

Hard hands tightened on his hips.

"Everything."

Magic. It could only be magic, Trey thought, as Jordan's mouth sought his, and fireworks went off inside him. His cock grew thicker and harder. His muscles trembled as if he'd run a marathon. And he clung to the other man as if afraid he would disappear. Their lips and tongues clashed in a sweet fire that claimed Trey's heart and shattered all the arguments in his head that this couldn't happen, not after so many years had passed.

When their mouths parted, Trey stared down at Jordan. What he saw in the other man's eyes made him realize that Fate screwed up the mailbox numbers for a reason. He drew a deep breath.

"There's a lot of catching up we need to do."

Jordan nodded cautiously.

"There's a lot we don't know about each other, including whether we're compatible in bed."

With a snort, Jordan's hips moved and their cocks rubbed together, pressing tightly, deliciously through the double layer of denim.

"Okay, so maybe that part's a given," Trey said with a chuckle. "But there's other stuff, jobs included."

Green eyes held an expression so serious Trey shivered again at its intensity.

"I'm in law enforcement. You're in law enforcement. What's the big deal? *Fly*, Trey. You know you want to. Here. Now. Be with me. We'll figure out the rest later and every day that comes after."

Trey had always been a planner. He planned everything right down to the last detail. It had been his way of life for as long as he could remember. But right then, with Jordan's green gaze pleading with him, with his body pressed tight to the other man's and his cock throbbing against Jordan's, with all of the dreams and desires he'd locked away in his heart finally seeing daylight, Trey let go and flew.

CHAPTER FOUR

SOMEHOW THEY GOT FROM the couch to Jordan's bed, but Trey could never be sure afterward how it happened. Both their T-shirts had disappeared, and Trey found himself unable to get enough of Jordan's golden skin. He rubbed the other man's chest, his fingers stroking over the hard ridges of muscle. He plucked at the flat, coppery nipples until they peaked, and Jordan moaned at his continued stimulation of what appeared to be a very sensitive part of his body.

For his part, Jordan seemed obsessed with everything below Trey's belt. He'd touched Trey briefly on the chest and back, licked his nipples for a scant few moments, and then pressed the flat of his palm to the zipper of Trey's jeans. With a loud groan, he began to rhythmically rub his hand over the bulge of Trey's denim-covered erection. His other hand squeezed Trey's ass and pulled him tighter and tighter against him.

Hips moving urgently, they writhed together as they kissed and kissed ... drew shaky breaths and kissed some more. Trey really couldn't get enough of the other man's mouth. Jordan's kisses made him feel on top of the world. Unique. Special. Wanted ... and more. He decided he could be happy kissing Jordan for the rest of his life.

Kisses weren't enough for Jordan, though. He popped the top button of Trey's jeans open and pulled down the zipper. With both hands, he delved beneath the denim, pushing it away. He rubbed both palms over the thin cotton of Trey's briefs, where his cock strained to be set free. When Jordan yanked the briefs down, Trey kicked them and his jeans away. Vaguely, he heard the thud of his pants as they hit the floor. But mostly, his senses were taken up with the feel of Jordan palming his cock.

"Oh, fuck!" he moaned as Jordan stroked his length. "More, Jordan. I need more!"

With his free hand, Jordan yanked at his own jeans, and Trey felt the button fly give way. Moments later, nothing lay between them. Hot skin on skin. Masculine and oh-so-enticing. Trey rubbed his naked body against Jordan's, and they both moaned. He got his fingers around the thick stalk of Jordan's cock and stroked. For long moments, they kissed and let their hands do all the talking.

Trey realized that Jordan's cock had a bit more length than his own, but he seemed to be thicker. Not that he cared. He'd never been a size queen, and what Jordan had was more than enough to please him.

"Oh, baby. I wanna fuck you."

Jordan's rough whisper filled Trey's ears and made his cock twitch. He squeezed Jordan's buttocks with one hand. "I was gonna say that."

Jordan raised his head and stared down at Trey. "You're a top?"

"Does it matter?"

"I don't give my ass up to just anyone," Jordan replied gruffly.

Trey raised his brows. "Fly in the face of convention, Sergeant Smithson."

"You're really a top?" Jordan repeated.

Giving him back his own words, Trey smiled seductively. "I don't give my ass up to just anyone."

They stared at one another for a brief moment, and then a wicked expression crept across Jordan's handsome face. "Whatever I do to you, you can do to me. Deal?"

"I can't believe we're having this conversation," Trey grumbled. "Just fuck me, okay?"

What happened next left Trey breathless. Jordan slipped down between Trey's legs and sucked his cock deep into his wet, willing, talented mouth. His fingers teased Trey's sensitive hole, making him writhe with pleasure. When Jordan pulled off and licked his balls, Trey sank his fingers in the other man's hair. When Jordan's tongue flicked at Trey's puckered entrance, he gasped. No one he'd ever been with had made him nearly delirious to be fucked.

By the time Jordan slid a condom over his cock and slipped lube-wet fingers into Trey to prep him, their moans and groans were in perfect unison. When Jordan spread Trey's thighs and pressed the thick head of his cock through the tight ring of muscles that led to Trey's heat, they both shuddered and went still.

"Oh, my fucking God. I've got my dick in Trey Beaumont."

Jordan's words would have been insulting had they not been spoken with a reverence that made Trey's heart turn over. Hard, hot kisses peppered his throat and neck, up over his jaw to his mouth. The kisses melted Trey like butter in a hot pan. He'd wanted this man for so very long, and now, Jordan filled his arms and his body. Every fantasy he'd ever had about Jordan had already been surpassed. The man's touch, his words, his every movement and oh, my God, his kisses, took Trey's previous infatuation and chucked it out the window, replacing it with a bone-deep desire to belong to Jordan.

When Jordan moved, Trey clung to him, moving with him. The press of Jordan's cockhead over his prostate made Trey's own cock leap and spurt pre-cum. He held Trey's legs open, thrusting his hips harder and harder as his cock speared deep within Trey. Friction from the brush of Jordan's hard abs against Trey's straining erection sent spirals of heat rushing through his veins. But the one thing above all that Trey noticed as Jordan fucked him was that the other man watched him intently. Watched him and couldn't stop kissing him.

The wet slap of flesh on flesh punctuated with pants and moans of pleasure sounded like a symphony in Trey's ears as he bucked beneath Jordan. What Jordan did to him went beyond sex, and Trey knew no other experience would ever top what he'd found with his former crush.

"God! Trey, gonna come," Jordan panted. "Need you! God, baby, need *you*!"

His mouth sought Trey's, and their tongues tangled. Trey wrapped his arms around Jordan, hips rising to meet the other man's downstroke. Jordan cried out and bit Trey's lower lip before pressing frantic kisses all over his face. Trey closed his eyes and concentrated on the pulse of Jordan's cock deep inside him, and then flames engulfed him from his spine throughout his groin and to his balls. He came hard, his body convulsing.

The aftermath of their orgasms left them cradled in each other's arms, kissing softly and nuzzling each other. No man had ever evoked such tender emotions from Trey. They filled him up to the top and spilled over. He didn't ever want to leave the haven of Jordan's body wrapped around his.

"My God. That had to have hit the Richter scale."

Jordan's words came out muffled by Trey's shoulder. He smiled but didn't reply. Moving and talking had become the very last things he wanted to do. He just wanted to bask in the afterglow of the most phenomenal sexual event of his life. Long minutes later, Jordan carefully pulled free of his ass and got up to dispose of the condom, returning with a warm, damp cloth, which he used to clean Trey. Afterward, they lay in Jordan's bed, wrapped in each other's arms, content just to be with each other without words. Finally, Trey tipped his head back and met Jordan's gaze.

"I never knew sex could feel like that," he said, his voice filled with awe.

A beautiful smile lit Jordan's face, and he hugged Trey tightly. "That's because we were flying, baby. Didn't I tell you to let go and fly?"

Trey chuckled. "You did, but I didn't believe you until I experienced it. Next time, I'll make you fly, okay?"

Jordan cupped Trey's face in his hands and kissed him. "I'm so glad you're not just anyone."

Happiness rose within Trey, and the part of him that cautioned about getting involved with a man he hadn't seen in six years fell silent while his heart cheered.

"Not so conventional now, am I?" he murmured before taking Jordan's lips with his own.

EPILOGUE

Two months later

CASEY'S WEDDING HAD GONE off without a hitch. He and his wife beamed happily at their guests from the head table. At one of the tables closest to the bride and groom, Trey and Jordan picked at their plates of food and sipped champagne from the same glass. Jordan had teased Trey that it was the only way to drink the expensive beverage with the added benefit of being a test run for when they got married.

Jordan hadn't asked and neither had Trey, but the whole getting-married thing seemed to be an accepted future occurrence for them as a couple. They'd spent the weeks leading up to Casey's wedding going on conventional dates as well as spending a lot of time in each other's beds. Neither of them had said the three little words yet, but like getting married, it was assumed.

For his part, Trey knew how deeply he loved Jordan, and his lover's actions told him the man felt the same. Jordan couldn't bear to spend a night sleeping alone unless one of them had to work. Trey knew they had a ways to go yet, but his confidence in his feelings for Jordan knew no bounds.

Reaching out one hand, he snagged Jordan's and brought it to his lips. Then he let their entwined hands lay on top of the white tablecloth while he leaned in close to Jordan's ear.

"You know that flying-in-the-face-of-convention thing you like to throw at me?"

Jordan nodded but didn't speak. He just smiled happily.

"I don't think you'll ever be able to accuse me of being conventional again."

One dark brow winged up, and Jordan's smile turned wicked. "Oh, no?"

Trey shook his head. "Nope." He drew a deep breath and

squeezed Jordan's fingers. "I love you. Always have. Always will."

Jordan sucked in a breath, and his eyes widened. After a moment, his breath came out in a whoosh. "I love you, too. From the first moment I saw you and until the moment I take my last breath."

"Sounds like wedding vows to me," Trey teased, his voice soft and low so only Jordan could hear him.

His partner stiffened, his eyes going dark with emotion. "Are you asking?"

"Are you saying yes?"

"Oh, fuck, *yes*! Yes!" Jordan breathed excitedly before he leaned in and pressed his mouth to Trey's.

Hot, hard, and possessive. Filled with tongue and demanding lips. Hands roughly holding heads, they kissed as if no one else in the world existed. A loudly cleared throat and tap on the shoulder broke them apart. With dazed eyes, Trey noticed Casey and Alex standing next to them, grinning with undisguised glee.

"You two got something to say to us?" Casey asked, his blond brows quirked up in amusement.

"Go the fuck away, you two. I just got engaged," Jordan growled, frowning at their friends.

Alex grinned and held out his hand. Rolling his eyes, Casey pulled a twenty-dollar bill from his pocket and slapped it into Alex's palm.

"Don't forget to send us invitations to the wedding!" they crowed as they walked away.

Trey stared at their retreating backs. He glanced over at his new fiancé. "You don't think they had something to do with your invitation being in my mailbox, do you?"

Jordan shook his head. "That would be tampering with the mail, a federal offense. Your jurisdiction, not mine, Agent Beaumont."

His gaze returning to his partner's, Trey smiled. "Not mine, either, I'm afraid. And we've got no evidence, so who'd believe us, anyway?"

Leaning his forehead against Trey's, Jordan let out a deep sigh. "The only thing that matters to me is that you love me. I'm going to spend my life with you, Trey Beaumont."

With an intimate grin and the stroke of his hand over the inseam of Jordan's suit pants, Trey rubbed his nose against his lover's. "That would make me beyond happy, Jordan Smithson. Now, can we slip out and go home? I want you to show me again how to fly."

Jordan kissed him briefly and stood, holding out his hand. Just as he had the night he'd taken the invitation to Jordan's condo, Trey put his hand in the broad palm and let Jordan pull him to his feet.

"We'll just fly in the face of convention together, shall we?"

Trey had only one answer to Jordan's question. He kissed him.

Award-winning author **Lex Valentine** writes across genres from contemporary to urban fantasy in M/M, M/F and M/M/F. A native of California, Lex lives in a canyon in Orange County with her long haired, tattooed husband and a bunch of cats she collectively calls "babies." She loves loud rock music, builds her own computers, works for a 100+ year old cemetery, and has a propensity for having very weird, vivid dreams about Nikki Sixx, although he's never naked in them to her great disappointment. A member of the Romance Writers of America, Lex is active in her local Orange County chapter.

Lex loves to hear from her readers. Her door is always open at lex@lexvalentine.com or on her Facebook author page.

Website: www.lexvalentine.com
Facebook: facebook.com/lexvalentineauthor

AN APRIL FOOL'S FORBIDDEN AFFAIR

SABRINA JEFFRIES

New York Times Bestseller, RITA® Finalist

WIDOWER MASON BRANDT, THE twenty-nine-year-old Earl of Westville, was sitting with his feet propped up on an otto-man, a brandy in one hand and the racing calendar in the other, when the woman he'd avoided for weeks burst into his study.

Miss Augusta Hunt, his late wife's sister. God help him.

The twenty-two-year-old female was *supposed* to be fifteen miles away at his family seat, reading to Mother about Hottentots from one of her prized travel tomes. She should *not* be here in his study, breathing hard from a race up the stairs, with her eyes emerald-bright, her lovely bosom at his eye level, and her lush lips tempting him into—

Belatedly he rose. "Good evening, Augusta." *Don't think about her mouth. Or her bosom. Or what you ache to do to both. She's Esther's sister, for God's sake!* "What wild adventure brings you into the wicked city?"

If he'd hoped to garner a blush from the woman, it didn't work. Her cheeks remained pale as lilies. "Forgive me for barging in, but the matter is urgent. Do you still have connections at *The London Monitor?*"

That sounded ominous. After Esther's death of an ague year before last, her orphaned siblings, Augusta and Lionel, who'd al-ready been living with them, had become solely his responsibility. And he took his responsibilities seriously. "Why?"

"Lionel told me this morning that he was going to spend the night in town with you, but one of our servants mentioned seeing him go off with two friends. So I searched his desk and found these." With a flourish, she tossed three papers onto the ottoman.

He picked up the first, an old newspaper clipping about a prank played on a prominent apothecary. Some imbecile had invited two hundred tradesmen to be at the apothecary's house by a particular hour to offer their wares. Mass chaos had ensued when they'd all come.

With his curiosity now thoroughly roused, Mason read the next—a draft for an announcement, full of edits:

On April 1st, at ten a.m., Mrs. Bowman, a ~~well-known~~ famous descendant of the artist Rembrandt, will be ~~pleased~~ delighted to entertain the public with a free showing of her valuable collection of ~~her ancestor's~~ the artist's paintings, hitherto unseen by anyone outside of her family, to take place at 47 Park Lane. Tea will be served.

Mason glanced uneasily at Augusta. "Who, pray tell, is Mrs. Bowman?"

"A prominent barrister's widow with a daughter whom Lionel fancies." Augusta paced the room, clearly in high dudgeon over … whatever this was.

Trying not to notice how fetching she looked in her traveling costume, he forced his attention to the draft. "Does this Mrs. Bowman really have a collection of 'hitherto unseen' Rembrandts?"

She eyed him as if he were daft. "There are no Rembrandts. That's the point."

"Of what?" Normally he could follow Augusta's wandering train of thought, but he'd had a bit too much brandy for that tonight.

"Of why he's angry at Mrs. Bowman. He wants to marry Pamela, and—"

"Marry! But he's not even out of Eton yet."

"I know! So does Mrs. Bowman. That's why she forbade him to see her daughter. She feared that his intentions weren't honorable. And being Lionel, he's all up in arms about the insult to his honor, calling her the 'Bowman Banshee.'"

A disturbing picture was beginning to form in Mason's head.

"But you haven't seen the worst of it." Augusta gestured to the last paper. "Look at the bill of sale."

A bill of sale? That couldn't be good. He stared down at a receipt from a few days ago for an announcement to be printed in *The London Monitor* on April first. Tomorrow morning.

Damn it to hell. "Surely Lionel isn't fool enough to—"

"Perpetrate an epic hoax to strike back at the 'Bowman Banshee'?" she snapped. "Apparently, he is. Dratted idiot. Lord only knows where he and his scurrilous friends are tonight. But so help me, when I get my hands on him, I shall throttle him senseless!"

"You and me both." Bloody stupid seventeen-year-old.

"*Now* you're concerned? I wrote you two weeks ago, asking that you visit Orton Hall during Lionel's school holidays to take him in hand, but you never even bothered to answer my letter."

"I've been … busy."

"Yes," she said caustically, gesturing to the racing calendar. "I can see how 'busy' you've been."

He bit back an oath. He could hardly admit that he hadn't wanted to go home if it meant seeing her, being with her … wanting her.

Sadly, marriage to her was out of the question. Wedding one's deceased wife's sister might not be illegal in England, but it was still taboo. It would tarnish their reputations and create an enormous scandal. He couldn't put that weight on her when she could still marry some fellow who *wasn't* her relation.

Besides, she'd never shown any romantic interest in him beyond the tender smiles and curious glances every young woman gave respectable gentlemen. So, regardless of his desire for her, he had to go on being the guardian he should be. Not the lover he wanted to be.

"So," she asked, "are you still friends with the owner of *The London Monitor*?"

That prodded him from his brandy-soaked woolgathering. "Charles Godwin. Yes." He headed into the hall where he ordered the waiting footman to call for his coach.

She was right on his heels. "Can you prevent them from printing the announcement?"

The quaver in her voice sent an answering quaver through him. It began to hit him how bad this was. If it ever got out that Lionel had been involved in such a monumental prank ...

As he strode for the stairs with her dogging his steps, Mason glanced at his pocket watch. "The paper has probably already gone to press. But I might prevail upon Godwin to hold it up. As long as I shoulder the cost."

A shocked gasp escaped her. "Oh, Mason, no! That sounds terribly expensive."

"No more than I deserve for neglecting my duties." *For desiring my wife's sister.*

She paused to cast him an apologetic glance. "I'm sorry, I shouldn't have blamed you. I'm just so worried—"

"I know."

"And I was peeved that you stayed away so long. I—*we*—missed you."

Trying not to read too much into that admission, he gestured for her to go ahead of him. Her auburn curls shook as she rushed downstairs with her skirts lifted just enough to give him a glimpse of ankle.

"We've caught it in time, I expect," he said to keep his mind off that tantalizing sight. "If we can replace the sheet containing the announcement, we'll be fine."

But that wouldn't solve the problem of Lionel.

"Doesn't setting type for even a single sheet take time?" she asked. "Though I suppose they could just ..."

He didn't hear the rest, too caught up in memories of his own schoolboy antics. Though none had been on this scale, they'd earned him a few canings. Unfortunately, that had only made him cagier about his rebellions, until—

"If we remove the announcement," he said, "Lionel will merely try it again, with another newspaper. Instead, we must give him a taste of his own medicine."

"How?"

"By subjecting him to more profound consequences." An idea was forming. "I'll change his announcement enough to look as if there'd been errors in the type. I'll put in a slightly different name, and, more importantly, an address *I* can control."

They'd reached the foyer now, and she faced him, looking perplexed. "I see how that deprives him of his revenge on Mrs. Bowman. But that will only teach him that the press makes mistakes. Assuming he even *sees* the misprinted—"

"Oh, he'll see it," he said as the footman brought his coat and hat. "Trust me, he and his friends will buy a newspaper first thing to view the effects of their handiwork. Or, if they don't, they'll go to Mrs. Bowman's, notice that no one is there to view their spurious exhibition, and *then* get a paper to figure out what went awry."

She pursed her lips. "And then what?"

"If Lionel has a conscience, he'll at least try to find out how badly his hoax mucked up the life of some innocent man or woman."

"Lionel does have a conscience. And I suppose it *would* be pricked if he went to the misprinted address and witnessed you fending off angry people. But I don't think—"

"My plan involves more than that. By the time I'm done with Lionel, he'll have learned a lesson he'll never forget."

He owed Esther that much. His late wife might have been a frivolous female whom he'd married in too much haste, but she'd done her best by him, and she'd adored her siblings. It hadn't been *her* fault that Mason's feelings for her had cooled later in their marriage.

Or that he'd recently grown enamored of her sister. It was simple proximity, that's all. Nothing more.

As he donned his coat and clapped his hat on, Augusta eyed him uncertainly. "So, what *is* your plan?"

"No time to explain." He headed out the door. "Just return to Orton Hall, and leave this to me."

"Absolutely not." Augusta hurried outside after him. "I intend to be with you tomorrow wherever you end up confronting Lionel."

"Augusta—"

"I mean it!" She swept past him to block his way down the steps. "You're *not* going to pack me off like some truculent child while you risk your money and reputation and heaven knows what else for my fool of a brother!"

"And what about *your* reputation?" He stared her down. "Your future could be seriously damaged if anyone sees you involved in this."

"I'm already involved. Lionel is my brother." Her tone turned sarcastic. "I can hardly escape the connection now."

"I still say it would be better for you to be off—"

"In the country, out of your hair? That's why this happened in the first place. Because you don't want us around." Her gaze dropped to where he was drawing on his gloves. "I suppose I understand why. We must remind you painfully of my sister."

"It has nothing to do with Esther. I told you, I've just been—"

"Busy," she said archly. "Right."

He sighed. "But this did happen because of my neglecting Lionel. That's why you ought to let me shift this burden from your shoulders, sweetheart."

The endearment slipped out before he could prevent it, and her eyes shot to his, glimmering with some unreadable emotion. "I don't want to give you another burden. I merely need someone to share it." As if realizing how that could be taken, she added hastily, "Besides, Lionel is the only family I have left. I have to be there when you talk to him. *Please*, Mason."

The words hit him like a sledgehammer to the chest. In the past six years, she'd lost most of her family. Yet she'd never asked him for anything except his help with her brother, a request that he'd ignored to his detriment.

She was right—she did have a stake in this. And for his neglect, he deserved to suffer the penance of having her with him. It would be a fitting one, since just the scent of her, crisp and fruity as apples in the night air, made his blood roar through his veins.

His carriage pulled up in front, reminding him that this matter required haste. "You can't go with me to the newspaper office; that is sure to provoke comment." When she opened her mouth as if to protest, he added, "But I'll send a message to Mother that you and Lionel are in town safe with me, and you can stay here tonight. Then, in the morning, you may come with me."

"Oh, thank you, Mason!" The smile that broke over her face spiked fire through him, but it wasn't nearly as bad as when she laid her hand on his arm and squeezed, making his every sense careen drunkenly.

For a moment, he exulted at the thought of having her to himself for a few hours, no matter what the reason. Or the cost.

Then he cursed his insanity. He was a besotted idiot, aching for the forbidden. And he would beat his desire into submission if it took him all night. Because he refused to let some ill-conceived prank of Lionel's provoke him into an unwise affair.

He refused to become anyone's April Fool.

Shortly after dawn on April first, Augusta roamed the drawing room at 117 Park Street, one of the town houses that Mason owned and leased. The tenants had been happy to let him take it over for a few hours in exchange for box tickets to the theater next week, even after he'd explained what he wanted to do.

Turn the place into a house in mourning.

It was a good plan. Assuming that Lionel hurried to the misprinted address after learning of the error, he'd surely be conscience-stricken to find the house beleaguered by strangers at a time when it was reprehensible that it should be so.

There was the added advantage that most other people who came to see the supposed Rembrandt collection would probably not even attempt to enter once they spotted the mourning trappings outside. For those who didn't assume that the exhibition was cancelled, servants were on hand to soothe ruffled feathers with ready explanations, plenty of tea, and the scores of crumpets Mason had purchased from a bakery.

Right now, the servants hovered about *her*, ready at a word to offer her refreshments. But all she could do was pace. It was better than standing out in the street watching Mason direct preparations to hoax the hoaxer.

Lionel. She groaned. What was she to do with her scamp of a brother?

Let me shift this burden from your shoulders, sweetheart.

Her breath caught in her throat. Mason had called her *sweetheart*.

She'd tried not to think of it as she'd lain in her bed last night, as she'd eaten an early breakfast this morning … as she'd ridden over here to join him. But the word rang in her head, a persistent bell tolling a most unreasonable hope.

Because her reserved brother-in-law had never called her anything so intimate. She'd always assumed he saw her as another burden, a leftover duty to Esther. And if sometimes he shot her a look oddly akin to yearning, she'd chalked it up to her own wishful thinking, born out of gratitude for how he'd taken her and Lionel in.

Never mind that during her come out, she'd compared all her suitors to him and found them lacking. Never mind that even before Esther's death, Augusta had felt a growing and decidedly un-sisterly fascination for her enigmatic brother-in-law. She'd told herself it was only natural. He was older, wiser. It meant nothing.

She knew better now. After so many weeks away from him, seeing him again last night had brought the truth painfully home. She was in love with him.

And he'd called her *sweetheart*. Did she dare hope he meant anything by it?

Her heart did a little skip. Which was utterly ludicrous. Mason was too sensible to take up with his deceased wife's sister. The world considered such unions immoral and scandalous.

Yet she didn't care. The very idea of being with him built a sweet pressure in her chest that made it increasingly hard for her to breathe.

"Everything's ready," said a voice from the doorway, and she forgot to breathe entirely.

Because Mason was back. And he'd never looked so cursedly appealing—chestnut hair tousled by the March winds, cheeks flushed from his exertions, and eyes the silver of moonbeams in the early morning light. Not to mention—

"Where's your coat?" she asked.

"My tenant's butler is repairing it. I caught the sleeve on a nail when I fell off the ladder, and ripped it right down to the cuff, along with my shirt."

"Fell off the ladder! Are you mad?" Her heart in her throat, she rushed over to him. "Why didn't you let the footmen hang the black crape? You could have broken your neck!"

"Nonsense. I only fell far enough to bruise my pride." He smiled indulgently at her, a smile that grew strained as she examined his arms. "And the footmen are all busy preparing for the hordes. I figured they could use the help."

She was so relieved to find no matching gash in the skin beneath his ruined shirt sleeve that it took a moment for her to realize he was staring down at her with what could only be called hunger.

Then a bleak expression crossed his face, and he walked swiftly past her to the window overlooking the street.

Perhaps she'd imagined that look. And really, it was disloyal of her to even imagine such a thing. She'd loved her bright and laughing sister, after all, even if Esther *had* been a flibbertigibbet. She shouldn't be coveting her sister's husband.

Still, Esther's last words to her had been, *Take care of Mason, my dear.* And how better to do so than to love him as much as Esther had?

Not that she had a choice. She couldn't stop herself from loving him, worrying about him. Wanting him. She was truly a wicked woman.

As Mason stared out the window, she said, "I do hope no one has the forethought to ignore the address in the paper and find out where Mrs. Bowman really lives. It does us no good if she suffers from Lionel's prank despite your machinations."

"She won't. I had them put the name in as Mrs. *Lowman*, another 'misprint.' And there are dozens of Lowmans in London."

"That's good, then." She glanced at the clock. "It's still only eight a.m. Do you think Lionel will show up here early and try to stop the so-called exhibit once he sees the listing in the paper?"

"Since your brother has never risen before nine in his life, I doubt it."

Mason's thick rumble of a voice resonated in her, from her skin to her bones. Half fearing he might see his effect on her, she pulled her shawl closer.

How she wished she had a more attractive gown. Women had been throwing themselves at Mason ever since Esther's death—beautiful women, with smaller waists, less brassy hair, and bigger bosoms than hers. How could she hope to compete?

Yet he'd called her *sweetheart*.

She steadied her shoulders. "You *do* think Lionel will come here and try to make things right, don't you?"

"He'd better. If he hides somewhere to avoid detection instead, I swear I will, at the very least, yank him out of Eton and put him into another school away from his rascal friends."

"I don't blame you," she muttered. "I only hope that when he sees the house in mourning, he'll regret what he's done."

"I'm more concerned with how he acts afterward. If he witnesses the havoc and slinks away, then we have deeper problems to address. If, however, he comes to the door and tries to make amends, I'll know for certain he has a conscience. That he has the potential to become a responsible young man."

It was a sound plan in theory. But ... "I don't know if I'd make too much of it if Lionel *does* slink away. After realizing he's inadvertently caused such pain to a family in mourning, he will surely be horrified. It *is* a rather extreme consequence for what was really only a prank."

He whirled on her. "*Only* a prank? That was meant to gull hundreds, perhaps *thousands* of people?"

"Yes, of course you're right," she mumbled.

When he saw the stricken look on her face, he let out a low oath. "Forgive me for being curt. Honestly, he's only behaving like every other idiot his age."

She eyed him skeptically. "I daresay *you* never did anything so foolish."

"I did, actually." His rueful smile twisted something in her belly. "When I was fifteen, my schoolboy friends and I played a spectacular prank on our pompous Latin professor. We hatched the bright scheme of taking the pins out of the hinges on his classroom door. We used wooden pegs to hold it in place, knowing that they would break when he made his usual grand entrance, and the door would, of course, come off."

His smile vanished. "And it did. It fell on him and broke his leg. Watching him writhe in pain cured me of playing pranks for good. It had a much more profound effect on me than the canings we were all given afterward."

The guilt in his voice made her want to take him in her arms and comfort him. Which she could not do, of course. "I'm so sorry, Mason."

"Don't be. I learned a valuable lesson." He straightened his spine. "And Lionel will, too. At the very least, he'll learn that pranks can have dire consequences beyond what he assumes. For example, he probably didn't even consider the very real possibility that this hoax could be traced back to his family and embroil *them* in a scandal."

She swallowed. "I suppose it *would* have reflected very badly on you if it had gotten out that he was involved, and considering how kind you've been to us—"

"It wasn't me I was worried about," he snapped. "It was *you.*"

When she gaped at him, he took a shuddering breath, then continued in a more controlled voice. "In a few weeks, you will have your first season since Esther's death. You have a real chance at finding a husband. But the last thing some respectable fellow will want is to take on a woman whose brother has proved to be so irresponsible and wild."

Her heart sank. Well. At least now she knew where she stood with him. He was already plotting to get her married off.

"You needn't worry about *that*," she said, fighting to hide her distress. "I have no intention of marrying." Not when she was in love with *him*.

His brow lowered in a frown. "That's absurd. Of course you must marry."

The firmness of his tone was a knife in her chest. "Am I that much a burden to you?" she said, trying but failing to sound flippant. "Are you in such haste to hand me over to some man?"

"Good God, no," he growled, then seemed to catch himself. "That's not what I meant."

With her pulse pounding in her ears, she edged closer to him. "Then what *did* you mean?"

He stared at her with a desolation that gave her pause. So when he turned away, as if to ignore the question, she grabbed him by the arm. "Tell me, Mason. Why must I marry? Why can't I just live at Orton Hall as your sister for—"

"Because I don't see you as a sister!" His gaze burned into hers, and when he continued, his voice held a raw edge. "Because I could *never* see you as a sister."

She froze, her blood flashing like a fever through her veins. Did he mean . . . *Could* he mean . . .

A muscle flexed in his jaw. "And it was utterly wrong of me to have said that."

He caught her hand as if to remove it from his arm, but she grabbed it, enfolding it in both of hers. Did she dare tell him how she felt?

She had to. "Thank heaven you did." When his gaze shot to hers, dark and wary, she gathered her courage and added, "Because I haven't seen you as a brother in some time."

A look of pure alarm flickered in his eyes, and she braced herself for anything. But then his gaze lowered to her mouth and turned covetous, and next thing she knew, he'd dragged her close enough to seal his mouth to hers.

Mason was kissing her. *Kissing* her! Her pulse leapt into a frenzied dance. His mouth was soft, then hard, then boldly urgent, pressing her lips apart. She gasped, and he took advantage of her surprise to plunge his tongue inside her mouth.

Heaven help her, what was this?

Amazing, that's what. Heart-stopping. Better than she'd ever dreamed. Mason drove his tongue into her mouth over and over, and she rose to the decadent pleasure, grabbing at his arms, determined to prolong the madness as long as possible.

When he locked one arm about her waist and slid his other hand about her neck to hold her against him from head to hip, she could hardly breathe for the joy of it. Mason was in her arms, ravaging her mouth with a greed that mirrored her own.

He was like those marauding sheiks she read about in her books, who ravished unwilling innocents. Except that she felt anything but innocent and unwilling. Because she would give everything to be marauded and ravished by *him*. To always feel the hard press of him against her, rousing a glorious ache in her breasts ... a shocking heat between her legs.

What was happening to her?

She made some mewling noise in the back of her throat, and he groaned.

"Augusta," he rasped against her lips. "Oh, God, Augusta ..." He caught her head in his hands. "We cannot do this."

"Why not?"

His beautiful eyes shone a stormy gray. "You know why. You're Esther's sister."

It took her a moment to come out of the fog of her need long enough to realize why that mattered. But when she did, she could have crowed her delight. If *that's* all that stood in their way ...

"I don't care about the rules of affinity, Mason," she whispered. "We are *not* brother and sister. It's ludicrous that first cousins can marry and no one blinks an eye, but people like us, with *no* connection by blood, aren't allowed to—"

She stopped short as she realized what she'd said. Oh, Lord. She'd practically proposed marriage to him. And for all she knew, his kissing her had just been some aberrant response to his lack of a night's sleep and their present close contact.

Releasing his shoulders, she pulled free of him. "Forgive me, Mason. That was beyond presumptuous. I realize you didn't mean anything by that kiss, and I wasn't trying to—"

"Damn it to hell." He raked his hand through his hair distractedly. "What do you take me for? Of course I meant something by it. I'm not the sort of man to engage in kissing lightly."

"Yes, but that doesn't mean you want … that you would like to—"

"Marry you?" His eyes softened, soothing her shattered pride. "If matters were different, I'd like nothing better than to have you for my wife."

Before she could even exult at that admission, he added, in a clipped tone, "But as it is, sweetheart, it's impossible."

Sweetheart. Such a delicious word. It gave her the courage to fight him. "I don't see why. It does happen, you know. Men do marry their late wives' sisters from time to time. Granted, they have to go to the Continent to wed in a church, and then return to England after the gossip dies down. But it's not as if it's actually illegal to marry one's sister-in-law."

"It might as well be. If anyone in the family objects, he or she can have the marriage declared void. And that would be a disaster. The children born in such an instance would be considered bastards in the eyes of the law."

She hadn't known that. But it didn't matter, and he knew it. "I have no family but Lionel, and you have no other family but your mother. Neither of them would object or try to void the marriage. Your mother likes me, and Lionel—"

"Might strike back at us for ruining his silly hoax by ruining our marriage."

Fear dropped like a stone into her stomach. "He wouldn't do that."

"You can't be sure. And I won't risk it. Not when there's a chance you could still marry some other man."

"You would just stand by and watch me do that?" She'd known he would be sensible about this, but she hadn't thought it would hurt so much. "Well, thank you for that *kindness*, but if I can't have you, I'm not going to marry anyone else."

When he blinked at her, she stared him down. "So don't fool

yourself that you're thrusting me aside for my own good. The only person you're doing this for is you. Because you're afraid to risk some gossip and scandal for the sake of love."

"Love?" He stared bleakly at her. "This isn't about love. It's about desire, about the lure of the forbidden."

"For whom? You?" Tears clogged her throat. "Because it's certainly not about that for *me*."

"Augusta, you're still young. It's easy to mistake desire for love at your age."

His placating tone made her want to lash out. "Because that's what you did with Esther? What Esther did with you?" She was sure she'd hit the nail on the head when he flinched. "I'm not Esther, and I'm certainly not you. But if you feel only the 'lure of the forbidden' for me, it's probably best that I know it now."

Her heart hammered so hard she feared it might burst out of her chest. "Even so, it doesn't change what I feel one whit. I love you, Mason. And that's not going to go away simply because you shove me into some other man's arms."

Then, turning on her heel, she left the room.

I love you, Mason.

Over the next few hours, he couldn't get the words out of his head, even after ten o'clock came and went with no sign of Lionel.

His plan was falling down about his ears, and all he could think about was Augusta's words. Before she walked away and began avoiding him as thoroughly as he'd avoided her the last few weeks. He felt the bite of her absence like an asp to his chest.

She loved him. Or rather, she *thought* she loved him. That's all it was.

You're afraid to risk some gossip and scandal for the sake of love.

No, she was wrong. He wasn't afraid of anything. Except the possibility of never getting to kiss her again, hold her again.

He swore under his breath. *Desire*, damn it! Nothing more than that. It had a powerful allure, but that didn't mean it should dictate his actions.

Frustrated, he strode to the window to look out for the hundredth time, then froze. Lionel stood across the street, staring up at the broad swaths of black crape they'd placed so carefully. His face was ash-white, and he was alone. If his friends had come with him, they were long gone now.

Leaving the window, Mason went in search of Augusta. He didn't have to go far. She practically ran into him as he came out.

"Lionel's here," she said in a low voice.

"I know."

Her worried expression made him ache to pull her into his arms and wipe it away, make it all better for her. Make her *life* better for her.

And that's when he knew. It wasn't mere desire he felt. It was something damned well more.

A knock came at the front door, making them both jump. One of the servants headed toward it, and Augusta opened her mouth as if to call him back.

"Let him answer it," Mason murmured. "We need to see what Lionel intends."

She nodded, but he could feel her distress like a blow to his gut. It hurt. How could it hurt like that? He'd never felt that way for Esther.

Yes, that was the problem precisely. He never had.

The door opened, and the footman recited his rehearsed speech. "There is no exhibit here, sir. The paper got it wrong. And seeing as we've had a death in the family—"

"Actually, that's why I've come." Even from where they stood, they could hear the regret in Lionel's voice. "I wish … I *need* to speak to the master of the house. It's important."

The footman glanced to Mason, and Mason nodded.

As soon as Lionel walked inside, he spotted Mason and Augusta. He stopped short, shock spreading over his face. But it was rapidly replaced by fury.

He marched up to Mason with hands clenched at his sides. "You! You did this … this terrible thing to ruin my life!"

"Lionel!" Augusta cried. "Don't speak to Mason like that. His quick thinking saved you from a possible scandal."

Lionel flushed. "He 'saved' me from the woman I love."

Mason wanted to shake the towheaded rascal. "And this is how you treat the *mother* of the woman you claim to love? By playing an April Fool's Day joke on her to upset her life and bring shame upon your family?"

"It wasn't a joke!" When they eyed him askance, Lionel muttered, "It wasn't, I swear. It was supposed to *look* like one, but we were really just trying to keep her mother occupied with all those people so that Pamela could slip away and run off with me to Scotland."

They could only stare at him, stunned.

"It was an elopement." A scowl knit his brow. "Until you ruined it, that is."

"An elopement?" Augusta cried. "You're only seventeen!"

"I'm almost eighteen," Lionel protested.

"That's still too young to marry, you fool!" Mason hissed. "What were you thinking?"

"It's *not* too young." Lionel squared his shoulders as if that would somehow make him older. "And I was thinking that I didn't want to end up like you two."

They gaped at him. Then Mason rasped, "What do you mean?"

Lionel's eyes, the same green as his sister's, bore into him with obvious contempt. "Anybody can see that you're mad for Augusta. The way you talk about her, the way you treat her ... Why, you stare at her practically all the time, thinking nobody notices, when, really, *everybody* notices."

His blood pounded in his ears. "Like who?"

"Me. The servants. The Dowager Countess. *Everybody*. And when you're gone, Augusta moons about the house and snaps at me. Meanwhile, you're here in London probably mooning about the town house and snapping at ... I don't know ... somebody. All because you're both desperate for each other and too *stupid* to do anything about it."

Mason could hardly breathe. Here he'd thought he'd been hiding his feelings so well. Good God.

Lionel thrust out his chin. "Well, you and Augusta may enjoy pretending you don't feel anything, but *I'm* not going to live my life like that. *I'm* not going to let silly things like my age or Mrs. Bowman's stupid objections or gossip or any of that keep me from being with Pamela. I *love* her. And that's all that matters to me."

"Don't waste your breath speaking of love to Mason," Augusta put in. "He only believes in the 'lure of the forbidden.'"

The pain in her voice reminded him of the idiotic lies he'd told her. And himself.

He stared at Lionel. This pup had more courage than he'd ever had. At least Lionel was willing to face his feelings, foolish though they might be.

"Stay here," he commanded the lad. "This discussion is *not* over. But your sister and I need a moment alone."

Grabbing Augusta by the arm, he pulled her into the drawing room and shut the door. When she faced him warily, he couldn't stand it one minute more.

He walked up to her and kissed her hard, showing by his actions what he'd been unable to admit before. He put everything he felt into that kiss, even as she remained stiff in his arms.

Then she shoved him away. "Don't," she said, her eyes haunted. "Not if you only feel—"

"I don't." Catching her hands, he drew her back to him. "You were wrong about Esther, you know. It wasn't desire that attracted me to her. Believe it or not, it was her flighty nature. Father had just died, I'd just inherited the estate, and the weight of it all struck me hard. I felt utterly unprepared for the responsibility."

Her face filled with understanding. Because she, too, had lost her parents young.

"I was lonely and panicked, and your happy-go-lucky sister was exactly the antidote for that. So I rather capriciously married her." He swallowed hard. "But once I found my feet, once I grew into my duties, I realized I needed someone steadier. By then it was too late to do anything about it."

He dragged in a heavy breath as he realized a truth he'd never dared admit to himself before. "So when she died, I felt ... enormous guilt over that disloyalty. Then I started having feelings for you, and I felt like I was trampling her memory somehow. I told myself that I merely desired you. That I could ignore desire, could control what I felt."

Her hands had started to tremble in his, and he squeezed them hard. "I was wrong." He flashed her a sad smile. "Don't misunderstand me—I loved your sister in my own way. But it was nothing to the way I love you."

Drawing her hands to his lips, he kissed each of them tenderly. "I do love you, Augusta Hunt. I believe I have for a long time. That's why I avoided answering your letters and going to Orton Hall. I was terrified to admit how much I loved you, how much I *needed* you. And I do, you know. I need you like fish need the sea and birds need the sky. Don't make me face a life without you in it."

Though her eyes glistened with unshed tears, she didn't throw herself into his arms just yet, instead dropping her gaze to their joined hands. "What about ... the rules that matter so much to you? The scandal and all that?"

He tipped up her chin with one finger. "Trust me, if your idiot brother can engineer a scheme as elaborate as this one just to be with the woman he loves, I can weather any scandal and brave any gossip. As long as you're willing to do it with me."

At last, a smile broke over her face. "Yes, Mason, oh, yes. I can do anything to be with you."

Never had he heard words so sweet. They made him want to leap, to run mad through the streets. He settled for kissing her again, reveling in the eagerness with which she met his desire.

Within moments, their kiss grew hotter and bolder and more intimate, and God only knew where it would have led if the door hadn't swung open with a bang.

"Hey, that's my sister you're kissing!" Lionel cried. "You'd better mean to do right by her."

As Augusta drew back with a blush, Mason sighed. Time to finish dealing with Lionel. "Or what?" Mason said. "You're already up to your chin in hot water, lad. I wouldn't start making threats if I were you."

When Lionel blinked, Mason added softly, "But don't worry. Your sister and I *will* be marrying." It took everything he had to force a stern expression to his face when inside he was dancing for joy. "You, however, will not."

A storm spread over Lionel's face. "Now see here, you can't stop—"

"Oh, yes, I can. If I have to, I'll lock you up to prevent it. For *now.*" When that got Lionel's full attention, he went on. "You will finish at Eton before you go near Miss Bowman again. In exchange, I will speak to her mother about your suit and make it clear that your intentions are honorable. *If* she allows it, you may start courting her daughter once you've graduated."

Lionel let out a relieved breath.

"But you will not be marrying her until you reach your majority and come into your inheritance, is that understood?" Mason snapped. "By then, you should be capable of supporting a wife."

"That's three years off!" Lionel cried. "She'll forget who I am. She'll find some other fellow."

Augusta stepped forward. "If she does, then she didn't love you enough to make you a good wife anyway." She slid her hand shyly in his. "And you want a woman who will wait for you, who'll walk through fire for you. Trust me in that."

Mason smiled at her, his heart soaring. "You should listen to your sister. She's a very wise woman."

Augusta beamed at him, then released his hand to draw Lionel off. "And now, dear brother, we should talk about how you mean to repay my future husband for all the trouble and money you've cost him with this ridiculous stunt."

As Mason watched the siblings spar, something dawned on him. Only an idiot would have let a woman as wonderful as Augusta slip out of his grasp.

So he'd narrowly missed being an April Fool after all. Thank God.

Sabrina Jeffries is the *New York Times* bestselling author of 38 novels and 9 works of short fiction (some written under the pseudonyms Deborah Martin and Deborah Nicholas).

Whatever time not spent writing in a coffee-fueled haze of dreams and madness is spent traveling with her husband and adult autistic son or indulging in one of her passions—jigsaw puzzles, chocolate, and music. With over 7 million books in print in 18 different languages, the North Carolina author never regrets tossing aside a budding career in academics for the sheer joy of writing fun fiction, and hopes that one day a book of hers will end up saving the world. She always dreams big.

You can find Sabrina online at:
www.sabrinajeffries.com
www.facebook.com/SabrinaJeffriesAuthor
twitter.com/SabrinaJeffries
www.pinterest.com/sabrinajeffries/boards/

WRONG ADDRESS, RIGHT GUY

DIANE KELLY

Golden Heart® Winner

Stood Up. Again.

A THROBBING BASS LINE vibrated the wall between my tiny top-floor flat and the one next door, threatening to send my Kit-Cat clock crashing to the floor. The black cat's eyes moved side to side, ticking off the beat as my neighbor sang along with raunchy hip-hop lyrics, her tipsy, off-key caterwauling wafting through the open window of my bedroom. I rolled my eyes. I could have been mistaken, but I think the plastic cat on my wall rolled his eyes, too.

Nicole and I had been neighbors for two years, and her pre-date ritual was as familiar to me as the reddish-brown freckles scattered across my nose. Nicole considered herself the next generation Carrie Bradshaw, slurping homemade cosmos as she spackled on her makeup and slid into yet another skin-tight micromini dress for yet another date. I was no prude, and to be totally honest, I'd kill to have as many men interested in me as Nicole had. I drew the line at casual sex, however. Nicole, on the other hand, drew no lines. Judging from the various names she'd shrieked during orgasm, she'd slept with three different men in the last month. Part of me was jealous. Another part of me feared she'd catch some kind of crotch cooties and that they'd travel through the air vents in search of fresh flesh to infest.

Like Nicole, I had my own pre-date ritual.

Step one: Shower with my lavender body gel, praying that the ancient pipes in the brownstone would provide sufficient water pressure for a full rinse.

Step two: Squeeze a glob of gel into my palm and run it through my curly brown hair. No sense trying to fight corkscrew locks with such a strong will of their own.

Step three: Drop the towel, step naked onto the scale, and kick the damn thing back under the cabinet when it shows I haven't lost a single ounce despite starving myself all week.

Step four: Slap on some lip gloss and mascara and dress in a cute outfit, something with a sweetheart neckline and full skirt to hide my overly generous hips.

Tonight's selection was a bright red number that brought out the warm undertones in my hair and skin. I added a black pashmina and a pair of four-inch black stilettos. The shoes tortured my feet, but my boyfriend, Brock, always requested I wear them. He said the shoes made my ass perky. When's the last time a man made any effort to make his ass perkier for a woman? That's what I wanted to know.

Lastly, there was step five: Round up my little dog for a final potty break before Mommy went out for the evening. Sinatra was a black-and-white Shih Tzu-poodle mix. I suppose that either made him a poo-zu or a shit-poo. Either way, the dog was a furry little heartbreaker. The beagle downstairs had been trying to catch his eye for weeks, but he hardly seemed to notice her, even when she rolled over onto her back in her best centerfold pose and wagged her tail.

Sinatra and I made our way out of the apartment, down two flights of stairs with a rickety handrail, and out the front door before settling on the stoop of the brownstone we called home. The place sat in the middle of a row of virtually identical brownstones in the Clinton Hill neighborhood of Brooklyn. Though not as popular or populated as the more trendy areas, these quaint, quiet streets held their own appeal. Especially for a woman like me. A thirty-year-old who'd never been married. A woman who'd grown tired of the crowded Manhattan nightclubs and bars and singles scene. A woman who'd gladly trade a posh dinner at a fancy five-star restaurant for a frozen pizza cooked at home and shared with a man she loved while watching *Jeopardy!*. If the clue was Katelyn Harrington, then the answer was *Who's the most lovelorn woman in the world?*

Yep, I was unlucky in love. What's worse, I knew it. Here I was, once again, sitting on my front steps waiting for Brock.

He was late.

As usual.

You'd think a guy who sold clocks for a living could take a moment to check the time.

Brock worked as a sales representative for a commercial clock company, selling wall clocks, timekeeping systems, and desktop devices that could instantly translate the hour into local time anywhere in the world by simply typing in the name of the city and country. Hoping to earn the Hawaiian vacation offered to the East Coast's top salesman, Brock worked long hours. Ironically, though Brock peddled timepieces, he rarely made time for me. His precious paychecks seemed more important.

At least the weather had cooperated tonight. Mid-April was always a crapshoot in New York. We could have a snowstorm as easily as sunshine. Fortunately, Mother Nature had decided to take it easy on us this year. Tonight was refreshingly cool but not cold.

As I sat there, watching for Brock to emerge from the subway stop on the corner, I made a decision. If he stood me up again tonight, this relationship was over. I might be ready to settle down, but only with the right man. If Brock couldn't get his act together, couldn't make me a priority in his life and stop taking me for granted, he obviously wasn't that man.

The phone in my hand buzzed with an incoming text. I glanced down at the screen, which displayed a message from Brock.

Running L8 with sales call. Reschedule?

I debated my response. My first impulse was to suggest he perform a nice swan dive off the Brooklyn Bridge. My second was a less fatal but still meaningful *kiss my ass*. But what did I do? I sent him a cryptic response instead.

Sure. April 31st at 13:00 p.m.

In other words, no. Never again. Put that in your time clock and punch it, Brock.

A few seconds later came Brock's befuddled reply. *Huh?*

I didn't bother clarifying things for the jackass. This relationship, if our occasional encounters could even be called that, was over. He'd been *L8* for the last time.

I shut off my phone, shoved it into my clutch, and kicked off the stilettos that had bent my feet into agonizing arches.

The door to the brownstone next door flew open, and Nicole emerged in thigh-high boots and a snakeskin print dress comprising approximately two square inches of spandex. She cackled into her cell phone. "You're a naughty boy!" Another cackle followed as she click-clacked down the steps to the sidewalk.

When she noticed me sitting on my stoop, she said, "Hold on," into her phone, covered the mouthpiece, and turned her glitter-lidded eyes on me. "Hey, Katherine. You gonna be out here for a while?"

I didn't bother correcting her on my name. If she didn't have it right by now, she never would.

I glanced down at Sinatra, who was sniffing around in the small patch of ivy at the bottom of the steps, having yet to do his business. "At least a few more minutes."

"Great," she said. "There's some guy coming over, a blind date one of my coworkers arranged. His name's Tim or Troy or Tom or something like that." She waved her hand as if his name didn't matter. "Anyway, I got a better offer. If you see the guy, can you tell him something came up and I can't make it?" Without waiting for a response, she resumed her phone conversation, hailed a taxi making its way up the street, and climbed into the cab.

A hot fury boiled up in me. How dare Nicole flake out on her blind date at the last moment! Being stood up sucked. It was hurtful and humiliating. I knew that better than anyone. And how dare she expect me to break the date for her! The least she could do is have the courtesy to call the guy herself.

Sinatra had rolled onto his back in the ivy now and wriggled to and fro. I rubbed his belly with my bare foot, and he playfully nipped at my toes. Sure, I wasn't a sexy bombshell like Nicole, but with my freckles and bouncy curls I was undeniably cute in an all-American-girl kind of way. I was also responsible, caring, and low maintenance. I'd even been called witty on occasion. Why couldn't Brock have appreciated me like Sinatra did?

A deep male voice interrupted my thoughts. "Could you tell me which one of these brownstones is 1663?"

CHAPTER TWO

Petty Theft

I LOOKED UP TO see a thirtyish guy standing on the sidewalk halfway between Nicole's brownstone and mine. Though not exactly male model material, he was attractive in a boy-next-door kind of way. He stood around five feet ten and wore jeans, brown loafers, and a green-and-white-checkered button-down that brought out the emerald color of his eyes. A lightweight gray jacket was draped over his arm. His dark hair was cut short and just beginning to give way to male-pattern baldness. His smile was warm and friendly. In his hands was a bouquet of yellow and white daisies wrapped in cellophane.

He glanced up at Nicole's bedroom window. The sill was lined with empty wine bottles. Cheaper than curtains, I suppose. A trio of lacy bras hung from an improvised clothesline strung across the frame. Must've been laundry day. Nicole had neglected to turn off her stereo when she left, treating the block to an earful of her pop tunes whether they wanted it or not. A frown flickered across his face as he took it all in.

As I watched, his gaze traveled from her window to mine, and the frown faded. The polka-dot curtains in my window were cheap but cheerful. A stack of paperbacks sat on the sill. Three romances for when I felt lonely, two cozy mysteries for when I felt cerebral, and one thriller for when I felt especially brave.

His expectant gaze returned to me. It was no wonder he was confused about the addresses. Many of the numbers had fallen off the buildings years ago. My landlord owned most of the block, and he was too cheap to replace them. The only number left on Nicole's brownstone was a 6. The only one left on my building was a 5.

I stood. "Are you Tim? Troy? Tom?"

"Trent," he replied with a smile. "Are you Nicole?"

Hell, no. But unlike the sleazeballs Nicole normally brought home, this guy appeared clean and employed and disease-free. He'd brought flowers, too. What a sweetie. He didn't deserve to be disappointed, did he? Of course not. Neither did I. Why should both of us spend the evening alone when we could have a nice time together?

Rather than lie outright, I simply smiled and said, "I'm your date for tonight."

Was it just my imagination, or did his eyes narrow for a brief moment? Before I could tell for sure, he offered me both a grin and the daisies. "Well, then. If you're my date, these are for you."

"Thanks." A blush warmed my cheeks as I took the flowers from him. How long had it been since a man had brought me flowers? I couldn't even remember the last time. Brock thought he was doing me a big favor buying ribbed-for-her-pleasure condoms.

Sinatra finished his wriggling and trotted over to sniff Trent's shoes. Trent knelt down and scratched the dog behind the ears. "Hey, little fella."

Sinatra replied with a grateful *arf!*

"What's his name?" Trent asked.

"Sinatra," I told him. "I love old swing music. My grandparents lived with us when I was young, and they'd always dance to it in the living room on Saturday nights." I remembered watching them from my perch on the piano bench, seeing the twinkle of love in their eyes as my grandpa twirled my grandma around. I hoped that one day I'd find someone I cared that deeply about. Of course I didn't expect to still be hoping at age thirty …

"What a coincidence," Trent replied, standing. "I play saxophone in a swing band. We cover some old Glen Miller tunes."

"What about Count Basie?" I asked. "Benny Goodman? Duke Ellington?"

"Those, too."

Wow. What were the odds of meeting a guy with the same unusual musical tastes? A hundred to one? A thousand to one? I supposed statistics didn't really matter. Romance was a spiritual matter, not a mathematical one. All a person really needed to know was that one plus one could equal a damn good time.

Trent cocked his head. "I'm surprised I got any traction with the sax. When I mention that I play in a swing band, most women peg me as a nerd."

"I can relate. When I tell guys I like classic singers like Billie Holliday, they assume they're not getting laid."

A smile tugged at Trent's lips. "Are they right?"

"That's for me to know and you to find out." I tossed him a coy smile. "Come on up. I'll put the flowers in some water." I hoped my instincts about Trent were right, that he was a nice guy and not a serial killer. Mentally crossing my fingers, I snatched my stilettos from the step.

"Sexy shoes," he noted.

Jeez. What was it with men and high heels?

"I bet they kill your feet," he added.

"They do," I replied. "How'd you know?"

"I dressed in drag for Halloween once after losing a bet. Wore a pink prom dress from a vintage clothing store and a pair of spike heels. Paraded around in them all night in Times Square. My toes hurt for a week."

"Ouch."

He shrugged. "On the bright side, I made fifty bucks taking photos with tourists."

"Clever."

"I won't be offended if you want to put on a pair of comfortable shoes instead. No sense hurting yourself just for me."

I fought the urge to kiss him right then and there. "How the heck are you still single?"

He chuckled and shrugged.

I opened the door to the brownstone. Sinatra trotted in, leading the way as Trent and I followed him into the foyer and up the stairs. I unlocked my door and stepped inside, holding it open for Trent. Sinatra grabbed his favorite chew toy and settled in his comfy doggie bed in the corner.

Trent glanced around my combination kitchen/living room, taking in my small cherry-wood bistro table, pillow-covered purple loveseat, and antique rolltop desk. "Nice place."

"Thanks." It wasn't much, but then again, I didn't need much. Sinatra and I spent most of our time here curled up together on the couch.

Trent wandered over to the record player I'd inherited from my grandparents when they'd passed away and began flipping through the albums stacked beside it. "You've got quite a collection of vinyl here."

"I've just about worn those records out."

I retrieved a vase from the kitchen cabinet, blew off the accumulated dust, and filled it halfway with water. After snipping the ends off the stems with a pair of kitchen shears, I plunked the daisies into the vase and used my fingers to separate them for best effect. I set the vase in the middle of the table and stepped back to admire them. The flowers brought a touch of spring inside, brightening the room. I supposed I should feel guilty. After all, I'd essentially stolen them from Nicole's date, whom I'd also stolen. But these acts of petty theft were justified, right?

CHAPTER THREE

What Number Is That?

AFTER DITCHING THE STILETTOS in my closet and exchanging them for a pair of black flats, Trent and I headed out to nearby Myrtle Avenue. The street was lined with shops and restaurants, including my favorite, a Middle Eastern café called Zaytoon's. Brock refused to eat unfamiliar foods and always took me to chain restaurants for dinner. Trent, on the other hand, proved to be much more adventurous. When I suggested the place, he immediately agreed.

"Sounds great."

The hostess seated us at a table by the open front window, where we could watch the people and activity on the street. We ordered mint tea and an appetizer of hummus, chatting as we used pita chips to scoop up yummy mouthfuls.

"What do you do for a living?" Trent asked between bites.

Whoever had set him up with Nicole must not have told him much about her. She worked as an assistant for a television producer in Manhattan. I, on the other hand, had a much less glamorous job.

"I'm a social worker," I told Trent. "I work with the elderly, making sure they're getting the services they need, encouraging them to stay active and involved in social activities, that kind of thing."

Though my job might not be prestigious or sophisticated, I loved it with a passion and was proud of my work. The older people I visited on the job told me intriguing stories of life in Brooklyn in the early 1900s. One of them, a spry woman named Idabel who was now in her nineties, had landed a role as an extra in the 1938 movie *Shopworn Angel*. Several scenes were filmed at Coney Island.

I took a sip of my tea. "Idabel had been on the beach sunbathing with friends when the director recruited them for the show. She got to meet James Stewart between takes. Said he was the nicest, most handsome fellow she'd ever met and that he ruined her for all other men."

Trent raised a cocky brow. "I suppose I'll do the same for you, huh?"

"Of course," I said, playing along. "Henceforth, all other men will pale in comparison."

After giving Trent a few details about my job, I asked what line of work he was in.

"I'm a computer programmer," he said. "A code-head. I spend my days immersed in ones and zeroes." He went on to tell me that he worked for a software company that wrote programs for the healthcare industry. When he finished, he offered an apologetic smile. "Are you bored yet?"

"Not at all," I said. "You had me at *code-head*."

"And you had me at *henceforth*."

We shared a laugh. We might not be the most fascinating people in town, but that didn't matter. We were nonetheless enjoying each other's company, as well as the falafel.

After dinner, Trent paid the bill, and we stepped out onto the sidewalk.

"How about a walk in the park?" I suggested. Trent and I had split the baklava for dessert. Might as well burn off some of those calories lest my already generous hips become even wider.

"Good idea."

We walked a few blocks west on Myrtle until we reached Fort Greene Park, the oldest park in Brooklyn. The site had once been a fort used in the Revolutionary War and the War of 1812. The locale was turned into a public park in the mid 1800s due in large part to the efforts of Walt Whitman, when he worked as editor of the *Brooklyn Daily Eagle* newspaper. With its sense of history, the place was one of my favorite spots in the city.

We turned in, strolling along the walking path, enjoying the spring evening. As the night cooled, my pashmina proved to be no match for the dropping temperature.

When I shivered, Trent held up his jacket. "Put this on."

We meandered along, past the Prison Ship Martyrs Monument,

a tall, light-colored column erected to memorialize the deaths of thousands of men and women who were taken captive and forced onto prisoner ships anchored in the East River during the Revolutionary War. Many died onboard due to starvation and disease. Not exactly uplifting or romantic. But two months from now, when the monarch butterflies returned from their migration south, the park would be alive with movement and color.

"I came here all the time with my parents and grandparents when I was a kid," I told Trent. "A butterfly landed on my head once, and my older brother told me that if I moved, it would sting me. I was only seven and kind of gullible, so I believed him. I stood stock-still for fifteen minutes until it flew away. Of course, I got revenge on my brother when I found out he'd tricked me."

"What did you do?"

"Bought a bag of plastic bugs at the dollar store and put them in the box of Froot Loops. He freaked out and spilled his cereal when the fake roaches dropped into his bowl. My parents grounded me for a week afterward. Totally worth it, though."

"So you're the youngest?"

I nodded. "It's just me and my brother. How about you?"

"I'm the youngest, too. I have three older sisters."

Good to know. Guys with older sisters came pre-trained. They put the toilet seat down, dropped their dirty laundry in the hamper, and even helped out with the cooking and dishes. Brock was the middle of three brothers and had a doting, indulgent mother. He'd never lifted a finger to help me cook or clean. Really, why had I put up with him?

I knew why.

Because I'd been lonely, maybe even a little desperate.

As many people as there were in New York City, it was still hard to find a worthwhile guy. Fortunately, I'd come to my senses about Brock earlier tonight, and glancing over at Trent, I was damn thankful I had.

Trent reached down and took my hand in his, cutting his eyes my way to gauge my response. My smile told him all he needed to know. His touch was welcome and warm and comforting.

"Where do you live?" I asked Trent.

"Windsor Terrace."

His neighborhood, like mine, was one of the quieter areas of Brooklyn. Though once a primarily Irish and Italian neighborhood, Windsor Terrace now comprised an interesting mix of cultures, as well as architectural styles. His neighborhood and mine were separated by only a twenty-minute train ride or a ten-dollar cab fare. Dating Trent would be convenient. Of course, I was getting way ahead of myself here.

Who knew if tonight would even lead to another date? He had taken my hand, though, a sure sign he was attracted to me. Then again, the guy had no idea who I really was. He thought I was Nicole. Once he found out the truth, that I'd misled him, he'd probably be pissed off and never want to see me again. The thought made me heartsick, but I pushed it from my mind. Why not enjoy the night, even if it might be the only one the two of us would ever have?

We walked on, past another of the four bronze eagle statues situated about the park. A soft breeze blew past us, carrying the strains of a classic Dizzy Gillespie tune to our ears.

"You hearing what I'm hearing?" Trent pulled me to a stop and tilted his head. "What number is that?"

I listened for a moment. "'On the Sunny Side of the Street.'"

"That's it. Let's go!"

We took off in the direction of the music and soon found a crowd of people scattered on blankets and in lawn chairs in front of a portable stage. Most of the men and women were in their seventies or eighties or even older, some in wheelchairs or electric scooters. But this fun-loving crowd wasn't going to let arthritis, bunions, or a misbehaving gallbladder keep them from having a good time.

A quartet performed on stage, including a drummer, a keyboardist, a cello player, and a fourth musician with a trumpet, clarinet, and saxophone situated on stands in a semicircle around him.

"I've heard these guys before," Trent said. "My band played warm-up for them at a jazz club in Manhattan a few months ago."

The quartet finished up the song and immediately launched into another classic number.

Trent lifted his chin to indicate a grassy spot under a tree nearby. We took seats on the ground and leaned back against the rough bark of the trunk to enjoy the music. A gnarled hand waved from nearby, and I spotted Idabel among a group of people who frequented the local senior center. I waved back. She pointed at Trent and gave me a thumbs-up.

"What's that about?" Trent asked, sharing a smile with the elderly woman across the way.

I lifted my shoulders, sheepish. "I shared my dating woes with Idabel."

I'd told the woman that Brock was blond, so she knew the man next to me wasn't him.

Trent waved to Idabel, pointed at me, then returned the thumbs-up sign. I fought a laugh but lost, too flattered not to giggle. Trent knew how to make a girl feel special.

He draped an arm around my shoulders and edged closer. We sat for an hour, listening to the music and having a wonderful, relaxing time. Could this unexpected, unplanned night be any more perfect?

When the band wrapped up their show, Idabel waved us over. My heart pounded in my chest like the *boom-boom-boom* of the band's bass drum. *Please don't let her say my name!* If she called me Katelyn, the jig would be up, and my date would be over.

When we reached her, she stood and gave me a warm hug. "Great to see you, honey."

Honey. Thank goodness.

"You, too, Idabel." I turned and raised a hand to indicate Trent. "This is Trent."

He shook her hand and she smiled. "You've got yourself quite a girl there, Trent."

Although his words were directed at Idabel, his gaze was locked on me. "I was just thinking the same thing myself."

CHAPTER FOUR

Cutting a Rug

AFTER BIDDING IDABEL AND the other seniors good-bye, Trent and I walked back to my place, hand in hand. We took our time, in no hurry, enjoying the fresh air and slower weekend pace.

As we turned onto my street, I spotted Nicole coming up the sidewalk from the other direction. She had her arm around the waist of a tall, thin guy with shaggy hair who, in turn, had his arm draped over her shoulders. Judging from their stagger, the two were three sheets to the wind.

We met each other between our brownstones. I nodded in greeting but kept walking, hoping to avoid a conversation. No such luck.

"Hey, Katherine," Nicole said, reaching out a hand to stop me. "Did Tim or Troy or whatever come by? Did you tell him something came up?"

Uh-oh.

I dared a glance at Trent. To my surprise, he *didn't* look surprised.

"Um … yeah," I said. "I … um … took care of things for you."

"Cool." With that, she and her date stumbled drunkenly up her stairs. Nicole let loose one last cackle before yanking open the door to her brownstone and disappearing inside.

Trent turned to me. "I dodged a bullet with that one, huh?"

"You knew?"

"Of course. Your brownstone has a number 5 on it. There's no 5 in 1663."

"Why didn't you say something?"

He lifted a shoulder. "'Cause you're cute."

"Really?"

"Really. And because the guy who set me up with Nicole told me she was a sure thing." His nose crinkled in disgust.

To most guys, a sure thing would be a plus. It said a lot about Trent that he wasn't merely looking to get laid. Still, I was curious. "Why'd you agree to go on the date, then?"

"To get the guys at work off my back. It's been a while since I've taken a girl out. Guys being guys, they've been giving me crap for it."

"The women at my office are the same way. Always asking about my love life." Of course, I knew they meant well, even if I did find their inquiries to be a bit personal and presumptuous.

Trent eyed me. "So your name's Katherine?"

"Actually, it's Katelyn," I said. "Nicole never gets it right."

"Ugh. Another reason not to like her."

We shared a laugh.

His gaze traveled from my face, up to my window, and back. He raised a hopeful brow. "Can I come up?"

"You know you're not getting lucky, right?" Not on the first date, anyway. "The only thing I'll give you tonight is a glass of cheap wine or a cup of coffee."

"Damn." He swung his arm in an *aw-shucks* motion, his grin belying his words.

He followed me up the stairs once again. While he set about opening the wine, I took Sinatra out for a potty break. When I returned to the apartment, Trent had two glasses of moscato poured and Artie Shaw's "My Blue Heaven" playing on the record player.

Trent handed me one of the glasses and raised the other to make a toast. "To blind dates."

I clinked my glass against his. "Hear, hear!"

After a few sips, Trent set his glass down on the kitchen counter. He picked up my lightweight bistro set and moved it up against the wall. He did the same with the shipping trunk that served as my coffee table. The center of the room now clear, he held one arm out toward me, the other up at his shoulder. "May I have this dance, Katelyn?"

I set my glass down next to his and performed an impromptu pirouette, spinning into his open arms.

"Wow," Trent said. "You've got some impressive moves."

I waggled my brows. "I'm just getting started."

Trent and I danced through the whole album before exchanging it for Glenn Miller and "Rug Cutter's Swing." The record spun at 78 RPM's and so did I, performing the turns and twists my grandmother had taught me and having the most romantic time of my life.

In the brief silence between songs, a banging sound came through the open door of my bedroom, the undeniable sound of Nicole's headboard slamming rhythmically against the wall next door.

I tilted my head. "Any second thoughts about not getting lucky?"

Trent shook his head. "None at all. Besides," he said with a broad smile, "I did get lucky tonight."

He spun me around one last time, pulled me in to his chest, and lowered his lips to mine.

A former tax advisor, **Diane Kelly** inadvertently worked with white-collar criminals. Lest she end up in an orange jumpsuit, Diane decided self-employment would be a good idea. Her fingers hit the keyboard and thus began her "Death and Taxes" romantic mystery series. A graduate of her hometown's Citizen Police Academy, Diane Kelly also writes the hilarious K-9 cop "Paw Enforcement" series.

Diane's books have been awarded the prestigious Romance Writers of America Golden Heart® Award and a Reviewers Choice Award.

Be the first to receive book news by signing up for Diane's newsletter at www.dianekelly.com. "Like" Diane on Facebook at www.facebook.com/dianekellybooks, and follow her on Twitter @dianekellybooks.

ABOUT RWA

Romance Writers of America:
The Voice of Romance Writers

ROMANCE WRITERS OF AMERICA® (RWA) is a nonprofit association whose mission is to advance the professional interests of career-focused romance writers through networking and advocacy. Founded in 1980, RWA has grown to one of the largest writers associations in the world. RWA represents more than 10,000 members who live in 38 countries. RWA provides programs and services to support the efforts of its members to earn a living from their writing endeavors.

If you are interested in becoming a part of this diverse and growing community, visit www.rwa.org for more information.

Like RWA on Facebook:
www.facebook.com/romancewriters

Follow RWA on Twitter:
@romancewriters